CAPTIVES OF THE CURSE

THE KYONA CHRONICLES BOOK TWO

DEBORAH GRACE WHITE

LUMINANT PUBLICATIONS

CAPTIVES OF THE CURSE

By Deborah Grace White

The Kyona Chronicles Book Two

Copyright © 2020 by Deborah Grace White

First edition (v1.0) published in 2020
by Luminant Publications

ISBN: 978-1-925898-23-1

Luminant Publications
PO Box 201
Burnside, South Australia 5066

http://www.deborahgracewhite.com

Cover Design by Karri Klawiter
Map illustration by Rebecca E. Paavo

For Reuben
Always keep exploring beyond the boundaries of your world.

Forest of Rune
Kynton
Dragon Realm
VAS.
Kerr
Montego
GREAT RIVER
Przvat
KYONA
Nerita
Argath
Alezae
MARSHLAND
NORTH L
SOUTH L
BALENOL
BASE TREE
N
S
E
W

North Wilds
ILISA
VALORIA
DRAGONCAVE
LOCH ARINE
Arinton
Basal Headlands
Wyvern Islands
Bryford
ANDS
ANDS
Nohl
Rasad's Bastion
Jeweled Peaks
Thirl
THORANIA
Logging Camp
SPICE FIELDS

CHAPTER ONE

Jonan stood on the rolling deck, his feet steady beneath him. When he had first boarded the ship he would have been unbalanced by swells as large as these, but three weeks on the ocean inevitably had an effect.

His eyes scanned the horizon, his glance straying back northward, in the ship's wake. Not for the first time, he found himself wondering what Calinnae and Elnora were doing at that moment.

Something boring and diplomatic, he assured himself firmly. *You're not missing anything.* He sighed. But he was missing something. He was missing his best friend. Shaking his head, he returned his gaze to the horizon ahead of him. As exciting as the events of the past months had been, he didn't want to dwell on the adventures behind him. Even if they did involve dragons and broken curses and magic swords. He wanted to look to the future.

Not that he regretted his part in the quest to reestablish the corrupted bloodline of his home country. He was glad, of course, that Cal had come into his own. And although Cal was somehow, impossibly, king of Kyona now, he knew it changed nothing between them. Cal had always been like a brother, and he would have gladly given Jonan a home and a role in the court at Kynton.

But Jonan had no interest in such a life. Back when he'd thought he was the one destined to be king, he had lain awake at nights filled with dread over it. Now that he was free, he had no intention of shackling himself to the absurdity of court intrigues by choice.

Besides, the best thing about being caught up in the events that had swept his old life away was that he had finally escaped the tiny fishing village where he'd grown up. He had always dreamed of sailing across the sea to explore the lands beyond. Now that he was finally doing it, the last thing he wanted to do was look back.

He sighed again and stretched his stiff limbs. It was only the period of inactivity, he reflected. He had boarded the vessel with excitement, ready to discover and conquer without hesitation. But three weeks of bobbing up and down over endless waves rather dulled the sense of urgency.

"Oi! You there! Throw me up that rope, would you?"

Looking around, Jonan spotted the sailor who had hailed him, and hastened to comply. He had a warmth toward the man, despite the sailor's rough ways. He was the only one who ever sought Jonan's assistance. Jonan felt a prickle of frustration as he watched the sailor busying himself partway up the mast. The unwillingness of the ship's crew to give him even the smallest of jobs was another cause of his current aggrieved state of mind.

He had assumed that he would be able to work his way across on a fishing or trading vessel, but apparently experienced seamen didn't place any particular value on offers of help from untrained outsiders. The master of this ship had been willing to give him passage for a fee, but it was made clear that he was to stay out of the way. With that offer he had to be content, and he hadn't hesitated to part with a large number of his coins.

The only alternative would have been to barter the silver chain around his neck, and Jonan hadn't wanted to do that. He fingered it absently now, unable to explain why he wanted to keep it. The royal signet ring that once hung from it now rested on Cal's finger, where it belonged. Jonan didn't regret losing the royal identity he briefly thought was his. But he couldn't quite part with the empty chain.

So he had paid in coins. It rankled a little to know that he had so quickly needed the gold that he had been hesitant to accept. But he supposed he should be grateful that he had left Kynton with many more coins than he had possessed when he left his hometown of Nerita not so long before. There were some advantages to being the best friend of the new king.

And despite the few coins left in his pouch, Jonan's heart was as light as his pocket. It was true he had no idea what he would find at his destination, or how difficult it might be to return, but he wasn't worried. He was sure he'd find a way to make it work. Things usually had a way of sorting themselves out.

"Need anything else?" he called up to the sailor.

The man grunted. "Some pitch wouldn't go astray," he acknowledged. "It's in the big storeroom, in the stern."

Jonan nodded, already on his way to the ladder that led below deck. Three weeks of aimless wandering in a confined space was more than enough time to be familiar with every aspect of the ship's layout. He had never actually entered the storeroom in question, but he knew exactly where it was.

He passed a number of other crew members on his way, but no one spared him a second glance. The storeroom occupied one end of the stern. Something about it was vaguely familiar, but he was certain he hadn't been inside it before. He wandered deeper into it, running a hand along the shelves as he searched for the jars of pitch that he knew would be there somewhere. Finally he saw them, right at the back of the space, on a shelf at knee height. He squatted down, picking up a half empty jar.

Before he stood up, however, he was distracted by the curved wooden wall of the ship behind where the shelf was attached. Just like the rest of the ship, the wood here looked old and worn. It was such a leaky bucket that he would have hesitated to accept passage on it if he had been one to worry about such details. You wouldn't get Cal onto this ship in a hurry, he thought with a grin.

His eyes flicked back to the part of wall that had attracted his attention. Loops of metal that he hadn't noticed anywhere else were bolted to the wood. They were so rusted and old that their original purpose was unclear, but they didn't hold his gaze for long. He was more interested in the space between them. Something had been carved in large letters into the wood. It was barely legible, clearly carved a long time ago. Whoever left the mark must have made it very deep for it to still be visible at all. Squinting at it, Jonan thought it must be a name, although it wasn't one he had ever heard before.

Alben.

Looking more closely, he realized that the "b" didn't look right. Inside the round part of the letter was another circle, contained within the "b". For a moment he wondered if it had been an accident, but the strokes were so deep and deliberate, it seemed unlikely. He glanced at the wall elsewhere at this height and saw that there were other markings too, but none in which legible letters could be made out. He looked back at the name. Alben. It had a strong feel to it, he thought.

Acting on a strange impulse, he reached his hand out and touched the letters, wanting to feel the groove they had left in the wood. Immediately he felt a surge—a strange feeling he couldn't define. For a moment he felt as though his hand had been soldered to the wall, and he couldn't have removed it if he tried. His hand looked strange though, unfamiliar against the wood, which seemed suddenly strong and sturdy. Glancing down he saw heavy iron shackles around his ankles, and he pulled his hand back with a stifled cry.

Reality returned at once. The wood was again weathered and splintered, and his hands and feet were his own. He had pulled back from the carved letters with such force that he had fallen back against the wooden floor. For a long moment he just sat there, trying to shake off the strange vision. The most disconcerting thing hadn't been what he had seen, but what he had felt inside his own mind. He had suddenly lost track of Jonan of Nerita, and looked out through entirely different eyes. He should have felt shock at the unexpected sight of chains restraining him, but he hadn't. Instead he had felt a powerful anger and determination, softened only by the mental image of a sweet and pretty face. The girl's features had seemed as familiar as his own in the moment, but now Jonan couldn't even recall them.

He stared at the markings again. What had just happened to him? Was he getting cabin fever at last, or was some kind of magic involved here? He could think of no other explanation. He had heard Cal describe such visions, but he had never experienced anything like it himself. And he could think of no reason for him to have any magical connection with this decrepit old trading vessel.

Looking around, he saw the pitch on the floor where he had dropped it. In his daze he had forgotten all about his reason for coming below deck, but he supposed that the sailor would be wondering where he was. He snatched the jar up and, with one last uneasy look at the carving on the wall, he hurried out of the storeroom.

Once back up on deck, he felt the strong sea wind clear his

mind. It was easier to think straight up here where he could see the sky, overcast though it might be. He made his way over to the sailor, who had descended from the mast and was focused on securing the rope Jonan had previously handed up to him.

The man grunted his thanks when Jonan handed over the pitch. He didn't comment on the delay, instead beginning work on a damaged barrel, putting the pitch to good use. Unsure whether to ask any of the questions swirling around his head, Jonan hovered nearby, neither engaging his companion nor turning away from him.

The man seemed unbothered by his presence, but after a few minutes he glanced in Jonan's direction, seeming to guess that the youth was leaving something unsaid.

"If this wind holds, we should reach Nohl early tomorrow," he offered.

Jonan started. "So soon?" He felt a smile growing, temporarily forgetting the strange moment he had just experienced below deck. "That will be a relief."

The sailor chuckled. "Aye, I figured you'd had about enough of the sea. This life isn't for everyone."

"It's not the sea I'm sick of," said Jonan quickly. "I just don't like having nothing to do." His companion smiled indulgently, and Jo felt a bit foolish. He had seen for himself how hard these seamen worked, and he supposed that they would love to have nothing to do for a spell. But he couldn't help it if they were unwilling to let him share the load.

"Who's waiting for you at the other end?" the sailor asked. Jonan wondered if it was the prospect of arriving on land at last that had made the older man suddenly more interested in conversation.

"No one," Jonan answered in surprise. The sailor looked at him sharply.

"I thought you were getting off at Nohl."

"That's right," Jonan affirmed, nodding. "I thought I'd see a little of Balenol." The man was staring at him now, and Jonan felt his own brows draw together in confusion.

"Thought you'd see a little of it? Balenol is not the country for some foolhardy adventure, kid. Not for a Kyonan. If you just wanted to wander around, you shouldn't be making for the South Lands."

Jonan shrugged, unconcerned by these strictures. He'd been drilled in caution all his life, and he'd never let it slow him down before.

The sailor was still shaking his head, but he didn't persist. Jonan's welfare was no concern of his.

"What's the capital like?" Jonan asked curiously. "Nohl, I mean."

The man shrugged. "Don't know. Never been there, have I?"

"What do you mean?" Jonan asked. "I thought you said you've been crew on this ship for years. Don't you sail this route all the time?"

The man grunted his assent.

"Then how..." Jonan trailed off, and the man sighed.

"We're Kyonan, kid. We don't linger in Nohl. We drop our cargo, then we continue straight on to Thorania. Methinks you should do the same. I'm sure the captain will let you continue on if you ask."

Jonan frowned at the mention of the country that bordered Balenol. There was something behind the man's words that he didn't fully understand. But the more the other man discouraged Jonan from exploring Balenol, the more he found himself wanting to do it.

"No thanks," he said succinctly. "Nohl is my stop." He started to turn away, but he suddenly remembered his strange vision in the storeroom. If this man was in the mood for conversation, it was too good an opportunity to miss.

"I saw something below deck," he began. "There was a..." He had intended to explain about the marking, but as the sailor looked at him questioningly, he somehow lost his nerve. "There was a metal ring attached to the wall. What would its purpose be?"

The sailor shrugged. "For the chains, I imagine."

"Chains?" Jonan felt an ominous foreboding.

"Aye," grunted his companion. "This ship was a slave vessel once."

Jonan recoiled from the man involuntarily, realizing why the room had seemed familiar. He had been on a slave vessel once before, and the captives had been held in large cells in the stern of the ship.

"And you crewed the ship?" Jonan demanded, not bothering to hide the anger rising up inside him.

The man spat, although his expression remained unconcerned. "Nar, I don't hold with that type of trade, myself," he said. "It's a sad thing when a man turns on his own countrymen. 'Sides, no guarantee you won't end up in shackles yourself when you take up with them traders."

Jonan slowly uncurled his fists, only realizing as he did so that he had balled them in the first place. "But I thought you said you've worked this ship for many years. Hasn't the slave trade only started operating again in the last few decades?"

"Aye," the soldier spat again, his attention apparently more on the barrel than on the conversation.

"So how long ago was this a slave ship?" Jonan asked with a frown.

The man sighed, apparently growing weary of the interruption. "When it was new, I figure," he said. "Dunno how long back. Couple hundred years, maybe."

"A couple hundred years?" repeated Jonan, startled. "Surely this ship isn't that old?"

The sailor threw him an amused glance. "Were you thinking it was new, lad?"

"Hardly," said Jonan dryly, casting a glance around at the state of the vessel. "But I didn't think ships could last that long."

"Mostly they don't," said the man. "But they'll last as long as you like if you keep maintaining them properly. I expect this one was among the best when it was first made. A lot of ships either go under before their lifespan can be tested or fall apart from overuse and under-maintenance. I reckon this one took some damage though, and lay unused for a long time.

"The last captain acquired it fifty some years ago, I reckon. Guess he figured it was cheaper to fix up an old relic than build a new boat. It was well repaired then, and it's been pretty well maintained most of the time I've sailed on it. Still, it's pretty sorry these days. Daresay we'll end up at the bottom of the sea one of these times."

Jonan raised his eyebrows. The seaman didn't seem too bothered by the idea, as he calmly continued his work. He seemed to have reached the end of his account, and Jonan had no more questions he cared to ask. But his mind was buzzing. Could it be possible that the mark Jonan had seen really had been left by a slave on a voyage away from Kyona a couple of centuries ago? It seemed unlikely that the carving could be so well preserved. But then Jonan thought of the strange flash he had seen. If some kind of magic was involved, who knew what was possible? The other marks had certainly not lasted as well. It was a shame he hadn't explored that storeroom earlier.

Jonan felt a small stirring of excitement. It was bewildering, but he eagerly welcomed the sense of looming adventure after the weeks of inactivity.

CHAPTER TWO

The thought of being so close to land at last sent Jonan to his bunk that night with a spring in his step. As usual no one paid him any heed as he settled in for sleep. He wouldn't miss the taciturn nature of the sailors any more than he would miss the endlessly empty horizon.

He was up as early as anyone the next morning, and his sense of excitement grew as the first glimmer of dawn confirmed the sailor's words from the day before. Land was indeed well and truly within sight. As the light grew and the distance decreased, Jonan could clearly make out a large harbor, bustling with activity despite the early hour. Dimly he could make out a vast city beyond the harbor. He could even catch glimpses of the enormous jungle that surrounded the city, looming out of the darkness, promising unknown dangers and excitement.

He had been packed and on deck well before he needed to be, his traveling cloak rolled up and shoved into the rucksack slung over his back. As they had sailed further south, the air had become warmer, moisture clinging to his skin even during the hours of darkness. Early though it was, even his light tunic felt like too much material.

He could hardly wait to feel solid ground beneath his feet, so he was confused and disappointed when the ship dropped anchor a significant distance from the large quay. As usual no one volunteered any information to the passenger.

Looking around the deck, he saw that preparations were being made to lower the rowboats into the water. His confusion increased when he realized that the small boats had been filled with cargo, presumably while he slept. Additional cargo was piled on the deck, apparently brought up from the bowels of the ship. He watched in consternation as sailors climbed into the boats, taking no personal packs with them. He had assumed that everyone would be eager to rush ashore for leave, but he could see no indication of it.

The boats made their way through the water, their progress swift with strong hands to work the oars. Jonan's amazement increased as he saw other small vessels approaching from the harbor. The boats met in the middle of the expanse of water, and an exchange of goods began. Jonan was surprised that they risked losing cargo into the depths with such a haphazard handover, but the practiced speed with which the operation was carried out demonstrated that it was not the first time for anyone involved.

Empty of their initial loads, the rowboats turned about and made their way back to the ship with even greater speed, their now laden counterparts making more labored progress back toward shore.

His surprise had kept him silent while he watched this bizarre changeover, but when the sailors began to pile another load of goods into the rowboats, Jonan realized he would need to assert himself if he didn't want to be forgotten.

Glancing around, he saw the sailor who had spoken to him the day before, assisting with the loading of cargo. He approached him quickly, seizing his opportunity before the rowboats left again. He didn't know how many trips would be needed.

"What's going on?" he asked.

The man responded with the grunt that seemed to be his preferred method of communication. "Offloading the goods."

"But why offload them in the water? Surely it's easier to dock at the quay? Or even send the rowboats all the way to shore?"

The man actually paused his efforts for a brief moment, giving Jonan a steady look. "You really have no idea where you are, do you lad?" Jo thought he looked genuinely concerned.

"This is Nohl, isn't it?" he asked, his brow furrowed. "The capital of Balenol."

The man's grunt almost seemed to hold a laugh this time. "Yes, the capital of Balenol. And the capital of the slave trade. Like I said yesterday, it's no place for any Kyonan who still has his freedom."

Jonan stared. "You mean you're afraid to go ashore for fear of being taken into captivity?"

The man shrugged. "I don't know as I'd say afraid, exactly. We've been doing our own type of trade with Balenol comfortably enough for a long time. But the system works because everyone knows what lines to cross and what lines to leave well enough alone. Kyonans don't come to Nohl just to explore. I told you, you'd do best to keep on with us until we reach Thorania. Not such a risky place for a friendly visit."

Jo didn't bother to respond to the advice. "I guess I'll hitch a ride on the next rowboat," he said instead. "I don't particularly want to swim to shore."

The man just shrugged again. "Suit yourself. Just make sure they don't sell you along with the cargo when you change boats."

Jonan couldn't tell whether the man's dry tone signified that he was joking, or just that he had little expectation of being heeded. Either way, Jo thanked him for his help and pushed forward to secure a place on a boat that was about to be lowered into the water. He may have appeared to take the warning lightly, but his every sense was on the alert. He had no intention of being pressed into slavery and every intention of finding out the full extent of what was going on in Nohl.

A voice in his head that sounded strangely like Cal's told him that he was being foolish not to take the sailor's advice and move on to Thorania. *I won't do anything rash*, he promised this voice of reason. *I'll just look around a little.*

The sailors in the boat he approached cast him sour looks, but no one said anything as he climbed in. Again, the progress was swift as they made their way toward the boats already waiting at the appointed place of exchange. When they pulled alongside the other vessels, Jonan was impressed at the efficiency of the process. He hadn't been able to see the details from his vantage point on the deck of the ship, but the waiting Balenan boats carried special wooden boards with vertical edges that slotted over the rims of the two meeting vessels. Their dual purpose was clearly to keep the boats securely lashed together, and to provide a walkway for transferring goods.

Jonan waited until the cargo had been moved before springing lightly across the platform. "Room for a passenger?" he asked cheerfully. The Balenan sailors looked at him with surprise, but no one protested. The Kyonans didn't give him a second glance, their oars dipping purposefully into the water as soon as the board had been raised.

"Where you going, kid?" asked one of his new companions, the accent strong and unfamiliar.

"Into Nohl," said Jonan easily. "I'd be grateful if you could just drop me off at the port." The man looked at him curiously, but Jo didn't elaborate. He may not be much given to caution, but even he had picked up that it would be unwise to emphasize his lack of a plan or specific destination.

The trip to the quay was accomplished in minutes, and Jo lost no time in leaping onto shore once they had pulled up alongside a small wharf. With a quick thanks to the sailors, he took off down the pier with falsely confident strides, trying to look like he knew where he was going. He blessed the feel of solid ground beneath his feet again, but he couldn't help a jittery rush of nerves as he glanced back at the Kyonan ship out in the water. It hadn't moved, but already it looked inaccessibly far away. He had felt the call of adventure when he and Cal had fled their home a couple of short months earlier, despite the terrible circumstances. But never had he stepped into the unknown as fully as he did now.

He'd always had a fondness for ships and the ocean, and he would have liked to have lingered and watched the bustle of activity unfolding in the harbor around him. But he judged that it was best to put some distance between himself and those who had seen him arrive so very alone, before someone decided to follow him or worse. He had a vague idea of finding lodgings for the night, but his curiosity to explore the city left him in no hurry to make inquiries.

He had seen from the ship that a large river opened up into the port. It appeared to run right through the city before emptying into the sea, and the port had evidently been built on the river's mouth. He began to follow it away from the harbor, keeping the fast-flowing waterway on his right.

He was not surprised to find that the neighborhood nearest the port appeared grimy and poor. For whatever reason, that trait seemed to be universal, he thought, picturing the only decently sized seaside city he had visited in Kyona. He looked around him with interest as he walked, noting that the area seemed crowded and full of activity, even first thing in the morning. At first he felt very conspicuous, and he couldn't help but notice many eyes watching him curiously as he passed. He didn't stop either to explore or to speak to anyone, pushing on with a quick gait deeper into the city, toward what he supposed to be the center of the action.

After walking for some time, Jonan realized that the river was curving away to the left, turning eastward. Wanting to continue his course toward the center of town, he crossed over one of the many bridges that spanned the water at regular intervals. It took a few minutes for him to notice what was different on this side of the river. Gradually he became aware that the dwellings were becoming more affluent, the general surroundings progressing from filthy toward pleasant. He was also a little relieved to see that he was not the only Kyonan around. A small number of his countrymen could be seen moving about the streets, recognizable with careful scrutiny from their skin, a few shades paler than the warmer caramel native to the Balenan people.

At first Jonan felt glad to stand out less, but he quickly realized that he was still attracting attention. It took him a few blocks to work out why. His clothes, nothing fancy to begin with and now dirty and travel worn, were no more impressive than those of the other Kyonans. But unlike him, each and every one of them walked with a certain shuffling gait, shoulders slumped and heads down. He tried in vain to catch the eye of any number of them as he passed, but no one seemed willing to raise their eyes from the cobblestones at their feet. He realized also that they were being watched much more closely than their Balenan fellows by the mean-looking guards whom he could see positioned at regular intervals along the streets.

It was only after he witnessed, with growing indignation, the proprietary manner in which a well-dressed Balenan berated another Kyonan that he realized the truth. They were, of course, slaves. A quick glance down the next time he passed a countryman showed that the man wore a shackle on his ankle, clearly a permanent fixture to allow chains to be fitted at any time. Jonan sucked in a breath. It was hardly a surprise to come across evidence of the trade that he had heard so much about in recent weeks, but he had not really expected to be the only Kyonan in the entire city who wasn't a slave. He felt a stirring of unease.

Nothing rash, he reminded himself. *I won't go looking for trouble. Just try to blend in.*

Noting the curious looks that still followed him, Jonan decided to veer off the street he had been following, which was clearly a main thoroughfare. He ducked down a side alley, trying to continue with the same collected strides.

Somehow the defeated demeanor of the Kyonan slaves rattled him more than anything else. Surely there was more fire in the blood of any Kyonan. Young and full of life as he was, Jonan found it hard to imagine a scenario where he would ever stop fighting such a fate.

He knew that Filip, from whom Cal had reclaimed the throne, had been a cruel king who cared nothing for his people. But he was still staggered to see the extent to which the slave trade had flourished at the expense of the citizens of Kyona.

With no idea where he was going, Jonan was taken by surprise when the back street he was following suddenly opened into a miniature courtyard, the dirty cobblestones offset by greenery that sprang out of raised beds around the small square. He had just entered the space when someone stepped out of another side street nearby, the unexpected movement making him jump.

"There you are! What kept you?" greeted the newcomer, his voice lowered.

Jonan looked at him in surprise. The boy looked several years younger than himself, and he was certainly Kyonan. His accent betrayed him as much as his complexion. Unsure how to respond, Jo looked him up and down, starting a second time when a girl stepped into the square behind the newcomer. She looked slightly older than Jonan, but not by much. She was peering at him closely, and she suddenly started as sharply as Jo had done.

"Cody, he's not one of ours!" she hissed.

"What do you mean?" asked the boy, looking from her to Jonan in astonishment. "He must be. Isn't this the meeting point?"

"Look at his arm," she insisted, her hand straying toward her hip even while her eyes remained fixed suspiciously on Jo's face.

A sharp intake of breath brought Jo's gaze back to the boy, apparently called Cody, who was now staring at Jo's arm, exposed as it was by his light tunic. Glancing curiously at the two other youths, Jo realized that they each bore a tattoo on their forearms, the black ink stark against their pale skin.

The girl spat onto the ground. "He must be working with them," she said, moving menacingly toward Jo. He caught a glint of steel and realized that her earlier movement had been reaching toward a concealed weapon.

But the boy looked more curious than suspicious. "Nah, can't be," he said. "Too young. If he's a new arrival, he must be a slave."

"I'm not a slave," said Jonan shortly, deciding it was time to take an active hand in the conversation.

"What did I say?" hissed the girl. Her expression was murderous, but she made no move to attack.

"Are you slaves?" Jo asked, his voice level.

"Not today," said Cody, his expression hardening. The defiance in his eyes gave Jonan's spirits a lift. It was exactly what had been missing from every other Kyonan he'd seen in Nohl.

"What's it to you?" asked the girl, still aggressive. "Who are you, and what do you want here?"

"I'm Jonan," he said. "I just arrived in Nohl this morning."

"From where?"

"Kyona, obviously."

His interrogator narrowed her eyes. "And you came of your own free will?"

Jo shrugged. "Sure." He noticed that the girl was gripping her weapon, a long knife, with unnecessary tightness.

"What more evidence do you need?" she shot at her companion. "We should take him out now, before he can cause any trouble for us."

"Surely that's for Scar to decide," said the boy, still regarding Jo with interest.

Jonan hid a smile. "Scar" was such an appropriate name for the leader of a resistance gang, which was surely what these two belonged to. He pictured a battle-worn man with tall shoulders and a ruined visage. He would have to make sure not to chuckle over the title when he met this imposing personage, because he didn't actually want to get on the wrong side of the only Kyonans in the country with any spirit. He wondered if the man actually did have a scar, or if the name was assumed for effect.

"I'm not looking for trouble," said Jo mildly. "And as you can see, I'm unarmed." He gestured down his person. "I'm quite willing to come with you, though," he added with a touch of humor, "if you want to let your leader decide what to do with me."

Cody looked heartened, but the girl's eyes were narrower than ever. "I bet you are," she hissed. She glared at her companion. "No way we're showing him the way back to base."

"We could blindfold him," suggested Cody hopefully, but Jo was hardly surprised that this suggestion found no favor. "Well, what do you want to do?" the boy continued, exasperated. He glanced at the knife the girl still held, and his gaze became stern.

"We're not going to take him down just for being Kyonan. That's their job."

She sighed. "Fine," she said, her tone resentful. "Let's get out of here, then. They're not coming, something's obviously gone wrong."

Without another glance at Jo, the two started to disappear back down the alley from which they had come.

"Wait!" he called after them, and they paused, looking back at him warily. "Are—are you just going to let me go?"

The girl raised an eyebrow. "Would you rather we roughed you up a bit first?"

"Hardly," said Jo, refraining with difficulty both from rolling his eyes and from challenging their ability to do so. "But what if you're wrong? What if I'm a threat after all? What if I follow you?"

Cody chuckled, his expression indulgent. "You can try, Jonan of Kyona," he said.

"All right," Jonan tried again. "What if your Scar wants to interrogate me after all?"

"Don't let it worry you," said the girl witheringly. "We'll find you without any difficulty."

"But—" Jo tried in vain to think of another argument to convince them to take him with them, but they had already melted into the shadows. He sighed but stayed where he was. He believed them that it was no use attempting to follow them. After all, he had no knowledge of his surroundings to help him, and they were clearly very familiar with the streets.

But he was keenly disappointed by the missed opportunity. The chance encounter had seemed too good to be true. He had boarded the ship weeks ago with no intentions beyond a vague desire for adventure, and an inexplicable certainty that there was something out there for him. But something had been solidifying in his mind since his strange experience in the ship's storeroom the day before. It wasn't purely stubbornness that had made him more eager to come to Nohl in face of the sailor's discouragement.

And although he hadn't articulated it to himself until now, the growing sense of purpose had only strengthened as he took in the true state of the Kyonan cause here in Balenol. He knew that now Cal was king, his friend would act as decisively as necessary to stop the traders' raids on the Kyonan coast. But Cal was far away, and even if he could stop the frequent abductions of Kyonan youth, that left all the victims already in Balenol. With his usual optimism, Jonan felt certain that there must be something he could do about the fate of all his countrymen in captivity here. It felt good to have a focus for his energy, and to have fallen in with whatever resistance was already in place within hours of arriving would have been fortuitous indeed.

But it could be a lot worse, he reflected as he made his way out of the small courtyard. At least now he knew that there was a resistance, and his next task was to figure out how to find them again. He realized that his steps were leading him back to the main street, and he decided to let them. Skulking around back alleys might increase his chances of running into an underground gang, but he needed to get to know the city first.

He hadn't been able to get much of a sense of Nohl in his glimpse from the ship, but he had seen an imposing looking castle rising from what appeared to be the center of the capital. Once he had actually entered the labyrinth of stone buildings, he couldn't see far enough ahead to see in which direction the castle lay, but he had done his best to head for the center of town, figuring that was where the action would likely be.

Sure enough, the increasing busyness of the main road he was walking down suggested that he was heading in the right direction. People jostled one another in their haste, merchants calling out above the din to advertise their wares and pedestrians, Balenans and slaves alike, hurrying about their own business. Most of the traffic seemed to be heading further south into the city, and Jonan allowed himself to be carried along on the wave.

After a short while, he realized that the road opened out up ahead, and looking up he once again saw the castle. The road was even more crowded here, and it took a while for the crush of people to filter into the space ahead. But slowly and surely Jonan inched forward, until he emerged into an enormous central square. He had never seen such a large paved area in his life. The square seemed to be as large as the castle itself, which rose up on the far side of the gigantic courtyard.

For a moment Jonan was distracted by the sight of the castle. He had spent a few days in the castle at Kynton just before leaving for the coast. Although he wasn't generally much interested in fancy buildings, he had found the old fortress beautiful and pleasant, despite the tyrannical nature of its previous inhabitant. But this castle gave off quite a different presence. The stone was solid and intimidating, its uncompromising mass somehow portraying aggression rather than security. There were no colorful pennants, no flowers growing in strategically placed boxes. Every angle was harsh and unforgiving, and function had clearly been given precedence over beauty in its design.

All of this Jonan took in at a glance before his eyes dropped to the action happening in the square. Instantly all thoughts of aesthetics were forgotten. He had assumed that the crush of people moving this way indicated that there was a morning market or some other attraction operating in the castle's courtyard. But it was now evident that a different type of spectacle altogether had attracted the crowds.

CHAPTER THREE

The central space of the square was not occupied by market stalls or a decorative fountain, as he might have expected. Instead, the scene was marred by fixtures that spoke volumes about the city he had entered. The stocks he knew the function of, and indeed one or two were currently occupied. There was no hangman's noose, but a raised platform boasted a curious structure with a wickedly sharp horizontal blade that made Jo's stomach turn over even without knowing its exact function.

But most of the attention was focused on a whipping post set to one side. A boy even younger than Cody clung to it. The boy was clearly Kyonan, presumably a slave.

Glancing around, Jonan realized with a surge of anger and revulsion that the area was crowded because many people had come specifically to watch what appeared to be a familiar event. No one seemed distressed by the sight, and some were even looking excited. He took a deep breath to steady himself, trying to master the fury that rose up at the spectacle. *Nothing rash. Keep your head down.*

Jonan was too far back to hear the details of what was

happening, but he could see the figures through the crowd. Even from this distance, the poor boy looked terrified, his already pale northern face even whiter than it should be. A soldier who was built like a bear stood nearby, holding a lethal looking whip, and addressing the crowd. Jo could only imagine that he was cataloging the victim's supposed crimes.

Without conscious thought, Jo found himself inching forward through the throng. He was close enough to hear the soldier's voice when the man suddenly stopped, turning to look behind him as someone hailed him from the direction of the castle.

"Lord Wrendal," the soldier said, inclining his head respectfully. Jo didn't need the man's obsequious tone or the title to recognize the middle-aged newcomer as someone of high status. Lord Wrendal's air of haughty authority radiated off him, and his elaborate clothes proclaimed more about his wealth than his taste. Jo didn't usually think much about anyone's attire, but even to him the thick court clothes seemed out of place in this humid climate.

"What do we have here?" Lord Wrendal demanded imperiously.

The soldier began again to list the slave's offenses, but Jonan's eyes slid past Lord Wrendal to the person standing behind him, and with an involuntary intake of breath he suddenly lost track of the conversation.

The young woman looked to be about Jonan's age, although she was so elegantly dressed, he couldn't be sure she wasn't older. But it was her, not her dress, that caught Jonan's attention. He realized that he was staring, and part of his mind berated himself for it, but he couldn't seem to look away. He'd never been much prone to making eyes at the girls back home, but no girl he'd ever met had been anything like this stranger before him.

She was absolutely stunning, her chestnut hair flawlessly matched in color with her impossibly large eyes, the deeper brown an ideal enrichment of the caramel color of her skin. It was all set off to perfection by the deep golden gown she wore, the cut much more revealing and the fabric much more sheer than the dresses favored in Kyona's climate.

It wasn't just that she was attractive. Her beauty was startling. And it was clearly not just Jonan who thought so. Murmurs of appreciation seemed to pass through the crowd, and glancing away from her at last, Jo could see that many eyes were now fixed on the young woman.

"Lady Wrendal is here," came whispers from around him, and it was immediately obvious why no one looked as stunned as Jo felt. She was a familiar fixture.

If she was aware of the attention she was attracting, she gave no sign of it as she watched the scene with cool disdain. Focusing on her face, Jo saw a resemblance more of expression than features between her and the man she was following.

"Must we linger, Father?" she asked, her eyes barely flicking to the unfortunate slave before settling on her father with a slightly petulant look.

Jo felt his own expression sour, and he turned his eyes resolutely away from her. In itself, beauty impressed him no more than rank. The most alluring face held no appeal if it concealed a cold heart.

Lord Wrendal raised his eyebrows at his daughter. "Would you have me neglect my duty as Overseer of Slaves? The swift administration of justice is a crucial part of keeping order."

Justice? Jonan didn't know whether to laugh or cry.

The young woman didn't answer, and Lord Wrendal turned back to the soldier.

"Ten lashes, you said? Insubordination is a serious offense. Surely fifteen would be more appropriate."

"As you wish, My Lord," said the soldier, his eagerness making Jo's stomach churn. The slave had started to shake, but to his credit he remained silent as the soldier resumed his position before the whipping post.

Jo had thought that the nobleman and his daughter might continue on their way after passing judgment, but this Lord Wrendal evidently wished to see his orders carried out. The two of them remained standing to the side while the soldier swung once, twice, three times.

The watching crowd started involuntarily at the first crack of the whip, but it was the sound of it hitting the boy's flesh that echoed so forcefully through Jo's mind that he knew he would never forget it as long as he lived. On the fourth lash the slave cried out in agony, unable to keep it in any longer. Jonan was impressed that he had managed to stay on his feet, but by the sixth lash he fell to his knees. Watching in horror, Jo couldn't see how this boy could withstand ten such lashes, let alone fifteen.

From where he stood, the Overseer and his daughter were positioned just behind the spectacle, almost directly in Jonan's line of sight. As the soldier raised the whip for a seventh lash, Jo's eyes flicked to the young Lady Wrendal. He wasn't sure whether it was her expression of calm distaste or the jeers from the crowd that enraged him more, but suddenly something clicked into place inside him. He felt his rage bubble to the surface, and casting aside all thought of caution, he surged forward, his internal promise of restraint forgotten.

"Stop!" he cried commandingly, and suddenly all eyes were on him.

He thought he caught a glimpse of a startled expression on the generally languid face of the young noblewoman, but he wasn't interested in her reaction, instead focusing his attention on the soldier.

The man looked at him in astonishment for a moment, his

arm still raised and his surprise apparently holding his tongue in check.

"Can't you see he can't take it?" demanded Jonan. "What kind of justice do you call this?"

Slowly a look of amusement replaced the shock on the soldier's face. "You'll have to wait your turn, rat," he said, and the momentarily stunned crowd resumed its jeers. The soldier returned his attention to the boy in front of him, bringing his arm down at last, but Jo was quicker.

Still fueled by his rage, he threw himself forward, raising an arm in instinctive defense as he placed himself between the slave and his tormentor. He expected to feel the lash on his arm, and he staggered more from shock than from pain as the leather carved into his back instead.

For a moment his senses were overwhelmed with confusion as he tried to understand when he had turned his back to the soldier and wondered how his arms had come to be wrapped protectively around the slave he was trying to shield. Then he felt a dual surge of both rage and terror as he saw a familiar yet unknown face raised to his, the fair hair matted and the eyes pleading for forgiveness as he read their silent message.

No! cried an alien voice inside his head. *You must not give up, Marine! You must stay with me!*

Jo returned to reality with a gasp, his first awareness centered on a strange sensation that seemed to rush up into him from the flagstones beneath his feet. A moment later he was conscious of searing pain in both his arm and his face, as the whip sliced across his forearm, curling around it before the tip flashed up and caught his cheek. He reeled under the blow, but he was more disoriented than anything. The pain hardly seemed to matter—he felt strangely strengthened by the rush of power that had passed into his feet and up his body.

Yes, he thought inconsequentially. Power was the word to describe that sensation.

He glanced behind him, trying to make sense of what had happened. The slave boy was once again visible, his eyes wide, and the sandy-haired girl whom Jonan had seen twice now in his mind's eye was nowhere to be seen. For a moment he could still feel her fragile body in his arms, experiencing again the unsettling emotions that had invaded his mind, love and grief and despair mingling together inextricably. Then the soldier's angry voice brought him back to the present.

"I thought I told you to wait your turn," the brutish man was snarling.

Jonan returned the glare, his every nerve still humming with the strange sense of power. "I've never been much good at waiting," he shot back, his tone intentionally insolent.

The soldier strode forward and seized the front of Jonan's tunic, bringing their faces uncomfortably close together. "I'll teach you to mind your betters, slave," he growled, his voice furious.

"I'm not a slave," spat Jonan. "And I do not recognize your authority over me." He saw the man's eyes flick down to Jo's uninjured forearm, as the gang members' eyes had done a short time before. The soldier's grip loosened slightly as his brows drew together in confusion.

Out of the corner of his eyes, Jonan saw Lord Wrendal approach. "What's the meaning of this insolence?" the noble demanded, and the soldier twisted his grip on Jonan's shirt, turning him to face the Overseer. "Who is your master, boy?"

"I am my own master," said Jo, his voice level but his eyes shooting sparks. He could feel blood dripping down his face and arm, but he ignored it. The line of the whip across his arm felt like it was on fire, but the sting was invigorating, reminding him of what he was fighting against.

"Unlikely," said Lord Wrendal dryly. "Every unattached Kyonan must register with me, and I do not know your face." The threat in his eyes was clear—he would not be forgetting Jo's face in a hurry.

"Is that so?" Jo asked flatly. "Well, I'm newly arrived in Nohl, and I was unaware of the requirement to register myself like livestock."

The nobleman's eyes narrowed. "You had better watch your tone, boy," he said.

"I thought I hit just the right note, actually," said Jonan flippantly. "I've never thought bullies deserve much respect, rank or no rank." The Cal-like voice of reason was shouting inside his head, but he ignored it. He was way past rash now, and if he was going to be executed, he might as well go down swinging.

He briefly registered the outrage on Lord Wrendal's face before the soldier, still gripping Jo's tunic with one hand, brought the other hand around to deliver a ringing blow to the back of Jo's head. His vision spun, but with an effort he brought his eyes back to the haughty face before him.

"You'll pay for your insolence," the Overseer promised. "And don't think I believe your lies. I monitor all arrivals, and I am not so easily deceived. One of our little rebel friends, are you? Well their number will be reduced by one tonight."

Jonan's ears were still ringing from the blow to his head, but he noted with interest that the nobleman's self-satisfied air had been replaced with the anger of a tyrant not in full control of his domain.

So the resistance had the Overseer of Slaves rattled. That was heartening.

Distracted by his thoughts, Jonan's fuzzy mind was slow to recognize the silent direction that the noble was issuing by a wave of his hand. Before he could react, two soldiers had stepped forward to grab him by each arm. Gritting his teeth against the pain in his injured arm, he struggled fiercely. All it earned him was more pain, as several soldiers converged on him. No one pulled a weapon—the Balenans seemed to enjoy using their fists. The more Jo struggled, the more he was pummeled, culminating in another, harder, blow to the head.

This time he was unable to remain on his feet, the sudden sharp pain in his knees the only clue that he was no longer upright. Black spots bloomed in front of his sight as he tried desperately to retain consciousness.

"He doesn't have the slave's mark."

Mild as it was, the new voice managed to reach his ears through the increasingly loud ringing. Lady Wrendal had apparently decided to weigh in on the situation. Jonan blinked rapidly, and her exquisite features swam into view, her eyes fixed on him with an expression of boredom.

Her father turned to her with an exasperated air. "Do not tell me you are naive enough to think him an innocent traveler."

She shrugged. "It surely would not be difficult to discover where he came from." She lowered her voice so that only those in the immediate vicinity could hear. "Are you certain you don't wish to at least consult Mundsen before doing anything irrevocable? After all, you said yourself that the situation in Kyona is...unknown."

Lord Wrendal gave his daughter a hard look. "I did not think you were listening, Daughter. I'm surprised you remember my comments." He also spoke quietly, but there was an edge of danger to his soft voice.

She shrugged again, her eyes traveling lazily over Jonan's kneeling form. "You wish me to take an interest in matters of state, do you not, Father? Prepare myself for a life at court? Are you so surprised when I do as you direct? Surely my *every* action cannot be a disappointment to you."

"Surely not indeed," said Lord Wrendal. Something in his

smooth voice made the hairs on the back of Jonan's neck stand up. "Very well, I will commend your efforts by humoring your suggestion. We will take him to Mundsen before we arrange for his execution."

Jonan was hauled to his feet, soldiers still gripping his arms firmly. As he was shoved along behind the departing form of the Overseer, he saw Lady Wrendal glance back at the scene behind them. Following her gaze, he saw the boy being carried silently out of the square by two other slaves. Jonan had not realized that there were any Kyonans other than himself in the crowd—they must be good at going unnoticed. He was glad at least that his intervention had spared the boy some of his punishment.

Jo's escorts made no attempt to be gentle, and it was all he could do to remain on his feet. Every inch of him ached from his beating, and his head was still strangely thick, the street before him seeming to slip and slide under his eyes. He had no sense of direction, but it was a mercifully short time before he found himself forced through the door of a small but official-looking stone building. The receiving room into which he was pushed was small, and after throwing him bodily to the ground in one corner and threatening dire consequences should he move, the soldiers retreated to wait outside the door.

Jonan contemplated defiance for the sake of it, but the throbbing in his head and the fire in his arm made him shamefully glad to be able to sit still. He wondered how the poor slave boy from the square was faring.

At the commotion, a willowy man in his middle age had hurried out of another room into the entrance area. Upon catching sight of Lord Wrendal, he bowed deeply, rubbing his hands in a nervous gesture.

"My Lord! What an unexpected honor. To what do I owe—ah, and you also, My Lady! Such undeserved favor to see you in my humble rooms." The man's eyes slid across to Jonan's bloodied form, and his eyes widened. Jonan met his gaze with steel in his own eyes. The newcomer was clearly Kyonan, but his obsequious sniveling left no doubt as to his loyalty, or lack of it.

"What is—what brings you here, My Lord?" the man tried again. "Not that I would wish to suggest—that is, I am always most pleased to welcome you to—"

"Ah, Mundsen," Lord Wrendal cut across the nervous babble, his tone stern. "This boy caused a disturbance in the square this morning, and my fair daughter," his eyes flicked to Lady Wrendal, their expression faintly derisive, "thought it best to consult you."

"In—indeed?" said Mundsen, his gaze both surprised and uneasy as it rested on Lady Wrendal's countenance. "I am most honored, My Lady, although I cannot imagine what need your esteemed father could have of my counsel."

"You flatter me, Mundsen," said Lord Wrendal dryly. "Surely as overseer of your people here, it is only natural for me to seek information from the Kyonan Ambassador."

Jonan's head was still spinning too much for him to lift it from the wall where he had let it rest, but he managed to raise his eyebrows nonetheless. This was Kyona's ambassador to Balenol? How could the existence of such a position even be justified when all other Kyonans in the country were apparently enslaved on sight?

"Of course, My Lord, of course," Mundsen hurried to respond, once again bowing low. "I would be glad to give any information in my power to assist you."

"You might have to bend down a bit further if you're going to properly climb into his pocket," Jonan interjected, his words coming out slightly slurred.

Mundsen looked offended, and Lord Wrendal crossed the room in two firm strides to box Jonan's ear as if he was an impertinent child. The ringing intensified, but not before Jonan had noted Lady Wrendal's expression as she watched him from behind her father. He was curious to see that she looked more annoyed than angry or offended. Even as the thought occurred to him, her face smoothed back into a bored expression, and she looked away.

"Once more and it's your head," growled Lord Wrendal, before turning back to his companions. Jo blinked in confusion. Surely that blow had been to his head? But it was hard to tell at this point—everything was a bit fuzzy.

"Well?" Lord Wrendal was demanding of Mundsen. "Do we have to conduct our conversation in this entrance hall?"

"Of course not, My Lord," said Mundsen, jumping into action. "Please, come into my rooms, make yourselves comfortable."

"I hardly think that's likely," said Lady Wrendal, her face once again betraying distaste. "I think I will stay out here, Father."

"You will not," said the older man curtly. "You wished to demonstrate your diplomatic instincts—here is your opportunity to do so."

For a moment she hesitated, looking like she might argue, but at the look in her father's eyes she capitulated, following a simpering Mundsen out of the room. Lord Wrendal paused in the doorway to look back at Jonan, who met his eye boldly.

"Stay where you are if you value your life." The words were delivered in a growl, then the nobleman was gone.

CHAPTER FOUR

Without hesitation, Jonan heaved himself up off the floor, restraining a groan at the increased throbbing in his head and the various other aches all over his body. He peered cautiously out into the street. He hadn't realized that more soldiers had accompanied them than the two who had held his arms. Half a dozen loitered outside. He shook his head with a sigh, trying unsuccessfully to shake off the fog.

Turning back inside, he moved silently toward the doorway through which the others had disappeared. As he approached, he could see that it led to a long corridor. Faintly he could make out voices further down. He crept along the corridor, stopping several feet away from an open door. He recognized the voice of the imperious Overseer, and gently he slid down the wall, settling his body on the floor where he could hear but not be seen.

"Enough of your fussing," Lord Wrendal was saying. "We do not want refreshments. We want to conduct our business and be gone."

"Yes, My Lord, of course, My Lord. What was it you wished to discuss?"

"That insolent pup out there," began Lord Wrendal. "He is one of your kind, but he does not have the slave mark on his arm. Could he nevertheless be a runaway?"

"Impossible, My Lord! All new arrivals are marked before their feet ever touch Balenan soil—there are no exceptions. And as you know, those born to the trade are marked in infancy."

Lord Wrendal grunted. "Is he then one of yours?"

"Certainly not, My Lord," returned Mundsen. "I do not employ scrawny youths."

Jo scowled from his place in the corridor. The man was no heavyweight himself.

"I thought not," said Lord Wrendal, his tone thoughtful. "It is a puzzle, then."

"Perhaps he was telling the truth," said Lady Wrendal, contributing for the first time. After a moment's silence she continued, presumably responding to a look of inquiry from the ambassador. "He claimed to have only just arrived in Nohl, as a free man."

"He is neither free nor a man," said Lord Wrendal shortly. "He is Kyonan, and an impertinent child."

"Newly arrived," repeated Mundsen, apparently deep in thought. "No human cargo has arrived in recent weeks, and I have certainly not requested or received additional personnel."

"It is a preposterous lie, designed to escape his just deserts," said Lord Wrendal, his tone dismissive. "I daresay the boy could be of use in the logging camps, but I am still inclined to silence his rebellious tongue more permanently."

"Yes, My Lord, if you wish it," said Mundsen. "I am sure you are right." But his tone was uneasy, and Jonan was clearly not the only one who had noticed it.

"Out with it, you fool," snapped the nobleman. "What's ailing your mind?"

"Nothing, My Lord, it's just...as I told you, the situation in my home country remains unclear to me. The last missive I received from my king gave no indication of impending change. Just the usual inventories of the human cargo, and confirmation of the regular exchange of goods in return. And then nothing. It is through my own sources that I have become aware of recent events, and my information is at best imprecise. I have had no official communication since the coup, and the wildest rumors are circulating about the nature of events..."

Jo smiled grimly, even as his insides boiled with rage. He supposed it should be no surprise to discover that the former king, Filip, had been condoning the slave trade, selling his own people for profit. But he felt a fierce satisfaction in the knowledge that whispers of Calinnae's successful overthrow of the usurper had reached Nohl. Let them sweat, these monsters who thought they could buy and sell fellow human beings. Especially the Kyonan traitor.

There was a pregnant silence after the ambassador's words, broken eventually by Lord Wrendal.

"I take your meaning, I suppose. You think this boy might be some kind of spy or emissary of this unknown claimant?"

"I do not know that I would go so far, My Lord," said Mundsen hastily. "I was merely reflecting that the new king is, as you say, utterly unknown to me. I do not know what to expect from this change. I understand him to be young, and inexperienced, certainly—"

Lord Wrendal snorted. "And fool enough to send a whelp like that to gather information?"

"It would be a strange decision," acknowledged Mundsen. "But the timing is certainly questionable, if he did indeed just arrive, and of his own choice. When was the last time any Kyonan traveled to Nohl for leisure? I cannot recall ever meeting such a person, and in my role I would expect to be aware of all Kyonan arrivals.

"I confess, I have been wishing I knew more of this new ruler. I have no indication of whether he will be content to continue in the ways established by his predecessor. To honor those agreements made before his time."

"He will if he knows what's good for him," growled Lord Wrendal. "King Siloam will not take kindly to deviations to our trade agreements. Not after two decades of harmonious interchange."

Jonan felt his hands ball involuntarily into fists. Harmonious interchange? He thought of the agonized cries of the boy in the square, and pictured the dejected shuffle of the slaves making their way through Nohl's streets. He had never been more glad of the success of the quest to reclaim Kyona's corrupted throne. Cal would set things to rights.

But he felt a stirring of unease. The problem was bigger than he had anticipated, and his friend would be operating blindly as far as the Balenan end was concerned. If only he had some way to communicate with Cal, but there was no way he would trust a message to any ship leaving this harbor.

He returned his attention to the conversation in the room, to find that Lord Wrendal was once again speaking.

"It is decided then. I will take no decisive action in relation to this Kyonan arrival. He will be given lodgings near the castle, where I can keep a close eye on him, and I will have a watch on him at all times. We will see what we can learn from him before we decide what to do with him."

"You are, as always, most wise, My Lord." The relief was evident in the ambassador's voice.

"Can we leave now?" The musical young voice was once again sounding petulant.

"You may wait for me outside, if you are going to complain," said Lord Wrendal shortly. "I have another matter to discuss with Mundsen."

Jonan's foggy mind had not kept pace with the conversation, and he had only just understood the significance of the scraping of a chair against stone when the figure of Lady Wrendal appeared in the doorway. For the briefest of moments, she stood frozen on the threshold, staring at him. Jonan met her gaze, willing his expression to remain nonchalant.

Her check in momentum was so short that he doubted the other two men would have noticed it. She continued out of the room, closing the door behind her with a fluid motion. Turning slowly, she fastened her eyes on Jonan, her expression sour. He suddenly felt a little foolish, propped on the floor as he was.

"Your boldness exceeds your discretion," she said tartly.

Jonan grinned easily back at her, his lightheadedness making everything seem surreal and slightly humorous. "I've never been known for my discretion, My Lady," he said impishly.

She narrowed her eyes at him, moving as if to wrap her arms around her body but then seeming to think better of it. Jonan was momentarily surprised by her discomfort, but he stifled a laugh as sudden understanding hit him.

"That's not the type of indiscretion I meant," he reassured her, pushing himself up off the ground with a wince. "Not that you need me to tell you that you're beautiful, I'm sure."

"I certainly do not," she said crisply. She turned on her heel and strode down the corridor toward the entrance room, Jonan keeping pace.

"That's a good thing, because I'm not going to do it." She raised an eyebrow at him, and he grinned impertinently back. "I'm not so easily impressed, you see. Beauty is only skin deep, after all."

"Fortunately, I have no ambition to impress you," she said, her voice hard.

They had reached the end of the corridor, and Jonan eased himself into an upholstered armchair. He saw a flicker of annoyance in Lady Wrendal's eyes. He didn't know anything much about court etiquette, but he was guessing he had violated some polite rule by sitting while she still stood. His grin broadened.

"You needn't think you present a very appealing picture yourself," Lady Wrendal said, eyeing him with disfavor. "You're repulsive, in fact." Her eyes lingered on the side of his face that was smeared with blood from the backlash of the whip.

Jonan shrugged, his cheerfulness unimpaired as he rubbed his injured arm against the chair, meticulously wiping his blood onto the upholstery. It dramatically increased the sting, but it was worth it. Lady Wrendal's eyes seemed caught on the sight. Jonan followed her gaze, and the sight of the blood brought back the image of the boy in the square. The cold anger that rushed through him cleared some of the fog still shrouding his mind.

"Thought I'd add to the decorations," he said, his voice suddenly hard. "Kyonan blood is the foundation of this place, but the furniture didn't match. Now it does."

Her eyes flicked quickly up to his, their expression impossible to read. He held her gaze for a long moment, and was surprised when she didn't look away in distaste or discomfort.

The standoff was interrupted by the sound of a door opening down the corridor, and Lady Wrendal quickly stepped back from him. She hesitated for a moment, her eyes sweeping over his seated position, then strode across the room to settle in a chair against the far wall. Jonan watched her in surprise. Was she trying to shield him from reprimand for taking a seat? If so, why?

He had no time to consider the matter further, as Lord

Wrendal exited the corridor into the small entrance room at that moment. His eyes fell first on the corner where he had left Jonan, then scoured quickly across the small space, noting his daughter in her seat, before settling on Jonan. His expression soured as he took in Jo's comfortable posture. He opened his mouth, but paused, apparently struggling to master himself.

Mundsen appeared behind him, a strangled cry of protest bursting out of him at the bloodied state of Jonan's chair.

Lord Wrendal silenced the ambassador with a look before turning to Jonan.

"I have considered your situation, uh—" He paused. "What is your name, boy?"

"Jonan," Jo supplied succinctly. The nobleman waited, but he seemed to realize after a moment that nothing more was forthcoming.

"Well, Jonan," Lord Wrendal managed to turn the name into an insult, despite his obvious effort to keep his tone level. "I have considered your situation, and I have decided to be lenient, given your unfamiliarity with the laws regulating your kind here in Balenol. You will not be punished for failing to register your presence."

Jo's eyebrows had gone up at the phrase "your kind", and he made no effort to acknowledge Lord Wrendal's speech.

The nobleman's eyes narrowed. "But any further displays of insubordination like the one in the square, and I will not be so forgiving."

The expectant silence drew out, and Jonan glanced around at the group.

"What, am I supposed to say thank you?"

Lord Wrendal's hand twitched, as if he was suppressing with difficulty the urge to again box Jonan's ears. Behind him, his daughter's face once again betrayed a flash of annoyance. Jonan felt a ghost of his earlier smile return. So he irritated her lady-ship, did he? So much the better.

"As a gesture of goodwill," Lord Wrendal continued, his teeth clenched, "you will be accommodated in the castle neighborhood. You are not under any circumstances to attempt to enter the castle unaccompanied."

"No thanks," said Jonan flatly. "I'll find my own lodgings."

"You will humor me in this matter," said the nobleman, a dangerous note entering his voice. Jo opened his mouth to again refuse him, but his eyes slid past the man in front of him to Lady Wrendal, still seated across the room. Her displeasure was clear on her face.

Jo hesitated. His first thought had been that staying anywhere near the court would make it more difficult to track down the resistance gang he had so briefly encountered earlier that morning. But on reflection, he realized that there may be advantages to being so close to the decision makers of the land. Who knew what information he might be able to glean? They were going to keep him under watch anyway, so either way his search would be hampered. Plus he probably didn't actually have enough gold to secure lodgings on his own. On balance it seemed smartest to follow along with Lord Wrendal's plans for now. The satisfying likelihood of his proximity getting under the skin of the haughty young peeress had nothing to do with it, of course.

"If you insist," Jonan said to the Overseer, his tone deceptively mild. He thought that Lady Wrendal looked suspicious at his sudden capitulation, but her father seemed satisfied.

A slave boy was summoned from the depths of Mundsen's offices, and charged with a message instructing that lodgings be prepared for Jo.

"You forgot to say please," Jonan interjected on the slave's behalf. The boy just shot him a terrified glance before scurrying from the room.

Jo thought that Lord Wrendal was only pretending not to have heard so that he didn't have to respond, but either way he strode to the doorway of the building, calling for the soldiers to fall in line. His movement seemed to be the cue for Mundsen to melt back to wherever he had come from.

Lady Wrendal stood slowly, but instead of immediately following her father, she approached Jonan with measured steps. There was stiff disapproval in her every movement.

"You do him no favors by encouraging him to be insolent, you know," she said, and it took Jonan a moment to realize that she was talking about the slave.

"Well, you're the authority on best slave behavior I'm sure, since your dear old father is their benevolent overseer. But there is a downside to preying only on the most vulnerable—you learn to underestimate what we're made of. You'll find that not every Kyonan has his spirit so easily broken."

As he spoke, Jonan pushed himself to his feet. He stood too quickly, forgetting the extent of his injuries, and for a moment his senses reeled. He reached out a hand and grasped Lady Wrendal's arm to steady himself, subconsciously seeking the support of the only other person nearby. She ripped her arm out of his grip instantly, letting out a hiss.

"Don't touch me!"

Jonan noted the way her eyes flicked to her father, his back to them as he stood in the doorway, speaking to the soldier who had whipped Jonan.

"Relax, *My Lady*," Jonan shot back. "I've already told you, you're not my type. I prefer warm-blooded Kyonans, not cold-hearted monsters."

Some emotion, brief but intense, passed over Lady Wrendal's face. Jo could identify anger, which he had expected, but he was thrown by the other impressions that flashed through his mind. Surely he was mistaken in thinking that she looked grieved more than irritated.

Before he had time to do more than ask himself the question, she had turned on her heel and followed her father out the door.

CHAPTER FIVE

Jonan opened his eyes, awareness returning slowly as he attempted to make sense of his surroundings. The way everything rocked made him think he must be back on the ship, but the space was too well-furnished for that.

He rolled over with a groan, wondering why his whole body ached, then suddenly everything came back in a rush. He sat bolt upright, wincing at the subsequent rush of dizziness. Once everything was the right way up again, he looked curiously around at his lodgings. It was a pleasant room, much nicer than anywhere he had slept before, with the exception of his few days at the castle in Kynton. His own room at home had held only a small bed and a rickety set of shelves. Large as it was, this room felt crowded to him, the large and comfortable four poster bed in which he was settled being supplemented by a plush armchair, a tall wardrobe, a heavy wooden chest at the foot of the bed, and a washstand complete with a basin of water and a looking glass.

The room was dim, but a glance at the window showed that the curtains were not drawn. Jonan stretched his stiff limbs, grimacing at their soreness. He felt disoriented. How long had he been asleep? And why had he been asleep?

He vaguely remembered being shepherded through the streets back in the direction of the castle, the soldier who had lashed him giving him murderous looks that told him that not everyone was ready to accept his new status as guest rather than rebel. His recollection of entering the building was hazy, and he had no idea where he was in relation to the castle or to Mundsen's rooms.

He heaved himself up and wandered over to the looking glass. He barely restrained a groan at the sight of himself. It had been weeks since he had seen his reflection, but he suspected that its unfamiliar appearance was less to do with the passage of time and more to do with the bruise blooming under one eye and the deep gash on his cheek from the whip.

His face was clear of blood though, and he realized upon closer scrutiny that his arm had been neatly bandaged. He suddenly remembered that as he had let himself fall onto the bed upon his arrival he had heard Lady Wrendal instructing someone to call a physician to see to his injuries. A flicker of surprise at the consideration had been his last conscious thought before he had blacked out. He felt strange at the thought of someone tending to him while he was unconscious, but he couldn't deny that he felt better than he had when he arrived in the room.

From the fading light outside, he could only assume that it was early evening. He wondered if the physician had drugged him for him to have slept so long. He glanced back at the bed and saw his rucksack sitting on the floor, propped a little too neatly in place. No doubt his belongings had been searched while he was out of it, but the thought didn't trouble him. He had nothing of interest for anyone to find, other than perhaps his chain, which a quick check reassured him was still around his neck.

He went to rub his face, but thought better of it, running a hand through his hair instead. Its dark waves flopped back into his eyes immediately, obscuring the beads of sweat that stood out on his forehead. Looking again at his reflection, he remembered Lady Wrendal's description of him with a grin. He thought repulsive was a bit harsh, but he certainly presented a disheveled appearance, even with his wounds dressed. He had let himself get a bit wild during his travels. With any luck that would allow him to keep well clear of any court nonsense Lord Wrendal might attempt to draw him into in hopes of weaseling out information about the state of Kyonan politics.

Another glance around the room revealed that a fresh set of clothes had been laid out for him. Such considerate hosts he had, he thought with an ironical snort. It was a bit overwhelming how quickly his circumstances seemed to have somersaulted. He was tempted to remain in his own clothes, despite their tattered and bloodied state, but he couldn't deny that the lighter fabric of the Balenan garb was appealing. Even at this time of day, the air was heavy with moisture, and his tunic clung to him with unpleasant stickiness.

After completing a simple wash at the basin, he changed quickly into the simple outfit, then strode to the room's only door. Pushing it open, he stuck his head into the corridor, looking in both directions. He was faintly surprised to see no soldiers stationed outside his room, but he knew better than to let himself relax. He had heard Lord Wrendal's intentions, and he knew that watching eyes would not be far away.

As if in response to his thoughts, someone rounded a corner and came into sight. For a moment Jonan wondered uneasily how they had known exactly when he would wake, but a second look demonstrated that this young Kyonan girl could hardly be his assigned minder.

"Hey!" he hailed her quietly, and she jumped, startled. "How are you doing?"

She just stared back at him with wide eyes. He felt a flicker of annoyance at her fearful demeanor, but immediately chastised himself for it. He might bemoan the lack of fighting spirit he had already witnessed in his enslaved countrymen, but he knew it was unfair to blame them for it. He was free.

"Sorry, I didn't mean to scare you," he tried again. "I was just wondering if you could answer some questions for me."

She hesitated, coming a few steps closer but stopping out of arm's reach.

"What can I help you with, sir?" she asked, her voice faint.

Jonan shook his head emphatically. "No need to call me sir," he said. "In fact, please don't. I'm not anyone official. I think I'm kind of here by mistake."

He saw her eyes flick to his arm in a gesture that was becoming familiar. Her expression hardened slightly, and when she spoke her voice was flat. "I saw Lady Wrendal bring you in here, sir, and she said to tell her when you woke up. I should go and do so."

"Wait," said Jonan quickly, pushing aside his surprise at the information that Lady Wrendal wanted further involvement with his situation. "Before you do, can you tell me where exactly I am?"

She stared at him. "In Nohl, sir."

"I told you, don't call me sir," said Jo shortly. "I know I'm in Nohl, but what is this building?"

"Oh," she said, her expression clearing. "It's overflow lodgings for the castle, si—, I mean—" she struggled for a moment, clearly unsure what to call him, then pushed on. "They use it for visiting envoys from other cities or even other countries, if the castle is too full, or if the visitors aren't important enough to be so near the royals."

"I see," said Jo thoughtfully. "Thanks." He was faintly relieved that he wasn't on the property of Lord Wrendal. It might make it easier to slip away unnoticed for his own explorations. He looked back at the girl. "Am I the only one staying here right now?"

She shook her head. "No, there's a small diplomatic group visiting from Thirl." When Jo remained silent, she explained further. "That's the capital of Thorania."

"I know," he said quickly. "Why aren't they in the castle?"

"Oh, the important ones are," she assured him. "It's just the extra aides staying here. Foreign dignitaries always bring way more people than they need. I guess a diplomatic delegation is a good excuse for people to explore outside their own kingdom, but I don't know why they bother with that these days, not here at least. There's not much to do in Nohl that they can't do in Thirl, as far as I know. This group has barely left the building the whole time they've been here."

"What do you mean, these days?" asked Jo curiously. "Did there used to be more to do in Nohl?"

"Not in Nohl," she said. "But the Balenan royals used to love taking visiting groups to explore the jungles, to show off 'its natural beauty and its productivity'." The sudden change in her tone suggested that the last phrase was a quote. There was also a bitter edge to her voice, and Jo remembered Lord Wrendal's mention of logging camps. Operated by slaves, presumably. "If you can call scheduled day trips exploring," the girl was continuing contemptuously. "But even that they don't do anymore. Not since..."

"Since what?" Jo prompted when she trailed off. She shot him a sharp look and didn't answer.

"Speaking of the Thoranian group," she said instead, "they'll be dining shortly. You were to join them if you woke up in time."

"All right," said Jonan, hiding his surprise at the inclusion. He locked away the unfinished conversation for later exploration. "Can you show me where to go?"

She nodded, and pulling his door shut behind him, he followed her down the corridor. For a moment they walked in silence, but Jo was eager not to waste the opportunity to learn as much as he could about this place.

"Can I ask you a personal question?" he said, and she started slightly at the sudden noise. She looked up at him warily, but since she didn't actually refuse, he barreled on. "You look pretty young. How long ago were you brought here?"

"What do you mean?" she asked cautiously.

"You're Kyonan, aren't you?"

"Of course," she said in surprise. "I'm a slave, aren't I?"

Jo's steps faltered slightly as he processed this way of putting it, but he didn't dwell on it. "So when were you taken from Kyona?"

"I wasn't," she said shortly. "I was born here."

"Here in Balenol?" Jo asked, his own voice surprised.

She nodded. "My parents were slaves, so I was born a slave."

Jo swallowed, the words "born a slave" triggering some of his previous anger. "Were?" he pressed.

The girl shrugged. "Or are, I suppose. I have no reason to think that they're not still alive." She glanced at him and saw his confusion. "You really are new here, aren't you?" she asked, a touch of humor in her voice. "I was taken away from my parents when I was small, like we all are. I was raised here in Nohl, but they didn't live in the city. They were out somewhere south, I think." She waved a hand vaguely toward the corridor wall.

Jonan tore his gaze away from her face, trying to hide his

horror. "Have you ever thought about trying to escape to go find them?" he asked.

She started again, and looked around nervously. "You shouldn't say things like that!" she hissed. "Especially not since Lord Wrendal and his daughter have been lurking around. Thanks to you," she added with a reproachful look. "I'm not looking for any trouble. I'm lucky to have been raised and trained as a housemaid, instead of sent to the logging camps."

"Lucky?" said Jonan incredulously. "Let me tell you something about where I grew up—your country! Children aren't taken away from their parents by bloodthirsty, greedy cowards! And there are no slaves. I admire you for trying to stay positive, but you can't call yourself lucky!"

She looked up at him skeptically. "No slaves?" she repeated. "There must be slaves."

"No, there aren't," he assured her.

"Who does the work then? The jobs the rich people don't want to do?"

"Well, rich people have servants, of course," conceded Jonan. "But they work for pay."

"You mean they get fed and given somewhere to sleep," the girl said. "So do we."

Jonan shook his head. "No, I mean they get paid with gold."

"Wow," said his guide, sounding almost dazed. "With actual gold?"

"Yes," Jo confirmed. "And they're not forced to stay. They can leave and find a different job if they don't like where they are."

"Wow," she said again, musing on this concept. She turned her eyes up to him again. "Were you a servant?"

"No," said Jonan, "I wasn't."

"You're someone rich then? Or a noble? You had your own servants?"

Jo shook his head. "No, I guess I was just in between. No one answered to me, but I didn't answer to anyone either."

"Sounds nice," she said wistfully.

"It was, I suppose," he acknowledged, quite struck by this view of his life.

"So why are you here in Nohl?" the girl asked him.

"Uh..." For a moment Jonan floundered for an answer, but he was saved by their sudden arrival at their destination. His guide fell silent as soon as she ushered him into a large dining hall, and before he could blink she had disappeared back into the corridor. Slaves seemed to be well trained in being invisible, he reflected.

The table before him already seated half a dozen people. Jonan had never seen a Thoranian before, and he looked at the group around him curiously. He couldn't see any obvious difference in appearance from Balenans. And there was no mistaking the by now familiar hint of derision in their expressions as they looked him up and down. It was clear how Kyonans were viewed in the South Lands.

He thought of the girl's comment, as if Kyonan and slave were interchangeable words, and his own expression hardened. If these Thoranians thought they could cow him with their disapproval, they would soon learn their mistake. He would scorn the good opinion of such people anyway.

Their food, on the other hand, he didn't scorn. He hadn't realized until he smelled the meal just how hungry he was. His meager breakfast on the ship felt like a week ago. His mind reeled at the thought. Had it really been only that morning that he had stepped onto the pier?

The Thoranians had already started eating, and he didn't wait for an invitation before helping himself to the contents of the platters in the middle of the table. The dishes were unfamiliar, but he was hungry enough not to care what he ate. He shoveled the food down, making no attempt to engage with his table companions. It was therefore left to one of them to initiate conversation.

"So, you're the newly arrived Kyonan envoy are you?"

Jo looked up in surprise. "Envoy? Not really. I'm just a traveler." He assumed an expression of false modesty. "But I am Kyonan, yes, thank you for noticing."

The others exchanged incredulous looks, and he could see that they thought him a liar, and a poor one at that, when he claimed he was just traveling through.

"Perhaps you bring news of this new king we have heard about," prompted another man.

"New king..." mused Jo, helping himself to some kind of banana that was much too dense and not nearly sweet enough. "I did hear something about that."

"Well?" the speaker said impatiently when Jo didn't elaborate. "If you've just come from Kyona, you must know more than we do. Do you know something of this king?"

"Know something of him..." Jo repeated. In his mind he saw a vivid picture of Cal in the courtyard of the royal castle at Kynton, his sword held high above his head, white hot dragon fire pouring from it, and the usurper on the ground at his feet. Jo hid a smile. "Not much, really. Apparently he's quite fierce."

The Thoranians glanced uneasily at each other. Jo had to restrain a chuckle as a memory surfaced, unbidden, of the time when a young Cal had been so moved by the performance of a traveling minstrel that Jo had caught him in the act of wiping away tears. He had sworn on his honor that his friend would never hear the end of it, but he realized suddenly that it had been years since he had ribbed Cal about it. He felt a deep sense of sadness at the missed opportunities.

"Oh yes," he said aloud, calmly. "Very fierce, from what I've heard." He chewed in silence for a moment. "As I understand it," he continued, watching their faces surreptitiously, "he has some kind of personal vendetta against the slave trade, too."

That was true enough, at least. After all Elnora, with whom Cal had fallen hopelessly in love, had grown up in fear of the traders, her childhood in Kyona's largest coastal city marred by their violence.

He had hoped for some kind of telling reaction to his words, so he was disappointed when he realized that his audience's attention was no longer on him. The scraping of six chairs suddenly filled the room, as each of the Thoranians sprang to his feet. Following their gaze in bemusement, Jo saw a vision of loveliness framed in the doorway.

Lady Wrendal. He reflected irrelevantly that she had arrived so quickly that her father's property must be nearby after all. He saw that her eyes were on him, and he took his time in looking her slowly up and down, his expression pointedly mocking. Then he continued eating, his movements unhurried.

"Stand up, you lout," hissed one of the Thoranian aides.

"Why?" asked Jo, looking between the man and Lady Wrendal with interest. "Is she royalty or something?"

"Close enough," muttered another one of the aides, inclining his head respectfully when Lady Wrendal glanced his way.

"Thank you for your consideration, sirs," said Lady Wrendal musically, "but we mustn't expect the manners of a man from an animal." She nodded graciously. "Don't let me interrupt your meal." They resumed their seats, and Lady Wrendal turned to Jonan, her expression hardening. "A word, if you please, Kyonan."

Jo regarded her curiously. "And what if I don't please?"

He wasn't sure what he enjoyed more, the sharp intake of breath from each of the men at the table, or the look of intense irritation that flitted involuntarily across the peeress's face before she managed to again smooth her features. In all honesty he was quite intrigued to hear what she wanted to speak to him about, but he simply couldn't resist playing to his audience.

"Do you have no respect, cur?" snarled one of the Thoranians, and Jo looked over at him, his expression mild.

"Of course I do," he said. "I have great respect for anything and anyone I consider worthy of respect."

The man seemed to swell before Jo's eyes, but whatever explosion was coming was cut off by Lady Wrendal's voice, which didn't sound quite as musical as usual.

"Well, I don't ask you to respect me, Jonan of Kyona, merely to speak with me for a moment. Then you can return to whatever worthless way you ordinarily spend your time."

"If that's all," said Jonan with a shrug, "I suppose I can condescend to oblige you." Ignoring the glares all around him he rose to his feet with an exaggerated sigh, trying to hide his curiosity as he made his way around the table.

Lady Wrendal stepped back to allow him to pass through the doorway, then shut the door behind her just as she had done at Mundsen's rooms. Jo waited expectantly, but she just stared at him for a moment, chewing the inside of her cheek in a gesture that struck him as less than ladylike. It seemed that having gotten his attention, she was unsure how to start.

"You seem to be developing a fondness for speaking with me in corridors," he offered by way of an opening sally.

She disregarded his words, but he appeared to have successfully unlocked her tongue. "I asked to be informed when you awoke," she said.

He nodded. "Yes, that girl told me as much. She was efficient in fetching you, it seems." He glanced wistfully back at the closed door. "I didn't even have time to finish my meal, and I was hungry enough to eat the slop you people consider edible, too."

She had scowled at his mention of the serving girl, and she ignored the rest of his speech. "I gather that you had significant speech with the girl," she said, an accusatory note in her voice. "Can you tell me why she seemed lost in daydreams when she spoke of you?"

Jo raised his eyebrows in surprise. "I don't know," he said. "Maybe *she* doesn't think I'm repulsive."

Something twitched behind Lady Wrendal's expression. "Or maybe," she said, her voice hard, "you used the short time you crossed her path to fill her head with ideas of insubordination that would achieve nothing but getting her killed."

Jo leveled a look at her. "Naturally you are most concerned for her welfare, oh Overseer's daughter."

"It is not I, but you who claim to be concerned for the welfare of your fellow Kyonans. If you cannot restrain your impertinence for your own sake, you might do so for theirs."

Jo shrugged. "I don't like playing a part, My Lady," he said.

"Yes," she said waspishly, "that much you have made abundantly clear."

Her met her look with amusement. "I recognize no right of yours to tell me how to conduct myself. After all, you called me indiscreet, but here you are, accosting innocent young men in private places." He assumed a bashful expression. "I'm not sure how much clearer I can be that your attentions are unwelcome."

"I would hardly call this corridor a private—" Lady Wrendal began, her voice a snarl, but she cut herself off, inhaling deeply. She took a moment to collect herself, her eyes closed and her shoulders stiff.

Jo watched her thoughtfully. "What did that man mean about you being almost royalty?" he asked, fully aware of the impertinence of his question. You're not some kind of a princess, are you?"

"Of course not," she said shortly, still looking irritated.

"Are you perhaps betrothed to the king?" Jonan persisted. "I thought he was middle-aged, but maybe that doesn't bother you.

I wonder what he, or your father for that matter, would think of you pushing yourself on a poor young traveler."

He thought he saw a look of unease flit across her features, quite different from the annoyance he usually provoked. "I am most certainly not betrothed to the king," she said, her tone clearly discouraging further discussion. "And that Thoranian man was right—you should learn to show some respect." She pulled herself together with an obvious effort, clearly not wanting to get further sidetracked. "In any event, I did not come here to discuss my life with you."

"What did you come here to discuss, then?" Jonan asked, quite at his ease.

She glared at him. "I wished to ascertain whether you had been successfully settled into your accommodations."

"I have," said Jo shortly, then waited. He didn't for a moment imagine that she had sought him out for purely that purpose.

"And are they to your liking?" she asked, her tone deceptively polite.

He shrugged. "They'll do."

She took a deep breath, as if willing herself not to lose her temper. "I spoke with the physician who attended you."

Jonan gave her a look of genuine curiosity. "Did you? I acknowledge, I was surprised that you thought to arrange his visit. I suppose I should thank you, but I wouldn't want to disappoint your expectations of me by showing so much humanity."

"He said," she pushed on as if she hadn't heard him, "that you should be strongly encouraged to rest for a few days." Their gazes locked for a moment, and he was certain she could see the amusement in his eyes.

She sighed, and he couldn't resist a smile. They both knew that he was not going to spend the next few days on bed rest. Her gaze traveled from his eyes down to his cheek. "I'm afraid he also said that the injury on your face and the one on your arm will certainly both leave a scar."

"I assume that by 'injury' you mean the lash of the whip intended for a frightened child who I suspect had committed no wrong other than being Kyonan?" clarified Jonan with unimpaired cheerfulness. "Ah well, you win some, you lose some. I don't mind a scar here or there myself."

"Don't you?" For some reason she seemed to find his answer amusing, but she didn't explain herself. "I'm glad to see you so unconcerned," she said instead. "The physician did not anticipate any other lasting detriment from your..."

"Beating," Jonan supplied helpfully when she hesitated over a word.

"Adventure," she finished dryly. After eyeing him thoughtfully for a moment, she continued. "In any event, you will have gathered that you have slept for most of the day and darkness has now fallen. I realize that you probably do not feel like going back to your bed, but you would be most unwise to venture outside this building tonight."

"Thank you for your guidance," said Jonan gravely. "I'll consider it carefully."

Her face twitched, unable to fully restrain her irritation at his obvious disregard for her warning, but she didn't press the matter.

"May I return to my meal now?" Jo asked with mock politeness when the silence stretched out.

She stepped to the side, clearing the way back to the dining hall, but as he began to walk past her, she reached out a hand and grabbed his arm. He looked from her hand to her face, his eyebrows raised, and she let go quickly.

"Is what you said true?" she asked abruptly. "About the new Kyonan king? Is he set against the slave trade?"

Jo rocked back on his heels, taking in the look on her face.

She was trying to maintain a calm facade, but she was clearly very interested in his answer. He supposed it shouldn't be a surprise that she had a vested interest in the matter, given her father's role.

He shrugged, keeping his tone carefully light. "It's possible that it's true. So much speculation surrounds his mysterious person, how can I be sure?"

She narrowed her eyes at him. "And you know nothing much of this new king, you say?"

He shrugged again. "How would I, a lowly traveler, more animal than man some might say, know anything of royalty, after all?"

She gave him an unexpectedly shrewd look. "So you're not entirely averse to playing a part," she said tartly.

Jo opened his mouth, but nothing came to mind. He saw the triumphant gleam in her eyes as she turned away, and felt aggrieved that she had emerged from the encounter victorious.

His mood didn't improve any when he found, upon returning to the dining hall, that the food had already been cleared away. So much for finishing his meal. With no desire to linger in conversation with the Thoranians, he returned to his room, not needing the services of a guide this time.

He wanted to explore the rest of the building, but that could wait for the morrow. On reflection, he thought that the real purpose of Lady Wrendal's visit was her warning against venturing out that night. Naturally he had intended to do so anyway, but her determination that he not go outside certainly added an extra layer of intrigue.

He knew that he would be watched regardless of the time, but he still thought it best to wait until the city outside had stilled for the night before venturing forth. That meant a wait of a few hours. He had never done well with inactivity, and he was fairly chafing for movement by the time he deemed it late enough. It was difficult to tell for certain, as his window opened onto a private pleasure garden rather than the street, but eventually he thought that a quiet had settled over the neighborhood.

He could only assume that there were soldiers at the door of the building, none being stationed outside his room. He was just wondering whether they would stop him from leaving or just follow him discreetly when he was startled by a quiet knock on his window.

Looking up, he did a double take at the sight of the young face on the other side of the glass. Crossing the room with quick strides, he threw the window open.

"Well, this is a surprise," he said with amusement. "Cody, isn't it?"

"That's right," said his visitor, sounding pleased at the recognition. "Got plans this evening?"

"Actually," said Jonan, a grin spreading across his face, "I find myself with nothing but free time."

"Great," said Cody, returning the grin. "Wanna come see my world?"

CHAPTER SIX

Cody declined the offer of coming inside, but Jo wasn't left long in suspense as to how the younger boy proposed to make good their escape.

"Can you climb?" Cody asked, giving Jo an appraising look.

"Yes," Jo assured him. He had actually always been very good at climbing.

"What about your arm, though?" Cody's tone was doubtful.

"It's nothing," said Jo hurriedly. "I'm fine."

Cody shrugged. "If you say so. Just don't fall. I would have to leave you and get out of here." He disappeared from the window, only to reappear after a moment, raising his eyebrows at Jo's unmoving form. "Well, come on then!"

Jonan hastened to follow his guide, clambering onto the window ledge with an agility that belied his injuries. He had realized that his room was on the second floor of the stately stone building, but he hadn't noticed that there was a third floor above it.

Looking up, he saw that Cody was already standing on the top of the frame that ran around the entire window, nimbly pulling himself up on a decorative ridge protruding from the stone between the levels. In no time at all, the boy had reached the window above Jonan's, and was reaching for the eaves above it. Jo did his best to copy Cody's movements, feeling his whipped arm wobble as he pulled himself up, despite what he had said.

He managed to get up and over the eaves without catastrophe, although he wasn't quite as silent in scrabbling up the tiled roof as his companion had been. Crouching low, Cody made his way halfway up the sloped surface, stopping soon enough to be hidden behind the ridge should anyone be looking from a nearby building. Glancing around, Jo could see that there were not many other buildings as tall as this one in the immediate vicinity. He thought he could dimly make out the castle ahead and to his right, but it was too far away to bring the risk of detection.

Cody waited patiently for Jo to catch up with him, then spoke in a whisper so quiet Jo had to lean precariously forward to hear him.

"They've got people watching the doors at each exit of the building. They really don't want you to wander off, do they? But fortunately," he grinned, "no one's watching the roof."

Jo grinned back, warming instantly to the boy's cheerful attitude. "How did you know how to find me so quickly, anyway?"

Cody smiled indulgently. "So quickly? Your little drama in the castle courtyard was hours and hours ago. We've known where you were all day, we just wanted to wait until dark to come fetch you."

"Well, I'm glad you did," said Jo emphatically. "I was just about to head out looking for you, but something tells me I wouldn't have found it easy to track you down."

"With a tail on you, we would have made sure you didn't track us down," said Cody flatly. "But we can talk more when we get there."

"Get where?" Jo asked eagerly.

Cody grinned. "Back to base, of course."

Jo felt a thrill of excitement. He had the feeling he was finally about to find himself among his own kind, in more ways than one.

"It'll be a little while before it's safe to get down onto the street," Cody was saying. "We'll have to jump. Follow me."

Jo followed without hesitation, even as he wondered if Cody could really be suggesting that they jump off a three level building. But as they reached the southern edge of the rooftop, closest to the castle, he realized what Cody was talking about. The buildings were quite close together in this part of the city, and the gap from one roof to the next was jumpable, for someone fit and strong enough.

Jo eyed Cody's boyish stature doubtfully, but a moment later it was clear that he had underestimated his guide. Cody leaped over the distance with surprising grace, landing as silently as a cat on the sloped roof of the next building. Jo swallowed once before backing up to get some momentum. It was a long way down, but he tried not to think about it. He cleared the gap successfully, but the clatter of his boots on the second roof made both boys wince and once again crouch low, holding their breath.

After a long moment Cody seemed satisfied that the noise had not attracted attention, and he shot Jo a reassuring smile. "Don't worry, you'll get the hang of it," he whispered encouragingly. "It's all about the way you absorb the impact. You've got to land on the balls of your feet and follow the momentum."

Jo nodded meekly, trying not to smile at the parental tone in the young boy's voice. The next jump required them to first lower themselves onto a balcony, since the neighboring building was only two levels high. Jo followed Cody closely across three more rooftops before the young Kyonan declared it safe to descend to the street. This feat was accomplished without too much difficulty given that the building they were creeping across had only one floor.

Once their feet hit the cobblestones, Cody took off at an impressive pace, flitting through the silent streets like a shadow. Jo tried to follow the way his guide avoided the sporadic pools of light thrown by the lanterns. The sky had cleared while Jonan slept, and a faint moonlight sped their passage.

It was hard to get a good sense of direction in the darkness, but Jo thought that they must have passed the castle some distance on their left. They ran on for only about fifteen minutes before Jo looked ahead and saw a wall looming up in front of them. He hadn't realized that the castle neighborhood was so close to the southern edge of the city. It had seemed central when he glimpsed it from the Kyonan ship, but Nohl was not as big as he had at first assumed. He was just wondering whether Cody intended to attempt to climb the wall when the younger boy veered to the side and stopped outside a small building that sat not far inside the stone barrier.

Instead of knocking, Cody let out a complicated whistle that sounded almost like a bird call. After a moment, the door eased open. Cody slipped in, followed closely by Jonan. The door closed behind them with a soft click, and Jo turned to see who had pushed it. A woman whom he judged to be about thirty was nodding a greeting at Cody, but neither of them spoke. She gave Jo an appraising look, still silent, before crossing the small space and kneeling down.

A quick glance around the room showed Jonan that he was in a simple dwelling. There was only one room, very sparsely furnished, and it appeared that she lived here alone. His curiosity was piqued—the mark on her arm denoted her slave status, and he could only imagine that it was not normal for slaves to have their own homes.

But there was no lingering for explanations. Cody hurried

forward to help the woman roll up a threadbare rug that covered part of the floor. A rough stone slab was revealed beneath it, set into the dirt floor. The woman lifted the stone with a quiet grunt, and a black hole yawned beneath it.

Jonan raised his eyebrows, impressed. With an encouraging glance back at him, Cody lowered himself quickly into the hole. Jonan nodded his thanks at their hostess before doing the same. He felt his feet touch the bottom sooner than he had expected, and realized that he would have to crawl to follow the tunnel that opened out from the hole. He could only just make out Cody's feet up ahead, and he pushed his aching limbs forward.

After a couple of seconds, he heard the stone slab being replaced over the hole, and the tunnel instantly became pitch black. Jo blinked rapidly in an instinctive response, but of course it made no difference. His skin prickled in the tight space. He couldn't tell if the rush of coolness that passed over him meant that the air was less warm down here, or just that his body was communicating the fear of blind confinement that his mind was too stubborn to acknowledge.

He crawled forward for what felt like an alarmingly long time, with only the quiet scuffle of Cody's movements to assure him that he was not alone. Eventually he realized with relief that the tunnel was starting to slope upward. Finally he heard a rustle ahead, and a moment later discovered why as his questing hands found foliage instead of dirt.

He emerged out of the tunnel, breathing deeply as he felt a knot of tension release. Looking around, he saw with another thrill of excitement that they had come up in the jungle. He glanced back and glimpsed the city wall between the trees. The jungle evidently grew right up to the wall.

Turning around again, he saw Cody grinning at him. "It's cool, hey?" the younger boy said. "You were pretty calm. I nearly had a heart attack the first time I went through the tunnel."

Jo laughed. "You definitely wouldn't want to have too big a gut. I guess all you rebels must be pretty fit." The release of talking again at normal volume was almost as great as the relief of emerging from the confined space. Somehow the humidity no longer felt so suffocating, despite the fact that there was even more moisture in the air out here in the jungle.

"Come on," said Cody. "It's not too far but we'd better be quick. There are scarier things than soldiers out here," he added, the impact of the warning substantially lessened by his accompanying wink.

Cody took off again, and it was all Jo could do to keep up in the unfamiliar terrain. He looked around him with fascination as they cut their way through the undergrowth, hoping fervently that he would have the chance to visit the jungle during daylight. Still, even the dappled moonlight seemed to provide substantial illumination after the close blackness of the tunnel. The trees were incredibly thick and tall for how close to the edge of the jungle they were. There was no wind, but soft rustles sounded all around them, and the hairs on the back of Jo's neck stood up from the unnerving sensation of being watched.

If he hadn't been confident of Cody's intentions he would have wondered if the boy was trying to lose him in the foliage, given the unpredictable way he was darting to and fro. Glancing back at him after a few minutes, Cody caught his look of confusion and shrugged.

"We can't take the most obvious route, or we'll leave a track over time."

Jo nodded. It made sense. His still-recovering limbs were starting to protest when Cody slowed noticeably in front of him. Looking up, Jo saw that they were approaching an enormous tree, its branches arching over them in a huge canopy. Vines climbed all around its massive trunk, and dangled loosely from the overhanging branches. He looked up for a moment, distracted by the sight, and when he looked down Cody was nowhere to be seen. He blinked, staring around in confusion. Surely the kid had been right in front of him.

He was still gazing at the empty space, nonplussed, when Cody's head suddenly appeared, apparently from inside the tree, wreathed in its usual grin.

"What—?" Jonan tried not to laugh at the improbable sight of Cody's head growing out of the trunk. Cody beckoned him forward, and as he approached he realized that there was a long slit in the bark, tall enough for a man to walk through, which wasn't obvious unless you were almost touching the tree. He passed through the gash in Cody's wake, and was amazed when they came out into a large open space. Evidently the tree had become hollow with age, and only its shell remained. He supposed it would be more obvious in the daylight, but it was still an impressive hiding place.

It was even darker inside the tree, of course, and Jo wondered if other rebels were lurking nearby. But Cody didn't hail anyone, instead skipping over to a spot near the middle of the space and stomping his foot in an uneven triple tap. Jo was surprised to hear the sound of a boot on wood, rather than the packed dirt he would have expected. Immediately a trapdoor swung upward, Cody jumping nimbly aside to avoid it.

Flickering light spilled out of the hole beneath the trapdoor, and a voice called up to Cody.

"That was quick! We weren't expecting you so soon."

"Yeah, we made good time!" Cody said cheerfully. "His injuries didn't seem to slow him down at all."

"Well bring him down," said the voice, and Cody once again beckoned to Jo. Walking over, he peered into the gap and saw another Kyonan, a few years older than him, holding a torch and standing on a small wooden platform. A ladder led down to the platform, and he could see the start of a rough staircase made of wooden planks.

He followed Cody down the ladder, and the other man closed the trapdoor behind them. Turning around, Jonan got a good look at the rebels' hideout and felt his mouth fall open in amazement.

If he had thought that the space inside the hollow tree was large, it was nothing to the space below it. A huge underground cavern had been excavated beneath the forest giant, whose mighty roots created a domed vault more impressive than any building Jo had ever entered.

The hideout was generously lit with torches on brackets all around the dirt walls, and to Jo's dazed eyes, it seemed full of people. One glance was enough to confirm that all of those present were Kyonan, and the slave mark could be seen on every arm. Most of them seemed young, but there was some variety in age. Many eyes followed their progress as Cody led Jonan forward, a spring in his step, clearly excited to be the center of attention.

"I've brought him, boss!" he said as they approached an alcove on the far side of the space. Jonan had been looking around, but he brought his gaze quickly back to what was in front of him, eager to lay eyes on the resistance leader.

The man who turned around was neither battle-worn nor particularly imposing. And he didn't look much older than thirty. Jonan felt slightly let down, but he did his best not to show it on his face.

"Good job, Cody," the man said, his voice calm and his eyes on Jonan. "Welcome."

"Thank you," said Jo, inclining his head. "This is an impressive operation you have here. I assume this is your base?"

"One of them," said the man with a shrug, and Jonan raised his eyebrows. Just how big was this resistance? "So you just got to Nohl, I hear?" the leader continued. "And you came straight from Kyona?"

Jo nodded. "Even in the short time I've been here, I've heard of the famous Scar. I'm happy to meet you so soon." He grimaced. "And I trust you'll prove to be more impressive than the other Kyonan representative I've encountered."

The man's look of surprise gave way to amusement at Cody's shout of laughter.

"This isn't Scar!"

Jo looked at him with furrowed brows. "It's not?"

Cody shook his head emphatically, still chuckling. "You really thought Raldo was Scar? That's funny."

"Why is it so—?" Jo began, but Raldo cut him off, directing a glare at the younger boy.

"That's enough, Cody," he said. "No need to laugh at him like that. It isn't polite."

"Oh, he doesn't care about polite," Cody responded, undaunted. He turned to Jo. "Do you?"

Jo couldn't resist grinning back. "No, I don't."

"All right, Cody," said Raldo with a long-suffering sigh. "Why don't you go and take your shift on the watch?"

"But—" Cody protested, clearly wanting to stay where the action was, but Raldo silenced him with a glare.

"Go."

Cody trudged off, muttering, and Raldo watched him with a hint of fondness in his eyes, waiting until he was out of earshot before speaking again.

"You'll have to excuse Cody," he said to Jo. "He came to us younger than most, and he sometimes needs a lesson in manners."

"No need to apologize to me," said Jo quickly. "I like him."

"Yes, most people do," said Raldo with a brief smile. "I was glad he managed to make his way to us so soon after he arrived. It's much easier when their spirits haven't been broken."

Jonan wasn't sure what to say to that, so he remained silent, and after a moment Raldo continued.

"As Cody said, my name is Raldo." He held out his arm, and Jo clasped it in the traditional Kyonan greeting.

"I'm Jonan," he said, and Raldo acknowledged it with a nod before continuing.

"Scar isn't here right now, but I was asked to send someone for you. We were all very interested to meet you once we heard about your display in the castle courtyard." Raldo's eyes flicked down to Jo's bandaged arm. "I hope your injuries aren't too serious."

"Of course not," Jo hastened to assure him. "I'm fine."

Raldo raised his eyebrows. "Well then, you're tougher than you look, if that won't offend you," he said. "The report I heard was that you took quite a beating."

"That's the least of my concerns," said Jonan. "I never imagined the situation would be so bad here. Is it common for them to do public whippings in the square like that?"

"Very common," said Raldo flatly. "It's entertainment to them."

Jo felt a surge of anger, and he wished he had a useful outlet for it. "So what do we do about it? Do you have a plan? What does this resistance actually do?"

"Whoa, slow down," said Raldo, looking amused. "You just got here. Which is a question in itself, actually."

"What do you mean?" Jo asked.

"How did you get to Nohl?"

"I came on a ship, from Kyona," said Jo, unsure what was behind the question.

"But what kind of a ship?" Raldo persisted. "A slave vessel?"

Jo shook his head. "No, it was a normal trading ship,

bringing various goods. I paid my way as a passenger, and they dropped me at the port in Nohl."

Raldo looked confused. "But why did you come? Are you truly some kind of messenger from this new king we've heard whispers about?"

Jo hesitated. It was tempting to stretch the truth and say yes, and Cal would probably back him up if he could. But who knew in what kind of ways Cal's hands might be tied now? Jonan would have to be careful not to make promises he couldn't keep.

"No," he said at last. "I'm really just a traveler. No one sent me. But now that I'm here, I want to help."

Raldo looked at him thoughtfully for a minute, and Jo couldn't read his thoughts in his expression. "Well, that's something at least," said the older man eventually. His voice dropped slightly. "If Scar is right to trust you so readily."

"He is," said Jo quickly. Raldo just smiled, and Jo realized how foolish it was to expect these people to take his word for it. Raldo had seemed almost to be speaking to himself, but he didn't strike Jo as the sort of person to use words carelessly. He must have had his reasons for making the comment about trust in Jo's hearing.

"You mentioned another Kyonan representative," said Raldo. "Did you mean the ambassador? Have you met him?"

"Yes, I've met him, the sniveling idiot," said Jo. He hadn't realized that others were listening to their conversation, but his words were met by a couple of harsh laughs, even as others nearby spat angrily on the ground.

"We don't have much love for Kyonan traitors," Raldo explained darkly. "They're even worse than the Balenans."

"I agree," said Jo, and he saw a few approving nods.

"So you're staying in a castle outbuilding," Raldo continued. "How did that happen?"

Jo shrugged. "Just a mistake, I think. Lord Wrendal and the

ambassador were worried I might have been sent by the new king, too. They decided to see what they could find out from me instead of just getting rid of me. The plan was to have someone watching me all the time, but I'm pretty sure no one followed me tonight."

Raldo shook his head. "They didn't. Cody might seem young and foolish, but he's more capable than you think. He wouldn't have brought you anywhere near here if he wasn't confident that you weren't being tracked."

Jo nodded, relieved. He would hate to bring any Balenans down on this hiding place.

"Well, Jonan," said Raldo purposefully. "It strikes me that we could make good use of their suspicions, if we're smart about it."

"What did you have in mind?" Jo asked eagerly. "I don't know where Lord Wrendal lives exactly, but I'm sure I can find out. Maybe if I search his residence—"

"No," said Raldo shortly. "That's not a good idea. And that's not what we need help with. But if they think that you might be someone official, it's an opportunity to get close to those in power here. See if you can find something out from them while they're trying to find something out from you."

Jo nodded reluctantly, his heart sinking a little. Political intrigue—it seemed he couldn't escape it even on the other side of the ocean. He would much prefer to try his hand at breaking into the castle or something exciting like that. But he wanted to prove himself to these resistance fighters.

"What do you want me to find out? If I can get close, I mean."

"Well, let's start with something specific. When you ran into Cody earlier today, he was waiting at a rendezvous point for a group of our people who were out on a job. We haven't heard from them, and we're very concerned that they might have been taken by Wrendal's people. In particular Stan, who was leading the group, knows a lot of things we don't want them to discover. We need to find out where they are."

Jo nodded again. "How many of them were there?"

"Five," supplied Raldo. "All pretty young, dressed to look like slaves. They were trying to get into the camp where the latest arrivals were brought, a couple of months ago. We try to get to new people more quickly than that if we can, to see if there's anyone worth trying to liberate right away, but we were prevented from acting sooner for various reasons."

Jo raised his eyebrows. "Aren't they all worth liberating straight away?"

"Of course they are," said Raldo with a frustrated sigh. "But we can only do what we can do." He met Jo's look squarely. "What do you think? Will you try to find out what you can?"

"Of course," Jo said quickly. "Like I said, I want to help."

"Good," said Raldo. "And I'm sure I don't need to tell you how important it is to be discreet. And not to let anyone find out what you've seen tonight."

"You don't," Jonan assured him, but he couldn't help a small sigh. "Although discretion is not my favorite trait."

Raldo returned the smile. "I hope, for our cause, you'll make an exception. And now I think you'd better head back. Cody can show you the way again. He never shuts up when he's in our territory, but the kid is better than anyone at being inconspicuous when he's in the city."

Jo grinned, making a mental note of the way Raldo said "our territory". "I should take lessons," he said aloud.

"Not a bad idea," said Raldo, nodding to a girl standing nearby. In a very short time she returned with Cody, who looked only too delighted to be called back from watch duty.

"Come on then," he said brightly to Jonan, barely restraining his impatience as Jo took a hurried leave of Raldo.

The trip back out of the lair and through the jungle was

accomplished in no time, and even the crawl through the tunnel didn't seem quite so interminable now that Jonan knew what to expect at the other end. The silent woman let them through onto the street, and again Jo was hard put to keep up with his guide. Despite his afternoon of sleep, he was feeling very weary. His injuries had been forgotten in the excitement of reaching the resistance hideout, but as he followed Cody through the streets, pain again throbbed in various parts of his body.

His movements were slower than before as he pulled himself up a windowsill in imitation of Cody's lead, and the leap from roof to roof felt like a heroic feat. On the last roof before his own building's, he caught up to Cody to find the boy crouching still, glowering off to the west.

"What is it?" Jo whispered, stopping alongside him.

"Huh? Oh, there you are!" Cody said. "Sorry, we should keep going."

"What were you looking at?" Jo insisted.

Cody indicated with a nod of his head. "That manor house there," he said. "It's where the Overseer lives. Devil of a man."

"Lord Wrendal?" asked Jo sharply, and Cody nodded. Jonan followed the boy's gaze and took in an imposing stone mansion with a large garden stretching out on one side of it, pushing it back from the street. Only a couple of buildings separated it from the castle's overflow accommodation. It was hard to make out much detail in the moonlight, but he locked the information away for future consideration.

"He doesn't live there all the time, of course," whispered Cody. "His main estates are out south somewhere. But he's in Nohl a lot more now, since...well, in recent years. Feels like he's always underfoot." Cody's scowl showed what he thought of the nobleman daring to show his face in the city.

A very few minutes later, Jonan lowered himself back

through his window with relief. Cody didn't enter, but he peered through to make sure that Jo was safely settled inside.

"Wait," whispered Jo as Cody's head disappeared. "How will I get in touch with you again?"

His only answer was a ghostly chuckle that wafted in through the humid air.

CHAPTER SEVEN

Despite the excitement of his midnight adventure, Jo slept like the dead for what was left of the night. He woke quite suddenly, the soft light suggesting that the morning was not too far advanced. For a moment he was disoriented, but not because of his new room this time. In the light sleep immediately preceding awakening, his mind had been gripped by dreams, swirling with impressions and emotions rather than concrete sights. The face of the sandy-haired girl from his strange visions, whom his thoughts had identified as Marine, had certainly swum in and out of his consciousness.

But it took only a moment for full awareness to return, and Jo leaped out of bed immediately. He was filled with a nervous energy and much too eager to begin snooping around to return to sleep. He splashed water onto his face from the washstand and quickly donned the clothes he had been given the day before.

He was just striding to the door to begin explorations when he was startled by a knock. He glanced involuntarily at the window, then shook his head at himself. It was fine when he was alone, like now, but he would have to be careful. Reactions like that might give him away, and he had to protect the secrets of the resistance now, not just his own.

He continued his course to the door, where the knock had actually come from, and pulled it open. A short and anxious-looking Balenan man was standing on the other side of it, and he instantly clucked in admonishment at the sight of Jonan.

"You should be in your bed, young man!" he protested, pushing his way into the room, followed by a Balenan boy who was clearly his assistant.

"Well, why did you knock if you didn't want me to answer?" Jo said reasonably, quickly identifying the man from his bag of tools as a physician.

The physician ignored the question, instead gesturing to the bed. "Sit," he said peremptorily.

"Actually," said Jonan, still standing by the door, "I was just going out."

The man glowered at him. "I have been charged with your care, and I'm here to check on your injuries. Sit."

"Yes, I picked that up, actually," said Jo tartly. "But maybe you could come back later, because I was just about to—"

"Listen here, young whelp," snapped the physician. "It may interest you to know—"

"I doubt it," muttered Jo, and the Balenan's scowl deepened.

"—that I am the royal physician. I attend the king himself, and I am not accustomed to being requested to attend to the injuries of slaves." His gaze lingered on Jo's uninjured arm. "Or slave emissaries, or whatever you seem to be." His face twitched in annoyance. "The effects of lashes—well-earned I have no doubt—are hardly my province. I cannot imagine why Lady Wrendal—" he drew a deep breath. "But in any event, I am here, and you will submit to my examination. Now *sit*."

The command was issued in much the same tone as might be used with a trained dog, and Jo felt his blood beginning to rise. He opened his mouth to give the physician the benefit of his well-formed opinions, but a sudden thought drew him up short. He had been tasked with gleaning information from those in power, and if this man really did attend the king, he was as good a place to start as any.

The physician read the sudden submission in Jo's eyes, and the smug look that came over his face nearly undid Jo's resolution. It took every ounce of his willpower to walk slowly back to the bed and lower himself onto it. He made a show of wincing a little as he did so, thinking that it wouldn't hurt for the Balenans to think he was more weakened by his injuries than he actually was.

Whatever he thought Jonan's state was, the physician did not have gentle hands, and soon Jo's winces were not faked as the man squeezed and prodded his way through the various cuts and bruises.

"Hmm, well certainly nothing broken, as I said yesterday." Jo refrained from pointing out that as he had been unconscious during the previous examination, he was in no position to acknowledge the man's consistency.

"What is this?!" the physician demanded, sounding outraged. Following his gaze, Jo saw that blood had seeped generously through the bandage over the arm that had received the brunt of the whip's lash. He hadn't even noticed it while he was getting dressed.

"I had the bleeding well under control when I left you yesterday," said the physician, as if Jo had made his arm bleed on purpose as an affront to the man's work. The physician unwound the bandage with deft hands, exclaiming again at the sight underneath. "The wound has been reopened! You're supposed to be resting. What have you been doing?"

"Resting," lied Jonan meekly. "Perhaps it happened in the night. I'm a restless sleeper."

The physician shot him a glare, evidently trying to figure out if he was being impertinent or just annoying. Still muttering darkly, he began to redress Jonan's wound, assisted by the boy, who still hadn't said a word.

"Did you say that Lady Wrendal is the one who sent you to examine me?" Jonan asked, frowning slightly.

"Never you mind," said the physician shortly, focused on his work.

"Why's she called Lady Wrendal?" Jonan persisted, undeterred by the man's unfriendly attitude. "Shouldn't that be the name of Lord Wrendal's wife, not his daughter?"

The physician sighed, clearly irritated by the distraction, but seemed unable to resist the opportunity to insult Jonan's ignorance. "Lord Wrendal's wife *was* called Lady Wrendal, obviously. I don't know how these things work in the *Kyonan* court—"

Jonan scowled at the man's insulting tone. Truth be told, he didn't know how they worked either, but he wasn't about to admit that to the physician.

"But here," the man was continuing, "the title passes down if the mother dies. Lord Wrendal's daughter will be called Lady Wrendal until she marries, unless her father takes another wife."

"Huh," said Jonan, smiling slightly to himself at the idea of how discomfited Lady Wrendal would likely be if she was supplanted by a stepmother. He looked back at the physician, contemplating how he could turn the man's willingness to speak to him to better account.

"Do you really attend the king?" He tried to sound impressed rather than just curious.

"Of course I do. Do you think I feel the need to make idle boasts to you?" He rounded on his assistant. "No, not that one, boy, the other one! Use your wits."

Jonan watched the assistant for a moment, as he scurried to

obey. "King Siloam, right?" Jo tried again once the physician looked slightly less hostile.

"Yes, King Siloam. You're not even sure of the name of the king?" The man's tone was derisive, but Jo just shrugged.

"He's not my king."

The physician's hands faltered for the briefest of moments, and Jo had the impression that he had captured the man's interest. Obviously whispers about the new Kyonan king were spreading quickly.

"So King Siloam, he's middle-aged, isn't he?"

The physician acknowledged it with a grunt, his eyes on his work.

"So does he have any family? I haven't heard mention of a queen. Does the king have children?"

"No, he doesn't," said the physician. "He hasn't married."

"Why not?" asked Jonan, surprised. "Doesn't he have to produce an heir?"

"The king doesn't have to do anything," said the physician shortly, "and it is not for you to question royalty, boy." He paused. "King Siloam could still father children should he wish to, provided he selected a young enough queen."

Disgusting, thought Jonan, but he remained silent.

"But there is no need for him to do so," continued the physician. "He has a perfectly suitable heir in his brother, Prince Rupert. And His Highness has three sons, all of whom have now reached adulthood and could take wives at any time, so the succession is not at risk."

"Three sons," repeated Jonan, trying to keep it all straight in his head. "Did Prince Rupert have no daughters?"

The physician hesitated for a moment, still not looking up from Jonan's arm. "No," he said shortly. "Only the three princes, Prince Giles, Prince Astor, and Prince Roland."

"So Prince Rupert will be king someday, or if not him, then his oldest son, Prince Giles," mused Jonan.

"It seems likely," said the physician, his tone still discouraging.

"And I assume they all live at the castle?" Jonan continued. His expression soured in spite of himself. "With an army of slaves to attend their every need, no doubt."

The physician's face twitched unmistakably at the phrase "army of slaves", and Jo regarded the man with increasing interest. Just how big a problem was the slave resistance becoming for those in power in the capital?

"Of course," was all the physician said aloud. "And it is an honor for those slaves who find themselves fortunate enough to serve in the castle."

Jonan snorted before he could stop himself. "And would you find it an honor to work without pay or freedom for my king in the Kyonan castle?"

"That is hardly an equivalent situation," said the physician with an unpleasant laugh.

"And why is that?" demanded Jonan.

"Everyone knows that Kyonans are by nature inferior," said the older man. "It is undisputed."

"I dispute it!" said Jonan hotly, forgetting his intention to be diplomatic. "How dare you say such a thing?"

"But—" started the physician's assistant, and Jo's gaze flicked instantly to the boy, his surprise stalling his anger for a moment. The boy looked like he was thinking better of speaking, but Jo pinned him with a glare.

"But what?" he demanded.

"Well," the boy looked uneasily at his supervisor, but the physician said nothing, apparently focused on winding a new bandage around Jonan's now re-dressed arm. "Everyone knows that Kyonans are born to be slaves. It's their function. That's why fate punishes them if they try to run away."

"That's outrageous!" started Jo, but he suddenly registered the assistant's last words. "What do you mean fate punishes them?" he asked with a frown.

"Consider yourself re-treated," interrupted the physician, addressing his words to Jo but frowning at his assistant. "I will return tomorrow, and I don't want to see any more re-opened wounds. I would advise you to remain in your room today and rest."

Jo just scowled, his reserves of civility exhausted for the moment.

The physician packed up his gear efficiently. But for all he seemed in a hurry to be gone, he paused at the door, looking back at Jo.

"You mentioned your king." He hesitated. "I hear that there's a new king in Kyona. A new line, in fact."

"An old line restored," corrected Jo, his tone discouraging.

"And what can you tell us of this new king?" the physician asked with a touch of impatience.

Jo restrained a sigh. He hadn't quite decided whether to give the same answer to everyone to give himself credibility, or whether to vary what he said to whom, in order to sow uncertainty. He settled for something in between.

"He's young. But from what I know, he's a person of great determination."

The physician didn't look satisfied, but he seemed to conclude from Jo's expression that there was no more information to be had. He disappeared through the doorway without another word, his assistant trailing behind him.

Jo waited only until the sound of their footsteps had faded before exiting the room himself. If anything he felt more sore from the physician's prodding, but he supposed it would help in the long run. He made his way to the same dining hall where he had eaten the night before, and found the Thoranian group finishing their morning meal. They cast him looks of disfavor, but he ignored them.

No one initiated conversation this time, and Jo was only too glad to wolf down his food and leave without having to engage with the surly strangers. He couldn't imagine that these foreign visitors would have any useful information regarding the whereabouts of the missing rebels.

Without any clear sense of purpose, he strolled out of the building, ready to explore the streets. The soldier who followed him made a passable attempt at being surreptitious, he thought, as he wandered in what he was pretty sure was the direction of the castle. He thought about how easily the resistance had seemed to find him, and he wondered if they might be watching even now. Glancing curiously around the crowded streets, he couldn't see anything that seemed suspicious. But then he didn't really know what to look for. He thought that he really would like to get Cody to teach him some tips for going unnoticed.

He found the castle courtyard without difficulty, but there was nothing of particular interest happening. Certainly no one was being flogged at that moment. He wondered if the showdown the day before had anything to do with it. Wandering back the other way, he decided to see if he could find Lord Wrendal's residence. He knew which direction it lay when looking from the rooftops, but it was a different matter to find it from the street.

He didn't know what he hoped to achieve by locating it, except for a general sense that it was good to know where to find your enemies. He took a number of wrong turns in his search, but he wasn't bothered. He was starting to get a sense for the castle neighborhood. Now that he looked around, there were a number of manor houses and other stately buildings. Clearly this was where the nobility had settled. The river and the less salubrious neighborhood on its other side seemed far away. Here the streets were clean, and the clothing richly made. Taking stock of the people walking past, Jo noted that it made the contrast between slave and owner more marked.

When Jo eventually found the Overseer's manor house, it took him a while to be sure that it was the right one. He stood at the imposing front gates for several minutes, pondering the vista within. Even from this limited vantage point, he could see that the gardens were impressive. Most likely Lady Wrendal spent her time sitting among flowerbeds being serenaded by admiring noblemen. The thought made Jo roll his eyes at no one in particular.

He was just turning away, wondering with a smile what Lord Wrendal would make of it when the soldier tailing Jonan reported on his visit here, when the gates opened. Looking up with interest, he saw a slave scurrying out of the entrance. Jo thought he looked vaguely familiar, and the impression was reinforced when the boy saw him and started, pulling to a stop.

"I've seen you before, haven't I?" Jonan addressed him with a friendly smile. "At the ambassador's rooms. Do you work for Mundsen?"

The boy nodded, his eyes round.

"I'm Jonan," said Jo, extending his hand.

Glancing nervously around, the boy took it. "I'm Jack," he said. He hesitated, then barreled on, clearly gathering his courage. "I'm glad to see you walkin' about, sir. You looked pretty messed up yesterday. I heard later that you got beat tryin' to stop them lashing one of us."

"Don't call me sir," said Jo, waving a hand dismissively. "And thanks, but I'm fine." He grinned at Jack. "Just needed to give my head time to stop spinning, that's all."

Jack glanced skeptically at his bandaged arm, and when his

eyes returned to Jo's face, they lingered first on the bruise under one eye, then the gash on the other cheek. But he didn't persist with his sympathy.

"Where are you off to?" Jo asked brightly. "Can I walk with you?"

Jack shook his head, but he looked more surprised than unwilling. "No need, mister. I'm looking for you."

"For me?" asked Jo quickly. "What for?"

"Mundsen's been at Lord Wrendal's place," said Jack, jerking his head back toward the gates. "They sent me to take a message to you."

"Well, that's convenient," laughed Jo. "Guess I saved you a walk."

"Guess so," said Jack, looking curiously at him. Jo had the impression that he wanted to ask what he was doing loitering at the gate but didn't dare.

"So what's the message?"

"Huh?"

"The message they sent you to bring me," repeated Jo patiently. "What is it?"

"Oh yeah," said Jack, "sorry. It's about tonight. Lord Wrendal's hosting a party or some such, and he wants you to attend. Cordially invited were the actual words," Jack gave a quick grin, "but I don't think you got any choice, really."

"He wants me to attend a party?" Jo asked, astonished. Could it be a ploy to get him away from interested eyes before doing away with him? It seemed more likely than a genuine invitation, but he couldn't imagine what need the powerful Overseer would have for such stratagems. Either way, it was too good an opportunity to miss. Lord Wrendal's crowd was precisely who Raldo wanted him to snoop around.

Jack was nodding. "Yeah, that's what he said. Mundsen will be there too." Jack gave a derisive snort. "He was practically drowning the Overseer in gratitude, but he knows as well as I do that the only reason he's invited is to be your minder, and give some reason to the other guests for why you're there. Make it seem like you're attached to the ambassadorship or sumthin'." There was a pause during which Jack peered curiously up at Jo. "Are you? Some kind of ambassador?"

Jo shook his head. "Nah, I've got nothing to do with Mundsen, that's for sure. What's his deal, anyway? I heard Lord Wrendal talk about Mundsen's 'people'. What did he mean? People who work for him, like you?"

Jack scowled. "I'm not one of his people. I'm a slave, assigned to him like anyone gets assigned. They meant his *personnel* as they call themselves. Think they're great because they're not slaves. But they're as good as. They got to register themselves, and get their own mark on their arms. And they're watched every move they make, just like we are. But it's true they got no chains on 'em, and they don't have to sleep at slave barracks. Some of 'em used to be slaves, of course."

He spat on the ground. "Turned traitor, working for Mundsen to get out of being one of us. They're supposed to watch us, but we know who they all are. They don't see nothing worth reporting. Mostly they just assist Mundsen with 'administering the system'—all the practical details of the slave trade, that means. But there's something we have that they don't."

"What?" Jo prompted when Jack fell silent.

"Each other," the boy replied simply. "At least the slaves mostly stick together. But not with them personnel. All the rest of the Kyonans hate them."

"I don't blame you," said Jo darkly. "So what do I need to know about this thing tonight?"

"Just to come here at seven," said Jack. "And to keep your eyes open, if you want my advice. I wouldn't trust a single one of 'em."

"Believe me, I don't," said Jo with feeling. He gave the boy a measuring glance. "Will you be there tonight?"

"Dunno," Jack said, giving him a sharp look. "Mundsen'll take someone along to wait on 'im hand and foot. I figure he thinks it makes him look less like one of us and more like one of them if he has a slave following him around. I could probably make sure it was me tonight. Why?"

Jo shrugged. "Just would be nice to have an ally."

Jack's eyes brightened, and Jo was sure that his instinct had not failed him in suggesting that this was a friend worth having.

"Dunno what I can do to help, but I will if I can."

"You don't have to do anything," said Jo with a smile. "But I don't know much about these people, and if you've been stuck in Mundsen's service for a while, I'm guessing you know more than they suspect you do."

Jack grinned. "You're not wrong."

"So I'll see you there?"

"You can count on me!" Jack assured him.

Jo thanked him solemnly, trying not to smile at the boy's enthusiasm. He watched Jack disappear back through the ornate gates, feeling his spirits lift at this opportunity to try his hand at a bit of espionage.

He would prove himself to Raldo and the gang and show these Balenans what he was made of at the same time.

CHAPTER EIGHT

When he found himself back before the same gates that evening, he wasn't so sure. He felt absolutely ridiculous in the formal garb he had been all but forced into by another messenger sent by the Kyonan ambassador. The stiff fabric was unbearably stifling in the humid air, and he didn't like the way it restricted his movements. He noticed that his arms were still bare. It hadn't escaped him that while Balenans might wear long sleeves, every Kyonan he had so far seen in Nohl was dressed in clothes that exposed the telltale tattoos on their forearms.

Good. Let them see and be reminded that he was the one Kyonan in the country who didn't carry a mark of any kind. He would have to trade on the uncertainty surrounding his status if he was going to successfully weasel out any inside information.

But still, he no longer felt any sense of confidence that he would be able to play the part and still be himself. He already felt like a stranger. He would just have to think of it as wearing a costume, he supposed, try to convince himself that there was no loss of dignity in putting on an act.

He didn't feel very convinced.

While he dithered outside the gates, other guests had been passing through, no one sparing a glance for him. He didn't take much note of them himself, distracted by the intimidating scene before him. The gates were thrown wide, but they somehow still managed to look forbidding rather than welcoming. The path through the gardens to the manor house was brightly lit by blazing torches at regular intervals, and lanterns hung prettily on poles throughout the gardens.

"Ah, I see you have arrived," said a haughty voice. Jo turned to see the ambassador approaching. "I am glad to see that you retain enough sense of respect to await me before entering."

Jo opened his mouth to retort that he had done no such thing, but he realized that he would hardly save face by admitting that he had been hanging back reluctantly because he felt intimidated. He settled instead for surly silence.

A slight movement behind Mundsen caught Jo's attention, and his eyes flicked behind the willowy man to catch a small grin directed at him. He returned it with the ghost of a wink, and Jack's face quickly resumed a neutral expression. Jo noted that Jack had also been dressed formally, in an official outfit not dissimilar to Jo's own. Mundsen's attire was far more elaborate, and he made an awkward stiff rustling noise when he moved. He looked like a pompous idiot, Jo thought with savage satisfaction. He supposed he could at least be grateful that he hadn't been expected to wear whatever that was.

He followed Mundsen through the gates and up the path, forcing himself to walk alongside the oily man rather than fall behind with Jack. The route from the gate was marked by torches. The lights veered off the main path leading to the front door of the manor house to guide guests down a smaller path culminating in large glass double doors that swung wide to display a ballroom beyond.

There was a small bottleneck at the entrance, as a Balenan

servant announced the names of the arriving guests to the room at large. His expression was so serious and his tone so formal that Jo had to bite back a laugh. The whole thing was utterly ridiculous. When the small Kyonan contingent reached the front of the queue, the man waved them through without a word, his expression sour. Mundsen looked like he had smelled something foul, but Jo was pleased to avoid being made more a spectacle than he already was.

The overall effect of the ballroom was dazzling. Crystal chandeliers hung from the ceiling, lit with hundreds of candles, and the sparkling light danced over everything. Swaths of colored material were draped in graceful curves from the roof beams, framing archways and snaking their way down pillars. There were no flowers, but lush green foliage sprouted from unlikely places, giving the whole room a tropical feel. Tables lined the edges of the space, laden with countless types of food generously interspersed with large bowls of punch. Jo wondered fleetingly if this was what a court ball would look like in Kynton. He had no way of knowing.

Everywhere Jo looked guests, men and women alike, were dressed in colors as vibrant as the jungle that surrounded Nohl. The men wore starched outfits that looked as uncomfortable as Jo's, but the women were the real attraction. Jo didn't know much about formal attire in Kyona, but he was sure that he hadn't seen anyone in the castle at Kynton wearing dresses such as the women here wore. The skirts were full, the sheer fabric floating gracefully in the languid air, but the arms and shoulders were left bare, and everywhere he looked the candlelight glinted off the warm tone of their skin.

And no one was more stunningly attired than Lady Wrendal. Jo's eyes picked her out immediately in spite of himself. To be fair, she was hard to miss in a crimson gown, set off beautifully by the palm fronds erupting from the alcove where she stood, surrounded by admiring young men.

It would have presented an appealing picture if not for the drably dressed Kyonan slaves ringing the edges of the room, standing ready to attend to their masters' every whim. Jo's expression hardened. No, as far as he was concerned, there was nothing to admire in this lavish scene.

But still...his eyes strayed back to the heavily laden tables. Since he was here, he may as well enjoy the food. The argument over his attire had taken so long that there had been no time to eat before he came, and his stomach was rumbling.

He took a step toward the delicacies, but Mundsen's hiss pulled him up short.

"Where do you think you're going?"

Jo raised his eyebrows at the other man. "Are we not allowed to eat? Surely the food is for the guests."

"Yes, the guests," spat Mundsen. "Which you are not."

"Then what am I?" asked Jo with a hint of amusement.

"You're...you're impertinent is what you are," said the ambassador sternly.

Jo laughed humorlessly. "That's not an answer." He smiled condescendingly at the official's angry expression. "You really don't know what to do with me, do you? What kind of a deal did you have with Filip, anyway? What could possibly make you prefer being the scum of Balenan society over being free in Kyona?"

"I am free here," Mundsen hissed. "And you should show some respect to our king."

"Our former king," corrected Jonan. "And believe me, he's former in every sense of the word." He looked with interest at Mundsen's conflicted countenance. The man clearly wanted to rip into Jonan, but all the uncertainties of the situation held him back. "I was there when the usurper was overthrown, you know.

I saw Filip die. I'd tell you how he was killed, but I don't think you'd believe me."

Jo could see the vein throbbing in Mundsen's temple, and he couldn't quite restrain a smile. It was satisfying to bait the despicable snake. He knew he was supposed to be diplomatic tonight, but no part of his plans included lending legitimacy to this traitorous excuse for an ambassador.

"You could try me," came another voice. "I might believe you." Mundsen's instant change in expression from enraged to obsequious was enough to identify the speaker, but Jo turned to look at Lord Wrendal anyway.

"I really don't think you would, My Lord," he said demurely. "It was quite a spectacle."

"I assume the new claimant disposed of his predecessor," prompted Lord Wrendal.

"No, he didn't actually," said Jonan. "He was saved the necessity by the timely arrival of his allies."

"Allies?" repeated Mundsen, sounding uneasy.

"Oh yes," said Jo serenely. "The new king wasn't operating alone. He has powerful allies. Very powerful."

A look passed between the ambassador and the nobleman, and it wasn't just Mundsen who looked uneasy now.

"But here I am chattering away as if you needed my information," said Jo. "Two such well-connected men as you, I'm sure there's nothing I can tell you that you don't already know. I can only imagine that you have eyes and ears everywhere." He watched Lord Wrendal's face and was pleased to see that his words had found their mark. It was clear that the nobleman was used to being the best-informed person in the room, and even more clear that he didn't like being one step behind.

Neither man spoke, and Jo continued on, quite at his ease. "You put on quite a party, My Lord. I was just going to help myself to some refreshments."

Lord Wrendal's jaw worked for a moment as he held in whatever barb he wanted to deliver. But he mastered himself and stepped aside, gesturing toward the food with a movement that was more grudging than gracious.

As Jo walked away, he heard Lord Wrendal mutter to the ambassador, "You seem to no longer be the most reliable source of information on the state of Kyona, ambassador."

Jo couldn't resist a small smile at Mundsen's sputtering protest, but he kept walking. Toppling the ambassador from his position wasn't his chief objective, but it would be a welcome side effect.

"That was amazing!" whispered an eager voice at Jo's side. He stopped in surprise, looking down. Jack had obviously taken advantage of his master's distraction to sidle after Jo. He smiled at the boy.

"Thanks."

"I didn't follow all of it," Jack admitted. "But I could tell you really made them sweat, and that's enough for me."

Jo grinned. "Makes a nice change, doesn't it?"

"Sure does," Jack agreed earnestly. He shot a quick look around the room. "A lot of 'em aren't too happy that you're here, in the middle of their world."

Looking around himself, Jo saw that Jack was right. Lots of faces were turned toward him, their expressions ranging from surprise, right through disgust, and all the way to offense.

"You better be careful," Jack was continuing. "But don't worry," he added quickly. "We've got your back."

"We?" Jo asked with a frown, his attention quickly back on the boy. "What do you mean?"

Jack grinned, his words fading to a whisper as he drew back against the wall with the other slaves. "Word spread pretty quick about what you did yesterday."

"Jack," said Jo warningly, but Jack was already gone. Jo

looked around uneasily, wondering what Jack had done and how much trouble it might get the boy into.

His attention was caught by Mundsen, standing alone and looking very sour. Jo scanned the room quickly and saw Lord Wrendal striding purposefully away from the ambassador. With a longing glance toward the food, Jo began to weave his way across the room, trying to keep the nobleman in sight without obviously following him. He figured that Lord Wrendal's choice of companions with whom to debrief his new discovery would be telling. Jonan wanted to know who among the courtiers he should be most interested in watching.

His way was hampered by a flurry of activity that accompanied the music that had suddenly started up. Jo hadn't even noticed the musicians waiting in one corner of the room, but it appeared that this event was to include dancing. Most of the other young people looked excited, and Jonan couldn't help but notice that Lady Wrendal was positively swamped with young men seeking her hand. He rolled his eyes. How easily impressed these fools were.

He had lost Lord Wrendal for a moment, but he spotted him entering an alcove across the room from where his daughter was accepting the hand of a young nobleman for the first dance. Jo sidled around the edge of the ballroom. It was difficult to be surreptitious when everyone he passed shot him venomous looks, but at least he was given a wide berth.

There was more lush foliage arranged tastefully at the edges of the alcove where Lord Wrendal now stood, greeting two other men who looked to be of his own age and rank. Jo thought that if he could get close enough, he would be able to lurk unseen within hearing range. The question was how to look natural just standing there, without it being obvious to others in the room that he was eavesdropping.

He saw a slave passing with a tray of goblets. A drink in his hand would make him blend in better, but it felt most uncomfortable to be served by his exploited countrymen. He sighed. Part of the game, he supposed.

"Hey," he hailed the young man as he passed. "Mind if I grab one? Which one didn't you spit into?"

The server turned shocked and fearful eyes on Jonan, but as soon as he saw who it was, his expression relaxed. "They're all safe, s'far as I know," he said with a grin.

"Thanks," said Jonan, grinning back as he took a goblet. "I owe you one."

"You don't owe me nothing," said the slave seriously before melting away into the crowd again.

Jonan was still pondering his words when he reached the spot he had been aiming for, but Lord Wrendal's domineering voice soon drove other thoughts from his mind.

"Yes, that's what I said. He specifically called them powerful allies."

"Surely he must mean Valoria," said another voice, naming the country immediately to Kyona's east. Jo didn't recognize the speaker, but he could only assume that it was another nobleman.

"Perhaps." Lord Wrendal didn't sound convinced. "Although it would be the first I heard of such an alliance. Only a short time ago we heard reports that Valoria was marching on Kyona in war, but that seems to have fizzled out."

"Fizzled out?" said a third voice skeptically. "Wars don't fizzle out. Why would Valoria withdraw so suddenly? Surely if Kyona had just had a coup, it would be the ideal time to press their advantage and attack. It's what I would do. Especially if the new king is as green as rumors say."

"You don't have to convince me, General," came Lord Wrendal's voice. "If I had my way, King Siloam would have your forces preparing for an annexation right now, while the moment is ripe. They say that Kyona has the most fertile fields in the North Lands."

"That may still be an option," said the General thoughtfully. "A brand new king, apparently unknown prior to his sudden appearance? The window of time during which he is vulnerable to being destabilized will be considerable."

Jonan stiffened. If these men thought that Kyona was as easily subjugated as the defenseless children they had stolen from their homes and pressed into service, they would find themselves mistaken. But he had no desire for them to find out the hard way. War was the last thing Kyona—or Cal—needed right now.

"You may be right," said Lord Wrendal. "And I am sure your troops are up to the task. But we all know King Siloam is not likely to put himself to so much trouble." The nobleman's tone was dry. "He lacks the vision." There was a moment of silence, then Lord Wrendal continued. "There may be other ways to capitalize on this new Kyonan ruler," he said. "Other ways to secure his allegiance and cooperation."

"The diplomatic option," came the second voice, with a hint of amusement. "Your specialty, of course."

"I only say that it may be possible," returned Lord Wrendal shortly. "If he is as young as they say, it shouldn't be too hard to maneuver him. He'll be locked into ongoing exchange before he knows what he's agreed to."

Jo felt his anger mixing with unease. He was sure these men were underestimating Calinnae, but at the same time they weren't wrong that Cal had no experience with the kind of games they were very practiced at playing. If only he could warn his friend.

"If you mean what I think you mean," said the other speaker, definitely amused now, "would you not have to sacrifice your present plans?"

"I'm sure that I *don't* know what you mean, Lord Grentan," said Lord Wrendal stiffly, and his companion let the matter drop.

"What of our problems closer to home, Wrendal?" asked the general. "If there's any possibility of trouble from outside our borders, I don't like having so many of my soldiers committed to this ongoing annoyance from your resistance."

"Hardly *my* resistance," said Lord Wrendal, sounding irritated.

"You are the Overseer, are you not? Surely you can bring them into line. They're absurdly problematic for a group of half-starved jungle dwellers. I've lost two dozen men to them in the last month alone."

"They're as big a nuisance to me as they are to you, General," returned Lord Wrendal tartly. "Our hunters are struggling to feed the labor camps. Half the jungle is too dangerous for them to hunt in now. And I can't even send slaves to do any foraging, because the cursed resistance will liberate any slaves who set foot in the jungle, killing their minders in the process."

"Most regrettable," said Lord Grentan, and Jonan thought he sounded smug at being the only one in the conversation who wasn't being personally bested by the slave resistance.

Lord Wrendal gave an irritated grunt. "I should be asking you for news, General. I thought you told me not three days ago that you had identified a cell of resistance rabble, and expected to apprehend them within days."

Jonan leaned involuntarily toward the three men, his ears straining.

The general acknowledged it with a frustrated huff. "We did. They infiltrated the camp of new arrivals, of that I am certain. There were half a dozen of them, and my men assured me they had them cornered."

"Well?"

"They took to the river, apparently. Downstream from the camp."

"Hm." Lord Wrendal sounded disappointed. "That is unfortunate."

"Indeed," said the General dryly. "No bodies were recovered, but that means little, after all."

"Most unfortunate," repeated Lord Wrendal.

"I daresay the deserter's fate overtook them," said Lord Grentan lightly.

"As it should," agreed the general firmly.

"My Lord Wrendal!" broke in a new voice, much louder than the others. "What a delightful evening! Everything so beautifully appointed."

"My Lord, General," Lord Wrendal muttered a leave-taking before responding at volume to the newcomer. "I am glad you approve."

Jo saw Lord Wrendal emerge from the alcove to greet the new arrival, the two of them disappearing into the throng.

"What do you think, General?" asked the nobleman left in the alcove. "Is Wrendal right that there's no immediate prospect of military action against Kyona? It would be nice to secure our cargo source more permanently, wouldn't it?"

Jonan ground his teeth at the phrase "cargo source", but he forced himself to maintain a relaxed posture. Although he was obscured from the sight of the speakers, he was visible from some angles of the room. He was receiving the occasional glance of disfavor from other guests. No one had actually challenged him, however, so he could only assume that it wasn't obvious that he could hear the conversation happening near him.

The General grunted. "It's difficult to say, especially without knowing more of this apparent ally of Kyona's. I cannot imagine King Siloam being in a hurry to engage, either way."

"His Majesty is...sometimes a little too content with the status quo, I think," said Lord Grentan hesitantly.

The General gave a bark of laughter. "You mean, as Wrendal said, that he lacks vision." There was a moment of silence. "And you're not wrong. But we should be glad he remains on the throne, not his brother. Prince Rupert has one disadvantage that the king is free from."

The nobleman laughed unpleasantly. "His wife, you mean? Yes, she would certainly disrupt matters were she queen. She's bad enough as a princess. I don't know what madness seized the prince. Or Wrendal for that matter. Although at least his wife didn't linger long enough to cause too much trouble."

"A familiar madness, I think." The General's voice was dismissive. "Beauty blinds many men."

"What of this new Kyonan arrival?" Lord Grentan asked after a minute of silence. "What do you make of him?"

"I'm not sure what to make of him," acknowledged the General. "He's certainly put Mundsen in a fluster."

"Not difficult to do," said Lord Grentan sneeringly. "I'm astonished, though, at Wrendal inviting him to an event like this."

"Wrendal knows what he's doing," said the General, clearly unconcerned. "He wishes to keep the boy close until he can find out what he knows. It's clear already from what Wrendal reports that the Kyonan knows much more than he has let on. I wouldn't concern yourself. The boy is being kept under close watch."

Jonan barely restrained a snort. Such close watch that unbeknownst to them he was listening in on their every word. Those in power in Balenol had clearly come to underestimate Kyonans drastically, and it was going to cost them if Jonan had anything to say about it.

"I daresay you're right," said the nobleman carefully. "Ah, my wife appears to be looking for me. With any luck one of our girls has sprained her ankle dancing and I'll get an early reprieve in order to take her home."

The general gave a dry chuckle, and the men parted ways. Jonan saw the unknown Lord Grentan approach a plump middle-aged woman in an elaborate gown, flanked by Balenans who were not dressed formally enough to be guests. Jonan wondered idly if it was a sign of compassion or merely of excessive wealth that these nobles at least seemed to employ paid Balenan servants as well as Kyonan slaves. Judging from what he had overheard from the nobleman, compassion seemed unlikely.

Jonan remained where he was for a long time, not wanting to attract attention. He had a great deal to think about, and his emotions were mixed as he thought over the conversation he had overheard. It had been an incredible stroke of luck to hear the discussion about the missing rebels, for surely that was who the general had meant. But unless what he had heard meant more to the resistance than it did to him, it didn't sound like he had good news to pass on.

The comments about Kyona's vulnerability made him deeply uneasy, especially as he couldn't see any way he could do anything to help Cal from here. And the final topic of discussion, regarding the royal family and even Lord Wrendal's wife, was intriguing and ambiguous, leaving him with more questions than answers.

His eyes strayed out across the dancers as he mulled it over, catching on the swirling crimson of Lady Wrendal's dress. She moved gracefully, of course, her status as hostess as much as her beauty making her the natural center of the action. She didn't dance with the same partner twice, someone new racing forward to claim her attention at the end of each song, all equally eager and equally ridiculous in Jo's eyes.

He felt a strange wistfulness as he watched the dancers. He

supposed Cal and Elnora would attend functions like this now, and dance together at them. It wasn't as though he had any desire to dance at this event, but he still felt strangely envious of his friends back home. He didn't envy Cal his partner. Much as he liked Elnora, Jo hadn't for a moment seen her as anything more than a friend.

But she and Cal were surely happy and settled, making a home for themselves in the pleasant country that Jo was appreciating more the longer he was gone from it. He couldn't quite figure out how his desire to strike out in search of adventure far from the restraints of Cal's new royal life had landed him neck deep in the slippery maneuvering of a court circle where he had to watch his every word with even more care than in Kynton.

"Enjoying the show?" asked a cheeky voice, and Jo looked down to see that Jack had once again sidled up to him.

"I don't know if I'd say enjoying, but show is right," he said scornfully. "They're about as absurd as a dancing bear in all their finery, aren't they?"

"I've never seen a dancing bear," said Jack doubtfully, "but I doubt they're as nice to look at as Lady Wrendal. What?" he said in response to Jo's raised eyebrows. "Like I ain't seen you lookin' at her this whole time."

"Not in admiration, I promise you," said Jo shortly.

Jack shrugged. "No harm in admiring what she looks like. She's the most beautiful girl in Nohl, everyone knows that. Doesn't mean you have to like her." His brows lowered in distaste. "Never had much to do with her myself, but they say she's as cold as her father."

"What's her story?" asked Jonan, thinking of the comments he had overheard. "Her mother is dead, isn't she? Who was she?"

"Yeah, her mother died forever ago. When this Lady Wrendal was a baby, I think. Her mother was called Violet, one of them Melton sisters. The younger one. Didn't do quite as well for herself as her sister I guess."

"Who are the Melton sisters?" asked Jonan.

"They're famous around here," said Jack. "Because they were nobodies, but they made impossibly good marriages. The Melton sisters were both very beautiful, they say. They were from a common family, but they both married above themselves, on account of being so nice to look at. Lady Violet married Lord Wrendal, but her sister, Princess Mariska, got a better prize. She married Prince Rupert. If she lives long enough, might even be queen one day, from what they say. Looks like King Siloam's happy enough to pass his crown on to his brother and his nephew."

While Jack spoke, Jonan had continued to watch Lady Wrendal. She had so far received all the attention with an unruffled countenance, her slightly cold manners perfectly crafted to assure her suitors of the honor she did them by accepting their tribute. But as he watched, a new figure approached her, apparently a late arrival to the party. Jonan observed Lady Wrendal with interest as she greeted this newcomer. There was no mistaking the warm friendliness that filled her face as she turned and gave him her hand. He seemed equally relaxed in her presence, unlike the starstruck courtiers around her, and he swept her into a dance with a smile, leaving her previous partner disconsolate.

"Who's that?" Jonan asked Jack curiously.

"Who?" asked Jack, following his gaze. "Oh, dancing with Lady Wrendal? That's Prince Giles."

"He's the oldest son of Prince Rupert, isn't he?" said Jo, remembering the physician's words that morning. "The one who'll probably be king one day?" Jack nodded. "So he's Lady Wrendal's cousin," Jo mused. "She's a cousin to the royals, but only through her mother, not her father." He smiled. "That must irk Lord Wrendal."

Jack laughed. "No doubt. He's sure made the most of the connection though, especially when it comes to his daughter."

"What do you mean?" Jo asked.

"Well, her mother died when she was a baby, like I said. Her brother was already old enough by then to not need babying, so he stayed on the estate out south with Lord Wrendal. But My Lord sent his daughter to Nohl, to be raised by her aunt. She was raised in the castle with the royal family, alongside Prince Giles and the others. She only came to live here in the manor a couple years back, when Lord Wrendal became Overseer and started spending more time in the city."

"Really?" said Jo with interest. "So she's almost like one of the royals." He watched the dancers, who still seemed relaxed and happy. "She seems to like Prince Giles. Probably she wants to marry him and become queen one day."

"Maybe," Jack shrugged, clearly not terribly interested.

"You seem to know a lot about where everyone fits," said Jo, shooting a look at his new friend.

Jack shrugged again. "Everyone knows that stuff. These people are the top of the social ladder when it comes to court. And I've spent way too much time around it all, the way Mundsen's always trying to weasel his way into Lord Wrendal's notice."

Jo grinned, more than ready to start making fun of the ambassador, but their conversation was cut short by a peremptory command.

"You, boy, get me a drink."

CHAPTER NINE

Jack was gone in a moment, hurrying to obey the order before Jo had even turned to look at the speaker.

"And you, something to eat. And be quick about it."

"No, I don't think so," said Jo flatly, his expression dark.

"Excuse me?" said the unknown guest, turning to face Jo with astonishment in his eyes. It quickly turned to fury as he took in Jonan's belligerent posture. "I said, get me something to eat. *Now*."

"Get it yourself. I don't exist to do your bidding," said Jo shortly.

The man took a menacing step toward Jonan. "That is exactly what you exist for, boy," he said, his voice becoming a bellow as his face began to turn red. There was a pounding in Jo's ears, but he was dimly aware that heads were starting to turn in their direction. So much for being inconspicuous.

"Now are you going to go get me some food, or am I going to teach you a lesson you'll never forget?" the guest was demanding forcefully.

"I think you'll find," said Jonan, his voice as cold and hard as ice, "that those are not the only two options."

"I will not stand this insolence," cried the man, raising his arm. He swung it forward, ready to backhand Jo across the face, but Jo was quicker. He reached up his own hand, gripping the man's arm mid-swing.

The guest pulled his arm free of Jonan's hand with a gasp. "You dare to touch me, you filth? I will make you regret the day you were born, boy!" He raised his arm again, but before he could make a move toward Jo, a small figure inserted itself between them in a gesture of silent defiance.

Jo opened his mouth to cry a warning to Jack, not wanting the boy to involve himself and bring down trouble on his head. But his words were stillborn in his surprise at finding that it was not Jack, but an unknown Kyonan boy who had thrown himself between Jonan and his aggressor.

The man was also staring at Jo's apparent champion, his anger momentarily suspended by surprise. The scene was frozen for a moment, then Jo became aware of another figure barreling forward. Jack joined the other boy, then two more others joined him, a girl and boy, neither of whom Jo recognized. Looking up in confusion he saw a ripple passing around the room, as a number of the Kyonans present began to make their way in his direction. He also saw that the little drama unfolding in his alcove had attracted the attention of most of the guests.

He involuntarily locked eyes with Lady Wrendal for a moment, her expression showing shock and some other unreadable reaction, then slid across to Lord Wrendal. His look was much easier to read. But perhaps that was because anger seemed to be his habitual expression. By now Jonan's little guard had grown to more than half a dozen people. The man in front of Jo was swelling before his eyes, and the other guests seemed to be vacillating between outrage and unease.

"We've got your back," said the first boy gruffly to Jonan, not taking his eyes off the guest in front of him.

"Jack, what did you do?" muttered Jo, addressing his new friend.

"You said you could do with some allies," Jack returned defiantly.

"I meant a friendly face, not an uprising!" Jonan hissed. "I don't want any of you getting into trouble for me."

"You didn't mind getting into trouble for one of us," piped up a girl nearby. "In the square yesterday."

"What is going on here?" Lord Wrendal had made his way over to the alcove, and his quiet voice was deadly.

"Nothing, My Lord," said Jonan quickly. "Just a...misunderstanding between me and one of your *other* guests." The man who had confronted Jonan had opened his mouth to unleash his outrage, but he hesitated at Jonan's words.

"Get out of here," Jo muttered to Jack. After a moment of hesitation, the boy retreated surreptitiously, his friends quickly melting away in imitation.

"I am not accustomed to being disrespected by slaves while attempting to enjoy a social evening," said Jonan's attacker, still irate.

"As Overseer, I would hope not," returned Lord Wrendal. "But I really cannot allow you to create a scene in my home, you know."

The man made an outraged noise. "It is not I creating a scene! This young whelp—"

"Ah yes," said Lord Wrendal, turning to Jonan as if he had just noticed him. "I see you have met our newest arrival in Nohl. He is quite the curiosity." The glare Lord Wrendal was leveling at Jo told him clearly that the older man wanted him to make himself scarce. Several stinging retorts chased their way through Jo's mind, but Jack and his crew were still hovering nearby, and he was keenly aware of the risk to them. Already angry mutters were rising around the room in the aftermath of the display of defiance.

With what he considered admirable restraint, Jonan turned and walked away without another word. He could see Mundsen on the other side of the room, his expression a mix of alarm and anger, but Jo steered himself in the other direction, making for a table of food. He still hadn't managed to eat anything, and he had a feeling this would be his last opportunity to experience Lord Wrendal's lavish hospitality.

He had just picked up some kind of baked scroll and was contemplating it when he was hailed by a new voice that had somehow already become familiar.

"That was quite a spectacle."

Jo stiffened at the disapproving tone, turning to face Lady Wrendal. "It wasn't my doing," he said shortly. "I was as surprised as you."

She gave him a long and measuring look. "I wouldn't exactly say I was surprised. You don't seem to be capable of going anywhere without creating a scene."

Her words hit a nerve, reminding Jonan of how genuinely he had intended to keep a low profile and prove to the resistance that he could succeed at subterfuge. "Do you usually accost your guests when they're trying to eat?" he said, his tone surly. "It's taken quite some doing to get to the food, and I need to keep up my strength. You never know when I might next be attacked."

"Yes, I hear that you're not quite recovered." Jo frowned at her, and she shrugged. "I spoke with the physician today."

"Ah yes," said Jo. "A warm and friendly man." He thought he saw the flicker of a smile on Lady Wrendal's countenance before her habitual cold expression returned.

"He was less than pleased. He said that your wound had reopened." She gave him an accusing look. "In fact, he seemed to think that you had been exerting yourself too much."

Jo shrugged, his expression innocent as he bit into the scroll. "He was just trying to blame me in order to hide his inadequate treatment, I daresay. I slept all day yesterday."

Her eyes were narrowed at him, but she didn't seem to have anything to say. Her silent judgment irked Jonan for some reason.

"What do you care, anyway?" he said with feeling. "Aren't I destined for execution? Surely it's not necessary for your victims to be in full health when you go to hang them?"

She looked confused. "Hang them?"

"You know," he said, imitating a noose being pulled tight around his neck. "Hang them from a rope around the neck so the neck breaks, or failing that, they suffocate. Isn't that how you execute people here?"

She looked faintly nauseated by his description, but her voice was quite expressionless when she answered.

"No, of course not. We chop their heads off with a blade."

There was a beat of silence. "That's disgusting," said Jonan, putting down his half-eaten food. He pictured the construction he had seen in the castle courtyard, and he found he was suddenly no longer hungry. "You people are barbaric."

"It's an execution," she said dryly. "It's not supposed to be pleasant."

"Still," muttered Jonan, trying to picture it. "What do you do with the head afterward?" he asked curiously.

"Who's barbaric now?" asked Lady Wrendal, raising one perfectly shaped eyebrow.

But Jonan didn't answer, his gaze sliding past her to the wrathful figure approaching them. His expression hardened as he braced himself for the inevitable explosion. Lady Wrendal took in his change in demeanor and shifted slightly to be in front of him as she turned. Seeing her father, she fell back to her previous position.

Jonan looked at her in surprise, distracted for a moment from the Overseer's approach. Her movement had been so slight it would be easy to miss it, but it had looked so much like a defensive instinct at work. Except that the idea of Lady Wrendal trying to protect him from anything was laughable, in a number of ways.

"You, boy," snarled Lord Wrendal, his face red. "What do you think you're doing, insulting my guests? I thought I told you what would happen if you showed me any more insubordination."

"Really, My Lord, it was all a misunderstanding," said Jonan calmly, meeting the Overseer's glare steadily. He felt himself to be on sure ground. If Lord Wrendal had really been willing to carry out his threats he would have done so in front of the guest whom Jonan had offended.

"It seems I overestimated you when I thought you could conduct yourself in a manner appropriate to polite society," Lord Wrendal said cuttingly. "You would be best to leave now."

Jonan couldn't help the flash of amusement that passed over his face. "I don't think overestimating me is your mistake, My Lord," he said. He noticed that Lady Wrendal's eyes were traveling over the rest of the ballroom as they spoke, and was unsurprised when her voice joined her father's.

"You should certainly leave," she said, her voice as cold as it had ever been. "Your presence is not welcome any longer." Following her gaze, he saw that many of the guests were looking at him with scandalized expressions, and a muttering like the buzz of angry bees was still filling the ballroom.

When Jo looked back at Lady Wrendal, he thought she looked faintly uneasy, and he wondered if she was worried about her social standing being affected by the gossip that would undoubtedly arise from tonight's events. He gave her a smile that was more a sneer.

"My deepest apologies, My Lady, for soiling your perfectly planned event with my uncomfortable presence."

Lord Wrendal growled. "You have already offended my guests—you will not disrespect my daughter in her own house. As she said, you should leave."

"I will be only too happy to oblige," said Jo sarcastically.

Without another word, he turned and made for the door. He saw Jack watching him anxiously from across the room, and sent him a reassuring wink. When he had reached the doorway, he couldn't quite resist looking back. Lady Wrendal was standing where he had left her, her face still betraying unease as she watched him leave. Well, he wouldn't shed any tears over the thought that he had ruined her evening.

The night was of course warm, but it was still a welcome relief to step from the enclosed space out into the moonlit gardens. Jo had intended to head straight back to his room at the castle outbuilding, but he found himself wandering through the garden in a circuitous route instead of following the path straight to the gate. There was so much to think through from the events of the evening.

He was touched by Jack's efforts on his behalf. After all, the boy didn't even know him. But he was also troubled by the implications. What would the consequences be for those Kyonans who had rushed to his aid tonight? Not long ago he would have loved to picture himself as a figure of defiance, inspiring others to follow his lead. But the vulnerability of these people, many of them little more than children, frightened him. He wasn't sure how he felt about the idea of becoming a rallying point for rebellion against such a powerful system of oppression.

He had stepped away from everything he knew in pursuit of

adventure, but he had to admit that his lack of knowledge and experience of Balenol was a weakness. He would do much better to throw his efforts behind the resistance that had grown up through the cracks in Nohl's polished facade than to offer those still in captivity some false hope that he could deliver them. But Raldo had told him to be discreet. After he had yet again created a stir tonight, would the resistance be willing to trust him with any responsibility?

He wasn't sure how long he wandered through the gardens, but when he heard the music stop, he judged that it was time to head for the gates. He had no desire to meet other guests as they departed.

He was starting to think longingly of his bed, but it was such a short distance from the manor to his building that he didn't feel the need to hurry. The streets were quiet, those citizens of the castle neighborhood not fortunate enough to be invited to Lord Wrendal's event having long since retired. No sound marred the stillness of the night, and Jo found it quite peaceful as he walked. His limbs were not so stiff tonight, his body starting to bounce back from his beating.

He had just turned off the street on which Lord Wrendal's residence was situated when he suddenly became aware of an indefinable certainty that he was being watched. He strained his ears, and sure enough in addition to his own footsteps he could hear the sound of someone attempting to move stealthily. On reflection, he assumed that it was the soldier who had been following him all day, presumably on Lord Wrendal's orders.

He rounded a corner and found that the new street was darker than the one he had left, devoid of the torches that could be found on tall poles placed sporadically throughout the neighborhood. As soon as he entered the shadows, he saw a sudden rush of movement to the side. Before he could do more than throw up his arms, two thickset Balenan men had emerged from a tiny laneway and jumped on him.

He wrestled furiously, attempting to throw off the larger of the two men, who had grabbed his arms and was holding them behind his back. But the man was much stronger than him, and he couldn't get free. Jo's other attacker approached warily from the front, and Jo managed to catch him in the stomach with a well-aimed kick. He saw the man bend over, wheezing, but a moment later Jo's vision spun as the first man released one of Jo's arms to deliver a ringing blow to his head. The hit disoriented him for a moment, and before he could make use of the temporary release, his hands were both secured firmly behind his back once again.

"Do it, quick!" hissed the man who was holding him. Jo blinked rapidly, his vision clearing to see the man he had kicked coming toward him again with a long dagger in his hand. Even as he flailed uselessly, part of Jonan's mind focused on the man's face, trying to place where he had seen him before.

He aimed another kick at his assailant, but the man dodged it. Jo was still straining fiercely against the hold on his arms, and he was caught by surprise when he was suddenly released. His own momentum sent him hurtling forward, the dagger held in the hand of his startled attacker slicing into his already-bandaged arm.

He gritted his teeth against the slashing pain, whirling to see what had become of the first man. To his astonishment, the large Balenan lay crumpled on the ground, a soldier standing over him. Before Jo could fully take in what was happening, two other soldiers had run forward to take on his other assailant, one of them wresting the dagger from his grip even as the other one knocked him senseless.

For a moment Jonan and the three soldiers just stared at each other, the scene silent except for their panting breaths. As

Jo got a good look at his rescuers, confusion mingled with astonishment. He definitely recognized the soldier who had struck down the first man. He was the same one whose whipping entertainment Jonan had interrupted when he had first arrived. Jo half expected the soldier to attack now, thinking that he had disposed of the others because he wanted the pleasure of taking Jo out himself. But the resentment in the man's eyes as he met Jonan's look said clearly that he hadn't been acting of his own initiative when he came to Jo's aid.

The soldier pulled his eyes from Jonan's face and turned to his companions. "Let's go," he grunted.

"Do we just...leave them?" asked one of the other soldiers, his gaze passing uncertainly from Jonan's bleeding arm to the prone forms on the street.

"Our orders were to prevent him being killed if he was attacked," said the first soldier shortly. "I don't intend to do any more than necessary." He spat on the ground, his glare once again leveled at Jonan.

The two other soldiers fell into line behind him, sending curious looks back at Jo as the three of them disappeared around the corner. Jo stood frozen in spot, his head reeling, and not just from yet another blow.

For all Lord Wrendal's scheming about finding out what Jo might know, he hadn't actually expected the nobleman to go so far as to protect him from other aggressors. And surely Lord Wrendal was behind the soldiers' intervention—it had been clear to Jonan the day before that these particular soldiers were the Overseer's personal lackeys. It seemed that Jo had hit just the right balance with his approach, letting drop enough information to raise questions in the nobleman's mind, but not enough to seem like his knowledge had been exhausted.

Jo looked down at the two men at his feet. They were not dead. He looked at the one who had held the dagger, the man's face now blank in unconsciousness rather than twisted in derision. The expressionless visage triggered a memory, and he suddenly realized that this was one of the Balenan servants of Lord Grentan, the nobleman who had been speaking with Lord Wrendal and the general. In his inert state, his face had returned to the emotionless mask generally adopted by servants.

As he watched, the man stirred slightly, and Jo decided it was time to be gone himself. He hurried through the streets, starting in spite of himself at every shadow cast by the flickering street torches. He reached his destination in minutes. There had been only a short window for his attackers to accost him. He wondered how long they had lain in wait while he wandered through the gardens.

As he let himself into the building, the adrenaline of the recent encounter began to wear off, and he found himself shaking slightly at the realization of how close to death he had come. It was sobering to owe his life to someone he neither liked nor trusted. He was relieved when he reached the relative haven of his room, pushing the door shut behind him with a satisfying thud. He felt exhausted, but it was hard to imagine dropping asleep in a hurry after what had just happened.

He had just pulled off the uncomfortable formal shirt when for the second time in as many nights he heard a gentle knock at the window. He strode over mechanically, opening the portal with no attempt to hide his surprise. It seemed sleep would have to wait, after all.

"Care for another midnight stroll?" asked Cody with a grin.

CHAPTER TEN

"Do I have a choice?" Jo asked the resistance boy with a grimace.

"Of course you do," said Cody, taken aback. "No one's forcing you, but I thought you wanted in!"

"I do," Jo assured him. "Sorry, you just caught me by surprise is all. I might need a minute to stop the bleeding."

Cody looked down, and his eyes widened as he took in the blood dripping from Jo's arm. "What happened to you?"

"Got knifed," said Jo succinctly, and Cody gave a low whistle.

"Let me help." The boy lowered himself smoothly in through the window, unconcerned by the lack of invitation or the fact that Jo was only half dressed. It was a good thing he didn't place too high a value on his privacy, Jo thought dryly.

"What, are you a physician now, as well as a spy?" he ribbed the younger boy, and Cody chuckled.

"Just wash it off in the basin, will you?"

While Jo complied, Cody looked around the room. Apparently he decided that the curtains would serve his purpose well enough. He pulled a short knife from his boot and sliced off a broad strip of fabric, which he then wound tightly around Jo's upper arm where the dagger had slashed him. It was a more colorful and much more haphazard accompaniment to the neat white bandage on his lower arm.

Jo flexed the limb painfully, trying not to wince in front of his audience. He could only hope he wouldn't suffer any permanent loss of function in the arm after all of this.

"That's better," said Cody approvingly. "Can't have you leaving a blood trail all the way to the safe house."

"Safe house?" asked Jo. "Aren't we going back to the base in the jungle?"

Cody shook his head. "Nah, Scar says there isn't time tonight. We're staying in the city."

"You mean I finally get to meet Scar?" asked Jo, his spirits lifting.

"Finally?" scoffed Cody. "You been here, what? Two days? This is only your second time visiting one of the bases. I could hardly believe Scar wanted to meet you tonight. Most newcomers don't get to meet the leader until they've proved themselves over and over again."

"Well I certainly haven't done that," said Jo, feeling suddenly disheartened again. He wondered if the resistance leader would be angry once he learned of Jo's failure that evening.

Cody seemed to take in Jo's change in mood. "Ah well," he said cheerfully. "There's always tomorrow."

Jo smiled at him. "Well, are you going to show me where to go, or what?"

"In a hurry now, are we?" laughed Cody. "Come on." And in an instant he was back out of the window.

Jo barely remembered to slip his light tunic on before following. It would make a strange first impression on this Scar if he turned up without a shirt on.

This time Cody led him in the opposite direction, away from

the southern city wall. Again Jo was filled with admiration for the stealthy way the boy flitted through the streets.

After a short while they crossed the river into the poorer district, and Cody slowed and began to move more cautiously. Jo followed his lead. Cody came to a stop at the edge of a small square not unlike the one where Jonan had first seen him. The square was lined with houses that pressed closely against one another in uniform blocks. Cody looked carefully around. Apparently he was satisfied that there were no witnesses, because he stole across the empty space, Jonan on his heels, and knocked quietly on an unremarkable wooden door.

It swung open without any visible sign of someone operating it. Cody and Jonan slipped inside, and the door swung softly shut behind them. A girl appeared from the shadow of the door, smiling tentatively at them but saying nothing.

After the experiences of the night before, Jo had expected to be led into a basement of some kind. But this time he was taken up. They climbed two flights of stairs and entered a sparsely furnished room. There was a trapdoor in the ceiling of the room, with a wooden ladder reaching down to the floor. Clearly the building had an attic.

Cody ushered Jo up the ladder, and he climbed quickly, his curiosity mounting. As with the jungle hideout, he was surprised to emerge into a space that was much larger and much better lit than he had expected. For a moment he was confused, picturing the small building they had entered and wondering how the attic could be so large. But casting his eyes over the long narrow space, he realized that the attics of the whole row of buildings had been merged into one large upper room. A number of lamps were burning, the absence of any windows apparently making it safe to light the space without fear of detection.

The room wasn't full of people the way the jungle base had

been, but there were several rebels ranged throughout it. Pallets on the floor in one corner suggested that some even slept here.

Jo turned to see Cody emerging from the trapdoor, followed by the unknown girl. Either they weren't expecting anyone else, or her curiosity was strong enough to prompt her to abandon her post at the front door.

"Here he is, Scar," Cody said, looking over at two people deep in discussion on the other side of the space, their backs to the entrance. "And he's quite eager to meet you."

"Actually," said a familiar voice, as its owner turned around, "we've already met."

Jonan took an involuntary step back, his eyes widening and his vision swimming for a moment. Cody reached out a steadying hand to prevent Jo toppling back through the trapdoor, but Jo was hardly aware of it. He knew his mouth was hanging open stupidly, but he couldn't seem to close it.

"You...you're Scar? Impossible." His voice sounded unnatural to his own ears.

"She has that effect on people," said Cody with a grin.

"Thank you, Cody, but I have it on good authority that Jonan is not so easily impressed," said Lady Wrendal wryly, approaching them with a stately stride. She had shed her crimson ballgown for a practical tunic and leggings in dark material, but her movements were somehow no less graceful.

Jonan was still frozen in shock when she stopped in front of him. He couldn't seem to bring his thoughts into any kind of order. The only coherent idea in his mind was the inconsequential one that he was doubly glad he had remembered to put his shirt on before climbing out his window.

Her eyes flicked down to the makeshift bandage on his arm, and her brow creased in concern. "What happened to your arm since I last saw you?" she asked.

After a moment Cody seemed to realize that Jonan, who was

still staring stupidly, was not going to answer, and he came to the rescue. "He said he got knifed."

There was a sharp intake of breath from Lady Wrendal. She reached a hand out toward Jo's arm, but he yanked it away on instinct, nowhere near close to trusting her enough to let her touch him. A flicker of distress passed across her perfect features, but she let her hand drop.

"On the way home from my father's house?" she asked instead. "It seems my instinct wasn't wrong. I'm glad I sent Father's soldiers to follow you."

"*You* sent—no," said Jonan firmly. The mention of her father had loosened his tongue. "You can't have done. And you can't be involved with the resistance." His eyes passed over her to the person she had been speaking with when he entered. He realized with a jolt that it was Raldo. Had the whole thing been some elaborate ruse designed to trap him all along?

"This is a trick," he said flatly.

She shook her head, and he noticed irrelevantly that her chestnut hair had been pulled back into a practical braid that was somehow equally as attractive as the gentle waves that he had seen earlier that evening.

"It's not a trick," she said softly, taking a step toward him. He stepped hurriedly back, and once again Cody had to grab him to stop him falling through the hole. Lady Wrendal sighed. "Come and sit down, and I'll explain everything," she said, her gentle voice holding no hint of the cold haughtiness he had come to expect. She looked around, and her voice became a bit less graceful. "And for goodness' sake, someone close that trapdoor before he backs right through it."

The girl who had followed Cody up the ladder hastened to obey. Lady Wrendal turned away from Jo and walked toward the edge of the room, where a few chairs were set around a simple table. Cody gave Jo a shove in her direction, and he found his feet moving without his permission, carrying him over to where Lady Wrendal was already seated. She gestured toward another chair, but he remained standing, watching her with suspicious eyes. She sighed again.

"I know you don't trust me, Jonan, but I truly don't want to be your enemy."

He didn't respond, meeting her look skeptically. He leaned against the wall in an attempt to look nonchalant, but quickly pushed himself upright again with a wince as his newly injured upper arm made contact with the stone.

Lady Wrendal once again gave him a look of concern. It was such an unfamiliar expression on her features that she looked like a stranger.

"Who attacked you? Do you think you'd recognize them again?"

"I don't think I'm the one who needs to answer questions," said Jonan shortly.

"Hey, I thought you were all right," said Cody accusingly. "You shouldn't talk to Scar like that."

"It's all right, Cody," said Lady Wrendal quickly. "He has his reasons. Can you give us a minute, please?"

Cody looked disappointed, but he shuffled off with a final glance at Jo. Lady Wrendal watched him walk away, only looking back over at Jo when the boy had joined Raldo on the other side of the room.

"You must be exhausted, Jonan, especially if you were attacked again tonight," said Lady Wrendal, giving him an appraising look. "Please, just...sit down."

Jonan hesitated for a long moment, then lowered himself into the chair across from her. She was right—he was exhausted.

Lady Wrendal took a deep breath. "I understand that you must have questions," she said levelly. "Ask me whatever you like."

"All right," said Jonan. "How did you get here so quickly?"

She looked surprised, but she didn't comment on the trivial nature of his question. In truth, Jonan just had no idea where to start.

"It wasn't difficult. I 'retired' for the evening soon after you left." She gave him a look. "You may not have noticed, but your antics cast a damper over the festivities."

"Am I supposed to apologize?" Jonan retorted. He knew he sounded surly, but he wasn't ready to let go of his resentment just yet.

"Of course not," she said, a hint of irritation in her voice. Contrarily, Jo found that the familiarity of the tone set him a little more at ease.

"Does your father know you're here?"

"Of course he doesn't!" She looked startled. "He thinks I'm asleep in my bed. He would likely poison me and make it look like an accident if he ever found out I had anything to do with the hated resistance." Her tone was blank as she spoke, but there was something in her expression that was hard to read. Jonan chose not to engage with it.

"So you're in the habit of sneaking out of your fancy manor house in the night to go running around with a bunch of renegade slaves?"

"Yes," she said simply.

"But this doesn't make any sense!" Jonan burst out, just not quite able to put the pieces together. "You're Balenan. Everyone else I've seen in the resistance is Kyonan. And you're not just Balenan—you're the daughter of the Overseer of Slaves!" He paused, but she just watched him silently, evidently realizing that he wasn't finished. "How does the daughter of the Overseer of Slaves come to be leading the resistance against him?"

She sighed. "That's a long story, too long for tonight. Just take my word for it that I want nothing to do with my father or anything he does. I think the slave trade is as despicable as you do."

Jo raised his eyebrows. "That's pretty hard to believe, from everything I've witnessed. You seem like a pretty dutiful daughter, *My Lady*. Or do you prefer Your Highness?"

"Enough, please," she said, raising her hand as if to ward him off. Her voice was weary, and the vulnerability of the gesture rattled him. "I don't want to play this game with you. I have to watch each breath I take every minute of every day, and I don't think I can stand it if I have to do that dance here. I don't like playing a part any more than you do."

He considered her for a moment. "You seem to be very good at it."

"Being good at something is not the same as enjoying it."

"I suppose that's true," he said cautiously. "So you really are this Scar? You really are the leader of the whole resistance?"

She shrugged uncomfortably. "Of sorts. Others, like Raldo over there, would be much better qualified to be in charge. But they seem to want me." She sighed. "Through no virtue of my own, I bring something to the table that no one else can."

"What's that?" Jonan asked. He tried to picture her as some kind of expert fighter, and failed.

She raised her eyebrows. "You said it yourself. I'm the daughter of the Overseer of Slaves."

Ah. Of course, it was information she brought to the group. How boring. He pictured her at her father's side, putting on that haughty air of disinterest, always trying not to let it show that she was listening keenly to every word.

"So you play the part to stay on the inside."

She nodded, still looking weary, and Jonan suddenly felt sorry for her. What an exhausting way to live. It had been enough of a challenge for him to navigate the social circle of the court for one night, and he had still failed. He could only imagine what the charade must cost her.

To his own surprise, he found that his mistrust was rapidly giving way to admiration, but he couldn't resist one last probing question.

"What about in the square the other day? You were sure in a hurry to get out of there when that poor boy was being flogged."

A look of such pain crossed her features that he felt guilty for bringing it up. "Maintaining the precarious balance I've built means I have to refrain from helping in a hundred small ways to have the potential to help in a much bigger way," she said. "It doesn't mean I don't care. I'm not the cold-hearted monster you think me." Again Jonan caught a brief look of anguish on her face, and he winced at the memory of his words. "And I don't enjoy watching children being beaten," she finished.

"You must be the only Balenan who doesn't," muttered Jo darkly, but she shook her head so vigorously that her braid whipped from side to side.

"No, you're wrong. They're not as bad as you think. Not all of them, anyway." Jo gave a snort of disbelief, but she barreled on. "Some of them are cruel, like my father. But surely it's the same in your country—positions of power too often seem to attract those with the blackest hearts. Many of those here in Nohl have been conditioned from birth as much as the slaves have. And not everyone thinks the way those in power do. People may not have the motivation to take a stand, but many would be willing to do things differently if someone led them in the right direction."

Jo raised his eyebrows, still incredulous. But he held his peace—his desire to argue with Lady Wrendal had evaporated.

"Believe me," she continued earnestly. "I want to see change, and as difficult as it is not to be able to do more, I'm trying to do everything I can to make it better."

He nodded, no longer able to doubt the sincerity in her eyes.

"I admire your courage, you know," she said with a small smile. "My hands were tied, but I wished I was free to take the lashes for that poor child."

"Well, I'm glad you didn't do that!" said Jo, startled. The reviled figure of Lady Wrendal had suddenly become warm-blooded and vulnerable, and for some reason he couldn't fully articulate, he found it greatly distressing to picture her slim form at the whipping post.

"That's generous of you to say, since those lashes seem to have been only the beginning of your troubles," she said, her forehead creased. She looked him up and down, taking in his various injuries. "It seems you were right this evening when you told me you might be attacked again at any moment."

He felt suddenly self-conscious under her scrutiny, and hastened to change the subject. "It's hard to believe you really are the infamous Scar, you know. You're definitely not what I pictured."

She smiled. "I think that's a good thing."

"It's a little much, isn't it?" persisted Jonan, a smile in his own voice. "Scar? It sounds very tough, but as a code name, it's not exactly apt, is it?"

She laughed aloud at that. "It's not a code name, and it's extremely apt. It's just my name. Scarlett," she clarified when he still looked confused. "My friends have called me Scar all my life. It's a nickname, nothing more. Honestly, a code name would probably have been smarter, but I'm counting on the unlikeli-hood of anyone making the connection even if something were to be let slip. It was just that when I first found the resistance, I couldn't handle being called My Lady every five seconds. I told someone to please call me Scar, and it stuck."

"Scarlett," Jo repeated thoughtfully, looking at her. "It suits you."

For some reason his gaze seemed to make her uncomfortable, and she looked away, a flush rising up her face.

"Much better than Lady Wrendal, anyway," he said, trying to lighten his tone.

She met his eyes again at that, her expression firmer. "I'm glad. I hate being 'My Lady', and I hate the name Wrendal even more."

"Is that because you didn't grow up in your father's household?" Jonan asked curiously. "You were raised at the castle with your cousins, right? The king's nephews."

"Been doing some digging, have we?" She raised her eyebrows at him, and he couldn't resist flashing her a grin.

"What? The mysterious Scar, via Raldo over there, commissioned me to snoop around and see what I could find out from these important types. I wanted to impress this battle-scarred warrior, so I got straight to investigating."

She grinned back. "I'm sure this fearsome commander would be impressed."

His face fell. "I doubt it. I made a mess of things at the event tonight. I really was trying to keep a low profile."

She laughed. "Yes, I could tell. And I couldn't help but feel sorry for you. You looked amazingly uncomfortable, although I'm not sure if it was the setting or the costume."

He grimaced. "Both. Why on earth do the men here wear such heavy fabric in this blasted heat? It's all right for the women—you were barely wearing anything at all compared to what girls wear back home."

She flushed again, but this time Jo could readily understand why. He wanted to slap himself. He wasn't usually so clumsy with his words.

"Come to think of it," he rushed on, trying to cover the awkward moment, "I can't imagine why the resistance needed me to try to gather information from that circle when they've got you hidden in the heart of it. And it was very convenient that I was immediately invited to an event at your father's manor." He looked at her suspiciously, but she shook her head, her expression serious.

"No, that wasn't me, it really was my father. I wouldn't have invited you. I'm amazed that he couldn't predict that things would turn ugly. Or maybe it was part of his plan, I don't know. He plays very deep, it's always hard to tell with him.

"Honestly the scene that happened was less dramatic than I feared it would be. And I thought I was lucky to get you out of there in one piece. Even if I did need to send soldiers after you to keep you from being ambushed."

"Thanks for that, by the way," said Jonan. "I assumed your father had sent them, and I must confess I'm relieved not to owe him my life." He gave her a steady look. "You I don't mind so much." She looked down, but her eyes snapped back to his at his next words. "I recognized one of the men who attacked me, by the way. He was at the party. A servant of one of the noblemen. Lord Grentan I think his name was. I could point the servant out again."

"Hmm," she said. "That's interesting. It doesn't hurt to know who we have to watch. I'm not exactly surprised." She was silent a moment, musing. "Lord Grentan is an inflexible man. He's obviously uncomfortable enough with the risk of you creating an uprising that he didn't want to await events like my father has decided to do."

"I really didn't put them up to it, you know," said Jonan. "I didn't want them to risk their safety for me."

"I believe you," she assured him. "I could see how surprised you were. But it's not so astonishing, really. What you did in the square was unheard of. I can't think of any other time someone has stood up for a Kyonan publicly and still been not only alive, but roaming free the next day. You instantly became a hero."

Jonan remained silent for a moment, his mind troubled as he pondered her words. He wasn't so sure he wanted to be a hero.

"What will happen to the slaves who stood up for me?" he asked abruptly. "What can I do to protect them?"

"Nothing," said Scarlett evenly. "You shouldn't do anything."

"But I have to do something!" Jo protested. "I can't let them get executed for trying to help me!"

Scarlett gave him a shrewd look. "Yes, I thought there might be a risk of you making a bad situation worse. I'm glad you're asking instead of rushing right in." She studied his troubled face for a moment then sighed. "It's commendable that you want to help them, Jonan, but trust me when I tell you that further intervention from you would be the worst thing for them right now. If their masters were determined to execute them, there would be nothing you could do to stop it."

"Would there be something you could do?" Jonan asked quickly.

Scarlett exchanged a glance with Raldo. "Maybe," she said. "If we had enough time to prepare, we might be able to liberate someone intended for execution. But I don't think it will come to that."

"Really?" Jonan asked dryly. "No offense, but from what I've seen of Balenans so far, they're pretty bloodthirsty."

Scarlett shook her head, her expression grim. "I'm not saying most masters have much compassion, but they're not all as quick to seek execution as my father is." She gave a barely perceptible shudder. "If any of them had been from his household, it would be a different matter, but none of them were."

She seemed to realize that Jonan was unconvinced, and her expression became earnest as she continued. "Whatever the masters want their slaves to think, Jonan, workers have value to them. Especially now, when everyone's unsure about whether they're going to be able to bring more over from Kyona. They have more to lose than gain from killing slaves as a disproportionate punishment. Rest assured that I will monitor the situation, with each and every person who stood up for you tonight. If any of them face execution for what happened, I will do all in my power to prevent it. But in my opinion, they're much more likely to get lashes, and perhaps some time in isolation."

Jonan nodded slowly, processing what she'd said. A short time ago he would have been horrified at the thought of anyone taking lashes for him, but when compared with a more final punishment, it was almost a relief.

"Just promise me you won't try to intervene," said Scarlett, her voice stern. "Leave it to me to manage the situation."

Jonan hesitated, not liking it, but unable to dispute her superior knowledge. He nodded reluctantly.

"Good," said Scarlett briskly, clearly ready to move on. She studied him in silence for a moment, her face losing the grim look that seemed out of place on her young features. "I hope you enjoyed the festivities while you could," she said. "Because I don't think my father will be inviting you to another such event in a hurry."

"At least something good came out of the night, then," muttered Jonan, and she chuckled.

"If only we were all so lucky."

He grinned easily back at her. "So, did I fail the test?"

"Of course not," Scarlett started, then caught the gleam of humor in his eyes and smiled in return. "Yes, you're right, it was in part a test. And actually I was impressed at your ability to play to your audience. But I also genuinely thought the extra pair of ears would be worthwhile. I haven't been able to discover anything about Stan and the rest of them, and—"

"But I did!" interrupted Jonan, suddenly remembering the real purpose of his assignment. "Your secret identity gave me such a shock that I'd forgotten all about it. But I overheard your father talking to some general and the nobleman who tried to have me killed about a small group of rebels who infiltrated the camp a few days ago."

"You did?" Scarlett exclaimed, her face a mixture of surprise and hope. She raised her hand in a subtle gesture. Instantly Raldo, whom Jonan hadn't even realized was close by, appeared as if by magic. "Tell us everything," she said earnestly, her full attention on Jonan.

"It's not very encouraging, I'm afraid," he said, then recounted everything he could remember about the discussion regarding the resistance. When he was finished, Scarlett and Raldo exchanged meaningful looks.

"They didn't find any bodies," Scarlett said.

"You think maybe they made it?" asked Raldo doubtfully. "But why haven't they returned, if so?"

"I don't know," said Scarlett. "But we have to check. If there's even any chance..."

"I agree," said Raldo quickly. "And there's no time to waste. I suggest we go tomorrow." Scarlett nodded her approval, and Raldo called another young man over from the other side of the room. "Go back to the base tree," he instructed the newcomer. "Have them put together a team ready for tomorrow. We're going to the rapids to search for Stan's group. I'll take them myself."

"No, I'll go," said Scarlett unexpectedly. The messenger nodded in acknowledgment and disappeared quickly down the trapdoor.

Raldo looked at Scarlett in surprise. "Will you be able to get away?"

"I'll figure something out," she said firmly. "I owe it to Stan." Her voice dropped. "I just hope they're alive."

She saw Jonan looking between her and Raldo with interest and sighed. "It was a mistake to let Stan go, and I knew it. The rest were young enough to pass as new arrivals, but..." she looked over at Raldo, "you know how Stan is about new shipments."

Her attention returned to Jonan. "In any event, Stan is one of our best strategic thinkers. We can't afford such a loss. Apart from the personal element, of course." She saw the questioning look on Jo's face and smiled. "We've become good friends. You'll see—or at least, I hope you will. Stan has a warm heart under that tough exterior."

"Well, let's hope they're all right," said Jonan, unsure what else to say. Raldo was scratching his forearm thoughtfully, obviously deep in thought about the planned rescue mission the next day. Jonan's eyes were drawn to the tattoo on Raldo's arm. He frowned at it, trying to pick what was wrong.

The slave mark that he had seen countless times now was a small image of two links of a chain, stretching horizontally up the arm. But Raldo's tattoo was off, somehow. As Jo studied it more closely, he realized that the top link of the chain was nothing more than an exaggerated flourish on the stalk of a letter b, the round part of the letter carefully crafted to look like the bottom link in the chain. But the feature of the mark that really caught his attention was the second circle contained within the rounded bottom of the b.

"Your mark," he exclaimed, and Raldo looked at him in surprise. "It's not a proper slave mark."

"No, I was never a slave," said Raldo.

"But...I thought..." Jonan was confused. "What does it mean, then? The letter b?"

Raldo raised his eyebrows, clearly impressed. "I'm surprised you can recognize that it's a letter. It's supposed to look like the chain tattoos the Balenans put on their slaves."

"I only recognize it because I've seen it before," said Jonan. "The b with the little circle inside it. It's part of a name, right? Alben."

He had not been conscious of any particular noise or movement in the room prior to his words, but it was impossible to miss the absolute stillness that fell over the space as soon as he had spoken. Looking around in confusion, he realized why. From Cody in the corner to Scarlett sitting across from him, every eye in the attic was trained unblinkingly on him.

CHAPTER ELEVEN

"How do you know that name?" asked Raldo, his voice hushed.

"I...I saw it written somewhere," said Jonan, looking around in consternation. "Why? Who is it? Is it someone important?"

"Alben the Liberator," said Raldo, his tone still reverent. "Yes, he was important. I suppose you could call him our founder."

"Was?" asked Jonan tentatively.

"Oh yes," said Raldo, "he passed to his ancestors generations ago."

Jonan's ears pricked up at the unusual phrase. He had heard it first among the mountain people of Kyona. The mountain people whom the rest of the country viewed with superstition because of their rumored magic. He remembered his strange visions, and leaned forward eagerly.

"He was Kyonan, then?"

"Of course he was," said Cody indignantly, approaching the table. "He was one of us. A slave," he added, seeing Jo's questioning look. "Then a rebel."

"Where did you see it written?" asked Scarlett, her brow

furrowed. "I'm surprised there's any mention of him in Nohl outside the resistance. He caused a great deal of trouble for the slave traders, and Balenol has an unfortunate history of expunging those records that don't reflect well on us."

"So does Kyona," admitted Jo ruefully. In his mind's eye he could see the plume of smoke rising from the Kyonan Hall of Records after he and Cal had escaped from it with an ancient manuscript. "But I didn't see it here in Nohl. It was on the ship I came over on."

Once again many pairs of eyes were trained on him in astonishment. He considered recounting his unnatural experience on the ship, but meeting Scarlett's wide eyes he couldn't quite bring himself to do it. She seemed ready to let him into the resistance, and he didn't want to spoil his chances by making her think he was crazy.

"The ship you came over on?" repeated Raldo. "How ancient was this vessel? And I thought you didn't come on a slave ship."

"I didn't," said Jonan. "It was a trading vessel. Of non-human cargo," he clarified darkly. "But apparently it was actually a restored wreck from a couple hundred years ago, and in its original life it was a slave ship. One of the cells had been turned into a storeroom. There were still metal anchors in the wall, where they used to secure the chains, and the name Alben was carved into the wall nearby." He nodded at Raldo. "The b had that little circle inside it, just like your tattoo."

"You mean, you came over on Alben the Liberator's actual ship?" said Cody in an awed voice. "People have been saying that you arrived right when the new king took over, as if by magic, and I think you really were sent by magic!" He looked around at the others appealingly. "Maybe he can break the curse! Maybe we can all go home!"

"Curse?" repeated Jonan, glancing between Scarlett and

Raldo. The two of them were exchanging a look, their expressions uneasy.

"Let's not get ahead of ourselves, Cody," said Scarlett quickly. "Life is full of many strange coincidences." She gave Jonan a searching look. "Although if it comes to that, I'm not convinced that the timing of Jonan's arrival *is* a coincidence."

Jo couldn't resist a smile. Scar's gentle friendliness hid a shrewd mind as much as Lady Wrendal's coldness hid a kind heart. "Please, call me Jo," he said pleasantly. "And tell me about this curse."

She hesitated, again looking over at Raldo. "Let's not worry ourselves over old superstitions."

Jonan laughed suddenly, and she looked at him, startled. "Sorry," he said. "It just strikes me as ironic. At the start of this conversation I was sure that there was nothing you could say that would make me trust you. And now I'm trying desperately to think of how to convince you that *you* can trust *me*."

"It's not that we don't trust you," she said quickly. "Far from it." She gave a rueful smile. "I really do believe that there's a curse, but the truth is I don't want to tell you about it for fear you'll think us all either insane or gullible."

"Actually," said Jonan, "you might be surprised. It wouldn't be the first time I've come across magic."

"I don't know about magic," Scarlett said uncomfortably. "All we know is that slaves can't return to Kyona, even once they've escaped."

"What do you mean can't?" asked Jo, frowning. "You mean the Balenans always manage to stop them?"

Raldo shook his head. "No, she means they physically can't. Many have tried, but no one has made it across the water." He saw that Jo was still confused. "The ship sinks," he explained simply. "Some Kyonans have made it successfully back to the

Balenan shore if the ship goes down soon enough after departure, but most have drowned."

"They call it the deserter's fate," said Scarlett softly.

"I've heard that phrase," Jo interjected suddenly. "Earlier this evening. They said that the deserter's fate must have overtaken the group of renegades."

Scarlett nodded. "They assume that Stan and the others drowned in the river. The deserter's fate is well known in Nohl. I'm afraid it's often been used to justify the slave trade, as though Kyonans belong in captivity." Jo suddenly remembered the words of the physician's assistant.

"And it's universally true, I'm afraid," Scarlett continued. "Ships carrying Kyonan slaves, freed or not, go down so consistently that no Balenan will even consider taking a single slave to serve them on a voyage."

She studied Jo's thoughtful face, her own expression a bit anxious. "We call it a curse, but I don't know if that's really the right word."

"Oh, I don't think you're crazy," Jo assured her quickly. "I've heard of such things before." He hesitated, still not sure he wanted to reveal how closely he had been involved in the usurper's recent overthrow. "I even heard that Kyona was under a curse," he said carefully. "And that it was only after it was broken that the real royal line could be restored."

Scarlett gave him a shrewd look that told him that she, at least, could tell he was holding something back. But it was Cody who spoke, his voice excited.

"Well, maybe that did it, then! Maybe the curse is broken, and we can cross the sea now."

"Maybe," said Jonan doubtfully. "But I don't know...this seems like something different to me." He looked again at Raldo's arm. "What does this Alben have to do with the curse?"

"Nothing," said Raldo in surprise. "At least—I suppose he

was sort of the one to discover its existence." He paused. "How much do you know about the history of the slave trade between the North and South Lands?"

Jo shrugged. "Not much. I only found out very recently that it was happening again. I had thought that the slave trade was stopped by a previous king in the real royal line, generations ago."

Raldo had begun to nod as Jo spoke. "It was. There was a period of thirty years when the raiders were growing in boldness, but that was a few hundred years ago. At first they took goods. They say Kyona is very fertile, and you cannot grow in this climate most of what is produced in the North Lands.

"But after a while, they started taking children and pressing them into service. Just orphans or street kids at first. Ones who wouldn't be missed. But the trade grew. At its peak new ships were arriving monthly, or so the stories go. But they had become too bold. The royals found out the extent of it, and they came down on the raiders mercilessly. Ships stopped making for Kyona."

"So the trade stopped," said Jonan.

Raldo gave a mirthless laugh. "The trade may have stopped, but the slavery didn't. All those already in Balenol were still stuck here. One of them was Alben the Liberator. He started the first resistance, while the trade was still at its peak. None of them ever made it back to Kyona, but some of them survived. That's who I'm descended from."

Jo had so many questions, it was hard to know which to ask first. "I spoke with a Kyonan girl who works in the building where I'm staying," he said slowly. "She said she was born a slave."

"Yes," confirmed Raldo. "Many of those taken in the initial trade remained in slavery, and their descendants have been forced to serve the Balenans ever since. But just as many of the

Kyonans you see now have been taken from their homes in this second wave of raids."

"Like me," chipped in Cody cheerfully. "I was only taken a year ago. I come from Alezae."

Jonan nodded at the mention of the large seaside trading town on Kyona's coast. He had been there. It was where he had first encountered the slave trade, and its influence on the town had been formidable.

"So when did they start taking people again?" he asked. "And why?"

"A couple of decades ago," said Scarlett. "Not long before I was born. It was only a trickle at first, but it's gotten much worse, as you've seen. As for why…greed, I suppose. Our economy is based on our timber trade, and logging camps are much cheaper to operate when you don't have to pay the laborers. There had been no diplomatic relations whatsoever between Balenol and Kyona since the trade was stopped generations back, but almost twenty years ago, the Kyonan king reached out to reestablish communication."

"That would be Hugo," Jonan mused. "Filip's father."

"Yes, him," agreed Scarlett. "He opened negotiations with our king. Apparently Kyona wanted to benefit from trading with Balenol. And what Balenol wanted in return was more workers."

Jo's mouth fell open. "You mean…the resurgence of the slave trade was initiated by Kyona?"

Scarlett nodded. "By the king, at least. Very secretly, of course," she said. "The abductions were still made to look like unauthorized raids."

Jo's mind was reeling, and he wasn't surprised to see the expressions around him growing dark.

"We didn't know any of this," Raldo cut in. "I imagine hardly anyone in Kyona even knows it. That piece of information is one of the many that Scar discovered in her inquiries after she came on board with the resistance a few years ago." He paused. "Not that we really were a resistance before she came on board," he amended. "Just a group of survivors, really, living a nomadic lifestyle in the jungle and trying not to be detected."

Jo looked at Scarlett with even more respect. So she really had initiated this resistance. She shook her head, seeming uncomfortable at the look Jonan was giving her.

"You exaggerate my role, Raldo," she said.

"I don't," he contradicted with a smile. "Before you came along, it had been too long since any of us had any hope. And what we've achieved in the last few years is incredible." He looked at Scarlett with warmth in his eyes, and Jonan looked away, feeling a stirring of some strange emotion he couldn't name.

She sighed. "You are generous," she said. "And we have achieved a great deal. But it's all for nothing if none of you can cross the sea."

"I wonder if there really is some magic involved," mused Jonan. "It would be interesting to know if this Alben came from the mountains."

"He did," said Raldo, staring at Jo. "That's what the circle inside the letter b is supposed to represent—the mountain rocks of his home. How did you guess?"

"People say the mountains have magic," said Jo, sitting up straighter. "Most Kyonans are very suspicious of the mountain people because of it."

Scarlett and Raldo looked at each other. "I didn't know that," said Raldo. "Most of the people who come through are from the coast, and there's not much discussion of the mountains."

"Could there be anyone in the resistance who would be directly descended from Alben?" asked Jonan excitedly.

"No," said Raldo, his voice curious. "Why?"

"Are you sure?" Jo pressed eagerly. "Sometimes there's a kind of magic in bloodlines. His descendants might have the answer. His descendants might *be* the answer."

Raldo shook his head. "I'm very sure, I'm afraid. Alben died without children. He never even married. The histories say that he loved a girl when he was young, another slave, but she died, and he never got over it."

"Marine," muttered Jo, remembering the girl from the visions. It was strange, because it had nothing to do with him, but he felt desperately sad to discover she had died after all.

"What?" Raldo asked, frowning.

"Nothing," said Jo quickly, not missing Scarlett's narrowed eyes as she watched him. "It's a shame he has no descendants, that's all. But still...if he came from the mountains..." He saw their skeptical looks and shrugged. "I'm from the coast, too, but I've been to the mountains myself. And there are definitely strange things going on up there."

"What do you mean strange?" asked Scarlett, and Jo hesitated.

"If I tell you, then you'll be the ones to think I'm crazy," he said with a humorous half shrug.

"Try us," she pressed, and he sighed.

"Fine. Dragons live in those mountains."

There was a long silence. Cody's eyes were as round as plates.

"Dragons?" repeated Raldo, his tone clearly communicating his opinion. "As in, the creatures from legends? Living in the Kyonan mountains?"

"Yes," said Jonan shortly. He couldn't really blame them for not believing him, and he didn't feel the need to give them all the details. A lot of people had seen the dragon Elddreki kill the usurper in Kynton, after all. He imagined that news would spread soon enough. Whether those in Balenol believed it or not was not his problem.

Scarlett looked at Raldo again before responding, and her voice was hesitant. "I don't mean to offend you, Jonan, but if your solution to our problem is to look for help from dragons…"

"It's not," said Jo quickly. He could see that they would not be easily convinced, and he didn't want to get into it. "I'm just saying that we shouldn't rule out the possibility of magic of some kind, with this curse and all."

"Even if you're right, I'm not sure how that helps us now," said Scarlett cautiously.

"Neither am I," Jo admitted.

Scarlett sighed. "Well, I don't know about you, but I need to sleep before the sun comes up. Especially if I'm going to lead this search tomorrow."

"I want to come," said Jo quickly. "On the search I mean."

She shook her head. "You need to rest. I'm not really sure how you're still walking around."

Jo scoffed. "You're making a big deal out of nothing. I'm fine."

"It's not nothing," she said firmly. "I was there in the square, remember? Not to mention whatever happened tonight." She gave him an appraising look. "I'm not sure when you last saw your reflection, but you're kind of a mess."

He grinned. "Repulsive, I've been told," he said, surprising a laugh out of Scarlett.

"That was a bit mean," she acknowledged. "But you started it, after all."

Jonan saw that Raldo looked confused, but neither he nor Scarlett stopped to explain the reference.

"I really do want to come," Jo said. "I promise I'll do as I'm told and not make any trouble. I'll even hang back if you say so." She looked uncertain, so he continued on. "Come on, you know perfectly well that I'm not going to spend the day in bed. And honestly I think I'm more likely to run into trouble wandering aimlessly around the city than out in the jungle with the team."

She smiled, apparently in spite of herself. "Well, that's probably true."

"In fact," Jo pressed his advantage, "having kept me alive this long, it would be positively irresponsible of you to leave me defenseless in the city without you while you go gallivanting off on adventures."

She laughed again, the merry sound lifting the muted mood of the enclosed space. Jonan grinned. He liked making Scarlett laugh. When she did, her face looked nothing like either the haughty Lady Wrendal or the serious rebel Scar.

"It seems I have to let you come, just so I can keep my eye on you," she capitulated with a smile. But her expression quickly became serious again. "Can you swim well?"

"Yes," Jonan said quickly.

"I mean it, Jo," she said seriously. "Speak up now if you're not a strong swimmer. I can't take you if that's the case—you'd be dead weight, and we can't afford that."

"I'm a strong swimmer," Jo assured her earnestly. "I told you that I come from the coast. I grew up in a fishing village. I learned to swim almost as soon as I learned to walk."

"But what about your arm?" she asked doubtfully.

"Honestly, the knife wound is not as serious as you think," said Jo winningly. "It barely grazed me."

He could see all her doubts return at the phrase "knife wound", and for a moment he thought she would refuse him after all. "Well, I suppose I can wait for the physician's report in the morning before deciding whether you're well enough to come," she said at last.

Jonan groaned. "Do you have to let that man loose on me every day?"

She raised an eyebrow at him. "Make it through a twenty four hour period without sustaining any new injuries, and then we'll talk."

He grimaced. She had a point. "He'll just say I have to rest," he said. He could hear the petulance in his tone, and Scarlett seemed to be trying to hide a smile.

"Well, let's get you home so you can do just that." He was surprised when she stood purposefully.

"Are you going to come?" he asked.

She looked at him in bewilderment. "Do you think you could find the way by yourself?"

He shook his head. "Definitely not. I just thought Cody..." He looked over as he said it, and saw that Cody also looked surprised.

"Cody can show you where to go if you prefer," said Scarlett, and Jo wondered if it was his imagination that she sounded a little bit disappointed. "It's just that he would have to return here again, whereas I need to go home anyway. I live a short distance from where you're staying, remember?"

"Of course," said Jonan, jumping to his feet. "That makes sense. I'm ready when you are."

She nodded, and after bidding a quick farewell to the others and briefly discussing plans for the morrow with Raldo, she led the way down the trapdoor. Jo followed quickly, trying to squash his sudden nervousness at the thought of being alone with this enigmatic individual. As hateful as she was, Lady Wrendal had been easier to know how to respond to.

But he needn't have worried. Just as on the journey there with Cody, the trip though the sleeping city didn't require much by way of conversation. And actually, he found Scarlett surprisingly easy to be silent with, which was not something he could say of everyone he knew. He couldn't help but watch her as she stole down moonlit lanes, flitting through shadows. Her movements were as stealthy as Cody's had been, but somehow nothing alike. She was much more graceful, reminding him of a sleek dark cat in her well-chosen black attire.

It looked to Jonan like the sun would be rising in only a couple of hours, and he fought back a yawn as he saw Scarlett glancing over at him. He didn't want to give her another excuse to exclude him from the next day's mission. Her knowing look told him he hadn't hidden it as well as he hoped, and he returned her gaze ruefully.

"How do you do it?" he whispered, as they entered the castle neighborhood. "Live a double life, one by day and one by night? When do you sleep?"

She smiled. "Years of practice. I function fine on much less sleep than I used to. It helps that fine ladies are not expected to be strong or active. No one thinks twice about it if I spend half the day 'resting' after an evening event like the one we just had."

Jonan looked sideways at her. "They underestimate you. To their cost, I'm sure." The steely edge to her smile was all the acknowledgment she gave. "When did you find the Kyonans in hiding, and start doing this?" he asked her.

"Three years ago." She considered for a moment. "Almost four."

"How old were you?"

Her smile of amusement told him that she was not deceived by his attempt to be subtle in discovering her present age. "I was fourteen," she said.

"That's very young," Jonan mused. He looked curiously at her. "What made you decide to do it?"

Her expression hardened slightly. "My father," she said concisely, and he could tell that she wasn't going to elaborate. After another moment, she stopped in the shadow of a tall building, pressing herself against the wall and indicating for him to do the same.

"There's your building up ahead," she whispered, and following her gaze, he saw that she was right. "Do you think you can get in undetected?"

He nodded, his eyes straying past his building in the direction of the Overseer's residence. "Yes, but maybe I should see you safely back to your own home first," he said with a frown.

Scarlett laughed softly, real amusement in her eyes. "What is this? Are you being chivalrous?"

"I don't know," said Jonan, taken aback. "I suppose so. Why is that so funny?"

She shook her head, still chuckling. "It's a good impulse, but a little misplaced, don't you think?"

"No," he protested. "I don't see why."

"It's not me who needs looking out for, Jonan," she said, light-hearted admonishment in her tone. "I've been doing this for years, and even you have to admit that you're way out of your depth."

"You don't know me at all," he said with mock dignity, "or you'd know there's no way I'd ever admit such a thing."

She shook her head, her smile indulgent. "Your intentions are good," she insisted, "but your situation is more dangerous than you seem to realize. As I think I've told you before, your boldness exceeds your discretion."

"So you did mean some of what you said when you were playing the ice sculpture," accused Jonan, raising his eyebrows.

She shot him a look of annoyance. "I meant a lot of what I said. Since the first moment I laid eyes on you, I've been trying very hard to keep you alive, and you don't exactly make it easy."

"Ha!" he said triumphantly. "There's that irritation I've come to know and love. I knew that couldn't all have been faked."

She rolled her eyes. "I meant it when I said that I don't want to be your enemy. That doesn't mean I don't find you irritating sometimes."

He grinned. "Yes, that is something that my friends and enemies generally seem to have in common."

"You're impossible, Kyonan," she whispered, her smile back in place. "Now go and get some sleep."

"Yes, My Lady, if you command," he shot back cheekily.

She shook her head, still looking amused. "I'll see you tomorrow."

He nodded distractedly, already looking around to make sure there was no one in sight. He stole across the front of the building and began to scale a lantern pole. By the time he had pulled himself onto a nearby balcony, Scarlett had disappeared into the night.

He followed the route Cody had showed him across the rooftops, flattering himself that he was already improving in terms of stealth. He tried to calculate how long it would take Scarlett to reach her home via the street, as opposed to his own trip across the tops of the buildings. He suddenly realized that she probably couldn't just enter by the front gates, and wondered what tactics she had in place for entering and exiting the manor unseen.

He reached the roof of his own building without incident and couldn't help hovering for a moment on the tiles, squinting toward Lord Wrendal's residence. He could dimly make out the shape of the manor in the darkness, rising up from the lavish gardens. He wondered where Scarlett's room was, and whether she would have to scale the building to enter through a window like he was doing.

As he eased himself into his own room, he stopped trying to wrestle through the avalanche of thoughts and emotions that had come out of the night's events. He was simply too exhausted to engage with a single one of them, and his throbbing head was demanding nothing but his pillow.

CHAPTER TWELVE

He could have sworn that his head had only just landed on its soft destination when he was suddenly startled into wakefulness by an insistent knock on the door.

Groaning, he pulled himself up and stumbled across the room, becoming more disgruntled than ever when he realized that it was the physician who had woken him. It cheered him slightly to see that the short Balenan man looked as grumpy as Jo felt.

He suffered through the examination with his mind still shrouded from sleep, barely even aware of the physician's strictures and exclamations. It was only once the man had packed up and left, Jonan's arm now neatly bandaged in two places, that Jo suddenly remembered that Scarlett had said he could take part in the planned rescue pending the physician's report.

He wondered uneasily what the fussy Balenan would have to say about him, but it was too late to worry about it now. He had hardly eaten anything at the event the night before, and his stomach was grumbling. It was hard to tell how long he had slept, and he hoped that he wasn't too late to partake of the morning meal that he assumed would be laid out for the Thoranian guests.

He was relieved on entering the dining hall to find the remains of the meal still spread across the table, and even more relieved to see that only a couple of his unfriendly fellow visitors were present, both clearly almost finished eating. He threw himself into a chair and attacked the food with gusto.

"What happened to you?" asked one of the Thoranians rudely, eyeing Jonan's double bandage.

"Huh?" he said, around a mouthful of some kind of sweet bread. "Oh, my arm." He chewed for a moment, stalling as he tried to remember the hasty lie he had concocted for the physician. "I sleep with a dagger under my pillow, just in case. You can't be too careful, right? But I rolled onto it last night."

"This is why Kyonans are born to be slaves," said the man derisively to his companion, who sniggered. "Too stupid to be left to themselves."

Jo scowled, a retort forming in his mind, but the conversation was interrupted by a voice outside the door.

"He's in there, My Lady, I saw him go in just a minute ago."

Jo's ears pricked up at the title. A moment later, Lady Wrendal's elegant figure appeared at the door of the dining hall for the second time. The two Thoranian aides jumped to their feet. This time Jo did the same, only remembering once he was standing that he was supposed to be playing a part. He hovered for a moment, confused, trying to remember whether his role required him to show her respect or discourtesy.

The truth was that he felt embarrassingly wrong-footed. He didn't think he was generally such a poor actor, but her presence unnerved him. Now that he knew she didn't deserve his scorn, her beauty was once again a bit overwhelming. Seeing her dressed for action in the rebels' hideout was one thing. Being confronted in the light of day by her polished form immaculately clad in a becoming gown of pale blue, her hair floating loosely around the soft lines of her face, seemed to be something else altogether.

"Gentlemen," she said, inclining her head graciously at the two Thoranian men. Her gaze traveled over to Jonan, and he almost staggered back at the way her expression hardened. She looked as haughty as ever, and he wondered for a moment if the night before had been nothing more than a dream. Or had she discovered something since then that had turned her against him?

"My father sent me to check up on you," she said coldly. "It seems I cannot be rid of you."

He blinked stupidly. Surely he was supposed to say something equally cutting. But the disrespectful quips that would have risen easily to his mind before were now nowhere to be found.

The Thoranian man who had addressed Jo earlier glanced scornfully at him. "We were just leaving, My Lady, but would you like us to stay? These Kyonans are not to be trusted, after all."

She smiled sweetly upon the man. "Do not put yourself to the trouble," she said. "I am sure you have important matters to attend to. I can handle this boy."

Jonan started to scowl at the insult, then stopped himself, remembering that she didn't really mean it. The next second he remembered that he was supposed to think she meant it. Wasn't he? He could feel his expression frozen unnaturally, but his mind was still struggling to keep up, and all he managed was to blink rapidly in response to her raised eyebrows.

"Halfwit," muttered one of the Thoranians, but the two men didn't linger, taking their leave of Lady Wrendal and exiting the dining hall.

A glance around confirmed that they were indeed alone, and Lady Wrendal's unpleasant expression instantly fell away.

"Are you all right?" she asked, looking faintly concerned.

Jo nodded stupidly, feeling more dazed than ever as he took in her completely altered demeanor. Her stiff posture was gone, and she leaned toward him almost confidingly.

"You're very good at that," he said faintly. "It's a little bit terrifying."

She gave a small humorless chuckle. "Thanks, I guess? You on the other hand could do with some work. No offense, but that was—"

"Woeful," finished Jo. "I know it was. I can do better than that, I swear. I just...need more sleep." He didn't really think sleep was the issue, but he could hardly tell her that her presence unnerved him all of a sudden.

"Boy was a low blow," he added with a bit of his usual spirit, and her laugh was more natural this time.

"I was trying to get a reaction," she admitted. "Besides, aren't you a boy?"

He smiled at what he assumed to be a teasing reference to his own clumsy attempts to discover her age the night before. "If I have the date right," he said, "I won't be in a matter of hours."

"Really?" she asked, surprised, and he nodded.

"But never mind that," he said, moving on to more important matters. "What did that old fraud say? Did he clear me for action?"

"Hardly," she said dryly. "I've just been speaking to him. I can only describe him as outraged, although whether he was more bothered by the sudden appearance of a knife wound or by the violation apparently committed upon your curtains, I couldn't say." She gave Jo a look. "He also seemed to find your explanation for how the injury was sustained to be...implausible."

He shrugged, returning to his food. "I wasn't sure if I was

supposed to be telling people that someone tried to do me in last night."

A ripple passed across her features, but she didn't comment.

"I hope you're not going to tell me to stay back," said Jonan. "What did the physician say?"

She sighed. "He said you should be resting, of course, but we both know that's not going to happen. He did back you up that the wound is not deep. Apparently you were lucky."

He smiled at her. "It wasn't luck, though, was it? Without the soldiers you sent, I would definitely have been done for."

She didn't return the smile, instead chewing the inside of her cheek, her forehead creased as she watched him eat.

"Aren't you worried about being caught out by your father?" Jonan asked curiously after a moment.

She looked at him in surprise. "Frequently," she admitted after a pause. "But what made you ask that?"

"You told those men that your father sent you to find me," he explained. "What if that got back to him? It's not so hard to imagine."

She smiled, but it didn't reach her eyes. "You don't give me enough credit, Jonan. I'm more careful than that. My father did send me here."

"He did?" asked Jo, startled.

She nodded serenely. "Of course. It seems you made some comments last night that have made him quite determined to discover what you know. This morning he uh...had a flash of inspiration that he might be able to use me to that end. He figures that you might be more likely to let something drop in front of a foolish girl than an imposing official like himself."

Jonan felt a grin rising. "And I suppose he came to this real-ization all by himself?"

"Of course," she said again, her expression innocent. "Every-thing he does is always his own idea. Only this morning he was congratulating himself on his foresight in deciding to keep you under watch instead of executing you."

"A man of great discernment, indeed," said Jonan dryly. His brow furrowed as he looked at Scarlett. "You saved my life on that occasion, too, didn't you? I hadn't put that together until now." He felt a warmth rising up in him as their eyes met. He wasn't sure what he'd done to earn her goodwill, but she was certainly a friend worth having. "Thank you," he said, his quiet voice full of sincerity.

She looked away from the warmth in his eyes, flushing. "You don't need to thank me," she said quickly.

For a moment Jonan wanted to argue the point, but he could see that he had made her uncomfortable, and that hadn't been his intention. "So what is Lord Wrendal's brilliant plan for how you're going to squeeze information out of me?" he asked instead.

"Would you believe," she said with a smile, looking up at him once again, "he thought you might like a tour of the city. Maybe even a glimpse of the jungle beyond."

Jo's grin broadened. "Especially a glimpse of the jungle beyond," he said. "Can we really get away without having an escort foisted onto us?"

"Well, you've got a soldier tailing you whenever you leave the building, not that my father thinks I'm aware of that. We'll have to lose him before we leave the city, but that shouldn't be too hard. And my attendant will be with us, of course." Jo raised his eyebrows inquiringly, and she clarified, her voice sardonic. "My personal slave." She saw Jonan's surprise, and smiled. "Her name is Bonnie. You'll like her. One of the very few who is part of the resistance but still officially in service instead of liberated and in hiding. Most people we don't trust to play the part, to be honest."

She gave Jo a look, and he returned it sheepishly.

"Sometimes I feel like she's my only friend," confessed Scarlett with a sigh. "But even with her I have to behave falsely so much of the time, whenever we're with other people."

"Really?" asked Jonan. "You seemed friendly with Raldo... and the others." The hasty addition didn't quite salvage the comment, and he could see from the strange look she gave him that his attempt to be casual had failed.

"Oh, of course I have friends among the resistance," she clarified. "But that's different. I'm not used to being able to talk freely in my normal life. You have no idea how strange it is to be real with you right now," she gestured down her body, indicating her attire, "as Lady Wrendal."

"Scarlett, you mean," said Jo, firmly resisting the impulse to follow her gesture with his gaze. "I thought we agreed that it suits you better."

"I prefer it of course, but when anyone else is around, you'll have to stick with Lady Wrendal, I'm afraid."

"I don't know," said Jo thoughtfully. "I suppose it's very disrespectful for me to call you by your first name, but doesn't that suit my persona? I could do it with a sneer if you like."

He had expected her to laugh, but she just shook her head, looking suddenly uneasy. "No, don't. There are some lines you shouldn't cross. If you get too familiar, my father will probably kill you himself."

Jonan smiled, thinking she was teasing him, but her expression remained serious, and he realized she wasn't joking. "Is he so fond of you?" he asked.

She snorted. "Hardly. My father is not sentimental, and he doesn't care for me at all. But he does care a great deal about his own honor. And I have value to him, even if not for my own sake."

Jonan was spared the need to respond to this chilling speech by the appearance of someone to clear away the food. The change in demeanor on Scarlett's part was seamless, her expression transitioning from earnest to bored with practiced ease.

"You needn't think I relish it any more than you do," she said coolly. "But are you going to come with me, or not?" Their audience of one had her back turned to them as she cleared the table, and although Scarlett's tone was petulant, her eyes twinkled as they met Jonan's.

"I certainly am," he said with the ghost of a smile.

AN HOUR LATER, he felt both more irritated, and more impressed, by his companion than he would have thought possible the day before. Now that he knew her manners were assumed, her cold unpleasantness seemed even more ridiculous, and he wondered how she could stand it day in and day out. No wonder she had seemed exhausted when he tried to bait her the night before.

One benefit, though, was that he had lost his initial awkwardness around her. With her continued rudeness, he found it easy to feign the reckless disrespect that had come naturally to him when they first met. And he couldn't help but feel a strange mix of admiration and sympathy for her. She had said that she hated being a noblewoman, but she was more trapped by her position than anyone around her could ever guess.

She had given him a cursory tour of the castle neighborhood, managing to skillfully weave in a lot of genuinely useful information in between the sarcastic insults. When they had reached the river, she declared that she had no intention of entering the dirty district on the other side, and they instead turned to follow the river south. After a short time it bent to the left, and they followed it all the way to the southeastern edge of the city.

Jonan was so fascinated by the enormous gates that marked this entrance to Nohl, that he temporarily forgot to be snide in his exclamations. The river was quite wide at this point, and its passage into the city necessitated an enormous breach in the solid stone walls. Massive wooden gates had been constructed to fill that gap. Although they currently stood open, Jo could see that when they were closed, they would hang out over the river, suspended without level ground to sit on. He thought that the bottom of the gates would actually be touching the water. Surely the gate must require regular repair, with the rushing torrent crashing against it. But it was probably quite effective. Attempting to swim underneath the gate would certainly risk death.

But presently the gates were wide, and the river was almost as heavily trafficked as the streets. Huge rafts floated through, made of vast lengths of timber, lashed together, with someone sitting on the makeshift vessel ready to negotiate with the guards at the gate. A path ran out on the western side of the river, a small gate set into the stone wall also open to allow foot traffic to come and go. Jonan could glimpse the jungle on the other side of the wall, tantalizingly close.

Scarlett responded to his questions coolly enough, but when he glanced at her he saw the smile in her eyes. Looking involuntarily back at the soldier who had been loitering for the last hour in a manner evidently intended to be inconspicuous, Jo thought it was a pity they couldn't have done this tour without watchful eyes.

Scarlett was apparently thinking the same thing, because as soon as they moved away from the gate, something strange began to happen. They had previously walked at a leisurely pace, but now they sped up, moving in spurts and taking what felt like an unnecessarily circuitous route through the riverside neighborhood. Glancing behind, Jo saw that the soldier was struggling to keep up. Bonnie, who had followed at a close distance behind them the entire time, seemed to have disappeared.

He had not caught a glimpse of the soldier for the last few turns when they emerged into a small market square, full of vendors' carts and bargaining purchasers. The imperious Lady Wrendal had previously shown little interest in anything around her, but she suddenly took a great interest in a stall selling bolts of fabric in various bright colors, located on the edge of the square, back toward the city wall.

Jonan had just obediently followed her behind a large width of cloth hanging from the stall's ceiling when she whispered, "Let's go," and slipped out the back of the stall down a small alley that Jo hadn't even noticed. As soon as she saw that he had followed, she took off running, following the direction of the alley, which was leading them toward the city's southern wall.

He kept pace with her easily, elation racing through him at the release of sprinting after so much time of measured rambling and artificial banter. They raced through a number of twisting backstreets before Scarlett pulled up short, putting up a hand to stop Jonan's forward momentum. They paused for a moment, catching their breath. Jonan couldn't help grinning at his companion, and she smiled back.

"Thank goodness," he said lightly. "I don't think I could have taken much more of Lady Wrendal today."

She grimaced. "Some days I can barely deal with her myself."

He was still chuckling as she led him past another few buildings, once again walking as they emerged onto a larger thoroughfare. He saw that the street they were now joining ran right along the southern wall of the city, and that the river was not far ahead.

"Well planned," he said, impressed, and Scarlett smiled.

"Yes, I've gotten to know my way around the city pretty well in my other life."

They had just reached the water when Bonnie appeared again. Her face was an expressionless mask, but she gave a tight nod in response to Scarlett's questioning look.

"Yes, milady," she muttered. "We're clear. The idiot is still wandering around the market square, looking panicked."

"Good," said Scarlett with a grim smile. She raised her voice slightly as they approached the side gate that was open in order to facilitate foot traffic alongside the river. "Well, if you must see the jungle, we can see it from here. Don't think I'm going to wander very far into it. You may wish to be crushed by a snake, but I do not."

"Lady Wrendal," said the guard on the gate respectfully as they drew alongside him. "Are you leaving the city?"

"Only briefly, I trust," she said, her tone querulous.

"Does...does your father know that you planned to leave the city today, My Lady?" The guard spoke hesitantly, clearly torn between fear of offending her now and the greater fear of being called to account later by Lord Wrendal.

She raised her eyebrows at him. "Of course." Her cool tone discouraged further questioning, and the guard stood hastily aside.

"Just be careful, My Lady," he said. "You know it's not safe to go any distance into the jungle anymore."

"Believe me," she said dryly, "I have no intention of running afoul of any...creatures." Her gaze lingered insultingly on Jonan. He wasn't entirely sure of the hidden subtext of the conversation, but he felt like a murderous scowl was a safe response. It felt very convincing on his face, too. He applauded himself for his increasing skills.

They passed through the gate, and a bend in the road quickly hid them from sight of the city wall. Jonan could only imagine that it would be a nightmare trying to keep any ground around the city clear with such a dense jungle on Nohl's doorstep.

The path was not busy, and after only a few minutes and a surreptitious scouring of the area, Scarlett beckoned the other two to follow her and plunged into the undergrowth. All three of them gained an instant bounce in their step at the absence of watching eyes.

"Phew!" said Jonan. "Feels good to be moving freely." Scarlett smiled as she looked over at him and took in his attempt to wrestle his way through a bush, but didn't comment. She somehow seemed to be navigating the jungle floor with much greater success despite her billowing skirt. "It must be frustrating," he continued. "Trying to pull off subterfuge when you're so easily recognized everywhere you go."

"Yes," admitted Scarlett with a sigh. "It is very frustrating. It's one of the biggest downsides of the position."

Jo, walking behind her, found his gaze shifting involuntarily from the back of Scarlett's head to the face of Bonnie walking beside him. The two still hadn't even been properly introduced, but the look of amusement that passed between them made it clear that she knew exactly what he was thinking. Somehow he suspected that Scarlett's position as Lady Wrendal was less responsible for her conspicuousness than her head-turning beauty.

Jo followed Scarlett beneath a low hanging branch, brushing a thick vine out of his way with a hand. "What did you mean about snakes?" he asked, trying not to sound nervous.

"Isn't it obvious?" Scarlett asked, confused. "There are snakes in the jungle, of course."

"Yes, but you said something about being crushed by a snake. Don't you mean bitten?"

"Nah," said Bonnie cheerfully. "She meant crushed. We get

these enormous serpents in here. They wrap themselves all around your body and crush the life out of you with their coils. Then they swallow you whole and digest you slowly."

Scarlett glanced back, and apparently she couldn't hold in a laugh at the look on Jonan's face. "Let me guess, the jungle is barbaric?" she teased, and he laughed reluctantly.

"I just hope you're leading me through a snake-free portion of it," he said fervently.

Bonnie grinned. "No such thing," she said, a twinkle in her eye.

"Oh, stop it, Bonnie," scolded Scarlett, her face forward again but the laugh clear in her voice. "Don't scare the poor boy, he won't want to come strolling with us again."

"Hey, I thought you didn't have to be mean now," protested Jonan, and she flashed him a grin.

"I'm just making the most of my limited window to call you a boy."

Jonan muttered under his breath, but let it pass. "So why did the guard say it's not safe anymore?" he asked instead. "Was it safer before? Has there been a recent rise in the population of man-crushing snakes?"

"Boy-crushing," Scarlett corrected. Bonnie grinned fiercely, but gave a serious answer.

"No, there's been a rise in the population of the resistance. A few years back, the Balenans loved to do day trips and such into the jungle, and the refugees living in here were always terrified of being caught. These days, it's a different matter. Since Scar started properly fighting back, it's the Nohlians who are scared to go into the jungle. They know we're out here, and we're not afraid to do as much damage as we can." She puffed her chest out proudly. "This is our territory now."

"I'm hardly the one who does the fighting back," said Scarlett dryly. "But otherwise she's right. The royals have even stopped taking foreign visitors for jungle tours, for fear of the guerrilla attacks. It used to be one of the main attractions of visiting Nohl."

Although Bonnie's expression remained smug, Jo thought Scarlett sounded a little bit sad. But he couldn't see her face, so perhaps it was his imagination.

"All right," she said, apparently done chatting. "Let's pick up the pace. We need to get to the base tree as quickly as possible. It's not far, but we're already behind schedule."

She took off at a surprising pace, wending between trees. Bonnie seemed to have no trouble following Scarlett's lead, but it was all Jo could do to keep up with them. Although he would never have admitted it, he was hampered by his fatigue and his throbbing arm as much as by the unfamiliar terrain.

In an unexpectedly short time, the two girls slowed. Looking up, Jonan could see why. He definitely wouldn't have found it on his own, especially as they were approaching it from a different direction this time. But now that they had stopped, he recognized the base tree.

The three of them ducked inside, and Scarlett tapped her foot on the trapdoor, which was covered with a layer of leaves. It swung open instantly, and she disappeared down the hole without a backward glance. Jo and Bonnie hastened to follow, and Jonan found himself back inside the impressive space.

Raldo strode forward to meet them as soon as they reached the bottom of the staircase. "You're here," he said, relief evident in his voice. His eyes flicked to Jonan, but he didn't comment on the final decision to include him.

"Yes," said Scarlett. "I'm sorry we're late. Is everything ready?"

Raldo nodded, gesturing toward a group of half a dozen youth standing nearby. They were armed, and they looked like a very determined bunch. When Scarlett looked in their direction, they all inclined their heads respectfully. She acknowledged the greeting with a gracious nod. Jonan watched her thoughtfully. It occurred to him that there was more similarity between her two roles than she realized.

"I'll just take a minute," she said to Raldo. She started to brush past him, but he stopped her with a hand on her arm, and she raised her eyes to his questioningly. The familiarity of the gesture wasn't lost on Jonan.

"I'm not sure about this," Raldo said, his tone betraying his unease. "I think I should be going, not you."

Scarlett shook her head. "I told you, I want to do this one myself."

"Well, perhaps I should come as well," he persisted, but she shook her head more firmly.

"You're needed here." When he still didn't look convinced, she smiled. "You worry too much, my friend," she said gently.

"You said that we can't afford the loss of Stan," he said. "We can afford your loss even less."

"Well, let's not lose either of us, then," she said reasonably, and pulled her arm out of his grip to continue on her way. She disappeared behind a screen on the far side of the space, and Raldo turned reluctantly back to look at the others.

"Jonan," he acknowledged, his eyes still troubled. Jonan nodded in return, but he didn't think Raldo was paying attention. The older man performed quick introductions, making Jo and the rest of the group known to each other. It seemed that Bonnie was already familiar with everyone.

Jo didn't think he had much hope of remembering anyone's name, but he did take note of who seemed to be the most senior of the group in terms of authority. He was observing this rebel surreptitiously, or he might have missed Raldo's quiet words to the young man.

"Remember. Don't let her take unnecessary risks."

The rebel nodded curtly.

When Raldo fell silent, Jo once again found his eye drawn to the man's tattoo. Now that he was paying close attention, he could see that a few of the other Kyonans in the underground base also sported the counterfeit slave mark.

"Can I ask you a question?" started Jo, and Raldo looked at him in surprise.

"Sure."

"If you and your people haven't been slaves for generations, why do you give yourselves tattoos at all, even if they're the mountain rock ones?"

"Because we're proud of who we are," said Raldo. He spoke sternly, but the effect was lessened by Bonnie's snort.

"Plus the survival of you refugees has always been dependent on being able to blend in with slaves when need arises."

Raldo granted her point with a smile. "Yes, there's also that. Before the resistance began in earnest, and freed slaves joined our numbers, there weren't enough of us to openly defy the Balenans. Not too many of the original resistance survived, and a nomadic life in the jungle is not an easy one. Only the strongest can thrive in such a setting. Still, some of us remain, generations later. We are a legacy of Alben and his work, I suppose."

Jo nodded, unsure what to say. He was saved the necessity of thinking of anything by the reappearance of Scarlett. She had changed out of her dress into practical clothes similar to those worn by the rest of the group, and she was twisting her hair up above her head as she walked. Jo couldn't help but reflect dryly that what with her Balenan coloring and her striking appearance, the change didn't really do much to help her blend in.

"All right," she said, her tone businesslike. "Let's go."

CHAPTER THIRTEEN

"What do you think?" Scarlett whispered to the grim-faced rebel beside her. "I'm inclined to wait them out."

The young man nodded curtly, just as he had when Raldo had spoken to him at the base. "I agree."

Scarlett turned and made a hand signal to the rest of the group. Jo didn't know what the motion meant, but he followed everyone else's lead as they lowered themselves silently until they were lying flat in the undergrowth.

"We're not far from the camp now," whispered Bonnie helpfully, apparently seeing his curiosity. "Did you hear the people nearby?" Jo shook his head, and she nodded, unsurprised. "It takes time to learn to distinguish jungle sounds from human sounds," she said. "But there are definitely people nearby."

"Do you think there are more of them than there are of us?" asked Jonan, still wondering why they were hiding. Bonnie had said earlier, after all, that the rebels weren't afraid to do as much damage as they could.

Bonnie shrugged, seeming to take his meaning. "Probably not. But if they're Balenan scouts from the slave camp, taking them out might alert others to our presence unnecessarily. We're trying to be stealthy, remember? Plus, we're almost at the camp, like I said. This isn't our territory now. That's why she's so on edge."

Jo followed the direction of Bonnie's gaze as she nodded at Scarlett. The leader had indeed seemed to get more tense the further the group had traveled through the jungle. They had moved swiftly through the tangled foliage for about an hour, heading south from the base tree, as far as Jo could tell.

He knew that everyone else was much more familiar with the terrain than he was. He had done his absolute best not to slow them down, with the result that he had gotten pretty battered as he pushed through branches and became tangled in vines. Even so, he wondered if it had been enough. Scarlett hadn't said a word to him the whole trek, but several times he had seen her eyes flick back to him, her tension seeming to increase on each occasion. He wondered if she regretted allowing him to come.

Almost as if she could read his thoughts, she glanced back at him now, her gaze seeming to pass between him and Bonnie with a barely readable reproach. Bonnie fell immediately silent, and Jo followed her lead. In another moment, even he could hear the sound of people approaching through the under-growth. Whoever it was didn't seem to be worried about detec-tion, as Jo could hear relaxed chatter.

Two men appeared between the trees as the thought occurred to him. They were clearly Balenan, and they were strolling southward while they talked. One of them had a bow in his hand and a quiver of arrows across his back. The other carried a much stranger burden—some kind of carcass was slung over the man's shoulder, legs dangling grotesquely.

The men passed by some distance from where the rebels were hiding, not glancing around them at all. Everyone remained frozen for several minutes after they had disappeared from sight. Then Scarlett relaxed visibly, the release in tension rippling out from her through the rest of the group.

"Just hunters," she said, and the rebel next to her nodded.

"What was that thing?" asked Jonan curiously, and Bonnie chuckled.

"A monkey," she said. "That archer must be pretty good— they're not easy to catch."

"Do they eat them?" asked Jo. Bonnie nodded, but further conversation was cut off by Scarlett's terse command to the group at large.

"Let's keep moving."

They continued on, turning to the south and going more slowly now as they picked their way carefully through the jungle. Having observed her in her persona of Lady Wrendal quite a bit now, Jo found it fascinating to watch Scarlett in her role of rebel leader. She was utterly focused, her ears clearly straining for any sounds, and her expression grim as she moved between trees. The rest of the group followed her closely, each one of them so obviously sensitive to her every movement that Jo was left in no doubt about their implicit trust in her leadership.

It was an entirely different type of tension, but Jonan thought that she seemed no more relaxed or comfortable in the jungle than she did in the city.

The ground had begun to rise steadily, and Jo could see brighter light up ahead, when Scarlett signaled for the group to stop. She and her right hand rebel crept through the trees in front of them, disappearing from view for a moment. Jo, waiting with the others, was surprised when he heard her softly calling his name. He hastened to join them, eager to know what was going on.

The trees stopped abruptly not far from where the rest of the group waited. Scarlett and her companion were lying on the ground at the top of the slope, just within the tree line. Jonan quickly placed himself beside Scarlett, taking in the scene below them.

They were at the top of a ridge, and the forest floor fell away again in front of them, the ground sloping down gently toward the river that ran swiftly past at the bottom. Jo had thought they had left the river behind east of the base tree, but clearly it curved back around. The space between them and the river was open, its bareness a shock after the dense terrain of the jungle. Clearly the whole area had been cleared for timber. Stumps could still be seen everywhere, along with the odd abandoned log.

But the main feature of the cleared slope was that it gave them an excellent view of the other side of the river. Jonan felt his eyes widen as he took in the scope of the logging camp. It was much bigger than he had pictured. The whole site was ringed by a tall wooden palisade, the wood sharpened at its top. Unlike in Nohl, the buildings here were not stone, but were all made of wood. Enormous piles of cut timber could be seen throughout the camp, with the figures of people, Kyonan and Balenan alike, weaving between them.

Sound carried across the empty space, with no foliage to deaden it. From where he lay, Jo could hear the shouts of the Balenans, occasionally punctuated by the lashing of a whip. His ears could even discern the clink of metal, and he realized that some of the Kyonans wore chains even while they worked. It was clearly back-breaking labor.

"Confronting, isn't it?" Scarlett said softly. Jo looked over at her and saw that her eyes were focused on the camp below, sadness in their depths.

"Yes," he agreed. "It is. I didn't think it would be so big."

"It's the largest of the camps," she explained. "It's one of the major logging sites, but it's also where they process all new arrivals."

"It must be a problem trying to get across this open space unseen," said Jo, but Scarlett shook her head.

"We don't have to. We're not going into the camp, we're going further down the river. You're just the only one never to have been here before, and I thought you'd be interested to see it."

"You were right," Jo assured her. "Thank you."

She nodded in acknowledgment, her eyes still on the scene across the river. She had nothing more to say to Jonan, and after a whispered exchange, she and the other rebel backed slowly away from the edge, Jonan in their wake. They rejoined the others in a moment, and the whole group began to move quickly through the jungle. They followed the edge of the cleared space, but stayed far enough back to be well hidden by the trees.

Before long they had left the camp behind. Their route began to curve back toward the river, and Jonan realized that the cleared space must have ended. As the sound of the water increased in volume, his guess was confirmed—they had traveled far enough that the jungle once again grew right up to the water. They picked their way along the bank for a few minutes, still keeping back among the trees. Jonan could just make out the torrent now, and he was puzzled as to why the rushing was still growing louder when they weren't getting any closer to the river.

In a very short time his question was answered. Scarlett paused, the rest of the group imitating her at a gesture of her hand, and Jo followed her gaze through the trees to the water. He sucked in a breath.

It was suddenly obvious why the nobles he had overhead at Lord Wrendal's manor were convinced that the rebels had not survived their escape down the river. Not far down from the camp, the already powerful current began to thrash and swirl wildly. Rocks protruded everywhere, and the roiling water danced around and over them in rapids more perilous than Jonan had ever imagined.

Scarlett apparently heard his gasp, and the glance she sent back at him was sharp. He remembered that he had assured her he could swim, and he schooled his features quickly. He hadn't been lying, of course—he was a strong swimmer. But still...he found himself staring at the rapids with apprehension and wishing his arm didn't ache so much.

Scarlett's glance had moved from Jonan to the rest of the group. She didn't say a word, but all around him he saw tight nods. Scarlett began to move through the trees, but she was stopped by a hand on her arm. The young man beside her was shaking his head.

"Let me go first, Scar," he said, his voice respectful but determined.

She hesitated, and Jo could see how much she wanted to take the lead. But after a moment she nodded reluctantly. Jo didn't miss the ripple of frustrated tension that passed over her, or the concern in her eyes as she watched the man make his way toward the water. Clearly she understood her own importance, regardless of how she had brushed off Raldo's protests. The weight of responsibility was obviously heavy on her young shoulders.

The rest of the group followed behind the leader, picking their way through the trees until they were almost at the water's edge. Looking upstream, Jo saw that the edge of the camp was still visible on the other side of the river, although too far away to make anything out clearly.

He could hardly hear anything over the thunder of the rapids directly in front of them, but the water immediately before their feet was actually fairly calm. A protrusion of rock further out in the stream seemed to have created a small breakwater, and the current eddied around it, water coursing gently from the main flow to lap at the near bank, carrying debris and dirty foam with it.

"There's a cave just a little bit further down—the entrance comes off this calmer water." The voice made Jonan jump. He hadn't even heard Bonnie's approach, but she had to put her mouth right next to his ear in order to be heard over the roar of the water. "It's a hiding place our people have used before. Not everyone in the team would have known about it, but Stan would. If they got across the river, maybe they made it in. Doesn't explain why they're still missing after three days, but I think she's hoping there might at least be a clue."

Bonnie gestured with her head toward Scarlett as she spoke. Jonan looked up and saw Scarlett's gaze flick to them, her face impassive as she took in their heads bent closely together in conversation. He wondered if she would again give them a silent reprimand for talking, but she turned toward the water without any change in expression.

"You can follow me if you like," offered Bonnie helpfully. "Just stay as close to the bank as you can, and don't get pulled into the rapids. There'll be no chance for you if that happens."

Jo nodded, grateful for her explanation. Without further discussion, the group began to slip into the river, the young man at the front and Scarlett close behind him. Jo had long since become overheated in the close jungle air, and the coolness of the water was a welcome relief. The river was deep almost instantly, and as soon as his body was in, he could feel the pull of the current trying to draw him out and into the rapids. Following behind Bonnie, he moved with determined strokes, putting all his strength into his movements and resolutely ignoring the immediate protest in his injured arm.

Scarlett looked back at him soon after he began to swim. He met her measuring look with what he hoped was a reassuring smile, but she merely turned to look ahead again. He felt a bit guilty. She had enough to worry about without feeling like she had to keep an eye on him as well.

The rebels moved swiftly, their figures hugging the bank in single file. Every now and then Jo checked on the progress of the man traveling at the front, and his own strokes faltered dangerously for a moment when he glanced up to see that the leader was simply gone. For a moment he was sure that the man had been swept into the rapids, but as he watched, he saw Scarlett dive under the water. Panic seized him for a brief moment when her head failed to reappear, but he quickly realized that the person traveling immediately behind her was too calm for Scarlett to be in trouble.

Fascinated, he watched as each of the rebels disappeared under the water at the same point. Bonnie, immediately in front of him, threw him an encouraging look before her head went under. Wishing that she had taken the time to explain a little more fully, Jonan took a deep breath and dived after her. The water stung his open eyes, but he was able to make out Bonnie's form in front of him, and he struck out after her. She had turned toward the bank, pushing deeper under the water. It took all Jo's courage to swim blindly away from the surface, with no idea where he was aiming for or how long he would have to hold his breath.

In fact it was a mercifully short time before Bonnie started to rise back up, Jonan gladly following. His head broke the surface, and he gulped in a deep breath. They had swum under some kind of rock shelf, and he was amazed to see that they had emerged into a small cavern. It couldn't be fully enclosed, as thin shafts of sunlight penetrated through from above, but it was still dim, and the close stone walls gave him a feeling of claustrophobia. He blinked rapidly as his eyes adjusted to the lower light.

Most of the group had already clambered out of the water

onto a wide flat space of rock, and he was quick to pull himself up as well. There was more than enough room for all of them to stand, so he was surprised by Bonnie's sharp voice.

"I thought the cave was bigger than this."

"It was," said Scarlett, her voice grim. "Much bigger." Following her gaze, Jo realized that what he had taken for the back wall of the cave was actually made up of a pile of loose rocks.

"A cave in?" asked someone, as several people gasped.

"It looks like it," said Scarlett, turning to the man who had led them in. "What do you think?"

His gaze moved appraisingly over the pile. "I think we can shift it without further collapse." He met her gaze. "It's obviously a risk though."

Scarlett looked at the rest of the group, her brow furrowed in concern.

"This is why we're here, milady," said Bonnie firmly. "If there's any chance they're in there, we need to dig them out. We're all ready to take a risk, or we wouldn't have come."

Scarlett's gaze traveled over the rest of the group as they nodded in support, her eyes lingering last on Jonan. He smiled encouragingly.

"All right," she said. "But be careful where you put the rocks. We don't want to block the exit."

They set swiftly to work, and Jonan was impressed at the efficiency of the group. Only two people actually moved rocks, the rest forming two small production lines, depositing their burdens on the edge of the rocky platform.

Jonan joined one of the lines, eager to be of use. He wondered uneasily how long it would take to move the debris, even if they could do so without causing a further cave in, but they had only been working for a short time when one of the people at the front paused, frantically waving a hand as he shushed everyone.

Straining his ears, Jo could hear it too. Although their group had all frozen, a scrabbling sound could still be heard.

"Hello?" called Scarlett eagerly. "Is anyone back there?"

A faint cry was heard in response, and the scrabbling increased. Likewise the group on the outside resumed their work, moving more quickly in their excitement. In a much shorter time than Jo had anticipated, a hole opened in the fallen rocks, and Scarlett leaped forward eagerly to climb up the debris. She reached the hole and grabbed at the rocks surrounding it, sending rubble flying down the slope behind her. After a minute her small figure disappeared through the hole. Her cry of greeting could be heard, and the rest of the group hastened to follow her through.

Jo went last, proceeding carefully up the uneven surface, checking as he went to make sure that everything seemed stable. When he finally reached the new opening, he stared in amazement. Scarlett had not been exaggerating when she said the cave was much bigger. The space beyond the cave in was ten times the size of the platform on which they had been standing. It was even darker inside this second area, but as he watched, figures gained definition in the gloom, to accompany the voices tumbling over each other as the rescue party greeted those within.

The air felt close and thin in here, and Jonan had to breathe deeply to fill his lungs. Everywhere he looked he could see people embracing and exclaiming, many of those who had been trapped crying in evident relief.

Involuntarily, Jo found himself searching for Scarlett in the mass of people. He located her against one wall of the cavern, kneeling down next to someone whose face Jo couldn't see. He climbed carefully down the other side of the rocks and wended through the throng to reach them, certain he was about to set eyes on the missing Stan.

When he drew alongside the pair, however, it seemed that he was wrong. The person leaning against the wall was a young woman, looking to be in her early twenties. She looked faint, and one of her legs was covered in blood, but she was conscious and responding to Scarlett's questions. Scarlett looked up as Jonan approached, and her small smile, the first he'd seen since they started on their mission, encouraged him to voice his question.

"Is Stan here somewhere?"

"Right here," said Scarlett's companion in surprise. "I'm Stan."

CHAPTER FOURTEEN

Once again Jo found himself blinking rapidly.

"You're Stan?" he repeated in surprise. He supposed that the revelation of Scar's identity should have prepared him for this possibility, but it hadn't occurred to him that Stan might be a woman.

"Yes," Stan repeated, still looking confused. "Who are you? Do I know you?"

Jo shook his head, even as he thought that he would have liked to have asked the same question. She looked vaguely familiar, but he couldn't possibly have met her before, given that she'd apparently been stuck in this cave for the entire time he'd been in the country.

"No, you don't. I'm new to the resistance. I'm Jonan."

"Oh," she said, her expression blank. She turned back to Scarlett. "How did you find us?"

"You can thank Jonan for that, actually," said Scarlett, and Stan looked as startled as Jo felt. "He overheard someone say that you had taken to the river. He didn't know about this place, of course, but as soon as Raldo and I heard, we knew you would have tried to get here."

Stan gave Jo a nod by way of acknowledgment, her expression reserved. He would have disclaimed any credit for the rescue, but Scarlett was still talking.

"We were still just as worried, though, because I couldn't imagine why you wouldn't have returned by now if you'd made it in here. A cave in never occurred to me."

"Or to me," agreed Stan dryly. "It was very unlucky. We got in here smoothly enough, and I don't think anyone saw us. But when we were leaving the camp, we cut loose a stack of those enormous lengths of timber in an effort to slow down the soldiers chasing us. It seemed like a good plan until some of the logs followed us into the water. We were lucky none of us were hit by any of them, but one of them struck the outside of the cave just as we were clambering through, and it caused a partial collapse."

"Stan almost got buried," came a new voice, grimly. Jo looked up to see an unfamiliar boy, who looked almost as weak as Stan did. "She insisted on bringing up the rear, of course, and she wasn't quite through when everything came down. Her leg took quite a hit from a falling rock."

Stan grimaced. "I've been useless in getting us out of here as a result. We've been working on clearing the debris, but it's not easy when you can barely see, and I was worried about causing more of a collapse."

"You can hardly blame yourself for being injured," said Scarlett sternly. "I'm just glad you're all alive. Three days is a long time to be trapped in here."

Stan laughed humorlessly. "Has it only been three days? It feels more like three weeks. We wouldn't have lasted much longer. Thankfully we had water," she nodded toward the back of the cave, and Jonan saw clear still springs dotted throughout the space, "but we're all pretty hungry by now, to say the least. We were almost through the rubble, but how on earth we were going to manage to get out safely in the state we're in I hadn't yet figured out."

"Well, we're here to help," said Scarlett firmly. "We'll get all five of you back to base in one piece."

"Six," corrected the unknown boy. "We picked one up at the camp."

Scarlett looked inquiringly at Stan, and the older girl nodded. "Thought you might be pretty interested in what she has to say."

"I'm sure you're right," said Scarlett, "but we can talk about it back at base." She hesitated. "What about you, Stan? In the camp. Did you...did you find what you were looking for?"

Stan shook her head, swallowing hard, and Jo saw Scarlett squeeze her friend's shoulder.

"I never know whether to be glad or sorry every time you say that."

"Glad," said Stan, her tone fierce. "Definitely glad."

Scarlett gave another squeeze, then stood up, addressing the cave at large. "All right, everyone. I know that you're all tired and hungry, but I don't think we should delay. I want to get you out of here straight away."

"No arguments here," said someone from the back of the cave, and Jo saw heads nodding everywhere.

"Good," said Scarlett. "Those of you who've been stuck in here, come gather with Stan over here." She turned to the young man who'd led the way into the cave. "You go and check that the coast is clear. The rest of you," she indicated the others from the rescue party, "let's clear a better path through the debris."

"What about me?" asked Jo quickly, as everyone sprang into action.

"Stay here with Stan and the others," said Scarlett. "Figure out who's up to getting out on their own and who'll need assistance."

Jo nodded quickly, glad to be given a task, and Scarlett disappeared off after the rest of the group. Soon the sounds of shifting rock once again filled the space.

Jo turned to find that Stan had been joined by five others. "How bad is your leg?" he asked Stan, and she shrugged.

"I'll manage."

"That's not an answer," said Jonan, amused. He was usually on the other end of this conversation, and it was strange to be playing this role.

She sighed. "It's pretty weak. I don't think it's broken, but it won't help me in the water any."

"So you'll need someone assisting you," said Jonan firmly. "What about the rest of you? Any other injuries?" He spoke to each of the rebels one by one, and ascertained that no one else had major injuries. He was impressed with how tough they all seemed despite their prolonged imprisonment in the cave, but his private assessment was that the youngest two members of the group looked pretty weakened and could also do with assistance getting out of there.

Having done as instructed, he had nothing more to do but wait for Scarlett to give the go ahead. He looked around but couldn't see her. The effort to clear the rockslide was still continuing. Returning his attention to the group around him, he saw a number of them looking at him curiously.

"So you're new to the resistance?" Stan asked after a moment, and he nodded.

"I didn't think I recognized you," said the boy who had spoken up earlier. "Jonan, right?" Jo nodded again. "Where did you join up?"

"In Nohl," said Jo. "Cody signed me up."

A few smiles passed around the group, and Jo could see that Raldo had spoken the truth when he said that most people liked the irrepressible young boy.

"Where are you from originally?" asked someone curiously. "In Kyona, I mean."

"Nerita," said Jonan. "You probably haven't heard of it. It's a tiny fishing village on the coast. Quite a long way west of Alezae." A number of his listeners nodded at the mention of the well known city.

"I didn't realize the traders were raiding small villages now," said a girl, and Jonan hesitated.

"I don't think they are," he said finally. "I wasn't taken from Nerita."

"Where were you taken from then?" asked someone else. "And how long ago?"

"Um..." Jo was even more hesitant now. "Actually, I...I wasn't."

"Wasn't what?" asked the boy.

"Taken."

There was a moment of confused silence. "What do you mean?" the boy eventually asked.

"I wasn't taken by the traders," Jonan repeated.

"Then how did you get to Balenol?" asked a girl.

"I came over on a ship," said Jo quickly. "Just not...not a traders' ship. A...a normal ship."

"But..." Not just the girl, but the whole group was looking at him as though he was speaking a different language. "Do you mean you came over by choice? By your own free will?"

"Well, yes," admitted Jonan. There was a stunned silence all around, and the girl's mouth actually fell open.

"But why?" she asked.

"Did you have no one who cared about you back home?" guessed one boy.

"Did you come to try to help us?" tried another one hopefully.

"Uh..." Jonan was unsure what to say. "Not exactly, no," he

admitted. "And my parents are dead, but I do have people back home…"

"Then what could possibly possess you to board a ship bound for Balenol?" asked Stan accusingly.

"Um…" Jonan looked around at the bewildered faces turned toward him, each one drawn and pale from their ordeal. His gaze traveled from Stan's injured leg to the slave mark inked into each person's arm. The word adventure had never seemed so foolish.

"Is everyone ready to go?" Scarlett broke the moment with her question, unknowingly coming to Jonan's rescue yet again. Jo quickly filled her in on his assessment, and she called forward some of the others from the rescue team to help the weaker members of the group.

"I can help someone," said Jo quickly, but Scarlett turned to him with a frown.

"No, you can't," she said sternly. "And you should know that. You're injured yourself. If your arm gives way in the water, I don't want anyone else's life to depend on you."

Jo couldn't help but read into her look the suggestion that he shouldn't have come. He felt hurt in spite of himself, but he swallowed any protest he might have made. As little as he wanted to admit it, she was right. He saw Stan giving him a hard look as well, and he was again struck by something familiar in her features.

Jonan was incredibly relieved to discover that after swimming back under the stone ledge, it was possible to swim further downstream within the sheltered waters to get around the rocky outcrop that hid the cave inside it. He hadn't relished the idea of trying to swim against the current in order to return the way they had come.

Still, the process of getting out of the cave, under the water and down the river took much longer with the weakened rebels in tow. When they emerged back into the sunlight, he saw that everyone else was casting anxious looks back toward the camp. He had almost forgotten the danger of detection while they were in the safely enclosed cave.

Once back in the jungle, the group started to move immediately, despite the exhausted state of those who had been trapped. Scarlett, once again taking the lead, glanced up at the sky then back at her companions. Her face betrayed her concern. She spoke a few quiet words to one of the rebels who had come with them from the base tree, and he took off at a jog into the trees, another boy at his heels. The remainder of them traveled on for some minutes before the two companions reemerged. They appeared to have been foraging, and they handed around bananas to the group from the cave.

Jonan found himself at the rear again, this time in company with the injured Stan, who was still being assisted by the young man whom Jo had previously identified as a leader. They had been traveling in silence for about fifteen minutes when Stan spoke. Her voice was quiet, but Jo was close enough to hear.

"I'm uselessly slow with this blasted leg. You should go ahead, get the rest back. I'll make my way all right."

The other rebel smiled grimly. "Nice try, Stan. We're not leaving you behind. You go as slowly as you need to."

"But—"

"But nothing," he continued firmly. "Stop trying to be a hero."

Stan actually smiled at that. It was the first time Jonan had seen a break in her normally hard expression, and her altered features triggered his recognition with such force that he actually stopped for a moment.

Stan and her assistant looked at him in surprise, Stan's eyebrows rising slightly when she took in the way he was staring at her.

"What are you looking at?" she asked, her tone slightly aggressive.

"Nothing," said Jo quickly. "Sorry." He fell into step beside them again, his mind racing. Could his suspicion really be right?

"So," he began cautiously. "I have to confess I wouldn't have guessed you were Stan."

She gave him a dry look. "I suppose you assumed Stan was a man."

He shrugged. "Well, it is an unusual name for a woman, isn't it?"

She just shrugged in return, her face tight as she navigated the undergrowth with her injured leg.

"Did you take on the name after you became a rebel?" Jo persisted. "Or is it your actual name?"

Stan was silent for a long moment, then sighed. "Not that it's any of your business," she said discouragingly, "but I chose it, sort of."

"Sort of?" repeated Jo inquiringly.

She sighed again. "It's a shortening. My full name is Constance."

Jo faltered in his excitement, and she looked over at him in surprise. "Where are you from?" he asked eagerly.

"Alezae." Her voice was cautious, her eyes narrowed suspiciously.

"Did you have family there?"

"Yes," she said slowly. "I have a sister. My parents are dead."

Jo's eyes were as wide as Stan's were narrow. "I thought you looked familiar, but I never would have guessed! That's what you were looking for in the camp! Your sister—not a what, but a who. You were checking to see if Elnora was there, weren't you?"

This time it was Stan who stopped in her tracks, the rebel assisting her stopping also as both of them stared at Jonan.

"You know Elnora?" Stan's voice was little more than a whisper.

Jo nodded eagerly. "I met her not long ago. She told me she had a sister called Constance who was taken by the traders."

Jo's eagerness started to turn toward discomfort at the look Stan was giving him. Her stony demeanor had altered completely, and he thought that tears were even starting to gather in her eyes.

"What's going on? Are you all right back here?" Scarlett's quiet voice broke in on their conversation. Her eyes rested on Jonan, a frown on her perfect features. "We can't afford any delay."

Jonan opened his mouth to protest, aggrieved by her assumption that he was the problem. But before he could do so Scarlett's eyes slid from him to Stan, and a look of astonishment replaced the frown as she saw the emotion on the older girl's face.

"Stan?" she asked, her voice uncertain. "Are you all right?" Scarlett looked shaken, and Jo was willing to bet she'd never seen Stan like this before.

"She's alive, Scar," Stan whispered. "And she's in Kyona. He's seen her."

Scarlett's astonished gaze traveled from Stan back to Jonan. "Seen who?" she asked, her eyes wide. "Elnora?"

He nodded silently, still a bit unnerved at the effect of his revelation on the stoic Stan.

"Well?" Stan prompted him, her eyes piercing him with their intensity. "Where is she? Is she all right?"

"She's...fine," said Jonan. "Better than fine." He hesitated. Stan was still watching him eagerly, but he wasn't entirely sure how to break the news to this strange rebel woman that the sister for whom she had been so afraid was about to become Kyona's queen. "She lives in Kynton now," he said cautiously.

"The capital?" asked Stan in surprise. "How did she end up there? Is that where you met her?"

"I'm sorry, Stan," Scarlett cut in softly, saving Jonan from the need to decide what to say. "Now isn't the time."

"But—" Stan started to protest, but Scarlett shook her head firmly.

"I'm sorry," she said again. "I know you have so many questions, but Jonan and I need to get back to the city. We're already pushing it as it is."

Stan looked between them in confusion. "He's going with you? Why?"

"Raldo will explain everything," said Scarlett. "I'm sorry to leave you, but the others will see you safely back to the base tree. Jo, Bonnie, and I will have to go ahead—we just can't afford to linger. That's what I came back to tell you."

Looking up, Jonan saw that the rest of the group had stopped too. Everyone was watching him curiously, a situation with which he was fast becoming familiar. He couldn't help but be glad of the reprieve, but he felt a bit guilty at Stan's wistful expression as he turned away.

Jonan, Scarlett, and Bonnie lost no time in separating from the others. The three of them made much faster progress now that they weren't hampered by the larger group. Jonan pushed himself even harder this time, and they moved through the jungle more quickly than they had on the way there. Not a word was exchanged until they reached the base tree, by which time the sun was getting low in the sky.

Raldo's obvious relief at Scarlett's safe return quickly became alarm as he took in their greatly reduced numbers. Leaving Bonnie to reassure him and explain the situation, Scarlett disappeared to reclothe herself as Lady Wrendal. Jo found the sight of her once again in her elegant dress surreal. The events of the morning, when they had so lightheartedly evaded the soldier following Jonan, seemed like they belonged to a different life. Which, Jo supposed, they did.

In no time at all, they were again moving quickly through the jungle, back toward the road that ran alongside the river. Jonan felt his heart sinking at the prospect of returning to the restrictions of his strange balancing act in Nohl. As sore as his aching limbs now were, he much preferred trekking through the jungle.

For most of the trip they moved in silence. Despite the successful rescue, the mood somehow seemed more somber than it had on the way in. Jonan noticed both of the girls giving him sidelong glances, and eventually his curiosity got the better of him.

"What is it?" he asked uneasily.

It was a moment before Scarlett answered. "You're just full of surprises, that's all," she said. "Do you really know Stan's sister?"

"Of course!" returned Jo in surprise. "I wouldn't be so cruel as to lie about such a thing."

Scarlett shook her head. "It's a strange chance that brought you to us," she said. "As long as I've known her, Stan has cared about little else other than getting back to Kyona to find her sister."

"Not that any of us can get back," interjected Bonnie darkly, and Scarlett sighed.

"No. It took quite a bit of convincing to stop her from just taking the chance and stowing away on a ship after she first came to us."

"It is a strange coincidence," said Jonan, trying to lighten the tone of the conversation. "I would never have guessed that your Stan was Elnora's Constance." He smiled sheepishly. "Or a woman at all in fact."

Scarlett smiled. "Who were you more surprised to find a woman? Scar or Stan?"

"You," said Jonan promptly. "You are most definitely the biggest surprise I've received since I got here." He glanced at Scarlett and was unable to read her expression. He mused for a moment. "Actually, I've been surprised at how many of the resistance are girls." He saw two pairs of eyebrows raised at him and hastened to clarify. "It's not that I don't think girls are capable or anything. It's just that I didn't expect such an imbalance in the numbers."

His two companions exchanged a look, their expressions hard. "I wish there were even more," said Scarlett shortly.

"What do you mean?" Jonan looked between them in confusion.

"Well," Bonnie started, "slavery is no life for anyone. But let's just say that girls have even more to fear. Which means there's even more incentive to rebel."

Jonan digested this information in silence, trying to hide the distress he felt at Bonnie's words. He could feel Scarlett looking sideways at him again, but he couldn't bring himself to meet her eye.

The minutes stretched out, and Jonan was relieved when Scarlett changed the topic. At least until he realized the new subject of conversation.

"So what can you tell me about the new king, Jo?"

Jonan hesitated. In truth, he probably knew more about the new king than anyone else in Kyona. But for reasons he couldn't fully articulate, he was very reluctant to reveal the fact that the new king was his best friend since childhood. The trouble was that dancing around the issue with Lord Wrendal was one thing —keeping information from Scarlett was quite another.

"Why do you ask?" he tried, knowing he couldn't avoid answering her forever, but not ready to be candid yet.

"Other than the fact that I'm as desperately curious about him as the rest of the resistance?" she asked in exasperation.

"Don't forget that I've spent the entire day with you, and the justification as far as my father is concerned is that I was supposed to be finding out information from you."

"Oh yeah," said Jonan lamely. He attempted a grin. "Is that your idea of cleverly weaseling information out of me, then? I imagine your father pictured more subtle methods."

"And what would you suggest?" asked Scarlett tartly. "Because you're such a master of subtlety."

"I don't know," said Jo innocently, hoping to make her laugh again. "He probably thought you would flirt with me a little or something. It seems like the least you could do."

Scarlett's expression froze in indignation, but any retort was cut off by a choking laugh from Bonnie.

"What?" she said when Scarlett turned reproachful eyes on her. "It's good for you, milady. No one else dares to talk to you so freely, in either of your lives."

"As nice as it is that someone approves of your outrageous ways, Jonan," said Scarlett, "I can't help but notice that you still haven't answered my question. I need something to tell my father."

"Well, what do you want to tell him?" asked Jonan, daunted by Scarlett's cold tone.

Her face twitched in irritation. "How about you tell me about these powerful allies he's so nervous about?"

"Uh..." Jonan hesitated. "I don't think we should start there actually. That's more something that we should build to."

She exhaled loudly, the sound frustrated. "Why are you being so evasive, Jonan? I thought I could speak plainly with you."

"You can," he said contritely. "I'm not trying to be difficult. It's just that...the circumstances in Kyona are so strange...I really think it's better not to enlighten your father more than strictly necessary at this stage."

For a moment she seemed unsure how to respond. "I don't mean to press you," she said eventually. "But it is strictly necessary that I give my father something. He will not...take kindly to me failing in this."

"What does that mean?" asked Jonan sharply.

"Nothing," said Scarlett quickly. "Just that if we make him suspicious it will make it significantly harder for me to work together with you in the future."

Jonan was not satisfied with this answer. Scarlett wouldn't meet his eyes, but he didn't miss the slight flush on her face, or the steady look Bonnie was giving him.

After a long moment of silent tension, Jonan spoke, his voice curt. "Tell him that the new king is called Calinnae. He is young, only just a man. He's inexperienced, but from all appearances he's responsible beyond his years. As your father knows, he was not raised as a royal. I can only assume that he therefore would be entirely unaware of any arrangements between the previous kings and the king of Balenol. Your father would be foolish to assume that this new king would be inclined to honor those deals simply because they're already in place."

"Thank you," said Scarlett softly, when Jonan paused.

"You're welcome," he answered, looking at her face as he walked. "And I'll tell you another thing. Whether or not you should pass it on to your father I'll leave to your judgment. You asked me once whether it was true that the new king is set against the slave trade, and I evaded the question because I didn't know who you were yet. Now I do, so I should give you a better answer. It's certainly what I've heard. Not that he should need a personal reason to be against it, but I heard that someone close to him was almost abducted by traders."

"That was the biggest mistake the traders ever made," said Bonnie, her eyebrows raised.

"Yes," agreed Jonan with grim satisfaction.

"Do you think he would help our cause?" asked Scarlett softly. "This King Calinnae?" Jonan was silent for a moment, and Scarlett sighed. "That's not an encouraging answer."

"No," Jonan assured her hastily, "it's not that. I think he would, but…"

"But what?" prompted Scarlett.

Jo sighed. "This curse idea bothers me," he admitted. "I don't see how the king can help if there's some magical barrier preventing Kyonans from crossing back over the sea. And the new king is a chance for a new start for the whole country. I would hate to see that endangered by some kind of curse. I just wish there was a way we could fix it from here."

"So do I," said Scarlett, her frustration evident. "So much so that I've dedicated my every action to that purpose. But it's not enough. Nothing I do will ever be enough!"

Jonan was startled by the passion in her voice, and even more startled to see tears standing in her clear brown eyes. His instinct was to reach for her comfortingly, but he wasn't sure she would appreciate his touch. He hovered, undecided, and the moment was lost as the road came into view ahead.

None of them spoke as they passed through the gate. Jonan noted with relief that the guard had changed shift since they had left Nohl that morning. Perhaps their prolonged absence would therefore be less likely to raise comment. He was not in the least concerned about any anger Lord Wrendal might direct toward him, but Scarlett's cryptic words had filled him with a deep unease about how little he really understood her situation.

They passed through the city in silence, Bonnie having fallen respectfully behind as soon as they were in sight of others. It was so much easier not to talk than to return to the artificial banter that would otherwise be required. Some time after they entered the castle neighborhood, Jonan became aware that a soldier had fallen in a short distance behind them. He wondered if the man would report to Lord Wrendal that he had lost them, or keep it to himself to avoid punishment.

When they reached Jonan's building, Bonnie stopped respectfully outside the door to wait for her mistress. She sent Jonan a cheerful wink as he passed her, and he chuckled quietly to himself as he mounted the stairs. Scarlett, walking beside him, sent him a questioning look.

Glancing around and seeing no one nearby, he shot her a smile. "Bonnie is great. You were right, I do like her."

Scarlett returned the smile, but the expression looked strained, her eyes hooded.

"I would probably have drowned in the rapids without her instruction," he continued. He had meant it as a joke, but when he saw that Scarlett looked anxious, he regretted bringing it up.

They were silent all the way to Jonan's door. Even once they stood outside it, Scarlett hovered for a moment, not speaking. Jonan waiting curiously for whatever she might have to say. He had been surprised that she had entered the building at all, and even more so that she had seen him all the way to his room.

"Jonan, I..." she started, clearly struggling for words. "I'm glad that Bonnie was looking out for you today. I'm sorry that I wasn't doing a better job of it."

"Don't be ridiculous," he protested, startled. She looked so uncomfortable that he reached out without thinking, putting a reassuring hand on her arm. "You don't need to apologize to me, Scarlett."

She had been staring down at his hand, but at the sound of her name she started nervously and pulled her arm away, her eyes darting along the corridor with an expression almost of panic.

"You can't call me that," she said sharply. "Not here. You never know who might be listening, and my father has a way of hearing about everything. I told you—I'm trying to keep you alive. And my father is not the type to forgive."

Jonan frowned at her, more uneasy than ever, although not on his own account. "What does that actually mean?" he said with a frown. "What will he do to you if you fail his stupid standards?"

"Not me," she said quickly. "It's you whose life is on the line, Jonan! And I mean that literally."

"Never mind me," said Jonan. "I always land on my feet. It's you I'm concerned about."

She took a step toward him, her distress evident in every movement. "You need to take the threat more seriously, Jo. You are in real danger, all the time."

"I do understand," he said gently. "You don't need to worry about me."

She shook her head ruefully. "I think I do. Even today, I shouldn't have taken you on a mission you weren't prepared for. I let you come, and then I didn't properly look after you."

"Nonsense!" protested Jo, not liking where the conversation was going. "I never expected you to look after me."

"No, I'm being serious," she said, not quite meeting his eyes. "I—I must have seemed—cold to you. I didn't mean to be, it's just that when I'm on a mission, there's a lot that depends on me. I have to be focused. I—"

"You don't need to explain," he said firmly. "And you certainly don't need to apologize. There's so much pressure on you, all the time. I thought when I first found out about your secret life that you got to be yourself when you were with the rebels. But after today..." He hesitated, suddenly worried he would offend her, but it was too late to stop now. "I think you play a part as Scar just as much as you play a part as Lady Wrendal."

She met his look now, her expression hard to read. "You told me before that you thought you should answer my questions now that you know who I am. But you're saying it yourself—you don't know who I am. And how could you?"

"That's not what I'm saying at all," Jonan contradicted quickly. "I just meant that, for what it's worth, you don't have to play a part for me. I'm not expecting anything from you."

"Thank you," she said, her tone as uncommunicative as her face. "But I don't think I know how to not play a part anymore."

And before he could say another word, she had turned on her heel and disappeared.

CHAPTER FIFTEEN

J o had plenty of opportunity to puzzle over Scarlett's cryptic comments, because he didn't see her again for a few days. In fact, he didn't see anyone of interest.

After his trip through the jungle with the rebels, he had slept solidly through the night for the first time since arriving in Nohl. Without having given it much thought, he had assumed that someone would make contact with him the next day, but this turned out not to be the case. A day spent in idleness was enough to restore all his restlessness, and he retired for the night dissatisfied and frustrated.

The only interesting thing that had happened had been the appearance of an unfamiliar red flower on the wooden chest that sat at the foot of his bed. He had returned from the midday meal to find the mysterious object placed there prominently. At first he had been excited, sure that it was some kind of signal from the rebels, and that someone would come for him soon if he stayed put. But as one hour turned into two, and no one appeared, his certainty leaked away.

No flowers or other decorations had ever been placed in the room before, and it seemed like it must be some kind of message. But what, he couldn't imagine. The thought that it might be poisonous, placed there by Lord Wrendal or some other enemy, crossed his mind. But it seemed too absurd to be likely.

Eventually his curiosity overcame his caution, and when he heard footsteps going past his room, he stuck his head out the door to see the young Kyonan girl who had previously showed him the way to the dining room.

She stopped when he hailed her, looking only slightly less wary than the first time. He hoped she hadn't gotten into trouble for their conversation.

"Sorry to bother you," he said quickly. "But do you know who put this in my room?" He held out his hand, and she stared down at the exotic red bloom sitting in it, her forehead creasing.

"No, I don't," she said. She looked up at him curiously. "Is it your birthday today? Happy birthday."

"What?" said Jonan, startled. "It's...well, actually, yes it is." He had forgotten about it himself, and he could feel the confusion painted on his face. "How did you know?"

"The hibiscus," she said, gesturing to the flower.

"What about it?"

"It's traditional to receive a hibiscus on your birthday."

Jonan wasn't sure whether to be gratified or embarrassed, and something in his expression must have communicated his consternation.

"What?" asked the girl, clearly surprised. "Don't people give each other flowers in Kyona?"

"No, of course they do," said Jonan, giving an awkward laugh. "It's just that...in Kyona, usually people only give flowers to girls."

"Oh," she said, smiling slightly. "Well, in Balenol, it's traditional for both men and women to receive a hibiscus on their birthday. People love birthdays here. They usually wear the flower all day."

"I see," said Jonan, staring down at the bloom. "Thank you."

She nodded and continued on her way, leaving him to reflect on the fact that only one person in the entire country knew that today was his birthday.

Whatever emotions the gesture might evoke, the realization that he had spent the day that carried him into adulthood in frustrated inactivity did nothing to improve Jonan's mood. He slept only fitfully that night, hoping and expecting at any moment to be awoken by a knock and to see Cody's cheerful face at the window.

When he woke the next morning, his light bedcover clinging to his body unpleasantly in the already moist air, he knew that he could not stand another day of waiting around. The idea of attempting to find either the upper room or the base tree on his own occurred to him, but he thought that the risk of being followed there by unfriendly shadows was too high.

He wandered out of the building, restraining himself with an effort from calling a cheeky greeting to the soldier who was lurking nearby. Jonan made his way toward the castle courtyard, finding that while the space was busy with the usual morning traffic, nothing of particular interest was going on. His eyes were drawn to the whipping post, and his mind inevitably returned to the events of his first visit to this spot.

His thoughts had been occupied all the previous day by the unsolvable problem of the curse. Unlike Scarlett, he had no hesitation in ascribing the curious block against Kyonans leaving Balenol to magic. Remembering his mysterious visions on the ship and in this square, he couldn't help but wonder if this Alben had more to do with it than the rebels thought. He still couldn't imagine what could have caused him to have seen into the long-dead rebel's mind. Cody had said that Jonan had appeared when he did by magic. Was it conceited to think that he might somehow hold the key to it all himself?

He stood for a moment in the middle of the square, looking thoughtfully at the unappealingly grim castle rising from the stone in front of him. He could only assume that whatever fastnesses were reserved for private royal use were located much deeper within the structure, because a trickle of people seemed to regularly come and go unhindered through the main entrance. There were certainly guards positioned either side of it, but they were taking only a cursory interest in the passersby.

Reaching a sudden decision, Jonan strode forward. A week ago he would have moved confidently, trusting in boldness and luck to convince those around him that his actions were legitimate. But a minute of observation was enough to make him realize that as a Kyonan, a bold approach would not help him to be inconspicuous.

Instead he lowered his gaze, fixing his eyes on the flagstones at his feet and imitating the shuffling gait he had often observed around him. He fell in behind a pair walking in the direction of the castle, staying close enough behind them that a casual observer could think he was their attendant, but far enough back not to attract their attention. As he neared the guards, he turned his arm inward a bit, in an effort to hide his lack of a mark. As he had hoped, the guards didn't even glance at him, and he passed through the portal without incident.

He looked up to find himself in a large stone entryway. The castle seemed no more inviting on the inside than it had on the outside. The wide space held little adornment, and the small number of windows made it dim and gloomy. Jonan hesitated for a moment, wondering whether to mount the large stone staircase branching up from the middle of the entryway or explore down one of the passages that ran behind it on the ground floor.

Deciding on the latter, he walked slowly forward, trying not to catch anyone's eye. As he traveled further down the passageway, he was heartened to see a number of other Kyonans. Following one surreptitiously, he found himself diverting off the main walkway and winding through a series of smaller passages, which became increasingly narrower and darker. Before long there were no Balenans to be seen.

"Do you need help?"

Jonan jumped slightly at the friendly voice. He hadn't even seen the boy approach.

"You look a little lost, that's all," the boy continued.

"Oh," said Jonan, recovering his poise and trying to look like he was supposed to be there. "Yes, actually. I'm looking for records, but I'm not sure where..."

"You mean the public records room?" asked the boy curiously, and Jonan nodded, pleased that his gamble had paid off and such a room did exist.

"You're in the wrong part of the castle for that," the boy informed him. "This is the servants' wing. You want to go up the stairs." The boy started describing the route to take, but quickly seemed to realize that Jonan would not be able to find it unassisted.

"I'll show you," he offered obligingly, and Jonan readily accepted.

It was easy to tell when they left the servants' wing for the more public part of the castle, because the lighthearted chatter of his guide instantly dropped away. They had mounted a narrow staircase by that time, and the boy led Jonan some distance down a broad walkway. They passed a few well-dressed Balenans, courtiers Jonan guessed, but no one paid them any attention.

Jo's new friend stopped outside a wide doorway, through which Jonan could glimpse shelves and shelves of manuscripts.

"This is it," he said, glancing at Jonan interestedly. "What are you here for?"

"To look at the records, of course," said Jonan in surprise.

"You can read, then?" The boy looked impressed as Jonan nodded. "Are you an attendant of a lord or something?"

Jonan hesitated. "No," he said slowly. He didn't really want to lie to this boy, but he wasn't sure what was safe to tell him. The matter was taken out of his hands, however, as the young Kyonan glanced down at Jo's arm, his eyes widening.

"You're him, aren't you?" he whispered, looking furtively around to make sure no one was within hearing. "You're the spy sent by the new king! We've heard about you. You're here to liberate us!"

"What? No!" said Jonan quickly. "The king didn't send me, I just came on my own."

The boy nodded quickly, but his expression lost none of its eagerness. "Of course," he said solemnly.

"No, seriously," Jonan protested, starting to feel genuine alarm. "You've got the wrong idea."

"I understand, don't worry," said the boy. But as his words were accompanied by the ghost of a wink, it was clear that he didn't understand at all. "I knew as soon as I saw your arm," he added. "I can't believe I'm actually talking to the unmarked liberator!"

"Listen," Jo started, but he couldn't think of anything to say to convince his listener that he had no power to liberate the slaves. He looked at the boy's enthusiastic expression, and his heart sank at the realization of how much expectation he had unintentionally created, and how drastically he was going to let all his countrymen down. How had he gotten himself into this mess?

"Can I help you somehow?" asked his guide eagerly. "What do you need from the records room?"

"Well..." Jonan decided in the moment that there was nothing to be gained by further attempts to convince the boy of who he was. "I want to find out more about Balenol's history." He glanced around as his guide had done a moment before and lowered his voice. "Especially about the slave trade, back when it all started."

The boy looked up at the sound of footsteps. The man wandering past paid them no attention, but the young Kyonan nevertheless ushered Jonan inside the records room. It was not as large a space as Jo had expected, and it took only a moment to establish that they were alone.

"I don't know what records you'll find in here," the boy said. "And I can't read, so I'll be no help with that. But I know a bit, from my training when I was small. What do you need to know?"

"When you were small?" echoed Jo. "Were you born here, then?"

The boy nodded. "Yep. My people were brought over from Kyona generations ago, apparently. I never knew my parents of course, but I was brought up by Kyonans just the same, and they told me how it was."

"What do you mean?" asked Jo curiously. "Who brought you up?"

"All the slave kids are taken away from our families," explained the boy. "But it's not like the Balenans want to have to care for small children. We all got raised in camps, by older slaves. There were forty of us in my group. Some of the others work here with me in the castle now." He shrugged. "It's almost like family, I guess."

"So what did they tell you about the trade?"

He smiled. "Well, officially they told us that Kyona swore loyalty to Balenol a few hundred years back, and agreed to serve them. But then the Kyonan royals broke faith and turned on their overlords. Apparently Balenol is a merciful country, so they didn't go to war over the broken treaty." The expression on the boy's face communicated what he thought of this obvious fabrication. "So anyway, the two countries stopped having anything to do with each other for a long time. But then a recent king in Kyona found out what had happened and wanted to honor the agreement again."

Jonan felt his face grow dark as he listened to this recital. What a warped and twisted version of what had actually happened.

"For as long as I can remember," the boy was continuing, "I've been told that loyal Kyonans will always serve Balenol, and those who try to break faith will be punished with the deserter's fate."

"You know all that's nonsense, right?" said Jonan, an angry edge to his voice. His new friend surprised him with a chuckle.

"Course I do. I'm not stupid. Plus, I got lucky with the Kyonans in charge of raising my group. They had a bit more spirit than some of the others. I said that's the official story we were told. But when the masters weren't around, they told us some other stuff." He grinned. "Much more interesting stuff."

Jonan eyed his instructor with increasing interest. "Did they ever tell you about someone called Alben?"

"Alben the Liberator, you mean?" asked the boy, surprised. "Sure, loads of times. He's our greatest hero," he added, a note of pride in his voice.

"What can you tell me about him?" asked Jonan.

"Well," the boy started, pulling himself up to sit on a nearby table, clearly settling in for a story. "He was brought over when he was young, around seventeen I think. The traders took him from Argath."

"Where's that?" asked Jo, joining the speaker on the table.

"It's a town in Kyona," said the boy with a shrug. "Some-where on the coast. Near the river, I think, toward the east."

"I've never heard of it," said Jo, "but then I come from the western part of the coast."

"I'm pretty sure it's still there," the younger boy said. "Every now and then you get people arriving who say they're from there."

Jo nodded. "Go on about Alben."

The Kyonan didn't need telling twice. He was clearly enjoying having an audience. "He had a girl, apparently, but I think she didn't come over with him. She came over later. He wanted to get free and go back home, with her as well, but she died."

"How did she die?" Jonan asked, and the boy shrugged, his expression sad.

"I don't know the details, but it's not hard to imagine. It's a hard life for us. Not everyone can make it. Those of us working here in the castle, or in households in the city, we're the lucky ones. It's not so different from being a servant, we just don't get paid and we get treated more harshly. But for the ones who end up in the logging camps...it's a hard life," he repeated, shrugging again.

Jo nodded, his own expression serious. "So what did Alben do? After Mari—his girl died?"

"He stopped trying to get home."

"What do you mean?" asked Jo, raising his eyebrows. "You mean he gave up and accepted being a slave?"

"Of course not!" protested the younger boy. "This is Alben the Liberator we're talking about."

Jo could see that he had offended his new friend, and he hastened to apologize, hiding a smile.

"He got free not too long after," the boy continued, "but he didn't try to go home. I guess he had nothing to go back to.

Instead he made it his mission to free all the slaves. Did some damage too. They say he started a full scale rebellion, and freed a lot of people. Not straight away, but in little bits and pieces. Over about twenty years or so."

"What happened to the rebellion?" asked Jonan cautiously, not wanting to reveal anything this boy didn't already know.

"I guess it fell apart when he died," the boy answered. "Those that were left after the big escape failed, I mean."

"What big escape?"

"Well, apparently the prince back in Kyona found out what was happening with the slave trade. He put a stop to it at their end, and Alben and everyone thought it was time for everyone who'd gotten free to escape back to Kyona. Only, you know," he shrugged, "it didn't work."

"Because of the deserter's fate?" asked Jonan quickly, and the boy nodded.

"They stole a bunch of ships and filled them with escaped slaves. Alben was on one of them, and he swore he would come back with an army and free all the rest. But they sank." The boy's expression was sad. "Every single one."

Jonan was silent for a moment, contemplating the awful impact of this mysterious curse. "So Alben drowned along with the rest?" he asked eventually.

"What?" The boy looked up, having been lost in his own thoughts. "Oh, no, he didn't drown. Some of them made it back to shore, because the boats didn't get far before they went down. Alben got caught, but a bunch of others escaped." He looked around again, ensuring himself no one else was listening. "They say they're still out there—their descendants, I mean. The Balenans claim they've turned savage, living in the jungle for generations. But I don't know...the Balenans say a lot of things about us, but from what I've seen, the Kyonans aren't nearly as savage as the locals."

Jonan couldn't agree more. Although he could think of one exception. "So what happened to Alben?" he asked.

"He was executed."

"What?" Jonan exclaimed, horrified. "You mean..." he touched his throat involuntarily.

"Beheaded, yeah," acknowledged the boy. He sighed sadly. "And that was the end of the rebellion."

No it wasn't! Jonan wanted to tell him. *Don't give up hope!* But he knew he couldn't betray the secrets entrusted to him. For a moment he was silent, mulling over everything the boy had told him. It was interesting to hear more of Alben's story, but he wasn't any closer to understanding the curse and how to break it.

"Do you know anything about Alben's life before he was taken by the traders?" he asked. "He didn't come from the coast originally, did he?"

The boy shook his head. "Nah, he came from the mountains apparently. I don't know where exactly. But he had to leave there."

"Why?" Jonan asked curiously.

"Because his village was destroyed. A rockslide, or an avalanche or something. He almost died, apparently. Imagine if he had! Even though they almost killed him, he never lost his love for the mountains."

"How did he survive?" Jo prompted.

"His mother saved him," said the boy. "Pushed him out of the way or something like that. Apparently he kept some of the rock that killed her. He used to wear it around his neck as a reminder of where he came from and what she did for him. It was his emblem, if you know what I mean."

"Really?" said Jonan eagerly. "A mountain rock? What happened to it when he died?"

The boy shrugged. "Dunno. I guess the Balenans would have

taken it. They must have recognized it—he was famous for always wearing it. Maybe they destroyed it. It was like a symbol of hope, it would've been a big blow."

"I wonder if we can find out," mused Jonan, looking around at the parchments.

"What, in here?" asked the boy, surprised. "You think there might be a record about him?"

"Maybe," shrugged Jonan. Scarlett had said that records about the rebellion wouldn't have been kept, but Jo wasn't convinced. Surely the execution of a dangerous rebel ringleader would be seen as a victory, worth recording.

Jonan began to wander up and down the aisles. His new friend trailed behind him, presumably just from curiosity, seeing as he was illiterate and therefore couldn't assist. Jo's eyes flicked over the various titles, his heart sinking as he realized how big a job it would be to comb through every potentially relevant record.

"Executions," he muttered. "Where are you?"

"An unusual topic for study," said a calm strong voice from the doorway. A sharp intake of breath drew Jo's attention toward the young Kyonan who had brought him to the records room, and he watched with surprise as the boy bowed himself backward and out of sight.

Looking over at the Balenan man who had spoken, Jo could see in an instant that he was someone important. The richness of his clothes and the two guards standing respectfully behind him were only confirmation. The real giveaway was his bearing. Although he couldn't be more than five years older than Jonan, he held himself as someone used to privilege and authority.

Nevertheless, he had a surprisingly pleasant face, Jonan thought, and his eyes held more curiosity than hostility as they rested on Jonan. They flicked inevitably down to his arm, apparently finding there the confirmation they sought.

"So you're our mysterious Kyonan guest," said the stranger, his voice steady.

Jonan thought he had seen the older man before somewhere, and for a moment he was silent, trying to place where it had been. It was so unusual for anyone to look at him or talk to him without an underlying hint of derision. The only other local to have done so was Scarlett. The thought triggered Jo's memory, and he suddenly realized where he had seen this man before. At Lord Wrendal's house, dancing with Scarlett.

Prince Giles, the oldest nephew of the king, likely to inherit the throne one day. No wonder the other Kyonan boy had been intimidated enough to disappear on the arrival of the newcomer.

So this was one of Scarlett's cousins, whom she had grown up with here in the castle. Jo remembered that Scarlett had greeted the man with unusual warmth at the event, and that he had speculated that she intended to marry him and become queen one day. He looked the royal over with increasing interest.

"Yes, Your Highness," he said, belatedly responding to the prince's observation. "I am Jonan." He tried to make his voice especially respectful, not wanting to automatically make an enemy of someone whom Scarlett seemed to like. He assumed that he was supposed to bow or something, but didn't know how to satisfy unfamiliar conventions.

If he had breached etiquette, the prince didn't comment on it. "This is a happy accident," he said instead. "I must confess that I have been curious to meet you, Jonan of Kyona. No one seems to know what to make of you. Rarely have I seen my uncle so lacking in answers."

Jonan looked up, startled, wondering how he had come to the king's attention. Prince Giles seemed to read his thought in his eyes, and smiled. His face was actually quite handsome,

Jonan admitted to himself grudgingly. Nothing to Scarlett's, of course.

"Not the king," Prince Giles was saying. "My maternal uncle, Lord Wrendal."

Ah. "Of course, Your Highness," Jonan said respectfully. "I understand that your mother's sister was married to Lord Wrendal."

"I see you have been doing some research before now," said the prince, his eyes passing calmly over the records around them. "You are correct. My aunt was married to Lord Wrendal until he was so unfortunate as to lose her to illness many years ago. But his loss was our gain, in some sense, as her death caused my cousin to come and live with us."

The prince was watching Jonan closely. He tried to keep his face neutral, suddenly hit with the uncomfortable feeling that Prince Giles had introduced his cousin into the conversation purely for the purpose of seeing Jonan's reaction. The royal's next words only reinforced this impression.

"She seems to take a considerable interest in you, my cousin." Prince Giles's expression was measuring. "It has made me doubly curious to meet you."

Jonan tried not to give anything away with his expression. He was alarmed by the prince's comment, as he had thought that Scarlett had gone to great lengths to convey the opposite impression. Jonan suddenly felt a burning curiosity about what conversation had passed between Scarlett and the prince regarding him. It was difficult to know what to make of this calm young man, his air of authority so different from that of his imperious uncle.

"And what makes you interested to read about executions?" the prince asked when Jonan remained silent.

Jo lowered his gaze, processing the change of topic. He would have to tread very cautiously. "Call it a morbid curiosity,

Your Highness," he said. "We don't execute by beheading in my country."

"Is that so?" said Prince Giles. "How fascinating."

Jonan restrained a smile. Neither the tone nor the face of the older man communicated fascination.

"Allow me to assist you in your search," said the prince, moving forward with a fluid gait.

Jonan hesitated, torn between astonishment and suspicion. But he didn't see what choice he had. "Thank you, Your Highness," he said carefully.

Prince Giles acknowledged his words with a regal nod. "Over here," he gestured toward a shelf, "you'll find a description of the...practicalities of beheading and its history as a form of execution. Or," he continued, walking casually over to another area altogether, "if you're looking for records of specific executions, you will find them here."

Prince Giles waited, watching Jonan expectantly, and Jonan understood. The cost of finding the information he wanted would be letting the prince discover what he was seeking. He paused for a moment, undecided. He wasn't at all sure what was in the prince's head. He wished he knew whether Scarlett's fondness for him had been genuine, or just part of her act.

Part of him thought that it would be madness to reveal anything to the prince, but the mention of Alben's mountain rock talisman had piqued his interest hugely. It seemed like the best lead he'd found, and he wanted to pursue it while he had the opportunity. Who knew how short a leash he would be kept on once his minder reported to Lord Wrendal that he had gone against the nobleman's express prohibition and entered the castle unaccompanied?

He moved toward the records regarding specific executions, not missing the flicker of interest in the prince's eyes. Jonan pulled out a book and began to browse through lists of name after name, unable to miss a certain theme.

"Do you ever execute anyone who's not Kyonan?" he muttered.

"What was that?" came Prince Giles's smooth voice, closer behind Jo than he had realized.

"Nothing, Your Highness," he said hastily, replacing the book. It was clear that he would need to go back much further. He wished he had an exact date for when Alben had lived, but no one seemed to know precisely when that had been. At least the records were well-organized, arranged chronologically. He pulled out the oldest, a neatly tied scroll, and smoothed it open.

He could see almost straight away that his instinct had not failed him. There were a number of entries on the page, but one about halfway down had been written in larger, bolder print than all the rest. The execution of Alben had clearly been a much celebrated event.

Next to the date it read:

*A*LBEN OF *K*YONA, *age 40: executed for insurrection*

The infamous rebel leader Alben was executed at dawn on this day, marking the end of his odious rebellion. Having set himself up in opposition to the crown, he was utterly defeated, leaving this world without companion, possessed of nothing but the clothes on his back.

He declined to make a last request, and passed beyond the blade in silence.

JONAN READ the words over twice, a chill creeping over him. It was a depressing summary of a life. Then he thought of Raldo, and the others in the base tree, and shook his head slightly. This cold entry was not the sum of Alben's life. He may have died childless, but he still had a living legacy.

Jonan's eyes were once again drawn to the phrase, "possessed of nothing but the clothes on his back". He frowned, disappointed. If Alben's executioners had taken possession of his talisman, they had not recorded it. Was it possible Alben had passed it on to someone else before his death? He sighed. It was a long shot.

"You seem disappointed, Jonan," said Prince Giles, watching his face. "Did you not find the information you were looking for?"

"I'm sure I don't know what you mean, Your Highness," said Jonan evenly, not quite meeting his eye. "All I'm looking for is a greater understanding of the history of this land."

"Indeed?" said the prince, his tone polite, but his expression full of a dark humor.

Jonan was saved the necessity of responding when the prince's eyes slid past his face to something at the door. Turning, Jonan was surprised to see Bonnie standing there. If she was surprised to see him, her face showed no sign of it. Of course, he knew her to be skilled at hiding her reactions. She didn't even look at him, just bowing her head respectfully in response to the prince's notice.

"Well?" prompted Prince Giles after a moment of silence. "You have a message?"

"Yes, Your Highness," answered Bonnie, not lifting her eyes from the stone floor. "My Lady says she will be glad to join you as requested."

"Excellent," said the prince briskly.

"And," continued Bonnie, in the same expressionless tone, "she regrets to inform you that My Lord Wrendal is otherwise occupied."

A small smile broke across Prince Giles's reserve. "Even more excellent," he said, and Jonan resisted the impulse to grin himself. It seemed he and the prince had one thing in common, at least.

Prince Giles's scrutiny returned to Jonan for a moment, although his words were directed to Bonnie.

"I believe you have encountered our guest before now. As he is new, he does not know his way around the castle. I'm sure he would benefit from your guidance as he finds his way back out to the courtyard, where I am sure he is missed."

The prince looked at Bonnie, and Jonan saw her nod obediently, her gaze still lowered.

"Yes, Your Highness."

Jonan smiled ruefully. The subtext was clear—straight to the exit, no detours. The prince had clearly been perfectly aware all along that Jonan was not supposed to enter the castle and that he had ditched his escort in order to do so. But Jonan wasn't complaining. It seemed unlikely that he would find any more information here than he already had, and he would gladly welcome the opportunity to speak with Bonnie.

He realized that the prince was watching him expectantly, so he dipped his head in what he hoped was a respectful gesture, then hurried to join Bonnie in the doorway. A glance back showed Prince Giles studying the scroll Jonan had been examining, a thoughtful expression on his face.

Bonnie led Jonan down a couple of corridors in silence, not betraying either by look or manner that she had ever met him before. Even once they had put some distance between them and the record room, she didn't make eye contact as she spoke to him, her face remaining impassive even while her voice was terse.

"What were you doing there Jonan?" she asked accusingly. "Milady is not going to be pleased that you were breaking more rules when you're supposed to be keeping out of trouble."

"You don't have to tell her," suggested Jonan winningly, and Bonnie snorted.

"If you think my loyalty is to you over her, then you're mistaken," she assured him. "But it wouldn't do you any good anyway. The prince will definitely tell her that he met you."

"Will he?" asked Jonan curiously. "What was your message about?"

"He invited her to dine with him," said Bonnie shortly, her tone discouraging further questions.

"Are they close?" Jo persisted anyway.

"Of course they are," she said shortly. "They grew up in the same household, remember?"

"So does she trust him?" Jonan asked.

"How about instead of asking questions, you answer mine?" said Bonnie. "What were you doing there?"

"Looking for information," said Jonan. "I thought there might be a record about Alben's execution, and I was right."

"Alben?" repeated Bonnie, clearly surprised. "As in Alben the Liberator? Why did you want to know about him?"

Jonan shrugged. "I'm just trying to find a clue about this curse," he said. "Same as everyone else."

Bonnie sighed. "I told her you wouldn't be capable of just sitting around and staying out of mischief. Better to keep you involved and keep an eye on you."

"Involved in what?" asked Jonan quickly. "What's going on?"

"Haven't you heard?" Bonnie asked, looking over at him in surprise.

"No," said Jonan, trying not to sound resentful. "I haven't seen or heard from anyone since the rescue mission."

"Really?" asked Bonnie, then gave a small chuckle. "Milady was more successful in restraining Stan than I expected, then."

"What do you mean?"

"Stan has been bursting with eagerness to question you

about her sister. I didn't think milady would be able to convince her to hold off coming to find you, but I guess Stan's injury would be slowing her down. I don't know what exactly passed between them. I don't go with her at night, usually. Part of my role is to cover for her if it seems like someone might discover her absence."

"But she fills you in, doesn't she?" asked Jonan eagerly. "What's happening?"

"They're trying to decide what to do about the slave camps," said Bonnie. "That girl who Stan and the others brought back had quite a tale to tell."

"What did she say?" Jonan pressed impatiently. He could tell that they were nearing the entryway, and he wasn't sure whether they could continue their conversation once they were outside.

"News of your new king has spread further than we realized. The camps are full of whispers. Most of them don't even know about the resistance, but they're starting to talk anyway, about rebellion. People are thinking that the time might be ripe, and there are almost constant small uprisings happening." She frowned. "I've rarely seen milady so worried."

"Worried?" repeated Jonan. "Why? Isn't it a good thing if everyone is ready for action?"

"Maybe," said Bonnie unconvincingly. "But only if the enthusiasm can be harnessed effectively. We don't have the resources to process that many liberated slaves at once, and an unsuccessful attempt at rebellion will end disastrously for those involved. Plus, many of the new ones don't believe the Balenan slave drivers when they talk about the deserter's fate, and who can blame them? They think it's just a tale to frighten them into submission. But if they try to escape back to Kyona themselves, they'll find out their mistake."

Jonan was silent, thinking it all over. It was more complicated than he had at first realized.

"And with all that's going on," added Bonnie, her tone again accusatory, "the last thing milady needs is to have to worry about you, too."

"She doesn't have to worry about me!" Jonan protested, but Bonnie just gave him a look. By this time they'd reached the entryway, and further conversation was suspended while they passed through the busy space. Once they were back out in the square, Bonnie looked him over consideringly.

"Whether she has to or not, she does worry about you, you know. She feels the weight of so many people relying on her, and it makes her nervous to have you so exposed, out here in her world. Most of the people she feels responsible for are hidden away in the jungle during the day. And here you are, wandering around as if you don't have a care in the world, as if there aren't plenty of people who would love any excuse to kill you."

"Well no one's killed me yet," said Jonan absently. "I don't know how she does it," he admitted after a moment, thinking of his interaction with the boy from the castle. "Deal with all those expectations. I'm starting to realize how overwhelming it must be."

"She's so used to hiding what she feels that I don't think even she realizes how much she struggles," said Bonnie dryly. "But it eats away at her. I can tell."

"Is she all right, Bonnie?" Jonan asked quickly, watching her face carefully. "Is she safe, I mean?"

Bonnie met his gaze, her expression veiled. "I don't really know how to answer that."

"Yes you do," said Jonan, unconvinced. "She told me once that her father would kill her if he found out about her involvement with the resistance. I thought she was joking, but now I'm not so sure. Is her life in danger?"

Bonnie didn't answer immediately. After a quick glance around the square she started walking in the direction of Jonan's lodging, and he followed her unconsciously, watching her face. She was clearly considering her answer carefully.

"He's a terrible man, Lord Wrendal," she said eventually, her words slow. "But he's not given to impulsive action. He would be very angry, and I'm not entirely sure what he would do. But he would only act in line with his own interests. She's an asset to him, and there are a number of ways he can make use of her. If he thought that her death would serve him best then, yes, I think he would kill her. But only if it would benefit him. And not in a fit of rage, if that's what you're thinking."

"He's a monster," said Jonan, appalled by this measured speech. "How can he have so little love for his own child?"

Bonnie shrugged. "I don't think he has much love for anyone. I mean, he certainly seems to like milady's brother better than he likes her. And he trusts him. Enough to leave him in charge back on the estate while Lord Wrendal spends so much time here in the capital, in his role as Overseer. I haven't had much to do with Scanlon, but from what I've seen, he takes after his father in all ways that matter."

"How did Scarlett escape intact?" asked Jonan. "Why is she nothing like her father?"

"Because he didn't raise her," said Bonnie simply. "Milady takes after her mother. Maybe because she was raised by her mother's sister, Princess Mariska. I hear that the two sisters were very much alike, in appearance and in temperament. And losing her sister only made Princess Mariska love her niece all the more in the grief of it. It's why the princes aren't as bad as you might expect. Their mother has a kind heart." Bonnie's tone turned dry. "Something that was unknown in royal and court circles before Princess Mariska and Lady Violet came out of nowhere and married into the upper ranks."

"Well the kind heart was passed on to Scarlett along with the beautiful face," said Jonan. "I just wish she didn't have to hide the best part of herself so much of the time."

"Me too," said Bonnie softly. She glanced over at Jonan, her expression thoughtful. "I like you Jonan. And I think you're good for her. It's rare for her to actually be seen, but you seem to see her. And you make her laugh. She doesn't laugh as Lady Wrendal, and she doesn't laugh as Scar either. But you're also dangerous for her."

"What do you mean?" Jonan asked indignantly. "I wouldn't hurt her."

"Not on purpose," said Bonnie. "But you're reckless. You have to realize that your risks affect more than just yourself."

Jonan was silent, wanting to deny her words but knowing that they were true. Through a series of circumstances that he still couldn't quite fathom, he found himself in a situation where his actions seemed to affect a vast number of people. He couldn't begin to articulate the alarm he felt at the discovery that a multitude of unknown slaves thought that he was an emissary sent by the king to rescue them. He was more glad than ever that he hadn't told anyone about his lifelong friendship with Cal. If he had, he was pretty sure that not even Scarlett would believe him that he hadn't been sent by the king but had just come on his own whim.

"Where is she now?" he asked Bonnie, as his thoughts returned to Scarlett.

She shook her head. "If you're thinking you want to talk to her, you can't. She's keeping a low profile after the other day, and any contact with you won't help."

"Why?" asked Jonan anxiously. "Did she get in trouble because we were gone so long?"

"Not exactly," said Bonnie evasively, and Jonan raised his eyebrows at her.

She sighed. "Her father wasn't entirely satisfied with the

information you gave her, so she decided to tell him the other stuff you said, about the new king having personal reasons for hating the slave trade. He's been in a foul mood ever since. He's dangerous when he's in this humor. He doesn't say much, but he's plotting." She hesitated. "You have to understand, there are some very powerful people who benefit enormously from the slave trade. They have a lot to lose if things change. Milady is keeping her distance from you, for your sake as much as for hers."

Jonan nodded reluctantly. He had no desire to endanger Scarlett. They had reached his building, and he hesitated at the door.

"Bonnie, can you get a message to Cody, or Stan, or anyone?"

"Yes," she said. "Why?"

"Can you do it without Scarlett knowing?"

She narrowed her eyes. "Yes," she said again. "But why would I do that?"

"Because she'll say no, but I know you want to protect her more than you want to obey her. And you've all but said yourself that I'm a liability as I am."

"What are you proposing?" asked Bonnie suspiciously.

Jonan flashed her a grin. "It's time for me to become a rebel."

CHAPTER SIXTEEN

Jonan could have sung for joy as he ran through the jungle with Cody that night. The release of tension that he felt upon leaving the city was immediate. The watching eyes of whatever dangerous creatures dwelt in the jungle were infinitely preferable to the surveillance that followed him everywhere he went within Nohl.

It had taken some doing to convince Bonnie to go behind Scarlett's back, and he hadn't been entirely sure that she would actually do it until he saw Cody's familiar face dangling outside his window.

But Jonan had not missed the full impact of Bonnie's words. Scarlett had been meeting the rebels over the last couple of nights, and she had been intentionally cutting Jonan out of those visits. He could hardly be surprised after his uselessness on the rescue trip, but that didn't make it any easier to swallow. His face burned with shame as he thought it over even now, and he was glad that Cody couldn't see him in the darkness.

The truth was that he wasn't used to thinking of himself as incapable, and he didn't at all like the realization that he had been more of a hindrance than a help. He had always been confident of himself—over-confident Cal had assured him many times—but he was now having to face the reality that he was as little prepared for the rebels' jungle warfare as he was for court intrigues.

He had wheedled Scarlett into including him on the rescue mission because he wanted to see the action, without a thought for the possibility that his presence might endanger others. But Bonnie's words had hit home when she said that the last thing Scarlett needed was to worry about him. He kept seeing in his mind's eye the image of Scarlett's face, serious and grim in her role as rebel leader, glancing back at him at regular intervals throughout the mission, clearly checking to see if he was coping.

He had been thinking it over ever since, and he had emerged with a determination to improve. Scarlett might want him to rest and keep out of it, but no matter how much he recognized the need not to endanger the others, that simply wasn't an option as far as he was concerned. So he had convinced Bonnie, and she had apparently convinced Raldo, that it was in everyone's interests to help him learn how to become a capable rebel fighter.

All that remained was to ensure that Scarlett wasn't intending to make an appearance at the base tree that night, and the way was clear for Jonan to make good his escape from the confines of the city and his strange life there.

So here he was, running through the undergrowth behind Cody, full of restless energy after spending the bulk of the day in idleness, and ready to spend every ounce of that energy in learning to fight and to navigate the harsh terrain.

He was not surprised to find himself ambushed by Stan the moment he entered the base tree. He had reconciled himself with the fact that seeking out the rebels would mean he would have to answer her questions about Elnora. Before he could even speak to Raldo, he found himself sitting down with her in a corner and being bombarded with questions. Stan's initial coldness was gone entirely. He could see none of the tough-skinned rebel in her demeanor—she was a vulnerable young woman, her eyes turned to him beseechingly and her voice painfully eager.

So he told her everything he knew about Elnora's life since her sister had seen her. He told her how Elnora had joined a street gang in Alezae for protection after Stan was taken by the traders. He told her how after several years she had run away from the gang, and made a life for herself on her own in Kerr. He knew from Stan's intake of breath that he didn't need to explain to her Kerr's reputation as the roughest city in Kyona.

He hurried on, assuring Stan that Elnora had survived her time there intact, and that he had met her there when she took him and his friend in, helping them out after they ran afoul of some local troublemakers. Her eyes lit up as he described Elnora's kindness in helping total strangers, and how they had invited her to join them in their travels as a result.

He skimmed over the rest of the story, just saying that they had traveled to Kynton, arriving in the capital in time to witness the recent overthrow of the false king, and that Elnora had decided to stay and settle in Kynton. He hinted at a relationship between Elnora and his friend, but left it at that. He had already decided that he couldn't tell her the identity of Elnora's intended, not if he wanted to avoid creating even more impossible-to-meet expectations than he already had.

She soaked up every word, and it was only with difficulty that he extricated himself from the conversation to find Raldo. Even so, she insisted on accompanying him, hobbling along on her injured leg.

Her presence turned out to be a good thing, as no sooner had she understood the purpose of his visit than she threw herself wholeheartedly into the project. Raldo, although more reserved, also agreed to facilitate Jonan's training, and Cody cheerfully promised to pass on everything he knew about being inconspicuous.

And so Jonan began a double life as secret as Scarlett's own. Every night he made his way to the base tree, soon having no need of Cody's guidance to get there. He pushed himself to his absolute limit, training to increase his fitness, learning to fight with a sword and a knife, and even trying his hand at archery. The only times he stayed away were when Bonnie warned him that Scarlett would be there, which was not as often as he had at first supposed. He was unwilling to waste even those nights, however. At his request Raldo arranged for someone to meet him in the jungle, teaching him as much as the darkness would allow about moving through the foliage undetected, tracking, and guerrilla attacks.

Sometimes Cody would even brave the city during the day. Jonan would lose his minder for a couple of hours, and the two of them would explore Nohl freely, Cody showing Jonan how to avoid notice both in crowds and in quiet corners.

The regular nighttime activity made the long boring days much easier to endure. When he wasn't sleeping off his nocturnal adventures, Jonan spent his time attempting to pursue his other project, to which he was no less dedicated, but with which he was having significantly less success. He had been impacted as much by the words of the unknown boy from the castle as by Bonnie's revelations. The assumption of the slaves that he had come to rescue them filled him with guilt over the truth—that he had come on his adventure without any intentions whatsoever.

Despite the fact that he wasn't who they thought he was, he was determined to help them. It seemed the only way to do this was to figure out how to break the curse. He was utterly convinced that Alben had something to do with it, even though no one else seemed to think it likely.

Raldo had confirmed that Alben had been known to wear a rock from his mountain home around his neck, but he couldn't see any connection between the item and the curse, and so showed little interest in helping Jo investigate what might have become of the talisman. Having seen what he had in the Kyonan mountains, Jo thought it would be wise not to underestimate any object that came from there. But his conviction wasn't of much use when no one had the slightest idea of the whereabouts of the rock, or even if it had survived.

In terms of the Balenan court, Jo kept his head down as instructed. Lord Grentan had not repeated the attempt to have Jo killed out of hand, and the rest of the nobles seemed content to ignore him. No one had openly challenged his presence in the city, limiting their protests to scornful sneers any time they encountered him. The sentiment was mutual, and Jonan was relieved to avoid the upper echelons of Balenan society as much as possible.

The slave community, however, was something else altogether. Jonan took every opportunity to speak to other Kyonans in the city, always careful not to reveal to them anything they didn't already know. It was clear that everyone was familiar with the basics of Alben's story, and everyone was almost painfully eager to assist him, but no one had much to say that Jonan could act on.

He persisted anyway, because he had a dual purpose in these conversations. Jonan had all but begged Raldo to let him help with the resistance's response to the looming crisis in the slave camps, and Raldo had finally entrusted Jo with a task. Starting with Jack, the slave who worked for Mundsen, Jonan built a network throughout the city's Kyonan inhabitants.

He was surprised and impressed with the level of communication between the various slaves, which he had first witnessed through Jack's ease in pulling together a small band of defiant youth at short notice the night of Lord Wrendal's event. Jack was delighted to assist him, and he seemed able to produce what felt like an endless stream of other young Kyonans eager to be part of anything the "unmarked liberator" might be up to. Jo felt a bit guilty at trading on their expectations, but as any attempt to persuade them that he wasn't anyone official was always met with conspiratorial agreement, he quickly gave up.

Although the people in this network were not part of the resistance, they were uncannily aware of much of what happened in Nohl. And not just in the city—some worked for slavers whose role took them back and forth to the camps, and it wasn't uncommon for slaves to accompany their masters on these trips. Jonan's conversations with these individuals soon confirmed what Bonnie had told him—rumors of the new Kyonan king were running wild throughout the camps, and from the perspective of the slavers, the situation had never been less stable. And little as Jonan liked to hear it, it seemed that he was discussed almost as much as the unknown king.

The discouragement he had felt at the defeated attitude of the slaves he had first encountered on arriving in Nohl was a distant memory. It was quickly becoming evident to him that for every Kyonan whose spirit was broken, there was another who burned with hidden defiance. The defiant ones were just better at hiding in plain sight. Jack and his fellows may not have been inducted into the resistance, but Jonan could only assume that this was because there had not been an opportunity for them to be made aware of it.

And even outside of the resistance, they could reliably identify individuals who would have both the courage and the connections to act if the whispers of rebellion came to a head. As one week stretched to two, then three, Jonan felt confident that if called upon to do so, he could pass a message around to a large proportion of Nohl's Kyonan residents, and in so doing ignite a spark that would spread the fire of defiance to every corner of the city.

Raldo had not authorized Jonan to tell these Kyonans anything concrete about the resistance, and he therefore had to tread with caution. The need to think carefully through every word before he spoke it was wearing, and Jonan found these conversations exhausting. Much more tedious, however, were his interactions with Lord Wrendal.

Bonnie had not been wrong about the nobleman's strong reaction to Jonan's revelations. Lord Wrendal was clearly scheming hard about how to ensure that the new king did not take decisive action to end the slave trade. He issued politely worded but inflexible invitations to Jonan on a semi-regular basis, and Jonan found himself enjoying Lord Wrendal's dubious hospitality much more often than he would have liked.

Sometimes he met Lord Wrendal at his house, sometimes he was taken through the castle, an environment evidently intended to intimidate, and sometimes he attended Mundsen's rooms. Walking the balance between not revealing anything that would damage Cal's cause and still portraying enough to make it seem like he had valuable information took every bit of the tact that Jonan had only just begun to acquire.

He was commenting on the new king's youth in one such conversation when, unable to resist following his interrogator's eyes, he found himself contemplating Lady Wrendal's elegant figure. Despite the appealing picture she presented, Jonan couldn't help but frown. He didn't like the calculating gleam in Lord Wrendal's eyes every time he looked at his daughter.

It had not escaped Jonan's notice that the nobleman often seemed to look at Scarlett on the occasions when she was present during these delightful chats. Nor had he failed to observe that she was always looking particularly magnificent when she appeared, as though her father hoped that the exquisite sight would stun Jonan into either compliance or careless speech.

But Jonan had come to know Scarlett much better than Lord Wrendal could imagine, and although she rarely spoke to him in her father's presence, her flawless appearance could not conceal from him how ill at ease she was when the three of them were in the same room. Jonan wished so much that he could reassure her, but of course he was as impeded by the Overseer's presence as she was.

Still, he felt his protective instincts rise at the way Lord Wrendal looked at her now, as though she were a bolt of cloth for sale at the markets, and he was trying to estimate her value. Regular exposure to the nobleman had certainly not increased Jonan's trust for the man. With difficulty he prevented himself from reaching to feel the dagger that he now always wore concealed on his person, to reassure himself of its presence.

Scarlett seemed to catch the abortive movement, and her eyes narrowed slightly. Due to his accommodation in the castle neighborhood, Jonan had seen her often in the previous few weeks, but they had little opportunity for real conversation. One reason for this was that she was almost constantly surrounded by admiring or obsequious courtiers. Her cool mask was always in place, so it must have been Jonan's imagination that he could see how weary the attention made her.

Lord Wrendal had evidently decided to turn a blind eye to Jonan's disobedience in entering the castle, and had made only a veiled reference to it, the menace in his eyes warning against a repeat of the behavior. But Scarlett had been present, and her reproachful expression had told Jonan that she at least had been filled in on the full story of his visit to the castle and his chance encounter with the prince.

Jonan couldn't regret his investigations, but he had felt guilty at Scarlett's unhappiness about it. She clearly had a lot on her mind already. He had noted the truth of Bonnie's words in the anxious cloud that always seemed to hover behind Scarlett's smooth features, but she had volunteered no information to him about what the resistance was up to. He swallowed his chagrin over her decision to withhold the information. He couldn't really blame her for thinking that he wouldn't be any help. She had no idea of how hard he had been working to change that.

Or at least he thought she had no idea. Her gaze at this moment was a little too shrewd, and the accusatory note in her voice when she unexpectedly addressed him was as consistent with her real identity as with her court persona.

"You look tired, Jonan."

"It's kind of you to notice, My Lady," said Jonan, pleased with his successful combination of an innocent expression and a slightly insolent tone. "I'm still not used to this climate, and I find it difficult to sleep at night."

He met her look steadily, smiling blandly back at the suspicion in her eyes. She was clearly not convinced, and he was not surprised when she made an excuse to walk with him when he left, a risk she rarely took.

"What are you up to?" she asked when they were clear of the house.

"What do you mean?" he said innocently, crossing his arms in a gesture that wasn't entirely natural.

Scarlett was looking him up and down with an uncomfortably piercing gaze, and he would prefer her not to look too closely at certain parts of him. He had told the rebels not to hold back in his training, so he could hardly blame anyone for the constant pain in his muscles. But his sparring session with Raldo the night before had been particularly brutal, and some of the bruises were starting to show.

"You know what I mean, Jonan," she said sharply. "Do I need to be worried about you?"

"No," he said quickly. "That's the last thing you need. You have enough to worry about." Unthinkingly, he reached for her hand, intending a gesture of friendly support. The alarm in her eyes as she yanked away from him distressed him more than he cared to admit. Her expression as she glanced around was almost terror.

There was no one in sight, but she still remained at an unnecessary distance from him. "How many times do I have to tell you to be careful, Jonan?" she asked, her voice strained. "When will you take me seriously?"

"I do," he insisted, but she was already walking away.

Jo was still feeling troubled by the interaction later that afternoon, when Bonnie sought him out. She came, as was their custom, to confirm that Scarlett was not intending to make a trip to the base tree that night. She was telling Jonan, concern on her face, that her mistress seemed unusually worn, when she seemed to notice his abstraction. She sighed.

"What is it Jo? You have that look on your face, so out with it."

"What look?" asked Jo defensively.

"The look that means you're about to interrogate me, usually about milady."

Jonan grinned sheepishly. "Is it my fault that you're such a treasure trove of knowledge?" Bonnie just rolled her eyes, so he continued, his expression becoming serious. "You told me once that her father sees her as an asset with several possible uses. What did you mean by that?"

To his surprise, Bonnie smiled. "Well, for one thing, you may have noticed that milady is almost supernaturally beautiful."

"I have," said Jonan shortly. Bonnie paused expectantly, her teasing grin inviting him to elaborate, but he maintained a dignified silence.

"You may also have noticed," Bonnie went on, "that she is close with the royal family, especially her aunt and her cousins, the king's nephews."

Jo nodded, and Bonnie shrugged. "Well, both of those things could be of great benefit to her father if he plays them right. To be honest, I think that's the real reason he took the role of Overseer and moved more permanently to Nohl."

"What do you mean?" Jo asked, surprised.

"He wanted to be near her," Bonnie explained, and Jo couldn't help letting out a snort.

"It would be the first I'd heard of any such fondness," he said dryly.

Bonnie smiled, but the expression was grim. "You know that's not what I mean. I should have said, he wanted to keep her near him, where he could keep an eye on her. As far as I know, he never showed the slightest interest in her throughout all of her childhood. But then, a few years ago, he comes for a trip to Nohl and discovers that his daughter is showing signs of turning out every bit as beautiful as her mother was. More beautiful, if gossip is to be believed. Next thing you know, he's moved into his manor house, and nothing will do but for him to have his beloved daughter to live with him, even though she was perfectly happy living at the castle, and they were perfectly happy to have her." Bonnie scowled. "She's certainly never been even the tiniest bit happy in her father's house, poor thing."

Jo frowned thoughtfully. "Why would he take her away from the royals, though? Didn't you say that her closeness to them was part of her value?"

Bonnie sighed. "I guess he wanted her close but not too close. They'd grown up like siblings, and that didn't really serve his purpose. By removing her from the family circle for those last few crucial years before adulthood, maybe he thought they would all suddenly see her differently."

"They?" repeated Jonan. "You mean the princes, I suppose. He hopes she'll marry one of them."

Bonnie nodded. "Of course. Preferably the oldest. She might well be queen one day then. And you can bet that Lord Wrendal would have plenty of ideas for how he could make use of that situation."

"Yes," said Jonan darkly. "I can imagine. Do you think she'll do it?"

"Not if she can help it," said Bonnie. "I'd bet my last coin that she has no interest in being queen."

"Well, I'm sure she knows what she's doing," said Jonan lightly. "I wouldn't bet against her."

"No, I wouldn't either," said Bonnie, but her expression remained heavy. "The trouble is, I wouldn't feel safe betting against Lord Wrendal, either."

Bonnie's ominous words bounced around Jonan's head for the rest of the day, and he was still distracted by them that night as he slipped through the sleeping city. Consequently he became aware only gradually of a sense of being watched. He came to a halt in a dark corner, looking around him uneasily. He wished he had been paying more attention, but he couldn't pinpoint when he had first felt the prickling at the back of his neck.

He could see no sign of anyone. He continued more cautiously, taking a roundabout route rather than heading straight to the house where the tunnel was concealed. After a while the feeling fell away. He wandered a few more blocks for good measure, but when he still couldn't detect anything he decided he must have been imagining it. He was on edge enough to jump at shadows, after all.

He passed through the tunnel without incident, and took off swiftly through the jungle. He hadn't gone far when, to his dismay, he once again felt a prickling sensation. This time he didn't look around him, just veered gradually off course, not so suddenly as to be noticeable.

The jungle always felt full of watching eyes, but his training in tracking had not been for nothing, and he could tell that something was different this time. His alarm grew. If someone really had been following him in the city, and was following him here now, had he just revealed the existence of the tunnel to Lord Wrendal's men? The very thought sent a cold rush over his whole body, despite the warm air.

He continued on for some ten minutes, still heading away from the base tree, taking a route he had taken before, on a nighttime training session with one of the rebels. Skirting around a particularly dense patch of undergrowth, he put on a spurt of speed, then threw himself suddenly sideways behind a moss-covered tree trunk. To the credit of whoever was following him, even once Jonan was utterly still, he could only barely hear their approach.

But barely was enough. As his uninvited guest drew alongside his hiding place, he threw himself in their path, whipping his dagger out in the process. Whoever it was had faster reflexes than he had bargained for, and his blade met steel as they pulled out their own knife. He could only be grateful that his assailant didn't have an actual sword, against which his dagger would be of little use.

Jonan disengaged his blade neatly, a detached part of his mind wishing Raldo could be present to witness his student putting their many lessons to the test. His opponent hesitated, and Jonan's dagger flashed forward again, aiming for the torso. The other person dropped suddenly, rolling smoothly to the side before springing up, blade raised in a defensive posture.

Jonan was hampered by the darkness, and he stumbled slightly as he spun to face the new position. He quickly drew back, out of reach of the other blade, as he regained his footing on the uneven ground. He peered at his adversary, and was not surprised that he had almost missed their presence. Whoever it was blended into the night, dressed in black from head to toe, even their face covered by the swath of black cloth wound around it. The figure was slight, and Jonan hesitated for a moment, surprised. He had assumed it was a soldier, but this person was smaller than him.

He regretted his hesitation a moment later, as the black-clad figure lunged toward him, knife flashing in the moonlight that filtered through the leaves above. Jonan stepped to the side as he repelled the attack with his own dagger, but his attempt to strike his assailant in the side as they plunged past him was unsuccessful. This person knew how to fight with a blade, and had twisted around and deflected his jab before he could blink.

For a moment the blades locked, then Jo's attacker pushed hard, forcing his blade upward and whipping their own blade back down. Jo stepped back hastily as he brought his dagger down to protect his chest, forcing the other knife to the side. He felt a sting as the metal sliced shallowly across his arm, but it was the slightest of wounds, and didn't slow him down at all.

Ignoring his opponent's intake of breath, he threw himself forward, trying to get in under their guard. The other fighter faltered, stepping back as well, but successfully held off Jonan's attack. Jo looked the dark figure up and down, then moved suddenly, his foot flying out to connect with a knee even while his blade continued to engage the other weapon.

The other fighter let out a grunt as Jo's foot found its mark, stepping back again, out of reach of Jonan's blade. He followed, ready to press his advantage, but was pulled up short by an alarmingly familiar voice.

"Enough Jo! Stop!"

He stumbled back himself, his blade dropping to the jungle floor from suddenly nerveless fingers. His opponent leaned against a nearby tree with one shaky hand while the other hand reached up to unwind the makeshift head covering, but Jo didn't need to see underneath to recognize whom he had been fighting.

CHAPTER SEVENTEEN

"Scarlett!" he cried in undisguised horror. "What are you doing here?"

"What am I doing here?" she repeated, her tone accusatory. "What are you doing here, Jo? You're supposed to be lying low!"

He ignored her words, unable to hide his distress as he took in her unnatural posture. She still leaned against the tree, keeping weight off the leg he had kicked.

"I hurt you!" he said.

"I'm fine," she quickly denied, guilt in her own eyes as she looked at the blood dripping down his sleeve. "I'm sorry about your arm."

He shook his head impatiently. "Don't be stupid, it's a scratch. Why did you let me hurt you?"

"To be honest, I didn't think you would be able to get me," she admitted dryly.

"But why did you attack me?" he insisted, feeling slightly sick at the memory of how his boot had connected with her knee.

"Well, if we're being accurate, you attacked me," she pointed out, but he just glared at her.

"Because you were following me! And you attacked back, Scarlett, you know you did. Why didn't you tell me it was you straight away?"

"Why do you think?" she said shortly. "I wanted to see what you would do. It wasn't like I was going to actually kill you, and I wasn't going to let you kill me either. But I suspected you were up to something, and I wanted to see just how far that something had gone. Clearly you've been busy." She gave him a long look. "I'm impressed, actually," she admitted finally.

"So am I," said Jonan with a reluctant laugh. "I didn't know you could fight with a blade."

"Seriously?" she asked disbelievingly. "I've been a leader of a group of guerrilla rebels for years, and you didn't think I'd know how to fight?"

Jonan shrugged. "I thought your role was more along the lines of information gathering."

"Well, I'm a woman of many talents," she said with a hint of irony. He regarded her in silence, unable to hold back an amused smile, and suddenly she grinned back at him.

"You have to admit, it was kind of fun."

He laughed readily this time. "Yes," he acknowledged. "It was a little. Much more fun that the type of sparring we do in our other lives." He shook his head. "But I wish you hadn't let it go that far. I'll gladly spar with you any time you like, but not with real blades next time."

"Deal," she said, but the smile quickly slid off her face as she looked him over. She put her dagger away, and her tone turned businesslike. "What are you doing out here, Jonan? Where are you going?"

"To the base tree, of course," he answered, surprised. "Where else?"

"This isn't the way to the base tree," she said. "You're heading out into the middle of nowhere."

"Give me a little credit," he said indignantly. "Once I realized I was being followed, I wasn't about to lead you straight there. Or, I mean, not you, but...whoever was following me...you know what I mean."

She raised an eyebrow, and he thought she looked a bit impressed. "When did you figure out you were being followed?"

"A little while ago," Jonan said. He pursed his lips. "I'm very relieved it's you, actually. I thought someone was following me in the city, but convinced myself I was imagining it. When I realized whoever it was had followed me out here, I thought I'd led someone through the tunnel."

She nodded. "I thought you seemed suspicious back in Nohl, so I stopped following you so closely. I took the chance that you were headed out here and made my own way to the tunnel." She gave him a measuring look.

"I could swear you didn't know anything about tracking or stealth when I took you through the city last time." She narrowed her eyes. "I can easily imagine who's taught you that. And it's not exactly news that you've gotten Cody well and truly onside, but I'm pretty sure he couldn't have taught you how to fight like that." She leveled him with a shrewd look.

At first Jo said nothing, but as the silence stretched out, he could see from Scarlett's expectant expression that she wasn't going to let him get away without giving her an answer. He sighed.

"Raldo," he said. "He's been training me. And Stan, a bit."

"When?" she said, her words tight and her face unimpressed. "Where?"

"Every night, just about," said Jonan. "At the base tree."

"But..." Scarlett looked confused. "I've been there, several times. I never saw you."

"Well, yeah, I stayed away on the nights you were coming," said Jo matter-of-factly. "I got the sense you might not approve. That's when I've been having a go at tracking and such."

"But how would you know whether I was going to..." her expression changed from confusion to annoyance as the truth hit. "Bonnie," she said grimly. Jonan didn't say anything, but she seemed to take his silence as confirmation.

"Unbelievable," she muttered, turning without another word and striking off in the direction of the base tree. Jonan hurried to keep up.

"Don't be angry with them," he said anxiously. "Any of them. They were just trying to help."

She said nothing, continuing to power through the undergrowth, her expression harder than he had ever seen it.

"Scar," said Jonan compellingly, but she ignored him. "Scarlett," he repeated insistently, his hand reaching out to lightly grab her arm. "Stop."

She turned to him, the cold look on her face making her look suddenly like Lady Wrendal, although she made no move to throw off his hand.

"We..." Jo hesitated as he took in her demeanor. "We didn't mean to make you angry."

"No," she said tightly, "because you meant for me to remain in ignorance. I can't lead if I don't have all the information, Jonan. I've been surprised that you were so compliantly keeping your head down. But when I saw you go for your knife today, I looked at you properly for the first time in a while. I don't know how I'd missed the bruises, or the fact that you're much more muscled than you were a few weeks ago."

"I am?" asked Jonan, gratified. He smiled, trying to lighten the mood. "Thanks for noticing."

But Scarlett was evidently not interested in pleasantries. "I realized then that you'd been up to something, but I little guessed the extent of it. I trusted you, Jonan. I let you into the resistance with hardly any testing. I know you're Kyonan, and I'll always be a Balenan, no matter how much I do for them. And I know I've been a bit distracted with everything going on. But it's still hard to believe that in such a short time you've turned all my best people against me."

"What?" said Jonan, startled. "Of course I haven't done anything of the kind!"

She said nothing. Her expression was still stony, but something flickered behind her eyes, and Jonan realized with alarm that there was genuine hurt and betrayal lurking beneath the angry front. He felt a surge of guilt and regret, and tightened his hold on her arm.

"Scarlett," he said earnestly. "No one has turned against you. Far from it! Every single member of that group," he nodded in the direction of the base tree, "is loyal to you to the point of death. They see you as their hero, every one of them! And they want to help you, to protect you. That's the only reason any of them are helping me. It's for your sake, not mine."

She frowned. "How does lying to me and going behind my back help or protect me?"

"Don't blame them for that," he said quickly. "That was all me. I knew you wanted me to stay out of trouble, but I also knew that your...good-hearted determination to protect everyone around you—including me—was blinding you to what needed to be done. I could see as clearly as everyone else could that I was a liability to you. And believe me, I don't blame you for not wanting to include me in what you've been up to. I know I was beyond useless in the last mission, and you can't afford to have someone on board you have to look after."

Scarlett had been looking down at his hand on her arm, her expression hard to read, but she looked up sharply at his words, her brow furrowed.

"But there's no point me being here if I can't help," Jo was barreling on. "I want to help, Scar. I want to figure out how to free the Kyonans. And I've been trying." His voice turned eager. "Training with Raldo and the others has just been at night. During the day I've been connecting with Kyonans across the city, finding out what I can, and trying to reach as many of those not already in the resistance as possible, through a further network."

"Whoa," said Scarlett, finally pulling her arm free and holding up her hand to stop the flow of words. "Slow down." She frowned at him. "What was all that about me seeing you as a liability? Is that what you think? Is that why you've been so uncomplaining about me not communicating with you?"

"Well...yes," said Jonan, watching in confusion as Scarlett made an exasperated noise. "What?" he asked defensively. "Would you prefer me to complain?"

That surprised a small laugh out of her. "No," she said firmly. "I wouldn't." She looked at him curiously. "You're very forgiving if you really do think I've been shutting you out because I thought you were useless. You have nothing to be ashamed of from the last mission. I'm not sure what you thought I was expecting you to do, but you didn't disappoint me in some way. It's true that you were more of a passenger than anything, but it's not as though you were any particular hindrance, and I was glad for you to get a sense of what we're up against. You're not a liability Jonan, you're an asset. One whose potential is still largely unknown."

Her eyes took on a shrewdly speculative gleam as she regarded him, and for a moment he was unnerved by her sudden resemblance to her father. Then she sighed, her expression softening, and any trace of similarity disappeared.

"You're also a friend, or at least I'd like to think so. For both of those reasons I want to keep you out of trouble. I don't even fully understand myself the knife's edge you're walking on. Honestly, I'm surprised my father has let you be for as long as he has."

"Well, he hasn't fully let me be," said Jonan. "He does have me followed all the time."

Scarlett made a noise of disbelief, gesturing around at the empty jungle. "All the time?"

"You know what I mean," said Jonan impatiently. "During the day. A soldier follows me everywhere I go. They don't seem to be the brightest—even for me it's not hard to tell I'm being followed—but they're always there, and I'm sure they report my movements to your father."

"They certainly do," said Scarlett tartly. "I'm glad you at least realize that much." She sighed. "You're right that a lot of the soldiers on that rotation don't take it too seriously. They're not used to having a very high opinion of Kyonans' intelligence, and they think it's a waste of time. It's fortunate that they've never had reason to suspect that you leave your room at night, so they haven't been checking too closely."

She frowned. "But don't get complacent, Jonan. At any moment your luck might run out, and one of the sharper ones might be on duty on a night when you decide to go for a midnight stroll. Believe me, my father is following with great interest your daytime explorations around the city. From what I can tell, he currently believes you're a spy, and he's convinced you know much more than you're letting on."

Jonan gave the ghost of a grin. "That's convenient. I'm not sure what he thinks I know, but surely we can use that to our advantage."

"Don't ever think you're in control when it comes to him, Jonan," said Scarlett, her voice sharp. "He's more devious than you realize, and he's always three steps ahead."

Jonan raised an eyebrow. "Then why am I still alive?"

Scarlett grimaced. "I wish I could say it was your maneuvering, or mine, but it's a big dose of luck as well." She shook her head. "You know my father was ready to execute you when you defied him the day you met. It wouldn't be the first time—he's bloodthirsty, he always has been." She looked away from him, her gaze becoming distant. "Did I ever tell you that he caught one of us once? A resistance leader, I mean."

"No," said Jonan quietly.

Scarlett sighed. "It was during a skirmish. I wasn't there personally. They tried to subdue him, but he fought too fiercely. My father gave the order to kill rather than let him get away." She returned her gaze to Jonan's face. "But I know he's regretted it since, wishing he had tried harder to take him alive. He's no fool, and he knows how much more valuable the man would have been if he'd been captured. It's hard to interrogate a dead man, and my father has remembered that in recent weeks. I can only assume it's part of why he's been so cautious."

Jonan gave her a shrewd look. "Remembered, or been reminded?"

Scarlett acknowledged it with a dip of her head. "I've found ways to subtly bring it to mind." She drew a deep breath. "But make no mistake—if he had the slightest suspicion of your nighttime activities, none of that would matter. It would be over in a heartbeat. And as soon as he has a more certain source of information about the state of affairs in Kyona—and it won't be long, because he started his own inquiries the moment he heard rumors of the overthrow—he won't indulge this fancy any longer. I can still hardly believe he's shown restraint for this long. Any day I expect him to decide to execute you and be done with it. It's a matter of when, not if, and any hope I have of protecting you depends on us having notice of his intentions. I have my ways of finding out what he's planning, but it won't help us if he makes a quick decision because you're careless and he finds out what you're up to."

"You worry too much," said Jonan lightly, aiming to ease her anxiety. He didn't doubt her words, and it wasn't exactly news to him that his life was in constant danger. But he had made the decision to throw his lot in with the rebels, and he intended to see it through. He was being as careful as he knew how, and he couldn't see any benefit from dwelling on the risks. "I'll be fine —I always land on my feet."

"If that's intended to reassure me," she said shortly, turning away from him and beginning to walk again, "you missed the mark. As if I need reminding that you don't take any of this as seriously as you should."

"I really do," he said earnestly, keeping pace with her. "I wish you would trust me when I say that you don't have to worry about me."

She sighed, but didn't otherwise answer, quickening her pace in spite of the injury to her leg. He followed her lead, and soon the two of them were jogging through the undergrowth. They reached the base tree in minutes. Scarlett tapped the code on the trapdoor, but then stepped aside to let Jonan precede her down the stairs.

As soon as he reached level ground, he was hailed by an anxious-sounding Bonnie.

"Jo, there you are! You should go. I didn't think she was coming tonight, but she's not in her—" He saw the moment Bonnie's eyes slid past him, her expression of dismay comical. "Oh."

"Yes," Scarlett repeated scathingly. "Oh."

Bonnie winced, but made a heroic effort at nonchalance. "There you are, milady. I was a bit alarmed when I realized your room was empty. I didn't expect you here."

"Evidently not," said Scarlett. She looked Bonnie over coldly, and Jo had to hide a grin. She was every inch the offended empress, her endless hours of playing the role of a haughty peeress standing her in good stead. Bonnie seemed to quail before her for an endless moment, then all of a sudden Scarlett's iciness fell away, and she spread her hands wide in a gesture of reproach.

"How could you, Bonnie?" she cried. "Keeping tabs on me all this time, hiding things from me!"

"Sorry, milady," said Bonnie sheepishly. "I meant it for the best."

"Don't be angry with Bonnie, Scar," came a calm voice. "She didn't do it to injure you."

Scarlett turned on the newcomer, a spark of her former outrage returning. "And you too, Raldo. I wouldn't have thought it of you. Why, may I ask, did you think it was a good idea to keep me in the dark?"

"We would have explained it all soon enough, Scar," he said imperturbably. "But the boy was right. He needed training or he was going to put you at risk. I kept it to myself because I knew it would make you worry, and you've had enough on your mind."

Jonan held his peace with difficulty at the word boy. Raldo might be in his thirties, but Jonan was pretty sure he was older than Scarlett.

"That wasn't yours to decide," said Scarlett stiffly.

"Oh, we're sprung, are we?" interjected a new voice cheerfully. "That's good, I won't have to worry about letting something slip anymore."

Scarlett just sighed, apparently having run out of outraged dignity. "Cody," she said wearily. "Of course you were in on this too."

"Of course, Scar!" he agreed brightly. "Someone had to teach our good old unmarked liberator how to hide in plain sight, or he was going to get himself into trouble sure as sunrise."

"What did you call him?" asked Scarlett curiously, at the same time Jo demanded, "Where did you hear that?"

Cody just grinned, biting into a papaya he had brought with him when he wandered over. "I been talking to people," he said thickly around his mouthful. "In the city."

Jonan scowled. "Have you just?" he said dryly, but Cody cut off anything else he might have wanted to say, his eyes taking in the blood on Jonan's shirt with interest.

"What happened to your arm this time, Jo?"

"Scarlett stabbed me," said Jonan promptly. "In the jungle."

Scarlett spluttered in protest as multiple pairs of startled eyes turned to her.

"Wow," said Cody uncertainly. "You really were angry we tricked you, huh?"

"No!" Scarlett cried indignantly. "Well, I mean, yes, I was. But I didn't attack Jo because I was angry at him." She turned reproachful eyes on Jo. "And I didn't *stab* him. I could see he'd been doing some kind of training, and I wanted to find out what he could do."

"And?" asked Raldo, betraying interest for the first time as he turned to Jo. "How did you go?"

"Pretty good, I think," said Jo modestly. "For a beginner, anyway. I mean," he lifted his arm, "I only got a light scratch."

Cody came closer and examined the shallow cut with an expert eye. "Yeah, he's right, it's just a scratch. Still," he turned to Scarlett, taking another bite of the fruit even as he looked at her reproachfully. "You shouldn't have knifed him, Scar. He's one of us."

"He got his own back, don't worry," she said wryly. On closer inspection Jo saw that she was still avoiding putting her full weight on her leg, and he felt another stab of guilt.

"Sorry again about that," he said with a cringe. "Although to be fair," he added sternly, "I didn't know it was you at the time, and you knew it was me all along."

"Yes, the cut was a miscalculation," she admitted. "I thought you'd deflect me." Her tone turned rebuking. "But it won't do you any harm to be reminded that you're not invincible." She suddenly grinned. "Or that you're not the only one with surprises up your sleeve."

He grinned back. He couldn't help himself. He bore her no malice for the inconsequential injury to his long-suffering arm, and there was something about her mirth he always found irresistible.

"Peace having been restored," said Raldo, his tone more than usually dry, "how about we catch Scar up on what she's missed?"

"Yes," said Scarlett, her expression becoming serious once again. "What was that you said about another network, Jo?"

Raldo led them all over to a corner, and Jonan quickly filled Scarlett in on his activities over the last weeks. She listened intently, her legs curled under her, catlike, on a packed earthen seat that had been dug into the wall. Jonan had to resist the urge to smile at her serious expression, so at odds with the posture.

He tried to take her impressed astonishment at the scope of his efforts as a compliment rather than an insult. But he couldn't help but think that she hadn't been entirely truthful when she'd said that she didn't think he was useless.

"That's amazing, Jo," she said finally. "All those connections. Who knows how they might come in handy? It's a shame you haven't found any more information on the curse, but it's not really surprising. We haven't had any breakthroughs on it in all these years." She glanced at Raldo. "Generations, even."

Her gaze returned to Jonan, an accusing glint appearing in her eyes. "I guess you didn't find anything all that helpful in the public records room, after all?"

He grinned unrepentantly. "So you heard all about that, did

you? I tried to convince Bonnie to keep it to herself, but you'll be glad to know she was far too loyal for that."

Bonnie chuckled as Scarlett gave him a look that on a less perfectly formed countenance would be called a glare. "I am glad," she said sternly. "But Giles told me about it too. He said that you looked at the record of Alben's execution."

"Giles, is it?" asked Jonan, raising an eyebrow and trying to sound nonchalant. Scarlett's bemused stare told him he had failed.

"What, are you offended that I didn't use his title?" she asked, her voice laden with irony. "I didn't realize you were such a stickler, Jonan. He's my cousin, I don't bother with the formalities."

"Well," said Jonan reasonably, "a cousin isn't a brother."

"You sound like my father," Scarlett muttered, a dark look on her face.

"Hey!" protested Jonan. "Surely I didn't say anything to deserve that."

Scarlett laughed reluctantly. "Sorry," she said. "I just don't want to talk about Giles. I get enough of that as it is. My father, well he—"

"Wants you to marry Prince Giles and become queen," finished Bonnie promptly. "It's all right, milady, we all get it. It's not exactly a secret." Bonnie sent Jonan a conspiratorial grin. "Jo and I were just talking about it this afternoon, in fact."

Scarlett flushed, not meeting Jo's eye, and even he felt a bit uncomfortable at being caught out talking about Scarlett's marriage prospects behind her back. He glared at Bonnie, but addressed his words to Scarlett.

"Bonnie was talking about it," he corrected. "I just wanted to know what had you so on edge today."

"Well, it was nothing to do with Giles," she assured him

shortly, her poise having returned. "Whatever my father's schemes might be."

"His scheming doesn't bother you?" Raldo asked, and Jo had the impression that he had been curious about this topic before now, but hesitant to bring it up.

"Not in that direction," said Scarlett firmly.

"Why is that?" asked Jo.

Scarlett smiled. "Because Giles has a mind of his own. My father is used to manipulating people, but he underestimates my cousin's will of iron. Trust me," she said dryly. "He's been stubborn as a mule since we were children. And he doesn't want to marry me any more than I want to marry him."

"Why not?" Jonan demanded, undeterred by the intrusiveness of the question.

Scarlett looked at him out of wide eyes, her expression slightly confused. "Does he need a reason?"

Jonan took in her slim form, somehow elegant despite being still curled up comfortably on her seat. She met his gaze steadily, her dark eyes seeming to sparkle in the light of the torches, the perfect lines of her face softened by the waves of hair, now released from the material that had covered her head to curl around her features in the damp air. She sat perfectly at ease surrounded by the people who most of her world scorned, and whom she constantly risked her own safety to help.

Jonan's eyes flicked to Raldo next to her. They shared a look, and although Jo saw his own amusement reflected back in the older rebel's eyes, both men kept their faces admirably impassive as they answered simultaneously.

"Yes."

Scarlett looked between them, uncharacteristically uncertain. "Well, he has reason enough. I mean...I grew up in his household. His mother was—still is—a mother to me. We see each other as brother and sister, and no amount of maneuvering by my father will change that." She paused. "We have even been told, often, that we look alike," she added. "Honestly, the thought of marrying each other is...kind of disgusting."

"I can understand that," said Jonan sympathetically. He had never technically had any siblings, but the brother-like relationship he had always had with Cal gave him a ready understanding of how being raised with someone could make them feel irrevocably like family.

"So does the prince know about your double life, then?" he asked. "About the resistance?"

"What? No," said Scarlett, startled. "Of course not." She sighed. "I can talk more freely with him than with almost anyone, but not that freely. I have sometimes been tempted...we talk around the edges of this issue often, and he's more sympathetic than you might imagine. But it's too big a risk to take. I can't be sure—it's a complex issue."

"Doesn't seem complex to me," said Jonan darkly, remembering the flogging in the square.

Scarlett shook her head slowly, her expression sad. "I'm sure it doesn't, from your perspective. But Giles was raised as a royal, as I was, effectively. The state of things here is all we've ever known, and as terrible as it is, the truth is that our economy is incredibly strong because of slave labor. Giles has been trained to think first of the good of the country." She sighed again. "Indoctrination about the deserter's fate doesn't help either."

Jonan was frowning at her words, but when she met his eye, his heart was softened in spite of himself by the hint of pleading lurking behind her calm words. "He's not a bad person," she said softly, "really. But it is complex, whether you want to admit it or not."

"You don't seem to suffer from any uncertainty on the topic," he pointed out, but she shrugged, her shoulders curving inward defensively, as if to shield herself.

"But I wasn't always like this," she said, her voice quiet. "I hardly thought about the issue when I was growing up. There's blood on my hands, too."

"There's no blood on your hands," said Raldo firmly. "You've done more than anyone for the slaves." He shot Jonan a reproachful look. But even though Jo felt a bit guilty for having brought the heaviness to Scarlett's face, he didn't want to waste the opportunity to have his questions answered.

"But why are you different now?" he pressed. "Why don't you see things the same way Prince Giles does anymore?"

Scarlett was silent for a moment before she answered. "You would have to be cold-hearted indeed to live with my father, to see the way he behaves, and not want to distance yourself from his philosophy on life. I never really questioned things when I lived at the castle, but it didn't take long after my father took me to live with him for me to question a great many things.

"And as for the way people interpret the deserter's fate," her eyes grew hard, "I have my own reasons for not believing that people can be less deserving just because of the status they're born with." Her expression turned thoughtful. "And I think Giles knows it, too."

Jonan opened his mouth to ask for clarification, but Raldo silenced him with a reproving look. Even though Scarlett hadn't objected to the personal nature of Jonan's questions, the reserved rebel leader obviously took issue on her behalf.

In the absence of further questions, Scarlett shook her head as if clearing the topic from her mind. "None of this matters right now," she said. "How did we end up talking about me and Giles, anyway?" She looked at Jonan with a frown. "You were going to tell me why you were looking at the record of Alben's execution."

"Was I?" Jonan said with a touch of humor, taking the change of direction in his stride. "If you say so. There's no great mystery. I was trying to figure out how to break the curse, like I told you."

She looked at him curiously. "Why are you so convinced it has something to do with Alben?"

"Because he came from the mountains, for one," said Jonan. "I've told you that there's magic there, I've seen it." He hesitated. "But there's more. I didn't want to tell you before, because I wasn't sure what you'd make of it. Honestly, I'm not sure what to make of it myself. But some strange things happened to me around the time I arrived in Nohl."

He hesitated again, looking at the many curious eyes trained on him. There was no turning back now. As briefly as possible, he described his mysterious visions on the ship and in the square. He kept his eyes on Scarlett the whole time he spoke, trying to gauge her reaction. Her eyes grew rounder as she listened, and she looked unnerved, but he couldn't see any sign of disbelief.

"That's incredible," said Raldo when he finished, regarding Jonan in amazement. "Maybe Cody's right. Maybe you really were sent here. But why? Do you know of any reason why you would have some magical connection to Alben?"

"No," said Jo quickly. Scarlett shifted slightly, and he saw that her eyes were fixed on him, her penetrating gaze holding the skepticism he had expected before.

"Honestly, I don't," he assured her. "I'd never heard the name Alben before I saw it on that ship, and as far as I know there's nothing in my own lineage to connect me either to magic or the mountains. In fact," he said, his voice slightly wistful in spite of himself, "there's nothing remarkable about my lineage at all."

She seemed to accept this, although her eyes still lingered thoughtfully on his face. "I still don't fully understand what all this would have to do with the curse, though," she said. "Even if you are somehow mysteriously connected to Alben."

Jo shook his head in frustration. "I wish I had the answers, I really do. I can't fully explain it, but I'm convinced he's at the heart of it."

No one else looked convinced, but Jonan's certainty was unshaken. He looked over at Raldo. Scarlett's comments about generations much earlier in the conversation had sparked something in his mind.

"I've been meaning to ask you something, actually," he addressed the older man. "Do you know for sure you can't cross the sea?"

"Of course," said Raldo, startled. "I mean, I've never tried personally, but plenty of others have. Why do you ask?"

"Well, just that Scarlett told me that first night that escaped slaves can't get back to Kyona, but you were never a slave, were you? It's generations since your people have been slaves. I wondered if maybe the curse doesn't apply to you."

"It does," said Raldo heavily. "A number of my people have tried over the generations. Some thought it worth the risk against the alternative of the lifestyle we're forced to lead. Always with the same result. I can only assume that it's because my ancestors who originally came here came as slaves."

"Exactly!" said Jonan. His voice was excited, and everyone looked at him strangely. "Sorry," he said quickly, dropping to a normal volume. "I know that's awful for you, I'm just excited because it supports my theory. It's as if the curse doesn't differentiate between you and your ancestors. Like your family line is treated as if it was the same person, despite spanning generations."

He looked around triumphantly, but all he was met with was blank looks.

"So?" said Cody eventually. "Why does that support your theory?"

"Because," said Jonan matter-of-factly, "it sounds like mountain power to me. That generational thing...that's how dragon magic works."

"And we're back to the dragons," muttered Raldo. Even Scarlett's expression had become hooded all of a sudden.

Jonan sighed in exasperation. "I'm not crazy," he said firmly. Scarlett opened her mouth to deny the implication, but he cut her off. "And I'm not gullible, either." He looked around at them all. "The truth is, I didn't give you all the details when I said I'd been to the mountains myself. In fact, there's a lot I didn't tell you."

"No kidding," said Scarlett dryly, but Jonan ignored her.

"I haven't just heard about dragons in the mountains. I've seen them with my own eyes. They are very real, trust me. They've been in isolation from humans for a long time, but that's changing now." He looked Scarlett in the eye. "When I was taunting your father with talk of the new king's powerful allies, that's who I was talking about. The dragons. It was a dragon who killed the false king, and half of Kynton saw it. News of their existence will be all over the country by now I'd guess, and it won't be long before it gets here, too."

His words were met with a stunned silence. Amazement could be seen on every face, but only Scarlett's held fear as well. "The new Kyonan king has dragons fighting for him?" she whispered, her voice hollow. "Balenol will be annihilated." Her eyes traveled around the group in a silent appeal. "I know my people have wronged yours monstrously, but not everyone in the country is evil. I don't exactly love it here myself, but that doesn't mean I want to see our whole way of life destroyed."

"No, no," said Jonan quickly, leaning forward to grasp her arm reassuringly. He saw Raldo's eyes follow the gesture, and he let go hastily. "I would be very surprised if Kyona wanted to mount a full-scale attack on Balenol," he said. "And even if the king wanted to, the dragons wouldn't fight for him against another country." His expression became rueful. "From what I've seen, they're not really all that interested in helping people, or getting involved in our petty life and death struggles."

"But…" said Raldo, clearly struggling to keep up. "You just said that a dragon killed the false king."

"Oh, well, yes," acknowledged Jonan. "That's true. But to be honest I think that dragon kind of went rogue on that occasion. Generally they prefer to leave us to ourselves." He looked over at Scarlett, trying to encourage her with his winning smile. "Calling them allies of the new king was a bit of a stretch, but I didn't think it would do any harm to give your father a scare."

She didn't respond, still looking dazed, but Bonnie piped up. "So the king has one rogue ally," she said dryly. "Not quite as impressive."

"Hang on," Jo protested. "You didn't see it all go down! That 'one ally' was pretty impressive all things considered. I mean, we're talking about a real live dragon! He swooped down out of the sky in the nick of time, and breathed fire out of his mouth to form some kind of stream connected with the new king's magic sword."

"Magic sword?" echoed Cody, his shock quickly giving way to excitement.

"Yeah, he's got a magic sword," said Jonan, unable to resist a grin at the younger boy's barely contained exuberance.

"How do you know all this?" asked Raldo, his tone suspicious. "You really were sent by the new king, weren't you? I knew you lied about that."

"No, I didn't!" said Jonan quickly. "I was telling the truth—I wasn't sent by anyone, I'm not here in any official capacity. And the new king wouldn't have a clue that I'm here, alarming the local authorities." Raldo's eyebrows remained raised, and Jonan grimaced. "But there is a little more to it than that."

"Well?" prompted Scarlett, as he hesitated for a moment, trying to think where to begin.

But he had no opportunity to answer her. A commotion at the trapdoor drew everyone's attention, all members of the group but Cody having their weapons in their hands within seconds.

But no enemy appeared through the hole. Instead, a girl Jo didn't know almost tumbled down the stairs, her eyes searching the space frantically.

"What's going on, Carla?" asked Scarlett sharply, and the girl's eyes snapped instantly to the rebel leader.

"Scar!" she cried, her relief evident as she rushed over to their group. "Thank goodness you're here! I've just come from patrol, near the river. There's trouble in the intake camp."

"What kind of trouble?" asked Raldo, stepping forward, his voice calm and clear.

"It's a full-scale revolt," Carla panted. "But it's not organized. Everything is in utter chaos, and they've called in reinforcements from the city. The slaves are all right on the edge. If this was a coordinated strike, I'd say it was a good thing, because I'd swear they're all willing to follow through, whatever it takes, and they'd probably have a real chance of overpowering the slavers. But it's not! I don't know what happened to set them off, but I don't think any of it was planned. When reinforcements come, they're going to give the order to kill rather than let any escape. If someone doesn't pull them together soon, a lot of people are going to die!"

They all stared at her for a horrorstruck moment, then Scarlett sprang into action, raising her voice above the outbreak of exclamations.

"We need to pull a team together, now! Anyone who's been on patrol in the last twelve hours, don't come forward, you can stay here and guard the base. Anyone who's fresh and willing to come, move this way."

People started to rush around the space, but Carla still looked stricken rather than relieved at this call to action. Her eyes flicked to Raldo, who was frowning down at Scarlett.

"I hope you realize you can't be part of this, Scar," he said firmly. She just shook her head as if flicking off a fly, her expression of grim determination unchanged. Raldo stepped forward and gripped her shoulder tightly. "I mean it," he said, his voice low. "You need to return to the city."

"That's not happening," she said curtly. "You can't stop me, Raldo. Someone needs to lead the group, and it's going to be me."

"I will lead the group," said Raldo, his tone uncompromising. Scarlett shook her head again, but before she could say another word, Carla cut in.

"I don't think you can lead this time, Scar," she said apologetically. "Remember that these slaves know nothing about you or even the resistance. How do you think they'll respond when a Balenan tries to rally them? I told you, this isn't an organized uprising—it's an angry mob. What if one of them recognized you as the Overseer's daughter? You wouldn't be able to help them. They'd be more likely to turn on you."

Raldo's face looked white, and Jonan could understand why. He felt his own color drain away at the thought of a mob of enraged captives venting their anger on Scarlett as she tried to help them.

"As I said, I'll lead," said Raldo even more firmly. He looked over Carla's shoulder at the bustle behind. "Yes, you three head out on patrol—check the gate, and the river."

"I only hope it will be enough," said Carla anxiously, watching as three rebels hurried toward the exit in response to Raldo's curt instruction. Another approached the leader swiftly, and Carla waited with evident impatience while the boy reported to Raldo on the group that was still assembling.

"I've never seen a camp so riled up, Raldo," Carla said, as soon as the boy had hurried off. "And they don't know you any more than they know Scar. I mean, I don't think they'd have any reason to turn on you, but they don't have any reason to follow you either. Anyone who goes in there should do so knowing that there's a serious risk that intervention is useless. We could all get caught up and killed along with the slaves."

"That's a risk we'll have to take," said Raldo grimly.

"Yes," Scarlett agreed. "And if you think you can convince me not to take the risk too, you don't know me at all. This isn't a low stakes reconnaissance mission. Do you know how many slaves are in that camp? How many lives are on the line?"

Raldo opened his mouth to argue, but Jo cut him off.

"I'll do it," he said loudly, and they both turned to look at him in confusion.

"Do what?" Scarlett asked.

"Lead the group," said Jo simply. "Rally the slaves. Get them out of there. I realize I don't know the jungle like you do, and I'll need help to get them somewhere safe if we can get them out, but I have something going for me that neither one of you has."

They both stared at him blankly, and he shrugged. "They certainly won't follow an unknown Balenan, and they might not follow Raldo. But they'll follow the unmarked liberator."

CHAPTER EIGHTEEN

It was immediately clear that neither Scarlett nor Raldo liked Jonan's plan, but he refused to back down. Short of physically restraining him, they couldn't stop him, and they were all perfectly aware that time was too short to allow an extended debate on the matter. When Jonan declared his intention of running ahead rather than waiting for the team that was still being put together, however, Scarlett reached her limit.

"Absolutely not, Jo, that's out of the question," she said, a panicked look in her eye.

"Think about it, Scar," Jo insisted, several steps toward the door already. "A group will be slower than an individual, even such a capable group." He nodded toward the rebels who were gathering around them, listening to Raldo's instructions. "And it's not numbers the slaves need, it's a rallying point. If we succeed in breaking out, we'll need assistance once we're in the jungle, but sending a whole group into the camp will just increase the chaos."

"So you think you're going alone?" Scarlett demanded indignantly. "There is no way I will allow that, and whatever you might think, I'm still in charge here."

"Well, not entirely alone," Jo conceded. "I'd never find my way there. But maybe Carla will be willing to show me?"

The rebel girl nodded curtly, hurrying to join Jo. But Scarlett was quicker, intercepting them before they reached the exit.

"Forget about it, Jo! It doesn't help anyone for you to get yourself killed."

"Have a little faith in me," Jo protested.

"This isn't the time to indulge your baseless belief that you're untouchable, Jonan," returned Scarlett, almost shouting in her agitation.

"I don't have any such belief," Jo denied, struggling to keep his own voice calm, to show her that he really was in earnest. "I'm not saying nothing can go wrong. But I don't think I'm any more likely to die than any other person who throws themselves into the middle of a disorganized slave rebellion. And someone has to do it."

Scarlett groaned, apparently not reassured by this view, but Raldo's expression was thoughtful as he looked over at Jonan. "He's right, Scar," he said. "You don't realize how far he's come. He's not as vulnerable as you think."

"Listen to him," said Jonan, with a gratified nod at Raldo. "And let someone else do something for once."

She measured him with her eyes for a long moment, finally giving in with a bad grace. "Fine," she spat, "but I'll show you the way, not Carla."

"That's not quite what I meant by letting someone else do something," Jonan muttered. But he didn't raise any serious objections—they had already wasted too much time arguing.

"Scar," started Raldo, apparently not inclined to show similar restraint, but Scarlett cut him off.

"Don't start, Raldo," she said tersely. "You won't dissuade me, and we don't have time."

He looked at her, his mouth set grimly. "Then I'm coming too," he said.

"No you're not," said Scarlett, equally grim. "You're leading the group that will follow us. They need someone in charge, and you know what needs to be done if there's a chance we might have a large group of disorganized liberated slaves to deal with before the night is over."

"I don't like it," he said, but again she cut him off.

"You don't have to." She turned toward Jonan, ready to leave, but Raldo reached out and gripped her arm.

"You're just showing him the way, right? Remember what Carla said!" She nodded, but he wasn't satisfied. "Promise me, Scar. Promise me that you won't enter the camp."

For a moment she hesitated, but taking in the look on his face she gave him a curt nod. Raldo released her, but as she turned to leave, his eyes slid across to meet Jonan's. Jonan didn't need words to understand their silent message, and he didn't hesitate to give a nod of his own. He would do everything he could to protect Scarlett, with or without Raldo's prompting.

If he had thought Scarlett was focused during their previous trip to the intake camp, it was nothing to her single-minded determination now. For all his training in recent weeks, he was pushed to his limit to keep up with her. But he wasn't complaining—he knew as well as she did how crucial every minute might be.

Without a group in tow, they almost halved the time it had taken them to travel this route before. Still, it felt like too long, and Jonan could feel that Scarlett was as tense as he was by the time she finally slowed down in the approach to the river. So far they hadn't exchanged a single word, but she took advantage of the reduced pace to convey as much information as possible about the layout of the camp and the best evacuation route.

"If you make it out, they'll have to split up," she said. "There are far too many to head for the base tree, and the bigger the group, the harder it will be to conceal their tracks."

"Yes, I've been thinking about that," said Jonan. "How will we get them somewhere safe without leading the slavers right to the resistance?"

"There are ways," said Scarlett shortly. "Raldo will be setting things in motion even now. Once the team catches up, we'll be able to split everyone into multiple groups. Some can make for the base tree, but we have other safe places. And if I know Raldo, he'll have people split off and start laying false trails well before any of the slaves join us. We should be able to confuse or even get rid of a number of pursuers that way. There's a large area of sinking mud not too far away, and a couple of large mounds of army ants in another direction. The jungle lake can be treacherous too."

Jonan didn't fully understand what was meant by these hazards, but he didn't care to ask. He just hoped fervently that he wouldn't have cause to discover for himself how treacherous these features of the jungle might be.

"When we cross the river," Scarlett was continuing, but Jo cut her off.

"We?" he said accusingly. "I heard you make that promise to Raldo, and just because he's not here, you needn't think I'm going to help you get yourself slaughtered by an angry mob."

She ground her teeth in frustration. "You, then. There's a spot where you can cross, upstream from the rapids. It's shallower, and there's a series of sort of stepping stones. Once you're across, the camp is not far. They know we're out here, so they always have sentries watching the jungle. We'll have to figure out a way to get you inside unnoticed."

As she spoke, they reached the edge of the trees. Her words died away, and her eyes widened as they stared over the cleared ground to the camp beyond. Carla had not been exaggerating when she had described the state of the camp as utter chaos. Shouts and screams carried across the empty space, mingling with the clash of metal and the thud of wood to form a confused melee. Bright spots lit the darkness with leaping orange and yellow, several of the buildings in the compound burning wildly. Jonan could see no fleeing figures in the darkness—it seemed that so far the slavers had been successful in preventing anyone from escaping. But it was evident that they were hard pressed to maintain any semblance of control.

"I don't think I'll have any trouble getting across the cleared area unnoticed," he said hollowly. "Something tells me no one is paying much attention to any possible threats *outside* the walls tonight."

"I think you're right," Scarlett whispered. She turned to him, her expression more serious than he had ever seen. "People are going to die tonight, Jonan," she said. "Innocent people. No matter how good a job you do. Do you understand that? If I send you in there, can you cope with that?"

He nodded, swallowing hard as he met her eye. "It's not the first time I've been in battle," he said quietly. "I'm not going to fall apart."

She nodded briefly, evidently deciding to take his word for it. "Good, because a lot more people will die if we do nothing than if you manage to rally them."

He nodded again, his expression hard and determined. "I understand what's at stake," he said. "I won't fail you. They'll have to kill me to stop me."

She looked at him, something flickering behind her eyes, but before she could say a word, a melodious whistling sounded in the jungle nearby. Jonan had thought it was a bird call, but Scarlett's head whipped around at the sound, and she pursed up her lips, mimicking it.

A moment later several rebels appeared by their side, exclaiming softly at the sight of them.

"Scar, Jo!" said Stan, leading the group. "Did Carla reach you?" She looked around, her brow creasing. "Aren't there any others?"

"Raldo is bringing a team close behind," said Scarlett briefly. "Jonan is going in alone."

"Alone?" asked Stan, startled. "Why?"

"I'll explain everything in a minute," said Scarlett. "If Jo's going to act, there's no time to waste."

She turned to him, the serious expression he had come to think of as her Scar mask slipping for a moment as she met his eye. She opened her mouth, then closed it. He smiled in spite of everything, certain he could read the dilemma in her eyes. She wanted to tell him to be careful, but she knew as well as he did that throwing himself into the middle of the chaos in the camp was anything but.

"Don't make me tell you yet again that you don't need to worry about me," he joked. She gave the smallest of smiles, but her expression lost none of its anxiety. He squeezed her arm reassuringly, much as he might have done to Cal in the same situation, and she pulled herself together with an effort, releasing him with a quick nod.

He moved away, but after a few steps called softly to Stan. She hastened to join him, a question in her eyes.

"She promised Raldo she wouldn't enter the camp," he said quietly, nodding his head toward Scarlett, who was being filled in by the rest of Stan's patrol. "Don't let her forget it, no matter what goes down."

Stan nodded, her eyes full of understanding and determination. "I won't."

He turned away again, but she gripped his arm. "Try not to die," she said ruefully, and he grinned.

"I will," he assured her. "And same to you. I don't want the job of telling Elnora I found her lost sister only to have to tell her you got yourself killed."

As they always did, her eyes sparkled at the mention of Elnora, and she sent him off with a smile.

He crossed the cleared space swiftly, moving with all the stealth he had learned from Cody. He could hear the pandemonium at the camp even more clearly once he left the trees, and he wasn't surprised to find no impediment to his passage from the trees to the water. He found the crossing Scarlett had described without any difficulty. Now that he wasn't under the trees, the moonlight provided substantial illumination. Even so, he crossed the river slowly, and with great care. He had no desire to be swept into the strong current.

Scarlett had been right that once across the river, he had only a short distance to go to reach the camp. And he had been right that with all their attention focused on keeping the slaves inside the walls, the Balenans didn't seem to be worrying about whether anyone might be trying to get in from the outside. The area between the crossing and the compound was also cleared of trees, but the space was filled with stacks of cut timber, the logs long and thick.

Skirting between these obstacles, he reached the edge of the compound without being detected, only hesitating once he stood right against the wall. He was a good climber, but he couldn't see any way to get a foothold on the smooth sides of the wooden palisades. Before he had time to become dismayed, his attention was caught by a violent battering that sounded closer than the main melee. Searching frantically in the darkness for the source of the noise, he saw a small side gate not far from where he stood.

He ran toward the gate, and had just reached it when a loud splintering sound heralded the emergence of the end of a large length of cut timber through the now ruined gate. Jonan dodged out of the way, expecting to see someone come rushing out, but there was no further movement, just increased shouting on the other side of the door.

He peered through the broken portal and saw why. The Kyonans who had wielded the log had been forced to drop it to defend themselves against two slavers who had caught up with them. They didn't have weapons, and even as Jo watched, one of them went down at the hands of an angry-looking Balenan.

Jo didn't wait to see any more. He squeezed through the hole and fell to the ground on the other side, his dagger drawn by the time he regained his feet. He rushed to the aid of one of the slaves, who was evading death by dodging and weaving out of the reach of the sword of one of the Balenans. Neither the slaves nor the slavers saw Jonan's approach, and he fell on the man at once, knowing that he would need to take him by surprise for his dagger to have a hope of success against a sword.

The man swung around a beat too late, his sword dropping uselessly as Jonan's dagger plunged into him, just below the rib cage. The man didn't even cry out, just jerking horribly, surprise frozen on his face, before he dropped to the ground and didn't get up.

Jonan swallowed hard, looking away from the man's body and the blood now pooling around it. He had killed before, in the brief but ferocious battle at Kynton, but he didn't think it was something he would ever get used to.

"Thanks," panted the other Kyonan breathlessly, and Jonan realized all at once that there was stillness in their immediate vicinity. He looked around to see that the other slaver had been taken down by three Kyonans, despite the fact that they were unarmed. A glance at the man's prone form was enough to show that he also would not be rising. Taking in the look in the eyes of the slaves who had brought him down, Jonan repressed a shudder.

Unlike the Kyonan Jo had just assisted, these were no youths, freshly arrived for processing, but grown men who had obviously spent a hard life in the logging camp. He suspected that they were not the only ones in the compound who were both able and willing to take their captors' lives with only their bare hands for weapons.

One of them reached down and retrieved the sword of the fallen slaver, while another gave Jonan a nod of acknowledgment.

"Where did you come from?" he asked, looking around in some confusion.

"Outside," said Jonan, jerking his head back toward the ruined gate.

The other three Kyonans stared at him in surprise, but the speaker was obviously not given to curiosity. "Well, that's where I want to be," he said curtly, moving toward the gate.

"Wait!" said Jonan quickly.

"For what?" the man demanded. "To get put back in chains? I don't think so."

"Wait, listen!" Jo cried desperately as the man again turned to leave. "Where will you go? Into the jungle? If they don't catch you, which they probably will, you won't last long out there by yourself." He glanced around, further into the camp, where chaos still reigned. "It's anarchy in here, but if we want to stage a successful uprising, someone needs to organize everyone."

"And who's going to do that? You?" asked the man rudely.

Jonan met him in the eye. "Yes."

He scoffed. "You'll get yourself killed, more like."

Jo shrugged. "Maybe," he said, "but at least I'll get myself killed trying to help my own people instead of running pointlessly through the jungle."

"Look, kid, I've got nothing against you, but I don't know who you are, and—"

"I'm here to help," said Jo quickly. "We can still salvage this mayhem, and get everyone out. There's a group of rebels in the jungle, just across the river, who can split everyone up and get them to safety."

"Rebels?" asked another one of the slaves in astonishment. "Here to help us? Kyonans, you mean?"

"Yes," said Jo impatiently. "And they know what they're doing. But they need more time, and we need a mass exodus, not a slow trickle. If you can hold the gate against the slavers—"

"Why should we believe a word of this?" asked the first speaker suspiciously. "More likely you just want to go back in there for someone you care about, and you want us to cover your exit once you get them out."

"I was never in there in the first place," said Jo in exasperation, "and I care about all of them, that's why I'm here."

"Look, Evan," said one of others suddenly, staring at Jonan's arm. "He doesn't have the slave mark. He doesn't have *any* mark."

Everyone's eyes flew to Jonan's face, and the young Kyonan whom he had saved from the slaver let out an audible gasp.

"It's really true! All that talk about the unmarked liberator! You're here to help us!"

"I am," said Jonan smoothly, but the older man was clearly not convinced.

"This rumor of the new king sending someone to end slavery altogether?" he said dismissively. "A pipe dream for people still too new to this life to know better. I'll believe it when I see it."

"You are seeing it," said one of his companions, his voice awed, and Jonan didn't attempt to correct him.

"What do you want us to do?" asked the youngest slave eagerly.

"Hold the gate," said Jonan promptly. "I'm going further in, to try to rally everyone to work together and get as many out as we can. There's a rocky stretch just a bit further up the river where we can cross..." his voice trailed off as he realized how impractical it would be for a large crowd to attempt to flee across the rocks at once, in the darkness, with the rapids not far away.

"No, that won't work," he muttered distractedly. "We'll have to think of a way to get everyone across the river, and quickly."

He was pulled from his thoughts by a loud shout, and he looked up to see a Balenan approaching them at a run. Jo positioned himself defensively, but before the man came within reach, the Kyonan who had taken the sword from the slaver leaped in front of Jonan, holding the blade up with more determination than expertise. The Balenan hesitated at sight of the weapon, and in the moment of distraction, another Kyonan appeared from out of the pandemonium and ran at him from behind, throwing his arms around the slaver's neck. The slaver gave a strangled cry, and before he could recover his balance, the sword had run him through.

The newcomer gave a curt nod to the assembled group, his eyes brightening as he took in the partially cleared gate behind them. He started toward it, but was stopped by the outstretched arm of one of the others.

"Wait," he said. "Don't just run out into the jungle." He nodded at Jonan. "He has a plan."

The man stared at Jo. "Who's he?"

"He's the liberator!" interjected the youngest member of the group excitedly. "He's here to free us, and he's got a team in the jungle ready to take us somewhere safe. He wants us to hold the gate."

The man stared at Jonan in amazement. "So it's true?" he said, wide-eyed.

"Yes, it's true," said Jonan, deciding that now was not the time to explain the subtleties of his identity.

"We'll clear the gate and hold it," said one of the men firmly.

Jonan's gaze swept around at them all. "Look," he said. "I can't promise you won't get killed doing it. You might. But I do know that a lot of our countrymen are definitely going to get killed if we don't rally everyone and get them out. I can't make you stay and help, and I wouldn't want to try, but I can't do this on my own."

"I don't know who you are exactly, kid," said the man who had been identified as Evan. "But no matter who sent you, I don't think you know anything about suffering and death that we don't."

"I believe it," said Jonan emphatically.

"So you don't need to tell us what's at stake," said the man dryly. He looked Jonan over for a moment, then turned his gaze toward the turmoil further in the camp. "If you can get them to the gate, we'll make sure they can get through it."

Jonan felt a surge of relief as the rest of the group nodded in agreement.

"And let us worry about getting everyone across the river," one of them added. "I think I know how."

"Thank you," said Jonan with real gratitude. He took off running without another word, noting as he did that the group had huddled together in conversation. A moment later, he was overtaken by the youngest one. Jo watched him pass in confusion, but had to be satisfied with the boy's reassuring nod.

Before long he was surrounded by chaos, buffeted by Balenans and Kyonans alike as everyone raced around in confusion. A slaver grabbed his arm, but he threw the man off, striking out with a foot for good measure. The slaver fell back, cursing, and instantly became distracted by another Kyonan attempting to run past.

Jonan pushed on. He wanted to find the center of the action, but it was hard to tell where that might be—everywhere he looked the scene was equally out of control. A rushing sound intensified the further he went, drowning out the other noises, and as he rounded a wooden building he could feel the heat of flames on his face. The fire was spreading quickly, the deadly blaze finding ready fuel in the wood that could be seen on all sides. No matter the outcome of the escape attempt, the camp itself was not going to be intact by the morning.

A violent retching noise made it to his ears, and glancing around he saw a young girl on all fours, perilously close to the fire, coughing in the smoke. Running over, he pulled her roughly to her feet, dragging her away from the inferno to where the air was clearer. It was the same on all sides—a jumble of individuals running wild, without clear purpose. Here and there he could see small groups that had banded together, and against the far wall of the compound he thought he could make out around two dozen Kyonans who had barricaded themselves behind a barrier of cut timber and upended wagons.

But there was no method to the madness, no exit strategy. As far as he could see, the slavers were mainly still trying to contain rather than slaughter the renegades, otherwise most of them would likely have been dead by now. As he watched, Jonan saw two slaves collide in the confusion, both of them falling to the ground and instantly being grabbed by separate slavers.

"Stand together!" he cried in frustration, but his voice was lost in the din. He saw a trio of slaves huddled nearby and ran over to them. "Get behind that barricade!" he shouted, pointing to the group on the far wall. They stared at him in confusion.

"We need to stand together!" he insisted. "Get yourselves behind that barricade, and take as many people with you as you can."

They glanced at each other, but no one seemed to have

anything to say, and after a moment they took off across the intervening space, shouting to those in their path as they ran, although the words were lost to Jonan's ears.

Jonan ran through the crowd, directing anyone he could get to listen to him to get behind the makeshift barrier. As his eyes roamed over the tumult, he realized that while most of the slavers were trying to round the slaves up, there were two or three who were not waiting for the official order, and were already aiming to kill. His eyes locked on one in particular, a short but stocky man, who even as Jonan watched ran his sword cleanly through the back of a young boy as the hapless slave was fleeing aimlessly.

Jonan felt a rush of anger, and he leaped toward the man without conscious thought. Turning away from the body of his victim, the slaver was confronted with Jonan's drawn dagger. His eyes passed from the blade to Jo's face in confusion, but he quickly recovered his surprise, bringing his sword up in front of him and forcing Jonan to jump backward out of reach.

Jo's blind fury subsided, and he quickly realized that while his opponent held a sword, there would be no hope of getting close enough to do any damage with his dagger. But even with a level head, he didn't want to leave the man to continue on his killing spree. He considered throwing his weapon, but he had undertaken very little training in that area, and his dagger wasn't a throwing knife. He would be unlikely to find his mark, and the risk of leaving himself unarmed was too great for such a gamble.

Even as he thought it, the slaver advanced, brandishing his weapon. Jonan thought the man's hold on his sword looked clumsy. This was no soldier, and Jo suspected that he hadn't had much call to use the blade. Still, his greater reach kept Jo retreating. He cast his eyes around for anything he could make use of, and the slaver took the opportunity to swing wildly at him. Jo raised his dagger instinctively, steel meeting steel. His blade held off the larger one long enough for him to fall further back out of reach, but his arm screamed in protest, the mostly healed injuries re-agitated by the unsustainable pressure. He knew he couldn't take many such hits.

But his questing eyes had fallen on a thin length of wood. It must have become detached from one of the burning buildings because the end still smoldered. As the soldier swung at him again, he dropped his dagger, reaching down to seize the plank with both hands. He brought it up just in time to deflect the sword, the contact sending sparks flying. The slaver fell back a step, cursing and raising a hand to his face, as embers flew into his eyes. Jonan lost no time, bringing the plank back and using it to deliver a mighty whack to his adversary's sword. In the man's distraction, the impact sent the sword flying out of his hand.

Jonan didn't hesitate. Dropping to one knee, he released the wood and grasped his dagger from the ground. His movement was smooth, and the same momentum carried him forward as he pushed up off his knee and lunged toward the disarmed slaver. Jonan's knife did its work in a moment, and the slaver dropped without a sound. Jo didn't stay to see if the wound had been fatal, taking off back into the chaos that still raged around him.

He could see that the area in his immediate vicinity was not as crowded as it had been, and the number of slaves behind the makeshift barricade had grown. Jonan grabbed at a nearby Kyonan, ducking just in time to avoid the young man's wildly swinging fist.

"It's all right," he shouted. "I'm trying to help. Get behind the barricade!"

Glancing around, the man seemed to understand, and took off with a nod, dragging a woman with him. Jonan ran on, trying to encourage the slaves to gather together. But there were too many—he had no idea how long it would be before the reinforcements arrived from Nohl to bolster the slavers, but he suspected he didn't have time to reach everyone individually. Plus, the slavers were already starting to realize what was happening, and were gathering together themselves, ready to subdue the growing group.

Looking around him in frustration, Jonan realized that a great many eyes seemed to be turned on him. Even with the melee, he got a sense of a whisper of momentum moving through the compound. People started surging toward him. Confused, he ran toward the group against the wall, and was heartened to see that many others were following him. Some, however, tore their eyes away from him to dart off into the darkness. He had no idea where they were going, but he didn't stop to try to figure it out.

As he neared the barricade, a group swelling around him, he heard whispers that seemed to reverberate out to join with shouts coming from further away.

"Over there!"

"Get over there! The liberator is here!"

"Get to the liberator!"

He had just reached the barricade when a voice close by spoke directly to him.

"We're as ready as we'll ever be. They'll follow you."

Looking up, Jonan saw the youngest Kyonan from the gate, and suddenly he understood. The boy had run back into the danger of the camp to spread the word and further Jonan's efforts. And the news had traveled as fast through the chaos as the flames that were leaping from building to building.

He didn't respond to the boy, looking instead at the now substantial group behind the barricade. Every eye was fixed on him. For a moment he hesitated, thrown by the weight of so much expectation, but a shout behind him drew his attention. Looking back, he saw a slaver racing toward him, weapon raised. With horror, Jo saw another Kyonan leap into the slaver's path while still some distance away, grappling with the man. Despite his shock, Jonan realized that he mustn't waste the precious moments that the slave's inevitable death would buy him.

"Come with me!" he shouted over the din, addressing himself to the group at large. "There's a way out!"

He doubted many could hear his words, but the basic message was clear. He set off at a run back toward the entrance through which he had come, conscious of the thunder of many feet behind him.

Balenans ran toward them from all sides, but they were unprepared for the force of the Kyonans' numbers once they were all moving together. The group burst through the disorganized resistance, speeding along in Jonan's wake.

When he neared the gate, he felt a huge surge of relief at the sight before him. Not all of the slaves he had spoken to were still there, but the gate was still held by Evan and one of the others. Half a dozen Balenan bodies on the ground told Jonan that they had been forced to fight for its possession.

Jonan put on a burst of speed, beating his companions to the gate.

"The river?" he panted, and Evan gave a curt nod.

"The others have made a path." He jerked his head toward the space beyond the gate, but Jonan didn't pause to investigate. Already the others were reaching them, and he didn't want to cause more of a bottleneck than was inevitable.

"Cross the river and STAY TOGETHER," he shouted at the first few as they ran through. "There's help on the other side!"

He repeated the message over and over as different forms raced past him. Increased shouting from the back of the group alerted him to trouble for those bringing up the rear. He looked over at Evan, and the older man didn't need to be told. He and a few others grabbed swords from the fallen Balenans and ran toward the commotion.

Jonan didn't stay to see the outcome. He raced straight past them back into the camp. He had expected to find a large number of Kyonans still milling throughout the space, but his unnamed ally had done his job better than Jo had anticipated. Still, some had missed the exodus, of course. Jonan barely paused as he passed each one, sending them toward the gate with a shout, and not waiting to see if they obeyed. There was only so much he could do. He had made it around most of the space when he was grabbed from behind by strong arms.

His dagger was still in his hand, and he slashed backward at his captor, hearing a quick grunt as the metal found a mark. The man released him for a moment and Jonan shot forward, but he was almost instantly seized again. One slaver held him fast while another wrested his blade from his grip.

"This one!" a rough voice shouted. "He was drumming them up, he's the one who started it!"

"Hang onto him," said another voice, "the Overseer will want to make an example of him."

Jonan struggled wildly, but he was much too outnumbered. He couldn't see who held him, not that their faces would mean anything to him. A new voice joined the group, panting as though from running.

"They've broken down the side gate! They're running out toward the river!"

"Well round them up!"

"There are too many!"

Jonan heard someone spit, then the voice that had ordered him to be held made itself heard again.

"Then eliminate any still inside."

"Are you sure?" asked someone uncertainly. "The reinforce ments will surely be here any minute."

"Of course I'm sure! You know the Overseer's orders. Better to kill them than let them escape. The river will get any who've already made it out, or if not, the jungle."

Jonan's mind whirred frantically, trying to think of a solution. He doubted everyone was out by now, the gate was too small.

"Wait!" he cried, trying to stall for time, but no one paid him any heed. What could he do? What would Scarlett do? She would think of some clever way to outwit them. Or Raldo—he would be able to fight his way out.

Two of the slavers had begun to drag Jonan toward the center of the camp, the others taking off in the direction of the gate. He continued to struggle wildly, no new ideas presenting themselves to him. His wrestling appeared to make no difference whatsoever, so he was surprised when one of his captors suddenly let go of his arm with a shout. Jonan didn't hesitate to make the most of the opportunity, bringing his free arm around to make contact with the man holding him on the other side.

The Balenan fell away quickly, and swinging around, Jonan saw why. As if summoned by his thoughts, Scarlett had appeared, Raldo close behind her.

"What are you doing?!" he gasped. "You can't be here!"

She ignored his words. "Are you all right?" she asked, her eyes scanning the space swiftly in search of further threats. Jo realized that their surrounds were suddenly quiet, and he saw that the two slavers were on the ground nearby. As he looked, one of them stirred, his expression disoriented as if from a hit to the head. His eyes passed between the three of them in confusion, widening as they settled on Scarlett.

"But you're—"

He never finished his sentence. Raldo had been hovering protectively near Scarlett, but at the recognition in the man's eyes, he didn't hesitate. He had a sword in his hand, and in a moment it had ensured that the man would never pass on his realization to anyone.

"Scarlett," Jo said, grasping her arm. "You promised you wouldn't come into the camp!"

She didn't quite meet his eyes, her face showing less than its usual poise as she took in the grim scene around them. "They said that you ran back in," she said, her voice sounding dazed.

"They?" repeated Jonan eagerly. "Did they make it out, then? All of them?"

Scarlett shook her head, pulling herself together. "Not all of them. Some were still trying to get out when we came through the gate. But Stan already took the first group back toward the base."

"Good," said Jo firmly. "Let's get the rest of them out. The slavers are going to kill anyone left inside."

That information got both Scarlett and Raldo moving, and within moments the three of them were racing back toward the action.

"You shouldn't have come in here," panted Jonan to Raldo as they ran. He could hardly believe Raldo had allowed Scarlett to take such a risk. "Why did you do it?"

"No offense," said Raldo shortly, "but I wouldn't have." He glanced over at Scarlett, running alongside Jo. "She wouldn't be deterred, so I followed her in."

"It seems you needed our help," Scarlett pointed out.

"It's not that I'm not grateful," said Jo, "but I knew the risk I was taking. I—"

"What's happening?" Raldo's sharp voice cut him off. Looking ahead, Jo saw what he meant. He had expected to come up against a mass of Balenan slavers at the gate, and had no plan as to how they were to get through.

But the scene before them was all but deserted. It seemed the last of the Kyonans had made it through, to Jonan's relief.

But the few Balenans in sight, instead of chasing them, were running in the other direction, back toward the compound's huge main gate.

"Where are they going?" he asked uneasily.

"Let's not stay to find out." Scarlett spoke firmly, once again mistress of the situation. "They might need assistance on the other side of the river." She glanced at her companions as they approached the gate. "Raldo, you join the group going toward the sinking mud. Carla could do with the assistance. Jo, you should be making for the base tree. Unless—" she looked at him sharply. "Were you compromised? Did anyone see your face who might recognize you in Nohl?"

They were passing through the gate as she spoke. Before Jonan had a chance to answer, they heard a commotion coming from the main gate. Jo had already left the compound, Scarlett close behind him, but looking back he saw Raldo glance sharply around before following.

"The reinforcements," he said, his voice grim. "That's where the slavers were going. We need to get everyone moving, *now*."

Jonan had no fault to find with that plan. Breaking free from the overwhelmed slavers was one thing. Facing off a squadron of trained and armed soldiers would be much more disastrous for the escaping Kyonans. Squinting ahead, he saw that they had almost caught up with the last stragglers. He could just make out the figures sprinting toward the river. They weren't heading for the rocky crossing, and in the darkness, it almost looked as though they ran straight into the water.

But when they got close, he saw that he had not misplaced his faith in the Kyonans he had met near the gate. They had indeed found a clever solution. Several enormous lengths of cut timber had been laid across the river, forming a makeshift bridge. It must have taken quite a number of people to achieve the effect, but Jo supposed that they were well used to lugging the logs around.

The last of the escaping slaves ahead of them had just set foot on the wooden beams when a thundering sound reached Jo's ears. Turning, he saw that mounted soldiers were rounding the outside of the compound, heading straight for them. At sight of the forms fleeing across the wood, the reinforcements let out a collective shout. Jo glanced from the approaching Balenans to the slaves gathering on the far side of the river.

"They need more time!" he shouted. "We have to take down the bridge."

Raldo nodded. "Once we get across, we'll push the beams out."

Jo hesitated, his eyes still on the mounted soldiers. "It might be too late by then."

"We don't have a choice," said Raldo sharply. "The three of us won't be strong enough to move them. We need help from the others." Jonan wasn't convinced, and he opened his mouth to argue, but looking at the older man, Jo couldn't help but notice that his eyes lingered on Scarlett. He had a feeling Raldo's insistence that they cross the bridge first had more to do with getting her to safety than with the practicalities of getting the planks loose.

They were almost to the river by now, and Scarlett's shrewd glance moved from the water to the approaching men, clearly calculating how long they had.

"I think Jo might be right, Raldo," she said. "We might have to—" Jo was watching her as she spoke, and he saw the moment her eyes slid past him to the oncoming threat. She stumbled, and both her companions slowed, throwing out their arms to steady her. They were at the water's edge, but Scarlett made no move either to cross or to attempt to dislodge the timber. She stood frozen, her eyes on the soldiers, and her hand shooting out to grip Jonan's arm in a hold that was somehow both vise-like and trembling.

"He's here," she whispered, horror in her voice.

"Who?" asked Jonan, looking around wildly, alarmed at the look on her face.

"My father."

CHAPTER NINETEEN

J o saw with a thrill of horror that Scarlett was right. Lord Wrendal's figure could be seen, leading the soldiers on a charger.

"It's all right, Scar," said Jo quickly, trying to speak reassuringly as he moved to place himself between her and the approaching riders. "Get across, I'll cover for you."

But she didn't move, immobilized by her terror. Her wide eyes were on her father's approaching form, and her hand still gripped Jo's arm.

"He's going to see me," she said, her voice shaking and her expression panicked. "He's going to see me!"

Jo exchanged a look with Raldo, and saw his own fear reflected in the other man's eyes. It seemed he wasn't the only one who had never seen Scarlett lose her head like this.

"Scarlett," he repeated, prying her hand off his arm and squeezing it encouragingly. "Get across the bridge."

She tore her eyes away from her father, clearly struggling to master herself. Her eyes met Jonan's, then her gaze passed to Raldo and on to the slaves on the other side of the river.

"There's no time," she said, her words faint. "We have to get the bridge down."

"Once you're across," cut in Raldo, but she shook her head.

"It's too late," she said, her voice rising hysterically. She dropped to her knees, trying to push the planks.

"Scar!" insisted Raldo, but Jo cut him off.

"There's no time!" If Jo could see that Scarlett wasn't going to listen, surely Raldo could too.

Raldo cursed softly, but dropped to his knees to help without another word. Jonan did the same, and one of the planks began to slide across the muddy bank. Someone on the other side seemed to realize what they were doing, and several people rushed to help at the far end.

Seeing this, Raldo pulled Scarlett to her feet roughly. "I've got this," he said, pushing her toward the rocky crossing further up. "Get across, now!"

Looking around, Jo realized why Raldo sounded frantic. The riders were all but on them. Scarlett started to protest, but meeting Raldo's eyes, Jonan seized her hand and began to run without another word. He could see the rocks up ahead, but it was too late. The riders had caught up to them, and some pushed ahead, forming a semi-circle that enclosed the three fugitives, out of reach of the crossing.

There was no time to think—still holding Scarlett's hand, Jo turned sharply, running back to Raldo. They arrived in time to see the last of the timber slide into the raging torrent, drawn instantly into the flood. If not for Scarlett's presence, Jo would have been glad in spite of his own peril. The time it would take the soldiers to get across the river would give the escapees a real chance at survival. And the squadron wouldn't realize the need for haste— they would never imagine the slaves had an organized exit strategy.

Jonan drew Scarlett behind him as he placed himself alongside Raldo, right at the water's edge. He had expected her to protest at being shielded, but she didn't make a sound, and he thought he could guess why. The soldiers had not pressed too close, enclosing the renegades in a loose ring, but Jo could still clearly see the identity of the well-dressed middle-aged man who was swinging down from his saddle, drawing a sword as he did so.

The look on Lord Wrendal's face spelled death as he approached with measured steps. The moon was hidden now behind clouds, and the night had become very dark indeed. The soldiers' faces were illuminated by the torches carried by some of their number, but the three individuals by the river were not in the circle of light. Jo could see no sign of recognition in the Overseer's eyes, either for his daughter or for Jonan. But within moments he would be close enough to get a good look, and Jo couldn't see how he could prevent Scarlett from being discovered any more than he could hide his own identity.

"Don't try to swim against the current." Raldo's curt whisper made Jonan jump in surprise. He had not realized the rebel had approached so close. "Swim with it, but angle yourself toward the far bank. Get her out before the rapids."

"What?" asked Jonan, confused. But before he could so much as look around, Raldo's arm shot out in a sweeping motion, and Jo found himself toppling backward into the dark churning water, Scarlett's hand still clutched in his.

The current instantly pulled at him as he fell into the cold torrent, and Scarlett's fingers began to slide away. But he grasped at them firmly, holding on as if his life depended on it until his head broke the surface. He drew a deep breath and saw with relief that Scarlett's head was bobbing nearby.

"Raldo!" she gasped, but Jo just shook his head. There was no time for discussion. Already they were being swept along at a terrifying speed, and it wouldn't be long before they were drawn into the rapids, with no hope of survival. He opened his mouth to tell her to swim for the far bank, but his head was pulled under again before he could speak. He kicked upward with an effort, coughing and spluttering as he once again encountered air.

The current was much too strong. He was terrified to let go of Scarlett, lest they both be swept away completely, but he knew they couldn't swim while still connected. He hesitated for a moment, but the decision was made for him as a strong surge in the current pulled them apart. For a moment Jo was once again submerged, but he fought his way quickly to the surface.

"Scarlett!" he called, but he couldn't see her. He struck out toward the far bank in blind terror, only just remembering Raldo's warning, and making sure to move with the current. He had taken only a few strokes when he heard a faint cry. Looking back, his heart somehow leaped and plummeted simultaneously at the sight of Scarlett, further upstream but closer to the wrong side of the bank.

Jo looked around frantically. The moon had temporarily emerged from the clouds, and in the sudden illumination, he saw that he was on a collision course with one of the lengths of timber that had formed the makeshift bridge. Thrown by the powerful torrent, one end of it had become firmly wedged in a rocky section of riverbank, on the far side from the camp. The plank extended diagonally out from this base point, buffeted by the river. Surely it wouldn't be long before it wriggled free and followed its fellows further down, toward the rapids Jonan could hear churning up ahead.

He abandoned his attempt to reach the shore, swimming instead with strong strokes toward the log. He allowed the current to carry him along its length some way, before throwing his arms around it. He held on grimly, pulling his forward motion to a stop with a supreme effort, disregarding the way the rough surface of the beam ripped at his skin. He glanced back—Scarlett was almost upon him, borne along by the rushing water.

Jo heaved himself partially onto the log in time to throw out his arm. Scarlett had seen him, and she was clearly putting every bit of strength she had into her strokes, moving toward him tortuously. As she was swept past, she reached for him. Jo's hand closed over her wrist, and she returned the pressure instantly. He hung onto her arm with one hand, his other arm still wrapped around the log. The current battered at him, and he let out an involuntary roar as he pulled with all his might in his attempt to bring her in toward the relative safety of the beam. His arm, imperfectly recovered from its many adventures, burned as if on fire at the unnatural strain, but he held on doggedly.

It was fortunate that Scarlett was stronger than she looked, because he couldn't have maintained the hold for much longer. But she was pulling too, and she grasped the wood with her free hand. Half pulling, half swimming, they inched along toward the bank. Jo was almost at the river's edge when he felt the plank begin to wobble. He threw an alarmed look back at Scarlett, and saw that she understood without the need for words. The two of them scrambled the last distance as quickly as their aching limbs would allow.

Jo reached the bank first. Letting go of the plank, he grasped an overhanging root and turned to offer Scarlett his hand. She grasped it readily, and the two of them hauled themselves up onto the mud. For a moment they just lay there, panting. A loud groan was followed by a splitting crack and a splintering noise, then the beam came free of the rocks and spun away into the flood.

The sound seemed to be the catalyst for movement, and Jo

and Scarlett both pushed themselves to their feet. Scarlett glanced frantically back into the river.

"Raldo?" she asked breathlessly, her gaze turning to Jonan in an urgent inquiry.

He shook his head heavily, no reassurances to offer. He didn't know what had become of their friend, but he was certain Raldo hadn't followed them into the river.

"We have to go back—"

"We can't, Scar," he said gently. She looked around wildly, as if searching for something solid to hold onto in the chaos of uncertainty, but she didn't argue with him. "It will be dawn in a couple of hours," Jo continued, watching her closely, half afraid she would throw herself back into the river in an attempt to find Raldo.

But he shouldn't have doubted her. The momentary panic that had seized her at sight of her father had passed, and the rebel leader was returning. For some reason it made Jo's heart ache almost as much as her blind terror had done.

"You're right," she said, her voice steady even while her hands shook. "We have to get back." She took a deep breath. "There are a lot of people who might need our help tonight."

"You can trust them to the others," said Jo firmly. "They know what they're doing. You need to get back to the city."

She pursed her lips, but didn't respond. She began to move through the undergrowth, Jonan following her lead. The moon had once again been engulfed by clouds, and rain had begun to fall.

Jo didn't ask Scarlett where she was taking them. Despite her collected front, he could sense that she was close to breaking point, and he thought it would be best to give her space. So he hung back as they pushed through the mud. But his eyes barely left her back, looking for any sign that she might need support, or welcome a comforting presence.

There was none. Her posture was as erect as ever, and her steps didn't falter as she pushed her way through the foliage, which was now dripping from the rain. Drops burst against Jonan's face from the increasing downpour that was making its way down in uneven splashes from the canopy above.

Scarlett glanced back, and Jo could see raindrops hitting her face as well. He could almost imagine that they were tears, for the slaves who had died, for Raldo's unknown fate, for the mammoth task ahead with those who had gotten away. But it was a fanciful thought. Scar the calm commander was back in full force, her emotions clearly locked away until they could be safely explored. If such a time existed.

He realized soon that she was following the river back toward the camp, keeping well back from the tree line. They didn't go all the way to the place where the slaves had crossed— merely close enough to establish that no one was left, and that the soldiers had not yet crossed over. Then Scarlett took off in the direction of the base tree, moving at an impressive pace considering the night's adventures.

Jonan knew she had taken a similar pummeling to him in the river, but no one would think it to see her move through the darkness. He was hard pressed to keep up, and he suspected she was pushing herself to her limit in an attempt to leave no space for thought. He could understand the impulse, but he couldn't help but wonder how she would cope the next day, and how she would explain her battered state.

Even with the increased pace, their progress was frustratingly hampered by the muddy conditions. To Jonan the time seemed to draw out interminably as they traversed the route back to the base tree. The tension stretched between them as they traveled in silence, unspoken fears keeping them company.

They reached the base tree without any sign of pursuit.

Jonan was impressed as he examined the ground surrounding the hideout.

"They did a good job of not leaving tracks," he said.

Scarlett looked at him for an uncomprehending moment before she seemed to process his words. Neither of them had spoken since the river.

"Yes," she said. "This rain might just save them."

Jo glanced sideways at her. "We were lucky it hadn't started yet when we were in the river."

"Yes," she repeated concisely. She had barely knocked on the trapdoor when it creaked open. The hubbub that poured forth instantly confirmed that one group at least had made it back here.

Jo swiftly followed Scarlett down the ladder, almost knocking into her on the wooden platform below. Looking down, he could immediately see why she had paused. The underground room was full of people, the unfamiliar crowd startling in the familiar space. Everywhere he looked he saw huddles of Kyonans, dripping wet and wide-eyed. Some looked exhilarated at their escape, but others seemed still to be in shock. He supposed they had a lot to take in.

Every eye turned toward them as they entered, a hush falling over the crowd. Scarlett was in front, and a whispered hiss passed through the assembled Kyonans. Jo saw some of those at the front physically recoil at the sight of the young Balenan woman.

"Isn't that—?" someone muttered, and Jo stepped instinctively forward, slightly shielding Scarlett with his body. When he came into prominence, an altogether different type of murmur passed through the group.

"That's him!" a boy cried. "The liberator!"

"He freed us!" another voice chimed in.

Jonan stared around him, at a total loss for what to say. The realization that these people saw Scarlett as their enemy and him as their heroic rescuer filled him with a myriad of emotions that he couldn't begin to articulate. He thought of the missing Raldo, who had sacrificed his own chance at escape to block the soldiers' pursuit of the escaped slaves, and then to allow Jo and Scarlett to get away.

He thought of Scarlett, and everything she had given over the last few years to help a cause in which she had nothing to gain and everything to lose. Not to mention the way she had come into the compound in spite of the danger because she had been told that Jo had run back in. He glanced involuntarily at her and was unable to read the flicker of emotion behind her calm front. The admiration in all the pairs of eyes trained on him suddenly felt like an accusation, and he fell back a step. He didn't want any of this.

Before he could think of what to say, a cry sounded through the space, followed by a ripple of motion as someone pushed their way to the front. Bonnie emerged from the crowd, racing up the steps toward them.

"Milady!" she cried in evident relief. "You made it! I thought —but are you all right?" She took in their bedraggled state, then looked around. "I thought Raldo was with you."

Jo saw Scarlett swallow hard, and realized that it was beyond her to give an answer.

"He was," he supplied. "But the reinforcements came. He stayed behind to let us get away."

"Then where..."

"I don't know," said Jonan. "I think he was captured." His eyes flicked involuntarily to Scarlett. "Lord Wrendal was there, Bonnie."

Bonnie's eyes flew to his, their expression startled. She looked over at Scarlett and seemed to understand.

"The morning will bring us answers, I imagine," she said

gruffly. "There's nothing more we can do tonight." She laid a hand on Scarlett's arm. "Stan has things well in hand here, milady. Messengers have been sent to the other bases, and hunters are ready to go as soon as the rain lets up. Let's get you back."

"I don't know if I can do it, Bonnie," Scarlett whispered. "I don't know if I can pretend after—"

"You can, milady," said Bonnie firmly. "You underestimate yourself. And in any event, you can't stay here. We have to get you home before the sun comes up."

"Home," echoed Scarlett, her tone bitter. She gave a short laugh, but the sound was hollow. Still, she made no effort to resist Bonnie's urging, turning back toward the ladder without another word. Jonan could only be relieved, as he could still see many suspicious looks being sent in her direction.

He followed the two girls up the ladder and out into the jungle. The rain was still falling, but he was so wet and mud-splattered already, it was hard to see what difference it could make. They had started back toward Nohl before Scarlett even seemed to notice him.

"Jo, should you be going back to the city?" she asked suddenly.

"Of course," said Jo, with a shrug. "Where else would I go?"

"But didn't they see you at the camp?" Scarlett insisted. "It might not be safe for you anymore."

"It was never all that safe, as you kept telling me," Jo pointed out. "I don't know if anyone saw me who could identify me in Nohl. But it doesn't matter. I'm not going to hide out in the jungle."

"Jo," said Scarlett, unexpectedly impassioned. "After every-thing that's happened, after all of this, will you still take foolish risks?"

"No," he assured her, his voice firm and calm. "It's not that I don't realize the risk, or don't care. But I've gone too far to turn back now. And I don't want to turn back. I want to finish this."

"But we don't know how!" Scarlett cried, her voice catching.

"I know that," said Jonan, still calm. "But I don't think I'll figure out how by hiding in the jungle."

Scarlett fell silent. In reality she looked too weary to argue further. Jonan met Bonnie's eyes over Scarlett's head. Her expression was shrewd, and Jo suspected that she could guess the additional reason he was determined to return to Nohl. He just gave her an infinitesimal shrug. He felt no need to explain himself. But the truth was that he had never seen Scarlett so vulnerable, and there was no way he was staying in hiding somewhere while she went back into the den of the beast. What-ever Lord Wrendal's reaction to the night's events might be, Jo wanted to be nearby when it happened.

The rest of the trip was completed in silence. The rain had increased to a torrential downpour, the first true deluge since Jonan had arrived in this tropical climate. The heavy sheets of water battered away at their heads, drenching them through. It made climbing much more dangerous, but the decreased visi-bility made it easy to pass through the city unseen. It was only necessary for Jo to take to the rooftops when his building was almost reached.

Although the group had split up a few blocks away, Jonan lingered on the roof of his building, trying in vain to see the others enter Lord Wrendal's property. When he noted the faint lightening of the darkness around him, and realized that dawn was about to break, he abandoned the attempt and slipped in through his window.

His body was weary, and every inch of him felt as though he had come fresh from his beating in the square all those weeks ago, but he didn't even attempt to sleep. He huddled in his room, his eyes fixed unseeingly on the wall as his mind worked through the unexpected events of the night. He had presented a calm face, but the truth was that he was deeply shaken by what he had witnessed. And it wasn't just the brutality of the riot in the slave camp, or Raldo's uncertain fate that haunted him. It was Scarlett's unintentional revelation.

He had known already that there was little love lost between her and Lord Wrendal, to say the least. But he hadn't known until tonight just how far it went. And he felt deeply alarmed at his discovery.

Despite her capability, and her brave front, Scarlett was afraid of her father. Not just wary of his poor opinion, or worried about the consequences of having her double life exposed. She was afraid of *him*, genuinely, desperately afraid.

And somehow, for reasons he couldn't explain, the realization made Jonan afraid himself.

CHAPTER TWENTY

It was difficult to tell when the sun had properly risen, the heavy sheets of rain preventing the darkness from fully lifting. Jonan had not lain down, but he had rumpled the covers to make it look as though the bed had been occupied, and had cleaned himself up in an attempt to conceal the night's adventures. He wasn't sure how much good it would do, as he had no clothes that could hide how much the log's rough bark had shredded his arms. There was also no way he could fully dry himself, but since it was still pouring, that would cease to be suspicious almost the moment he stepped outside the building.

As soon as he thought the dawn was advanced enough for his movements not to raise questions, he let himself out onto the street. The memory of Raldo's calm voice in his ear as the older man had sacrificed himself without hesitation burned in Jo's mind, and he could find no rest until the question of his friend's fate had been answered.

He stepped onto the rain-drenched flagstones, not bothering to locate the soldier set to watch him today. He had no idea whether he had passed through the fracas in the slave camp unrecognized. It was very possible that at any moment Lord

Wrendal's men would descend on him, and if that was the case he wanted to make full use of every minute of freedom left to him.

He thought of heading toward Lord Wrendal's manor, to see if Scarlett or Bonnie had been able to discover anything. But he was fairly certain Scarlett's connection with the rebels had not been exposed, and if his had, then any communication between them could be disastrous for her. And in any event, Jo could still picture Lord Wrendal's face as he dismounted next to the river such a short time ago. The image was enough to convince him that Lord Wrendal would be a good man to avoid this morning as far as humanly possible.

Jo moved instead in the opposite direction, toward the castle. As soon as he entered the courtyard, he could tell that his instinct had not failed him. This gathering point was the natural center of any drama unfolding within Nohl. He could hardly see the castle itself through the downpour of rain, and the sound of the hammering water all but drowned out the excited chatter of the growing crowd. But somehow neither sight nor sound was necessary to convey the tremor of activity passing through the space. It was evident that news of the events at the logging camp had begun to spread.

Jo saw a huddle of locals standing nearby, and approached them unthinkingly.

"What's going on?"

They turned astonished and disapproving glares on him, angling their bodies away as they continued to gossip. He turned away with a frustrated growl, losing patience with their prejudice.

He cast around until he saw a group of his own countrymen nearby, and hurried over to join them instead. Their faces were tense and anxious.

"What's happening?" he tried again.

"Some kind of commotion in the intake camp," said one girl, her eyes wide. "Word is all of the slaves escaped."

"Not all," said an older woman. "They caught one of them, trying to get across the river. Poor soul—he must have been the last out of the camp."

Jo let out a long breath. If these people were right, the authorities hadn't figured out that Raldo was part of the resistance rather than one of the slaves from the camp. That was a huge advantage. But his relief was short-lived, banished by the words of another member of the group.

"There's going to be an execution," the man said. "Any minute now."

"What? No!" Jonan shouted, starting forward involuntarily. They all stared at him in surprise. "Are you sure?" he pressed, trying to keep his voice level.

The boy nodded. "I work at the castle. I saw them taking him to the execution chamber not long ago." The boy shivered. "The Overseer was there, and I've never seen him so angry."

Jonan looked around, squinting through the rain, half expecting to see Lord Wrendal bearing down on them right now. His heart seemed to leap into his throat at the sight of the structure he had seen his first day here, the wickedly sharp blade suspended sickeningly in the air. He didn't want to look at it, but he couldn't seem to tear his eyes away.

"We have to do something," he said desperately. "We have to stop it!"

The rest of the group stared at him in astonishment. "What do you suggest we do?" asked one of them.

"I don't know—something!" Jonan's mind raced frantically, but no brilliant ideas appeared for how to save Raldo. "Where's the execution chamber?" he asked quickly.

"Right below our feet," said one of the slaves, looking at him curiously. "The castle dungeons extend out below the courtyard."

Jonan took off running toward the castle without another word. "You can't get in there!" one of them called out, but he ignored the cry, his panic overpowering his reason. But even if he had a plan, it would have been too late. He had barely taken three steps when a hush fell over the courtyard. A grim procession had emerged from the castle entrance.

Jonan's steps faltered as a wave of cold horror washed over him at the sight of Raldo, hands chained together as he was shoved along by an escort of soldiers. He looked roughed up, but Jonan saw with a fierce stab of admiration that the rebel's expression remained calm and his bearing proud.

For a moment Jo was unable to move, his mind trying desperately and fruitlessly to think of a way to rescue Raldo. The soldiers pushed the captured rebel roughly into place before the scaffold, then formed a guard on either side of him. Jo wasn't sure what they were waiting for, but it was clear that if he wanted to do something, he was almost out of time.

He propelled himself forward, joining the throng of people who were jostling for position at the front of the crowd. The soldiers shot menacing glares at anyone who got too close, but for the most part they ignored the onlookers, many of whom were heckling the prisoner. Their words were mostly lost in the ongoing downpour, but the sentiment was clear.

Jo shoved his way to the front, ignoring the outraged cries of Balenans who took offense at being elbowed by one of his kind. He found that he wasn't the only Kyonan present, although the others were keeping their heads down better than he was. Raldo's eyes scanned the crowd, his expression impassive until his gaze landed on Jonan.

His eyes widened in alarm. He gave a small start, as if to move toward Jonan, but stopped himself in time. Jo had come to know Raldo's priorities well enough to have no difficulty reading the question in the rebel's eyes. It was clear his panic was not for himself.

She's safe, he mouthed, and saw Raldo's shoulders instantly relax. The older man's resignation terrified him.

He struggled forward, no clear idea of what he was going to do, but unable to bear doing nothing.

"Enough."

Raldo's sharp voice drew Jo up short. After a moment of hesitation, he fell back under the ferocity of Raldo's expression. The rebel couldn't be more clear that he didn't want Jonan to intervene. And as much as he hated to admit it, even Jo could see that without a plan, he would only make it worse.

Of course the prisoner's exclamation had attracted the notice of the soldiers guarding him. One of them cuffed him over the back of the head for good measure, his gaze passing from Raldo to the crowd with a look of amusement.

"Can't take a bit of heckling?" he mocked, obviously believing Raldo's protest to have been directed to the Balenans still jeering at him. "Don't worry, there's much worse to come."

Jo's hands balled into fists at his sides, and he felt his breathing speed up.

"You can't do this!" he shouted, unable to hold it in. "I won't let this happen!"

Another one of the soldiers heard his voice over the melee, the man's eyes narrowing as they rested on the rebellious Kyonan.

"Watch yourself, boy," he spat. "There's plenty of room up here for you." His eyes swept the crowd, and he raised his voice. "And the same goes for any other of you Kyonans who get ideas about helping your little friend."

Jonan felt his control deserting him as a growl built in his throat, but again it was Raldo who brought him to his senses.

The older man's gaze was calm and unwavering as he locked eyes with Jonan for the briefest second, before appearing to address the crowd at large.

"No one can stop this," he said. "I don't want *anyone* to try."

"How gracious," sneered a soldier. He shook Raldo's shoulder roughly. "Now that's enough from you!"

Jonan's breath caught as Raldo once again met his eyes and he understood his friend's meaning. He scanned the crowd quickly for Scarlett. If she saw what was happening, if she tried to stop them from executing Raldo—she would surely be exposed, and Raldo's sacrifice would be for nothing.

As if summoned by his thoughts, Bonnie suddenly appeared at Jo's side.

"Bonnie!" he gasped, struggling to speak quietly enough not to be overheard. "We have to stop this."

Bonnie's eyes, red-rimmed and unblinking, were riveted on Raldo. But she drew her gaze back to Jonan with an effort. "We can't," she whispered. "It's too late."

"How can you say that?" Jo hissed furiously. "We have to at least—"

"She's coming, Jo," Bonnie cut him off. "She's beside herself, and I can't talk her down. She's going to get caught."

Jo's heart seemed to stop for an endless second, and his eyes passed involuntarily from Bonnie to Raldo. The rebel was too far away to hear their conversation, but he seemed to have grasped why Bonnie had come for Jo.

Go, he mouthed, his face showing real alarm.

Still Jo hesitated, terrified that if he took his eyes from his friend, it would somehow make Raldo's fate inevitable.

"Jo." Tears were running down Bonnie's face as she tugged on Jonan's tunic. "There's no time. She won't listen to me, but I think she'll listen to you."

The alarm in Raldo's eyes grew to panic as Jo stood motionless. In a sudden movement that caught everyone by surprise, the captive lunged forward, throwing himself into the crowd to the sound of the soldiers' startled cries.

"Promise me you'll protect her," Raldo demanded, his voice low and his eyes riveted on Jonan, who was less than an arm's length from him by the time the soldiers once again seized him.

Raldo barely seemed aware of the soldiers converging on him, their fists communicating their displeasure as much as their angry words.

"Promise me!" Raldo insisted, his voice rising above the increased chaos.

Bonnie tugged on Jonan again, and he lowered his eyes just in time to avoid the notice of those soldiers who turned from their prisoner to scan the crowd. They were clearly trying to identify who Raldo was speaking to. He counted to ten, his blood pounding in his ears, before he raised his eyes again. They instantly found Raldo's, and he gave a curt nod in acknowledgment of the promise, his throat tight.

Again Raldo's shoulders slumped in relief. Bonnie started to pull Jonan away from the front of the crowd, but he couldn't drag his eyes from the condemned man. Raldo met his look, and for the first time Jo saw vulnerability in the stoic rebel's face.

Don't...let...her...watch.

Despite the space now between them, and the fact that Raldo was clearly mouthing the words, Jo could have sworn he heard his friend's familiar voice. A pounding filled Jo's ears as he suddenly comprehended the awful truth that there was no stopping this.

Bonnie continued to tug Jo away as Raldo's attention turned to the crowd gathered in the square. He raised his voice, his next words addressed to the group at large.

"I am proud to add my name to the wall," he cried, his voice clear and strong. "Kyona!"

There was no answering cry, but a rustle passed through the square as all the Kyonans squared their shoulders, standing a little taller.

Jonan's mind was numb, but even he felt the ripple that passed through the assembled watchers a moment later. Every eye turned to the far side of the square, Jonan's gaze drawn there as well. He barely heard Bonnie's gasp, lost in his own horror at the sight of Lord Wrendal striding toward the prisoner.

But imposing as the Overseer was, he held Jonan's attention for no more than a second, because a smaller figure stumbled along in his wake. Scarlett was back in her usual daytime attire, but in her wide-eyed terror she looked nothing like the poised and haughty Lady Wrendal. Jo saw the panic in Scarlett's eyes as she took in the scene before her. Involuntarily, he followed the trajectory of her glance back toward Raldo. The rebel's eyes flicked from Scarlett to Jo. Their expression became compelling, the message clear with no need for speech.

You promised.

"Go," Bonnie hissed in his ear. "Before it's too late!"

Jo tore his eyes away from Raldo. Turning his back on his friend with the greatest effort of his life, he pushed through the crowd toward Scarlett. She had momentarily fallen behind her father, frozen in her horror, but she started forward again now, a cry on her lips.

Lord Wrendal didn't seem to have noticed her outburst. Every fiber of Jonan's being wanted to throw himself at the evil man, but he forced his feet to run around him in a wide arc instead, attempting to escape the Overseer's notice. Lord Wrendal strode forward imperiously, his eyes fixed on his victim, apparently oblivious to the crowd, curious Balenans and anxious Kyonans alike.

Scarlett's eyes were also locked on Raldo, and she didn't see

Jonan until he all but slammed into her, halting her forward momentum.

"Jo!" she gasped, "he's going to execute Raldo!" She made a movement as if to grasp his arm, stopping herself with evident effort.

"I know," he said grimly. "I know." He grabbed her wrist as unobtrusively as he could, trying to pull her back the way she had come, away from the scaffold.

"What are you doing?" she hissed. "We have to stop it!"

"We can't, Scarlett." His voice was gentle but firm, his promise to Raldo burning in his mind.

"We have to! We have to do something!" She tried to pull free, but he held onto her wrist, still pulling her away. "Jo, stop it!" she snapped, getting angry.

He stopped, dropping his grip on her with a furtive look around. A few nearby people were watching them curiously, although the pounding rain was helping in his attempts to keep Scarlett's presence from becoming conspicuous. Jo's eyes were drawn involuntarily to the scaffold. Raldo had been led up onto the platform. Jo could have sworn he heard the metallic ding of raindrops hitting the metal of the lethal blade.

"Scarlett, you need to get out of here," he said, his voice urgent and his throat tight.

"No! I'll—"

"What?" Jonan challenged. "What can you do?"

"I don't know!" She cast her gaze around frantically, tears beginning to gather in her deep brown eyes. "I'll—I'll speak to my father, I'll tell him—"

"Tell him what?" choked Jonan, fighting tears himself, his heart wrenched as much by her panic as by Raldo's fate. "What could you possibly tell him that would make it better, not worse?"

"I—" Her eyes met his, but she had no answer, and her voice died in her throat.

"It's too late, Scar," Jo whispered, "he's made his peace. You need to leave. It will all be for nothing if you're exposed, and you don't want to see this."

She shook her head frantically, but Jo could see that she no longer believed her own denial. He once again grasped her wrist and tugged her away, his movements more measured, but no less determined. They had almost left the square when he heard Lord Wrendal's voice raised above the din. Jo couldn't make out the words, but he guessed that the Overseer must be offering Raldo the traditional last request. Jo picked up his pace. It was moments away, then.

He saw Scarlett turn her head frantically, and he tugged her the last few steps without ceremony, pulling her around the corner of a building. He didn't stop tugging until they were halfway down a narrow alley, well out of sight of the crowd gathered in the square.

Glancing around him, he couldn't see a single other person. Everyone who was out of their beds seemed to have congregated in the courtyard. He turned his attention back to Scarlett.

"Don't try to look," he said firmly. "Keep your eyes on my face." After a frantic look around at the deserted area, she complied, and the horror in her eyes made holding her gaze feel like trying to keep a grip on burning metal. But Jo forced his own emotions down, keeping his expression steady as he gripped her shoulders firmly.

Even though they had left the square, they could still feel the tension building in the crowd. Scarlett reached for him, clutching the front of his tunic convulsively.

"Jo." Her whisper was barely audible over the rain. He had no words to comfort her, merely tightening his hold on her shoulders.

All of a sudden, they heard it. The swish then thud was as unmistakable as the collective release of tension. Scarlett's eyes widened for the briefest moment, then the last of her control fled, and she threw herself against Jonan's chest, tears bursting from her in a hysterical torrent.

His arms closed around her, drawing her against him. He was both relieved and regretful that his intervention on Scarlett's behalf had prevented him from witnessing the execution himself. It didn't feel true without seeing it, but he knew without doubt that it was over.

He rested his cheek on the top of Scarlett's head, holding her close as she continued to sob wildly against him. His own tears were flowing now, mingling with the rain that still fell onto his face. Nothing about the horrible moment felt real. Jo couldn't deny to himself that he had thought before now about what it would be like to hold Scarlett. But not like this.

For a matter of minutes, Scarlett's tears flowed unchecked, but too quickly she began to pull herself together. Eventually the sobs slowed, then stopped. Jonan made no move to release her, seeking comfort from their embrace as much as giving it. For a drawn-out moment she stayed as she was, her face buried in his chest, and her hands still gripping his shirt. Then slowly, her whole body still shaking, she drew back.

He dropped his arms reluctantly, trying to catch her eyes. But she was clearly trying hard not to look at him, her hold over herself still incomplete.

"Scarlett," he said softly, and she shook her head, her breath momentarily hitching again. He reached for her, but she pulled away, and he let his hand drop.

"Scarlett, I'm sorry," he tried again.

"For what?" she said, still not looking at him. "This isn't your fault. It's mine."

"Scarlett, that's madness," he said, his tone almost angry. "None of this is your fault. You take too much on yourself."

She stepped away from him, breathing in deeply and shuddering on the exhale. "Do you think I don't realize that he did it to save me? I was there, Jonan."

"That doesn't make it your fault," said Jo softly. "It was his choice. And I'm confident he'd make it again."

For a moment he thought she would continue to argue, but she didn't speak. He could see her struggling with herself briefly, then she schooled her features to the impassive face she usually showed to the world. He felt his throat constrict again, hardly able to bear the sight.

"I apologize," she said, and the sudden formality of her tone caught him off guard.

"For what?" he asked blankly.

"For..." She gestured between them. "For that. I just...lost control for a moment."

"I would have thought you cold-hearted for real if you hadn't lost control at such a moment," said Jonan quietly. Scarlett turned her head slightly away, not quite able to hide the pain in her eyes. "What are you thinking, Scarlett?" he pressed. "Why would you apologize for such a thing? This is me, not some courtier you have to dupe, or some rebel you have to be strong for."

She met his eyes at last, but she gave no response to his words.

"We need to return to the square," she said instead. "Before we're missed. We should return separately."

"Scarlett." Jo spoke warningly. "You don't need to see—"

But she was already striding away, back the way they had come. Stifling a curse, Jo set off in the opposite direction, darting down the first side alley he found, trying to beat her back to the courtyard.

He emerged into the crowd a moment later, jostled by the horde of people returning to their usual morning activities. He pushed his way through, unable to stop himself from looking toward the scaffold.

He immediately wished he hadn't. His insides contracted at the horrible sight before him, and he turned away, trying to get his bearings as he scanned the edge of the courtyard for the point where Scarlett would enter. He found the spot, but he could see no sign of her. He shoved his way through more vigorously, joining a stream of people exiting by the same route.

Caught up in the tide, he almost missed the two figures standing together down the side of a building. Fury washed over him at the sight of the Overseer, mingling with his relief that Scarlett had apparently never made it back into the courtyard. Jonan stepped out of the crowd, his hands balling into fists as he caught Lord Wrendal's words.

"Did you hide here the whole time, Daughter? Still squeamish, I see."

Scarlett said nothing, but Jonan could barely contain his anger at the thought that this monster of cruelty would mock his brave and selfless daughter for betraying a hint of compassion.

Lord Wrendal turned his head, becoming suddenly aware of Jonan's presence. "What are you doing here?" the Overseer growled. It was clear that his rage over the successful breakout at the camp hadn't been satiated by the execution.

"You just murdered one of my people," Jonan spat. "Did you think I would have no interest in that?" He stepped aggressively toward the nobleman. "Do you think my king will have no interest in that?"

"How dare you make accusations against me?" hissed Lord Wrendal. "I am above your reproach, whelp. And the sooner your precious king realizes that, the better for him."

He seemed to dismiss Jonan with the words, his eyes sliding

back to Scarlett. "Come," he barked, as though Scarlett were a disobedient dog.

She stayed where she was, her face expressionless, but a glimpse of flint in her eyes. Her father stepped toward her, and though his movements were measured, Jo could feel the fury rolling off him in waves. Lord Wrendal curled his hand around Scarlett's arm, the very smoothness of the gesture somehow making it infinitely more threatening than a rough grab would have been.

"You will not defy me again." His voice was calm, but even Jo could tell that its quiet tones concealed suppressed rage. Propelled by his own anger, Jo started forward, his hands still in fists at his side.

Lord Wrendal turned his head, maintaining his possessive hold on his daughter's arm while he took in Jo's belligerent posture. When the Overseer spoke, his voice was even quieter than before, but Jo would have been a fool to miss the danger behind the silky tone.

"Watch yourself, boy. Just give me one reason to take your head also, and I will do it gladly. Make no mistake—if I find you had any involvement in last night's events, I will not make it as quick and clean as that man's justice." His gaze passed from Jo's furious face to Scarlett's expressionless features, and his eyes narrowed. "And stay away from my daughter. I don't want to see you speaking with her ever again." He turned back to Scarlett. "I won't tell you another time, Scarlett."

She swallowed, looking from her father to Jonan before capitulating. She made no effort to resist this time as Lord Wrendal led her away from the square. Jonan stayed frozen where he was, his blood pounding in his ears and his hands clenching and unclenching convulsively as he watched them walk away.

He longed to go after them, to vent his rage and grief on the

Overseer, but he hadn't missed the pleading warning in Scarlett's eyes, and he restrained himself. It wasn't that he was deterred by Lord Wrendal's threats against him. It was becoming increasingly clear to Jonan that he had been in grave danger all along, and in that sense nothing had changed.

But he was much more concerned about Scarlett's well-being. It looked as though she had avoided suspicion for now regarding her involvement with the resistance. But Jo knew enough of her father to see that his fury over recent events had made him unpredictable, and more dangerous than ever. What he would do next, Jonan couldn't begin to guess. But something had clearly made him angry with his daughter as well, and any attempt by Jonan to defend her would surely make it worse. Raldo had paid with his life to protect Scarlett from discovery—it would be no action of a friend to jeopardize that now.

But he wished desperately that there was a way to get Scarlett out from under Lord Wrendal's power. Even now, watching her walk away with that unyielding grip still on her arm filled Jonan with an unspecified fear. He had promised Raldo to protect Scarlett, but it seemed to him that she was in constant peril, and he had no idea what to do about it.

And all that was without even considering her emotional state. However unjust it might be, it was not exactly a surprise that she blamed herself for what had happened. Jonan hated to think of her locked away, feigning indifference for her father's eyes, and showing a strong front for her friends, while her anguish ate away at her on the inside. He didn't know how deep her attachment to Raldo had run, but the loss of the rebel leader was certainly going to hit her hard.

Once the ill-matched pair had passed out of his sight, Jonan began to walk as well. The street, deserted such a short time before, was now buzzing with activity as the crowds who had thronged eagerly to watch the execution now wandered back out of the square. There was no sign of Bonnie, however, or any other familiar face.

Jonan couldn't bring himself to return to the castle courtyard —he had no desire for a closer look at the aftermath of the beheading. Rain was still pounding down, but it didn't seem to trouble the locals much. He supposed they were used to it.

He hadn't really decided where to go, and he followed his feet away from the square without thinking about it. As he walked, his thoughts flicked between Raldo and Scarlett and the rebels in the jungle. How were the escaped slaves faring this morning? Would the resistance have enough reserves to feed them? Perhaps tonight he would be able to sneak back to the base tree, to see how he could help. He found himself reflecting that Raldo would know how to organize them, then realized with a sickening jolt that Raldo was gone. How desperately they would feel his loss at such a moment! Jonan supposed that Stan would be taking charge at the base tree. He had never met the leaders in charge at the other bases, and could only hope they were capable.

He reached the overflow building before he had realized he was heading there. He would rest for a minute in his room, he decided. The intensity of recent events had made him momentarily forget that he had not slept at all the night before, but he found that he was suddenly unutterably weary. He hadn't intended to actually lie down, but the bed looked far too inviting to be ignored. He would lay his head on his pillow, just while he thought about how he could best serve Stan in her efforts to provide for her group of fugitives, and how to keep his promise to Raldo.

Just for a few minutes, he promised himself. There was no harm in a few minutes.

CHAPTER TWENTY-ONE

Jonan woke with a start and a smothered cry, shooting up in his bed as his eyes flew frantically around the room in an attempt to orient himself. Rain was still pelting the window, and it was impossible to tell the hour from the dim light that filtered through it. His heart pounded in his ears as he struggled to emerge from the dream that had gripped him.

He had been back at the whipping post, that much he could remember, once again shielding the long-dead Marine from a beating. But as he had wrapped his arms around her protectively, he had suddenly found brown eyes boring into his, and realized that it was not Marine, but Scarlett whom he held. And it had not been until he heard her cry of pain that he understood that it was her protecting him, not the other way around. He knew it wasn't real, but he shuddered at the memory of her taking lashes for him. And as she had cried out in pain again and again, he had heard a curt whisper, the voice clear and familiar even in dream form, although it would never sound again in real life.

Don't try to swim against the current. Get her out before the rapids. You promised. You promised!

Jonan took deep breaths, trying to clear his head and return to reality. He suddenly became aware of a pounding on his door, and realized that he had not woken naturally. He leaped to his feet but hesitated for a moment. It had not escaped him that his accommodation here may be at an end after recent events. But he shook his head sharply, clearing the last of the fog. If Lord Wrendal had sent someone after him, there was nothing to be done but face them.

He crossed the room in two strides and wrenched open the door. But it was no soldier who almost toppled in at the sudden motion.

"Bonnie!" he cried, surprised at her appearance, and even more surprised when she pushed all the way into the room and closed the door behind her.

"You're still here!" she said, relief evident in her voice. "When you took so long to answer, I was worried I was too late." Getting a good look at her, he realized that she looked exhausted, her face pale and her expression grim.

"What do you mean?" he asked quickly. "What's happening?"

She looked at him sharply. "You haven't heard? Where have you been?"

"In here," said Jo. "I fell asleep," he admitted. "What time is it?"

"It's almost dark," said Bonnie curtly, and Jo started. Had he really slept so long? He ran a hand over his face, trying to gather his scattered thoughts.

"Where did you go?" he asked. "In the courtyard. You sent me after Scarlett, then you just disappeared."

Bonnie drew a shuddering breath, a shadow passing over her face at the reminder of the execution. "Cody was there," she said curtly. "I saw him on my way to get you. Raldo was his mentor, his hero. I couldn't let him see…"

She was clearly struggling with her emotions as her voice trailed off, and Jo gripped her shoulder firmly.

"You did the right thing."

Bonnie shook her head, dismissing the topic. "There's no time to waste," she said. "Pack your things. We need to leave right away."

"Leave?" Jonan repeated, staring. "What do you mean? Where are we going?"

Bonnie sighed. "There's no time to explain. But milady wants you out of here immediately."

"Where are we meeting her?" Jo asked, throwing his things into his rucksack.

"We're not," said Bonnie shortly. "She's not coming."

Jonan stopped short at that. "What do you mean? Where is she?"

"At her house," said Bonnie. "She's staying here. But she wants you safely out of the city."

"I don't think so," said Jo flatly.

"Jo—"

"We've been over this before," said Jo, his voice firm. "I'm not going anywhere while she's under the power of that monster. And I think it's suspicious that she's trying to send me away all of a sudden. It makes me think she's planning something, something she knows I'll try to stop her from doing. She wasn't herself this morning."

Bonnie sighed. "I don't like it any more than you do, but she told me not to take no for an answer. And honestly, I think you should do what she says, Jo. She's not sending you away for no reason—I don't think you can stay here now."

"Why?" he asked quickly. "What's happened?" His voice

turned stern as Bonnie hesitated. "And don't tell me there's no time to explain, because I'm not going anywhere until you do."

"Fine," snapped Bonnie. "A ship came in an hour ago. A trader vessel."

"You mean—a slave vessel? From Kyona?" asked Jo eagerly, and Bonnie gave a curt nod.

"Yes, except there weren't any slaves on board." Her eyes lit with a fierce gleam. "Quite the opposite."

"What do you mean?" Jo pressed.

"It seems that the ship was expected in Alezae," said Bonnie with a grim smile. "By a large squadron sent by King Calinnae. The slavers have come back without a single Kyonan on board."

Jo's eyes gleamed, but he felt slightly disappointed. "I'm surprised he allowed the ship to come back at all," he said, and was taken aback when Bonnie's smile grew.

"I think he didn't kill the Balenans because he wanted them to carry a message." She gave an ugly laugh in response to Jo's inquiring look. "Every single one of them has been branded with the slave mark. On their foreheads."

"Yes, Cal!" Jo said, his fist curling involuntarily.

"Cal?" repeated Bonnie quickly, but Jo shook his head. "Never mind that. What does this have to do with me? Why did Scarlett send you?"

"Why do you think?" said Bonnie, exasperated. "If your position was precarious before, it's unsustainable now. You're only being kept alive because of the uncertainty of the situation in Kyona, remember? Now that this King Calinnae has showed his hand, what interest can Lord Wrendal have in keeping you around? I think the only reason he hasn't come for you already is that he's been too distracted to remember you. Scarlett wants you out of Nohl and into the jungle straight away."

"She's in trouble, isn't she?" said Jonan, ignoring the last part of Bonnie's speech. "I could tell he was on the point of exploding this morning."

Bonnie hesitated, and when she spoke she sounded afraid. "I've never seen him so angry, Jo. He's on the warpath. I don't know what he's going to do."

"What happened to make him angry?"

She stared at him incredulously. "What do you mean? Almost the entire camp escaped last night, and then the slave ship this afternoon—"

"No, I mean what happened to make him angry at Scarlett?" Jo clarified quickly. "This morning he talked about her defying him." A sudden horrible thought occurred to him. "He doesn't know she was involved, does he?"

"No," said Bonnie. "I'm pretty sure he has no suspicion of that, thankfully. But he was absolutely livid this morning about the whole thing. Even before this incident with the trading ship, he was convinced that the crown needs to take drastic action against Kyona to quell any attempts to stop the trade. He summoned milady from her room just after dawn and insisted that she use her influence with the royals to convince them to act against King Calinnae, but she refused. She doesn't usually refuse him anything outright. She usually...well, manipulates him, I guess. Prods his thoughts in a different direction and makes him think it was his idea. But she wasn't quite her usual self after the night's events. And now..."

"Yes," said Jo quietly, "I know. Did she love him, Bonnie?" Her eyes flew to his swiftly, and he shrugged apologetically. "I know I shouldn't ask, but better to ask you than her."

She was silent for a moment, her gaze a little too shrewd. "I don't think so," she said at last. "Not like he did."

Jo nodded. He had realized before now that Bonnie didn't miss much. He felt a strange relief at her words. He tried to tell himself it was just that he was glad Scarlett was spared the pain of having the man she loved executed, but that explanation didn't quite account for the guilt he felt when he thought of Raldo.

"So basically, yes, she is in trouble," he said, returning to the previous topic. "Her defenses are lower than they've ever been, and her father is already angry with her."

"More than angry," asserted Bonnie. "He was dangerous before, but now, with this ship that's arrived…"

Jo was silent for a moment, thinking it over, then he nodded in sudden decision. "That settles it," he said firmly. "I'm definitely not going anywhere."

"What?" said Bonnie, startled. "You have to!"

Jo shook his head stubbornly. "He's too unpredictable, and too dangerous."

"All the more reason for you to get out while you can, Jo," said Bonnie seriously. "You need to get somewhere safe."

"Not while Scarlett's in danger," said Jo, unyielding. "I promised Raldo that I would protect her, and she needs protecting from herself as much as from her father. Even if I hadn't promised, I wouldn't leave her to his mercy and save myself. Don't look at me like that—I don't see you heading for the jungle and abandoning her."

"Of course not, but it's not the same," argued Bonnie. "I'm not in Lord Wrendal's sights."

Jo said nothing, merely unpacking his belongings again with a calm determination.

"Jo!" said Bonnie, grasping his arm. "Stop. She won't let it rest. She's determined to get you out. I'm supposed to take you under the wall as soon as it's dark. If I go back and tell her you're still here—"

"Well, tell her I'll leave gladly the minute she does," said Jo reasonably. "I would be only too pleased to see her safely out."

"And what will she do then?" asked Bonnie sarcastically. "Spend the rest of her life as an outlaw in the jungle?"

Jo pursed his lips. "Maybe she could seek refuge at the castle. Her cousins might receive her." Bonnie opened her mouth to protest, but Jo cut her off. "You can't force me to leave, Bonnie," he said. His lips curved in a tiny smile. The gesture felt unnatural after all that had passed. "No offense, but I think I could take you in a fight."

"You joke," she said darkly. "But I think she would expect me to fight you rather than let you stay here."

"There's no reason for you to get in trouble," said Jo firmly. "I'll talk to her. Where is she?"

"You can't get to her. She's at the manor, in her rooms."

Jo gave her a look. "And of course there's no way to get in and out of the manor undetected," he said ironically. "You, for example, have never done so."

She smiled reluctantly. "Of course there is, but that doesn't mean I'm going to show it to you. She told me to get you to safety. Taking you into Lord Wrendal's house is the opposite. She'd have my hide."

"Bonnie," said Jo seriously. "If you look me in the eye and tell me you're more afraid of Scarlett's reaction to you disobeying her than you are of Lord Wrendal's reaction to her disobeying him, then I'll come with you out of Nohl right now." She hesitated, and he pressed his point. "You know her, Bonnie. You know she'll worry about everyone else, and think of her own safety last. We have to think of it for her." His voice became grim. "I won't let him hurt her. Not if I'm still alive." He caught Bonnie's gaze and held it. "Can you honestly tell me that she isn't planning to do something dangerous right now?"

Bonnie sighed. "She hasn't told me what she's planning, but I can't deny I'm nervous."

"Let me talk to her," Jo insisted. "Let me remind her that she doesn't have to do everything on her own."

Bonnie protested a little, as one honor-bound to do so, but Jo could tell that he had convinced her. In a matter of minutes, they were making their way through the rain-soaked streets, Lord Wrendal's manor drawing closer with each step.

Following Bonnie's direction, Jo peeled off before the main gates, making use of a gap that could be created in the fence by removing a loose iron rail. Bonnie, who had no need to explain her presence there, continued to the main entrance to serve as a distraction for the soldiers milling around. Thanks to the rain and the gathering darkness, once Jonan made it into the grounds it was not a difficult task to steal through the gardens to the building.

He hugged the outside of the dwelling, hoping that the spot in question would be as hard to miss as Bonnie had suggested. Sure enough, he found the tree she had described and scaled it without difficulty. From there it was a simple step to the narrow ridge of roofing that ran around the top of the first story, the walls of the second level rising from it. He padded silently along it for a short way, climbing over a low railing onto a shallow balcony that Bonnie assured him opened out from the receiving room of Scarlett's suite.

The glass double doors were closed, but Bonnie had told him that Scarlett would not have locked them, for fear of blocking Bonnie's route should she need to return unexpectedly. Only a sheer curtain was drawn across them, and Jonan could dimly make out the scene within. Scarlett was there, her skirts billowing behind her as she paced like a caged animal. Pausing only to confirm that she was alone, Jonan opened the door just wide enough to slip inside, closing it softly behind him.

Scarlett must have been distracted indeed, because she did not immediately notice his entry. Her strides had been taking her away from the window, and he was inside the room before she turned. A single glance was enough to show that unlike him she had not slept since the previous night's misadventures. She was wringing her hands as she paced, and her expression was anguished, her eyes wild and her face pale. Jonan had given some thought to what he wanted to say to her, but all of his careful words fell from his mind once he got a good look at her.

"Scarlett!" he cried involuntarily, starting toward her.

She started violently, her eyes flying to him in shock. "Jonan!" she said, her voice hoarse. He reached her in three quick strides, and took her hands in his. His eyes searched her face anxiously. He had never seen her in such a state.

"What are you doing here?" she asked him faintly. She glanced around, her expression nervous, before returning her gaze to his face. "It's not safe for you to be here. You're supposed to be far away. *How* are you here?" Her momentary panic was suddenly replaced by a familiar shrewd expression as understanding came. She pulled her hands away. "I think you've bewitched Bonnie," she accused. "She can't ever seem to do as she's told when it comes to you."

"It's not fair to blame Bonnie," he said quickly. "Did you really think I would run away and hide, and leave you here to face whatever explosion is coming?"

"I hoped you would," she said earnestly. He shook his head grimly, and her voice turned pleading. "You still can," she urged. "Please, Jonan." His heart twisted at the desperation in her voice. "I can't bear for you to be executed because of me, too."

"Stop saying that," he said firmly. "None of this is because of you."

She turned away from him. "We both know that isn't true. Was it only last night Raldo was saying I have no blood on my hands?" Her voice became choked as she said his name, and she turned suddenly back around, spreading those shapely hands in front of her. "Now they're covered with blood—his blood!" She buried her face in them, her shoulders shaking as she attempted to master herself.

He watched her helplessly for a moment. She seemed to be trying to keep him out with the gesture, but he couldn't stand to do nothing when she was in such distress. He stepped forward, placing his hands tentatively on her shoulders. As most of her dresses seemed to do, this one left her arms and shoulders exposed, and a spark seemed to race into his hands as they touched her skin. She stilled at his touch, but she didn't remove her hands from her face.

"You're wrong, Scarlett," he whispered. "You torture yourself for no reason. No one but you would ever blame any of this on you." His voice became firmer, as did his hold on her shoulders. "And I won't let you get yourself killed doing something dangerous out of your misguided guilt."

She dropped her hands at that, her expression blank. "I don't know what you mean," she said dully.

"Yes you do," he said, unimpressed. He let go of her and stepped back, getting a good look into her eyes. "What are you planning, Scarlett?"

She met his look but didn't immediately answer the question. "Did Bonnie tell you about the ship?"

He nodded. "It seems my king has made a statement," he said dryly. "I'm glad, but the timing is...inflammatory."

"Yes," she agreed shortly. "My father is...let's say displeased."

Jo couldn't resist a snort. "More like murderously enraged, from what Bonnie said."

Scarlett's voice remained steady, but he didn't miss the shiver that ran through her small frame. "She's right. He has become obsessed with maintaining his position, and the trade along with it. And this development, coming on the back of the revolt last night...Jonan, you need to get out of Nohl. It's easy to underestimate his anger, because his actions always seem so calculated. But his smooth manner hides a surprising bloodthirstiness. The execution this morning has done nothing to satisfy his desire for vengeance. When he remembers your existence, I am certain he'll have you killed. The only question is whether he has you tortured for information first."

"If this is supposed to convince me to leave," Jo said grimly, "you're not doing a very good job. From where I stand, everything you just said is all the more reason why I'm not abandoning you to him."

"Jo," she started, her voice once again sounding desperate, but he cut her off.

"I'm willing to go," he said, and she brightened. "I'd prefer to stay and face whatever is coming head on, but if you come with me, I'm willing to leave the city."

Her face fell again at this qualification. "I can't leave, Jo, you know I can't."

He shrugged. "Then I'm not going anywhere."

"What good will it do me for you to die?" she demanded.

"I don't have any intention of dying anytime soon," he retorted.

"Jo," she moaned. "You're not invincible."

"I know I'm not. But neither are you. You're strong Scarlett, but not so strong that you can do this on your own. Tell me, where do you fit into all this? What are you going to do next? Bonnie told me that your father is angry because you refused to lobby the royals for him. How long will he tolerate your refusal before he decides to compel you?"

"All the more reason for you to be safely out of here," she replied. "I shudder to think what he might do to try to compel me. If he found out that I—that I care about your safety..."

"You're not responsible for me, Scarlett," said Jo softly. He moved toward her again, but she took a step back, and he paused.

"I shouldn't have defied him openly," she said after a moment. "I usually handle myself better, but I just...I'll make it right though," she finished, her voice suddenly fierce.

"What does that mean?" Jo asked uneasily. "What are you going to do?"

She didn't meet his eye. "I've told him that I'll do as he asked. I've sent a message requesting Giles to come here to speak with me when he can get away. I can only imagine that the castle is in something of an uproar since that ship came in."

"You're going to cooperate with him after all?" Jo asked, surprised, but attempting to keep the reproach out of his voice.

"No, of course not!" she exclaimed, looking up at him. "That's just what I told my father." She took a deep breath. "I've given it a lot of thought, and I'm going to tell Giles everything. I'm going to ask him to help us."

"You are?" asked Jo, feeling faintly alarmed. "I thought you said it was too big a risk to take, that you weren't sure of him."

She made a fatalistic gesture. "I'm not. But I have to do something. All those slaves who escaped last night...without Raldo to lead, it will be so much harder. And there are still the other camps. My father wants the trade to continue, and he's willing to go to war with Kyona if that's what it takes. He has the ear of the king—he's put a great deal of effort into making sure he does—and the only reason we're not fighting already is that King Siloam is not the most...active of rulers. Getting free rein on policies is one thing. Convincing him to initiate a war is something else entirely.

"Still, this revolt doesn't help the cause—it supports my father's argument that drastic action is needed to maintain the status quo. The king listens to his brother more than anyone. My father isn't wrong that getting my cousins and uncle onside would be critical. That's why I have to try to get Giles to support the Kyonan cause. If he was willing to openly stand against the trade, I don't think King Siloam would go to war to protect it."

Jo listened silently, frowning as he wrapped his head around the dynamics. The idea of Cal having an ally among the royals here was certainly appealing.

"But what if he doesn't take our side?" he asked eventually. "What if you tell him everything and he decides his loyalty is to Balenol's prosperity, regardless of the human cost? Surely it's too big a risk to tell him everything?"

"I won't actually tell him everything," Scarlett said hastily. "Not details about the resistance, like where to find them, or who's in it. Just about my role. That I've been working with the slaves, and that I helped with the uprising at the camp."

"I don't like the sound of that," said Jonan, his frown deepening. "It sounds like you're trying to take all of the risk on yourself."

"Of course I am," said Scarlett. "It's only right since I'm the one deciding to divulge information. This way if it turns out to be a mistake, I won't have utterly betrayed everyone. It will be clear that I know more than I've said, of course." She swallowed hard, and her confident tone suddenly seemed a bit forced. "But if it came to the worst, I *think* Giles would protect me from the more...barbaric methods of trying to find out what I know."

For a moment Jo stood frozen, then he lunged forward, seizing her arms roughly. "You think? Scarlett, if there's even the slimmest chance someone would try to beat information out of you, then that's more than enough reason to abandon this plan altogether. Do you think I'll let you take that risk?"

"It's not up to you," she said firmly.

"Think about it Scarlett," said Jo, starting to feel desperate. "No matter how much you try to limit what you say, if Giles doesn't agree to help, you could still have done a lot of damage.

You will have put yourself in danger for no benefit to the resistance. We might be so close to a breakthrough, with Kyona finally willing to fight back—it's hardly the time to throw away everything you've worked for."

"If we go to war over this, a lot more people will be put in danger," she retorted. "And maybe this is the perfect time to reveal my involvement. Even if he doesn't want to help, Giles won't wish to harm me, but it's very possible he'll feel honor-bound to pass on my information to his father, and to the king. And if Kyona is bent on aggression, then in order to avert war, King Siloam will have to somehow manage to both mollify your king, and placate his own people. And if there's one thing I know about King Siloam, it's that he doesn't like being put in a difficult situation. He'd be only too glad to have a neat solution presented to him."

Jo frowned, maintaining his grip on her arms. "I don't follow. What's this neat solution?"

She shrugged, not meeting his eyes. "Your king will want amnesty for his people, but the Balenans are already calling for blood over this uprising. Executing a high profile Balenan traitor could answer both purposes. I could offer myself in exchange for a blind eye toward the resistance. Maybe even an official pardon, if your king has King Siloam scared enough." She smiled weakly, the gesture not reaching her eyes. "Honestly, I think my father will be angry enough when he finds out what I've been doing that even he would support that solution."

It took several long seconds for the full import of her words to crash down on Jonan's consciousness, and when it did the idea filled him with so much rage that he was momentarily unable to speak. His hands tightened convulsively on Scarlett's arms, his whole body shaking from the tension in his muscles. The strain passed through him into Scarlett with a ripple, and he could feel a tremble go through her.

"Solution?" he choked out at last. "That's not a solution. That's insanity. And you tell me I take too many risks? Listen to me, Scarlett—I will not allow any part of that to happen."

She still wouldn't look him in the eye. "It's not in your power to prevent it, Jonan."

He was breathing hard, her words hitting uncomfortably close to home. He was out of his depth when it came to manipulating the dynamics of the Balenan power structure, and he knew it. He had no idea whether Scarlett was right, and whether her execution or even violent interrogation was a likely outcome of her revealing her double life to Prince Giles. He hadn't coveted Cal's crown, had in fact been immeasurably relieved when the responsibility had been taken away from him. But never had he so desperately wished for the kind of power that a royal position would bring. Surely as king he would at least have had the ability to protect the people he cared about.

"But it's in your power," he said. "There's absolutely no reason for you to tell anyone anything about your role. I won't let you take the risk."

"You can't stop me," she said, her calmness terrifying him more than impassioned protestations would have done.

"Can't I?" he growled. He was still shaking with anger at the thought of Scarlett being executed, but he took a deep breath, attempting to master himself. He didn't want her to think his anger was directed at her. He didn't let go of her, but he relaxed his muscles with an effort. The reduced tension seemed to soften her belligerence, and she looked up at him at last, her expression vulnerable.

"I don't want anyone else to suffer because of me, Jo," she whispered.

"And you think no one would suffer if you were tortured and killed?" he demanded fiercely.

She shrugged. "My cousins would be upset, my aunt even

more so. But they've already lost me—when my father took me away and I decided to live this double life, and turn Lady Wrendal into nothing more than a part. Bonnie would be hit hard, but at least she could run to the jungle, and stop living on the knife's edge with me. My father would only regret my loss for the unexploited opportunities, but that's hardly going to convince me to be cautious."

"Your cousins—Bonnie—your father?" Jo choked out. "What about me? Do you think I wouldn't care? I will lose my own head before I let you go under that blade."

"Well maybe I feel the same way," said Scarlett with spirit. "You're allowed to risk your life for my sake, but I'm not allowed to do the same?"

"It's different—" Jo started, but she glared him down.

"Yes, it's different," she agreed. "I have much more reason to want to protect you, because I'm the one who pulled you into this dangerous game. You have no reason to risk your life for me. You don't know me—*I* don't even know who I am anymore!"

He pulled her against him in a fierce gesture, his heart hammering as if he had been running instead of standing still. "I know exactly who you are," he said, his voice a low and passionate growl. "And I would risk anything to protect you."

She looked up at him, her eyes suddenly swimming, their expression full of the beautiful blend of strength and vulnerability that characterized her. He could see her anguish, but he could also see warmth at his words, a desperate hope and longing at the idea of being worth so much to someone. All at once, and without thinking it through, he leaned down and touched his lips to hers.

She responded with equal abandon, leaning into him and returning his kiss with a passion that was almost frenzied. He matched her instantly, letting go of her arms so that he could wind his own around her waist, holding her firmly against his chest. She threw her arms around his neck, and the feel of her skin on his sent fire through his body. One of his hands found its way up her back to touch the skin between her shoulder blades, and she shivered at the contact, pressing even closer.

They were so lost in their embrace that neither one of them heard the door into the passageway open, or saw the imposing figure that appeared in the doorway. But they could hardly fail to hear Lord Wrendal's infuriated roar as it thundered over them.

"WHAT IS THIS?!"

CHAPTER TWENTY-TWO

Jo and Scarlett broke apart, gasping. Scarlett tried to pull away, but Jo held fast for a moment, trying to shield her with his arms. One look at her father's face, and he changed positions in a flash, placing her behind him. In the moments after Lord Wrendal's exclamation, during which the nobleman seemed frozen in shock, Jo realized that the Overseer had not come to Scarlett's suite alone.

Prince Giles stood slightly behind his uncle, clearly having come more quickly than expected in response to Scarlett's summons. The sight before him seemed to have broken through his princely reserve, and he stared at them with undisguised astonishment.

Lord Wrendal recovered from his stupefaction all too quickly. He strode forward into the room, death on his face, and Jonan stepped up to meet him, his own eyes blazing. He was humming with energy from the stolen kiss, and he felt not the smallest stirring of fear as he faced off the older man.

"You dog," choked out Lord Wrendal, his eyes rolling madly. "I will kill you where you stand."

"You can try," said Jonan smoothly, planting his feet firmly.

But Lord Wrendal was quicker than he looked. Before Jonan knew what he was about, the Overseer's hand had shot out and seized Jonan around the neck. He squeezed with a surprisingly strong grip, and stars burst before Jo's vision.

"Father, no! Stop!" screamed Scarlett, throwing herself into the fray and trying to prize Lord Wrendal's hand away.

"Get back, Scarlett," Jo choked, but she ignored him. He pulled his hand away from the hold on his throat, curling it into a fist and summoning every ounce of fading energy. With a supreme effort, he pulled his arm back and punched, sinking his fist into Lord Wrendal's middle.

The older man grunted at the impact, falling back a step and releasing his hold on Jo's throat. Jo drew deep gasping breaths, raising his fists ready to defend himself further, even as he attempted to maneuver Scarlett behind him again.

"You will die for this," promised Lord Wrendal, pulling his sword from its sheath at his side.

"No!" Scarlett cried, throwing herself in between them, to Jo's alarm. He grabbed her arm, trying to pull her back, but she shook him off. "You will not kill him!" she shouted at her father.

"How dare you defy me!" he yelled, spittle flying from his mouth, the look in his eyes more manic than ever. "You dishonor me! You may have a beautiful face, but you are as common as your mother was. At least she had virtue—even she would be ashamed to see how loose her daughter has become."

Scarlett fell back a step as if slapped, even as Jo surged forward. He felt his blood boil at the insult to Scarlett, and he raised his fists, heedless of the blade in the Overseer's hands. Before he could do more than let out a furious growl, a flicker of movement behind Lord Wrendal caught his eye. Prince Giles, up until now suspended by his amazement, had stepped forward also, his pleasant features tightened in anger.

Jo didn't wait to see who the anger was for. Still fueled by his rage and not thinking clearly, he whipped out his dagger, wanting nothing more than to kill the monster in front of him. But a knife was a poor match for a sword, wielded by someone who had actually been trained in its use. With a flick of his wrist, the nobleman sent Jo's blade flying across the room.

Scarlett again ran forward with a cry, and Jonan tasted fear for the first time as she hurled herself at her father. But enraged as he was, Lord Wrendal still retained enough sense not to run his daughter through. He seized her with his free hand, his voice shaking with anger.

"How dare you? Here I have an uprising on my hands, and all you can do is debase yourself with this worthless slave?"

"He's not a slave," she gasped out. "And he's worth a hundred times what you are to me. I won't let you kill him!"

Lord Wrendal released Scarlett, only to strike her across the face with the back of his hand. She reeled under the impact.

"See here!" shouted the prince, his voice outraged as he stepped forward, but Jonan could barely see him through the red haze that had filled his vision.

"Don't touch her!" he bellowed, just as a shout sounded from the doorway. Evidently Lord Wrendal's lackeys were in the house, and the soldiers had come to investigate the noise. Jonan ignored them, throwing himself at Lord Wrendal once again.

But the Overseer seemed to have regained control of himself. He lowered his sword, and at a quick command from him, a soldier surged forward, intercepting Jonan. Jo broke free, but another soldier quickly stepped up to help. It took three of them to subdue him, and even then they did so with difficulty. He didn't even look at them, his every nerve still screaming for Lord Wrendal's blood.

The nobleman watched the struggle silently, his face still furious, but his violence contained for now. He looked away only when addressed by a smooth, angry voice.

"You go too far, Uncle." Prince Giles had gone to stand next to Scarlett, his hand resting on her shoulder in a gesture both protective and restraining.

"I believe I have autonomy in my own household, Your Highness," said Lord Wrendal, the thin layer of respect in his tone barely concealing a threat. He turned to the soldiers. "Get him out of my sight."

"No!" Scarlett broke free of her cousin, running forward and attempting to pull one of the soldiers off Jonan. The man was unmoving in response to her efforts, but he seemed unwilling to physically restrain her without specific direction.

"It's all right, Scarlett," said Jonan quickly. "I'll be all right. There's no reason for you to get involved." His eyes bored into hers, willing her to read their silent message. *Don't do anything rash.*

"No!" She shook her head vehemently, reaching past the soldier and clutching at Jonan's shirt. The contact sent a spark into him. "I won't let this happen." She let go and turned back to her cousin. "Giles, do something! Do something!"

The prince frowned in response to her plea, his eyes passing between her, Jonan, and her father as he tried to put all the pieces together. He met Scarlett's impassioned gaze for a measured moment, then turned to Lord Wrendal, his voice calm.

"Surely there is occasion for restraint, Uncle. It must be considered unwise to take any irrevocable action before all the circumstances are fully understood."

"As always, I value your reflections, Your Highness," spat out Lord Wrendal. "But it is me and my household that have been insulted by this boy, not you. I must trust to my own judgment to respond." He took a deep breath, then gave Prince Giles a half-bow that seemed to cost him physical pain. "But certainly there is occasion for restraint, as you say. I can acknowledge that it would be hasty to kill the boy out of hand."

The Overseer turned back to Jonan, an ugly gleam in his eyes. "I have been too lenient with you, Kyonan, too patient." His voice was soft, but it carried around the room in a venomous hum. "I should have resorted long ago to more effective methods to find out what you know. You will die, rest assured. But before I remove that worthless head of yours, you will oblige me by sharing every piece of information it contains."

Jonan glared defiantly back. If Lord Wrendal thought Jo was going to tell him anything, he would soon learn his mistake.

But if he wasn't afraid for himself, Scarlett was clearly terrified for him. "Don't do this, Father!" she begged breathlessly. "I'll —I'll do anything!"

"Scarlett!" said Jo warningly, but he needn't have bothered. Her father was clearly not interested in what she had to say.

"You are my daughter," Lord Wrendal said sharply. "And you will do what I tell you without the need for bargaining." He nodded at the soldiers still restraining Jonan. "Take him to the dungeons. I believe the execution chamber is once again vacated. I will accompany you."

He turned to two other soldiers who were milling around outside the door, obviously taking in the dramatic scene with great interest. "Stay here," he barked, jerking his head back toward Scarlett. "Ensure she doesn't leave her rooms." His gaze lingered on Scarlett's face for a moment. "Watch the windows as well as the doors."

"Is that really necessary?" asked Prince Giles, still frowning.

"I will decide what is necessary within my own house, Your Highness," returned Lord Wrendal. The soldiers moved forward to loosely flank Scarlett, whose eyes were glued to Jonan's form in horror.

He met her gaze unflinchingly, trying to reassure her with

his steadiness. Inside his mind was racing frantically, his senses swimming at the sight of her surrounded by soldiers. He had promised to protect her, and instead he had put her in greater danger than ever with his presumptuous, impulsive behavior.

The soldiers began to drag Jonan out of the room. Lord Wrendal followed behind them, but paused at the threshold. Jo was still close enough to hear the nobleman's voice as he addressed his daughter, his words silkier and more menacing then ever. "I will deal with you later, Scarlett."

"If you touch one hair on her head," Jo growled as soon as Lord Wrendal was back within his line of sight, but Lord Wrendal didn't let him finish. Stepping forward with a furious stride, the nobleman delivered a sharp slap to Jo's face.

"Your presumption is an insult," he hissed, "and I will not countenance it."

He swept off without another word, the soldiers dragging Jo behind him as they descended a grand flight of stairs. They paused in the entryway to allow Lord Wrendal to bark out some orders to his terrified-looking servants, and Jo heard a quick step on the stairs behind him. Turning, he saw Prince Giles making for the front door. The prince slowed his stride as he passed them, his inscrutable gaze resting on Jonan for a brief moment, then he swept out into the night.

As the party passed the front gates, Jo caught sight of Bonnie, her eyes fixed on him in horror. He refused to meet her gaze, fearful of alerting his captors to their connection, but he hoped that she would go straight to Scarlett. He didn't like to think of her alone with only the soldiers and her fears for company.

Rain continued to soak the streets as Jo's escorts dragged him past his own accommodations and through the castle square. Darkness had fallen, but it was not so late that the streets were deserted, and a number of people watched curiously as Jo was hauled into the castle.

Jo had expected to be taken to the dungeons without delay, and was surprised when Lord Wrendal pulled up short in the castle's entryway, bowing low. Jo peered around the Overseer and saw two middle-aged men in richly embroidered clothes, conversing casually with one another as they walked across the space, guards walking in tight formation a short distance behind them.

"Your Majesty, Your Highness," said Lord Wrendal, rising from his bow, and Jo looked again at the men, his interest suddenly roused. He wondered which one was King Siloam, and which one Prince Rupert. He searched for a resemblance on either face to Prince Giles.

The shorter of the two men seemed not to notice Jonan and the soldiers, but the taller one was taking in the whole entourage with a raised eyebrow. Something in his penetrating look made Jo think of Prince Giles, and he decided this must be Prince Rupert.

"Ah, Lord Wrendal," said the other man lazily, acknowledging the Overseer with a gracious gesture. "How go your efforts? I trust you have things well in hand after the recent unpleasantness?"

"As to that, Your Majesty, the matter is most serious," said Lord Wrendal. "I am afraid there will be a great deal of action necessary to respond to the—"

"Yes, yes," said King Siloam, cutting the nobleman off with an unconcerned gesture. "No need to give me the details. I'm sure you will settle everything admirably."

"I will endeavor to do so, Your Majesty," said Lord Wrendal with another bow.

"I felt sure you would, Lord Wrendal," said King Siloam contentedly. "You are always so capable."

Jo blinked in surprise. Could this man really be the king? He had heard King Siloam described as lacking in initiative, but this indolence was beyond anything he had imagined. Surely the king could not be so disinterested in a mass slave revolt that had emptied the largest of the labor camps? Jo could suddenly see why Lord Wrendal had his work cut out for him in trying to convince King Siloam to go to war against Kyona. Jo had never understood how it could come to be that the king had no heir other than his brother, but setting eyes on him, he could readily imagine that King Siloam had just been too lazy to ever provide himself with a wife and children.

The king seemed ready to move on, but Prince Rupert was still looking at Jonan with a hard gaze. "What do we have here, My Lord?" he asked. "Are you punishing one of your slaves again? Some weighty offense, I assume?"

Lord Wrendal hesitated for a moment, and Jo had the distinct impression that he would rather not discuss the matter with the prince. "No, Your Highness," he said at last. "This boy is not one of my slaves. He broke into my house tonight and was discovered lurking in a private room."

Jo looked at his captor shrewdly at this truncated version of events. Lord Wrendal was definitely reluctant to discuss it.

"Broke in?" repeated King Siloam in mild surprise. "That is certainly shocking. The boy should undoubtedly be whipped."

"If Your Majesty will permit," said Lord Wrendal smoothly, "the matter is a little more serious than that. It is my intention to order the boy's execution. It would not do for these Kyonans to think they can force entry into our homes and make off with our possessions without serious consequence."

"Indeed it would not," said the king, evidently struck by this view of the matter. "I am sure you are right Lord Wrendal. You will do as you see fit." Jonan pursed his lips in disgust. Clearly the Overseer had a great deal of power and very little accountability.

"Yes, Your Majesty," agreed the man himself, with a final

bow. The king began to move away. Prince Rupert followed his brother without comment, but not before throwing another searching look over the whole group. Jonan met his gaze squarely, feeling that he had nothing to lose, after all. He found the whole dynamics of the royal circle more interesting than he would ever have expected. He only wished there was a way to communicate his discoveries to Cal. But at this stage, it would be nothing short of miraculous if he ever saw Cal again. The thought sent a sharp pang through him, its potency taking him by surprise.

Once the royal pair were out of sight, Lord Wrendal led the soldiers down a passageway that became increasingly darker and narrower. They descended a long narrow flight of stairs, the air becoming suffocatingly close.

It was difficult to keep any sense of direction, but remembering the words of the Kyonan in the square that morning, Jonan realized that by the time they reached the dungeons they were indeed directly below the castle courtyard. He was dragged to the furthest cell and thrown in without ceremony. He leaped to his feet instantly, wheeling around to find Lord Wrendal watching him through the bars, a dangerous glint in his eyes.

"I hope these accommodations are as much to your liking as the previous ones I so generously gave you," said the nobleman quietly. Jo glared silently back. "I think I will let you settle in for a day or two," Lord Wrendal continued. "You will want to be well rested for our next interview."

"I'm not going to tell you anything," Jo spat. "No matter what you do to me."

"We'll see about that," said Lord Wrendal, his voice soft. He gave a mirthless laugh. "What makes you think I'm going to do anything to you? I'm sure you will be much more communicative if it is not you personally who will suffer for your silence."

Jo's breath caught involuntarily as he took the Overseer's meaning.

"You wouldn't," he said reflexively. "She's your own daughter."

"Wouldn't I?" said Lord Wrendal, his voice grim. "As you say, she is my daughter. She exists to serve my purposes."

Jo threw himself against the bars in impotent fury. "I don't believe you," he shouted, but his words lacked conviction, and his tormentor clearly knew it. "You think you can manipulate her with your stupid schemes," Jonan growled. "But she's much stronger than you think. She was never going to marry her cousin."

A flash of annoyance passed across the nobleman's face. "Well she has certainly lost any opportunity to do so now that she has humiliated herself so disgustingly in front of him," he snapped. But a moment later his features cleared, and he took a deep breath. "No matter," he said lightly. "There are other 'schemes', as you put it." His look turned calculating. "Perhaps I can make good use of her apparent preference for your kind."

Jonan ignored the insult in the way the Overseer said the last two words, feeling suddenly uneasy. "What does that mean?" he demanded.

But Lord Wrendal merely smiled. "I don't think I'll trouble you with my plans," he said calmly. "I will see how things unfold. It may be that I am unable to keep our rendezvous, which would be most disappointing to us both, I'm sure. But I am confident that my assistant here will be happy to stand in for me."

He nodded to one of the soldiers standing nearby, and Jonan realized without surprise that it was the man he had first challenged in the square the day of his arrival. The soldier gave a grim smile, cracking his knuckles meaningfully. Jo ignored him.

"You think you're better than her," he spat at the Overseer. "But she is smarter, stronger and braver than you'll ever be."

Lord Wrendal dismissed his declaration with a lazy wave of his hand. "Yes, one of her more useful qualities is the fact that young men seem to be universally convinced of her worth. You're hardly the first eager young fool to be blinded by beauty." His voice turned pensive. "The real mystery is how *you* managed to ensnare *her*." He sighed. "I should never have let her aunt raise her. She has turned out with too much of her mother in her—hardly a desirable situation."

"Surely you're not admitting to a mistake, *My Lord*," said Jonan insultingly. "Don't tell me that even you were once blinded by beauty."

Lord Wrendal regarded him in surprise for a moment. "So you've been inquiring into my history, have you? You're smarter than I gave you credit for. But you are mistaken. I did not marry Violet for her beauty any more than for love." He said the word humorously, as though the very concept of it was amusing. "Although her beauty has proved most useful in posterity. No, I married her for the same reason anyone does anything—for what it could gain me. She and her sister were close, and her sister had defied all convention and married a prince. That connection has been more than useful enough to justify overcoming my natural distaste for allying myself to a commoner."

He frowned, speaking almost to himself, as if he had forgotten his audience. "It is distressing, however, to discover that her inferior breeding has passed to our daughter. Our son seems to suffer from no such weakness."

Jo suddenly remembered Scarlett's words about having reason to reject the idea that someone could be born less deserving than someone else. He shook his head, amazed by the depth of Lord Wrendal's blindness. He had clearly believed that his wife, who by all accounts had been kind and generous and sweet, had brought no value to their marriage because of her low birth. And he was certainly incapable of valuing the treasure he had in his daughter.

He thought his wisdom infallible, but the cruelty and arrogance of his beliefs had driven his underestimated daughter not only to question the entire premise of the slave trade, but to orchestrate the very resistance that undermined his power and plagued his life. And the very connection to the royals that Lord Wrendal had masterminded for his own gain opened the door for Scarlett to at least attempt to turn them against her father's interests.

"You are a fool," he said without heat.

He could almost feel sorry for the Overseer, thinking how precious were the blessings he had thrown away in his obsession with power. But then he remembered the shock in Scarlett's eyes and the way her hand had flown to her cheek when her father slapped her, and his face hardened again. No, he had no sympathy for this man.

"If you think I am interested in your opinion of me," responded Lord Wrendal smoothly, "you are even more of an imbecile than I had supposed." He leaned close to the bars, his expression unyielding. "You seem to have a great deal of faith in your luck, young man," he said. "But it will not save you from me. You will tell us what you know, and then you will pass beyond the blade where you can trouble your betters no more. And you can be very certain that you will never set eyes on my daughter again."

With that parting shot, Lord Wrendal turned and strode from the dungeons, his lackeys behind him, leaving Jonan to his thoughts.

CHAPTER TWENTY-THREE

Despite Jo's bold front, his thoughts were bitter indeed. He cursed his own selfish foolishness as vehemently as he knew how. He couldn't regret refusing to run away and leave Scarlett behind, but it was sickening to realize that it probably would have been better for her if he had.

Bonnie had told him that his recklessness was a danger to Scarlett, and Raldo had made him promise to protect her. But still he had impetuously insisted on running into danger, without thought of the consequences for others. He had known the risk he took in going into Lord Wrendal's house. Scarlett had warned him repeatedly about how her father would respond if he so much as heard Jonan use her name, but Jo hadn't even taken the precaution of locking the door before putting his arms around her.

Not that he'd intended to put his arms around her. He had certainly not gone to her suite with any thought of kissing her in his mind. It had just happened—another example of his impulsiveness getting the better of him. But when she'd looked up at him like that, her mesmerizing eyes seeming to beg him to save her from the danger that surrounded her, even while her firm words insisted she would not be deterred from taking the risk...

But it was better not to think about it right now. He was in enough of a mess already, and so was she. It wouldn't help either of them for him to dwell on the way her lips had responded so passionately to his, or how confidingly she had leaned into him, as though all she wanted was to be near him...he shook his head, trying to focus.

He found that he had no fear about his own danger. Somehow the matter seemed unimportant. It was Scarlett he feared for, and Bonnie, and Cody, and all the others in the jungle. At least Lord Wrendal still seemed unaware of either Scarlett's or his connection to the resistance. He wished he could believe that Lord Wrendal was bluffing when he threatened to harm Scarlett in order to get Jonan to talk.

But remembering the manic glint in the nobleman's eyes when he had discovered his daughter in Jo's arms, and the deepseated fear of her father that Scarlett had demonstrated the night of the riot, he could hold onto no such certainty. What Lord Wrendal meant by his new schemes for Scarlett, Jo couldn't guess, but he couldn't imagine that they were anything good.

He had plenty of time to berate himself as the long night stretched out. After having slept most of the day, he wasn't nearly tired enough to drift off on the hard stone floor, and he had nothing to do but fret in the darkness. His fears chased each other around inside his head until he felt like he would go mad. In the humid climate, the cell wasn't as cold as he had imagined all dungeons would be, but the air was dank, and he had the uncomfortable feeling of being slowly suffocated.

He thought of all the escaped slaves being sheltered in the jungle, and tried for the hundredth time to figure out how the curse could be broken so that they could return to their homeland. But no amount of mental strain could suggest to him a logical reason why mountain magic would create a barrier across the ocean. As the hours crept by, he sank into listlessness, recognizing at last his own arrogance in thinking he could somehow find the key.

And always his thoughts circled back around to Scarlett. What was she thinking at this moment? He knew her well enough to be sure she would be afraid for him, and would blame herself. But perhaps she was also angry with him—after all, she had constantly warned him to be cautious, and his recklessness had finally landed them in just the situation she had feared. Yet he couldn't help but wonder—was she thinking of him in other ways as well? Did she keep reliving their kiss as he did, fire racing through him in the darkness at the memory?

He had meant it when he said he would risk anything to protect her, and not knowing where she was or if she was safe was an infinitely worse punishment than being locked in a cell. His anxiety for her was a constant weight in his stomach. Was she still confined to her rooms? At least he could be thankful she wasn't in a damp prison cell, but he couldn't imagine that her lavish surrounds would be bringing her much comfort. What had her father done or said in retribution when he returned to his manor?

Jo could see that Bonnie had been right. Lord Wrendal would not harm Scarlett in a fit of rage. He was too calculating for that. But the thought brought Jo no comfort. Because it was equally clear that the Overseer would not hesitate to sacrifice his daughter if he thought it would best serve his interests.

Although dawn must have eventually begun to creep through the sky, Jo had no way of knowing it had happened. No natural light filtered into the dungeons, and the few torches burning on the walls paid no heed to sun or moon. He began to grow weary, almost weary enough to sleep, but he couldn't still his mind sufficiently to do so. He was by now very hungry, and his thoughts kept drifting without his permission to the meals his mother used to cook on special occasions.

He was thinking inexplicably of Cal, remembering the way they used to explore the seashore as children, and thinking that Scarlett would like the open air of his homeland, when he heard pattering feet.

Looking up, he saw a young Kyonan girl approaching. Her eyes were wide, and she looked skittish. She stopped just outside his cell, and for a moment she just stared at him.

"Hello," said Jo eventually, not getting up from where he sat with his back against the back wall of the cell. She jumped slightly at the greeting, and didn't respond.

"Is it day out there yet?" Jo tried again, and she nodded tentatively. "I don't suppose you've brought me breakfast?" Jo suggested hopefully.

The girl shook her head slowly. "No," she said, her voice faint. "I don't—I don't think they're going to send you any food."

Jo nodded. It wasn't exactly a surprise. "Why are you here?" he prompted, and the girl started.

"Oh. I came to bring you this." She held something out between the bars.

Jo pushed off the wall and approached her, curious. The object she held was a small metal implement, of a type he had never seen before. He picked it up eagerly, wondering if the resistance had sent this girl, but a close examination left him disappointed. It was too blunt to use as a weapon, and too large to be any good for picking locks.

"What do I do with it?" he asked blankly.

"You add your name to the wall," she said, as if it was obvious. "I mean, if you want to. I suppose you don't have to."

"What wall?" he asked slowly.

She nodded at a side wall of the cell. "That wall." She frowned slightly. "I guess you can't really see very well. Hang on." She shifted a burning torch to a bracket closer to Jo's cell. He turned slowly, not sure he wanted to see what was now revealed in the flickering light. But having looked, he couldn't seem to withdraw his gaze.

Most of the length of the wall was covered from floor to ceiling with markings carved into the stone. Not just markings—names. Each in a different hand, haphazard and disorganized, some in large letters, some small. Some were barely legible, faded with time, others clearly fresh.

"What—?" He turned back to the girl, but she was already gone. Approaching the wall, he examined the letters more closely. His eye was drawn to the last name in the marked length of wall, and his breath caught in his throat.

Raldo.

He remembered now that just before his execution Raldo had said something to the crowd in the square about being proud to add his name to the wall. Jonan hadn't understood, but it had seemed unimportant to pursue the thought at the time. He had been too busy trying to prevent Scarlett from witnessing the coming atrocity. That had been the first time he had held her, the moment he had realized in full force that he would do anything for this girl.

But no. He needed to think about something else. He touched Raldo's name softly, his heart full of his sorrow and gratitude for his friend, and a stinging guilt for how poorly he was keeping his promise to the dead rebel. Looking back over the wall, he realized that he must be looking at the names of every Kyonan who had ever been executed in Nohl, or at least those willing to add their names. Which was probably all of them, because from what Raldo had said, it was a mark of pride. Looking more closely he saw that there were many X markings interspersed among the names. Of course—many slaves wouldn't know how to write their names, but they would still want to leave their mark.

He supposed they might not all have been slaves. Some of the names might be Balenan, he grudgingly admitted to himself. Surely they sometimes executed locals. Thieves, or murderers, or traitors. But that thought brought him back to Scarlett, reminding him of her terrifying backup plan of handing herself in for execution as a traitor in exchange for a pardon for the others in the resistance.

A rush of cold passed over him despite the warm air, and he threw the utensil away with angry force. It hit the far wall of the cell and clattered to the floor. He glared at it, breathing hard. Mark of pride or not, he had no intention of adding his name to the wall. To do so would be to accept that he was going to be executed. And he was determined not to be, whatever Lord Wrendal said about his luck. He had no plan, no concrete thought on how to escape, but he wasn't going to die under that blade. He was going to get out of here, he was going to find Scarlett and protect her from her father, and he was going to break the curse so his countrymen could go home. If Raldo's was the last name to ever be added to this wall, it would be a fitting legacy for the brave and selfless rebel.

Oh, and one more thing that he had almost forgotten. Once it was all over, he was going to make Lord Wrendal pay in blood for what he had done—to the slaves, to Raldo, to Kyona at large, and most of all to Scarlett.

These invigorating plans and their accompanying burst of energy sustained Jonan for another hour or two, as he paced fiercely around the cell, dwelling with grim delight on all the bold actions he would take when he was free. There was no denying that his schemes got more and more bloodthirsty the hungrier and more uncomfortable he became. He was just dwelling on various possible punishments for the hated nobleman when his eye caught on the wall of names and a sudden thought occurred to him.

How far back did the tradition go? If this wall really showed the names, or at least marks, of every executed prisoner in Nohl's history, could there be another name he recognized beside Raldo's? He hurried back over to the wall, straining his eyes in the dim light as he followed the expanse of stone to the back corner of the cell. Most of the markings here were too faded to read, clearly having been carved into the stone long years ago.

For a moment Jonan felt disappointed, sure he wouldn't be able to make anything out at all, but as he ran his hand over the wall, he felt a surge of tingling power pass into his fingers, and his heart leaped in excitement. Leaning closer, he saw what he was looking for. He wasn't sure how he had missed it—it was substantially larger than the other names. All the surrounding marks might be illegible, but like on the slave ship, some latent magic seemed to have preserved the one he was looking for. It was faded some, certainly, but he could still make out the letters.

Alben.

He felt a thrill go through him at the name, as though it had been a close friend instead of a long-dead stranger. He touched the marking, and again felt a small burst of power go into him. Although he didn't know what good the name on the wall could do him, he suddenly felt emboldened, as though he was no longer alone in this prison cell. As though he had a friend in the execution chamber with him.

He leaned closer. There was the b with the second circle inside it, just like on the ship and on the self-imposed tattoos of Raldo's people. He touched his thumb to the letter, and gave an involuntary yelp at the strength of the spark that shot into his hand. He stared at the letter. His hand had jolted in his surprise, and he could have sworn the stone rattled a little. Leaning in, he examined the spot. He again put his thumb to it, pushing back and forth. The inner circle of the unusual b definitely wiggled a little bit.

His excitement grew. The circle looked like it was just carved into the stone like all the other marks around it, but could it be possible that it was actually a much deeper cut, grown over with the dust and moss of generations? He tried to pull at it further, but if it was a separate piece of stone, it was firmly wedged.

After a moment's thought, he remembered the item brought by the Kyonan girl. He hastened across the cell to retrieve the dull metal instrument, profoundly grateful that he had thrown it across the cell instead of out of it in his impulsive anger.

He set to work on the letter, the strange power throbbing indescribably at regular intervals. It wasn't the work of a moment, and if it had been a matter of idle curiosity, he wouldn't have had the patience to chip away at it for so long. But as it turned out, he had nothing but time on his hands, and it was anything but idle curiosity. Even though it felt like hours that he worked on it, his sense of excitement only grew as he became more captivated by his unformed hope about what he might find inside.

The circle of stone became looser and looser as he whittled away at the detritus that had built up in the cracks. Eventually, with a grinding scrape, the stone came loose in a short cylinder that he was able to pull out. With a rush of excitement, he saw a dark cavity behind. The hole wasn't big enough for his hand to fit through, of course, but he was able to reach a finger back and feel around. His questing touch hit something round and rough. He hooked his finger around it and pulled, causing it to shoot out of the hole and clatter to the ground.

Jo stared at the object, transfixed. It was a rough unremarkable-looking gray rock about the size of a coin, though not nearly as perfectly round. Jonan's heart seemed to stop for a moment before speeding up erratically, excitement like he had never known coursing through him. The impossible nature of his discovery should have filled him with disbelief, but instead he felt a curious satisfaction, as though he had been certain all along that he would reach this moment.

Alben had hidden his mountain rock talisman here before his execution. And Jonan, thrown without ceremony into the same execution chamber generations later, had found it.

CHAPTER TWENTY-FOUR

For a moment he just stared at the rock, mesmerized despite its ordinary appearance. Then he reached for it with his free hand, feeling a kinship with it, as though it really did belong to him instead of having been a chance discovery. He grasped it firmly, and he had only the barest instant in which to note briefly that it felt unnaturally warm before he staggered back under the onslaught that poured through him.

Images and memories flashed before his sight, seeming to be his own, although he had never seen them before. He was once again inside Alben's mind—he recognized its cadence from his two previous excursions into it, however brief they had been. The images were varied, but they were not a chaotic jumble. On the contrary, they progressed with order and clarity. Feeling the rock squeezed firmly in his hand, it seemed only natural that he should be shown its origin.

In some part of his consciousness, Jonan was still aware of his own mind, aflame with amazement as he watched on. But mostly he was submerged in Alben's self, remembering the dramatic and devastating day his mountain town had been destroyed by a rockslide. He saw the torrent of stone coming and felt the brief flash of certainty that his fourteen years of life were closing, and that within moments he would be passing to his ancestors. He was not alone, there was another boy with him—a contemporary, but not especially a friend. Liam, his name was. The information flashed through his mind and out, inconsequential in that moment of impending fate.

Then his mother appeared from nowhere, and he knew instinctively that her cry of fear was for him, not for herself. Before he understood her intent, she had pushed him out of the way, placing her own body in the path of the oncoming avalanche. He had toppled down a small incline, his momentum carrying Liam with him, the other boy an unintended recipient of his mother's sacrifice. Everything had become blurred as he tumbled, but he had thought he caught a glimpse of a vast dark shape in the sky above, wheeling over the chaos then out of sight.

It had been over in moments after that. Through Alben's eyes, Jo saw the mad scramble back up the fallen rocks, the horror-filled hunt for his mother, the discovery of her body, all life crushed out of it. Jonan saw hands that were not his own reach out from his body and attempt to shift the rock that covered her, his tears falling and anguish in his heart. He couldn't move it, but pieces broke off in his hands. Others appeared, grown men, much stronger than he was. They were able to lift the inanimate instrument of death, although its removal could not benefit his mother now.

He knelt unmoving at her side through the process, his hands still balled into fists around the rubble. It was a strange impulse that prompted him to put some of that rock into his pocket, but then he had always been sentimental. It was only later that he had formed the intention of carrying a piece of the rock around his neck always, a reminder of his mother's last, ultimate, gift to him.

Jo let go of the rock with a gasp, needing a minute to collect his thoughts. As he had hoped, the strange sights stopped immediately. He stared at the talisman, lying innocently on the floor of the prison cell. It was so unremarkable to look at. Was it only because of what he had just—impossibly—seen that he thought he could actually sense the magic emanating from it? He shook his head.

It was unnerving to be inside someone else's mind. Alben had been a person of strong emotion, and Jo felt shaken by the intensity of the feelings he had vicariously experienced. Alben's grief for his mother had mingled with his passion for the mountains and his anguish over the permanent loss of his home. Jonan had enough strong emotions of his own to deal with. He had no need of someone else's burdens to carry too.

But he was not one to be easily overwhelmed, or to shy away from the unusual. If this rock was inclined to magically give him answers, he would lap them up eagerly. He wondered if Alben himself had any suspicion of a connection between the rock and the curse. The very experience Jo was having at that moment seemed conclusive proof that there was mountain magic in the rock, but did Alben know that? Why had he hidden it in the wall of the execution chamber?

Jo grasped the rock again as he wondered, and it responded instantly to the direction of his thoughts. He saw the cell through Alben's eyes. Not much seemed to have changed. There was straw in one corner, a consideration Lord Wrendal did not seem to think necessary in the present day. Jo knew himself to be standing still, next to the wall with the markings, but at the same time he felt Alben's body move as he paced restlessly throughout the space, and he shared the older man's thoughts with an intimacy that felt intrusive...

I⊤ ᴡᴀѕ *hard to accept that this was the end of it all. So many years of fighting, so many slaves freed. They had been so close, or so he had thought. He clutched at his hair as he remembered the terrible events of the day. All those ships, full of Kyonans whom he had himself encouraged to board and sail for home in a desperate bid for freedom. And every one of those ships had gone down. He was haunted by the cries of his drowning kin. Again and again he had returned to the water, pulling as many as he could back toward the shore. He was a strong swimmer, but that didn't account for the fact that he had not tired. On the contrary, he had seemed to get stronger, his strokes more sure, with every repeated rescue.*

But it had not been enough. So many had died that day. And the Balenans had finally gotten their hands on him. He could only hope that those others who had made it to shore had been more fortunate, and had returned safely to their secret haven in the jungle. His throat constricted at the thought of his brave rebel band. They had trusted his leadership so implicitly, and so many had died today under his direction. But how could he have known? It had seemed like the perfect time, like it would have been insane not to have taken advantage of the victory that had just been won against the slave traders by the young Kyonan prince. Cael, was that his name? It was unfamiliar—the prince was only a very young man. He had been born a few years after Alben had been taken by the traders in Argath.

His thoughts turned black as he remembered that day, but he refused to spend his last minutes dwelling on the old betrayal. He had put it behind him, after all. He had found new focus, new energy in dedicating his life to the cause of the Kyonan slaves in Balenol. He had given everything he had toward the destruction of the heinous practice. But he had failed. He could make no sense of the disaster with the ships. How could they all have sunk? How could every single one turn out not to be seaworthy? They had stolen some of the best ships in

Balenol's fleet. It was almost as though there was magic involved. Almost like some curse was at work. He had heard of such things, long ago in his childhood in the mountains, but they seemed out of place here in Nohl.

An old, almost-forgotten longing filled him as he thought of his beloved mountain home, and he felt suddenly weary. He knew his hours were limited, his execution near, and it felt strange to spend any of his last moments in sleep, but he felt that he could not hold it off. He sank onto the straw, confused by his sudden exhaustion, but with no spirit left to fight as sleep instantly claimed him.

He fell at once into a dream, as though it had been waiting impatiently for his arrival. He was back in the mountains, and his heart ached at the familiarity of the clear cold air. He wanted nothing more than to wander through the well-known landscape, to visit his old haunts, but it seemed that was not the purpose of this vision. He had barely taken in his surroundings when a mighty rush filled the air, and he was hit by a gust of wind so strong that it almost blew him over. A dark shape obscured the sun, and he looked up, an involuntary cry of astonishment on his lips. He had heard of these creatures, of course, but only in legends. Never would he have believed he could see such a thing in real life. But then, this wasn't real life. It was merely a dream. Wasn't it?

The dragon regarded him steadily, its eyes calm but commanding in that reptilian face. Its monstrous form was covered in scales, so dark they were almost black, and the talons on the end of its feet were long and lethal. Truly this was not a beast to have as an enemy.

"Greetings, Alben of the mountains," said the dragon. "Or as they now call you, Alben the Liberator."

For a moment Alben just blinked stupidly, unsure how to respond to being thus addressed. Truly this was a strange and unexpected vision. Brought on by the strain of his impending execution, no doubt. But the thought made him frown in confusion. If this was a dream, he shouldn't know it was a dream while he was in it, should he? He shouldn't realize that he wasn't actually in the mountains, but was in fact in the execution chamber in the castle at Nohl.

"Greetings, Mighty Sire," he managed at last, unwilling to offend a dragon, even one appearing in his own subconscious vision.

"You draw near to your ancestors," said the dragon gravely, "and I do not wish to embitter your passing. But once you have gone to them, you will be beyond my reach either to reproach or instruct."

"Reproach?" echoed Alben faintly. He didn't know why he should feel so alarmed—after all, was he not sentenced to death in a matter of hours anyway?

"That rock you wear about your neck," said the beast. "You should not have removed it from the mountains. You have taken hold of a magic you do not understand."

"My rock?" repeated Alben in amazement, reaching down to touch the familiar talisman. "It has magic? But...surely people remove mountain rocks regularly. Do they not have quarries in the south of the mountains, even?"

"The area in the south of the mountains is no concern of mine," said the dragon dismissively. "And had you merely removed a rock from the mountains, I would not engage in speech with you. But that rock comes from the Dragon Realm, and it should not have left that realm."

"Then...the warnings were true?" asked Alben with a sinking feeling.

"Certainly," said the dragon, as calm as ever. "Your people were warned by the other mountain folk not to build their town so far to the north. They were told not to encroach on the Dragon Realm. In fact your town was right on the edge of our lands. Its destruction was inevitable."

"Inevitable?" The memory of his mother's death was fresh even across the intervening years, and Alben felt the briefest stirring of anger, despite the intimidating proportions of his companion. "Do you

mean you caused the rockslide? To punish us for building our town on the edge of your domain?"

"Punish is a word often misapplied by humans," said the dragon pensively. "With 'cause' you come closer to the truth, but still it eludes you. Undoubtedly certain actions have certain effects. Particular outcomes are caused by particular decisions." The creature sighed. "Such complexity," he said. "It would take more years than your lifetime spans to explain it all to your understanding." The words were not said as though to offend, simply as a fact objectively stated.

Alben blinked again, unsure what to make of this cryptic answer.

"Well," he said. "I'm sorry to have violated your rules in taking a rock from your realm. I was not aware of having done anything I should not have."

"Awareness, also, is a concept worthy of contemplation," said the dragon. Suddenly he inclined his head. "But I thank you for your words. And in return I will tell you that I did not wish for the curse that was unleashed as a result." The dragon opened its wings, as though preparing to take off.

"Wait!" said Alben quickly. "Curse? What curse? Is this something to do with the ships?"

But the dragon was already crouching, ready to ascend, and he did not answer the question.

"Farewell, Alben the Liberator. May you find peace with your ancestors."

"Wait!" Alben cried again, but he felt the ground falling away beneath him. For a moment he tumbled out of control, then he seemed to fall into reality with a jolt, his body stretched out on the straw in the execution chamber. For a moment he just lay there, panting. His senses still tingled, and his mind raced. That was no dream. It was a message.

He supposed the stories of dragons in the mountains of his home really were true, but the thought didn't hold much interest for him now. It was this mention of a curse that had caught his attention. He clutched at the rock around his neck in the darkness. It had been a part of him for so long, a symbol of his past. It was horrible to think that it was a stolen treasure, that it might even be part of a curse afflicting his countrymen. But as he squeezed it he couldn't quite believe it. The rock wasn't evil. It couldn't be. It wasn't the first time he had suspected that there was something unnatural about the rock, of course. After all, his chest still carried the scar, and in his memory he could still feel the burn of the rock against his skin when—but he had already determined not to think about that day. Not now.

He let out a growl of frustration. What good was any of this knowledge now, when it was too late for him to pass it on? If the rock was somehow connected with this curse, it should be protected, examined. If only he could entrust it to someone from his rebel band. But he would have no more opportunity to see any of them. He knew that perfectly well.

His eyes, casting around the room hopelessly, fell on the wall with the markings. His mouth set in grim lines. He was familiar with this tradition. Two dozen names had already appeared, along with numerous illiterate marks. His eyes pricked as he read scratches left by those he had known. Too many. And now one more. He would certainly leave his name. He was proud for it to appear alongside those already there.

It was after he had begun to carve into the stone that he had the idea. Where it came from, he didn't know. It seemed a little desperate, a little reckless, but what did he have to lose? For reasons of sentiment as much as for any possible connection with any curse, he recoiled from the idea of his enemies getting their hands on his rock once he was gone. Perhaps if he left it in the wall some friendlier hand would one day find it. Of course, he realized that anyone being held in this chamber would have as little ongoing use for the talisman as he did, but once the idea had occurred to him, it would not be shaken. He would leave it here, and he would trust to fate. It felt like a small act of final rebellion, and he relished it.

And it was his final act. He had accepted that. Many times over the years he had evaded capture in the most unlikely escapes, running one step ahead of death. But he had reached the end at last, and there was nothing to be gained by fighting it. It was hard to accept that this was how it would end, of course, but he knew what was coming. The ignominious march to the blade. The traditional offer of the last request, insulting in its futility.

There were things he wanted, many things. But nothing these Balenan monsters could give him. For a moment the thought distracted him as he continued to work at the wall. What did he most want, if any request were possible?

The question was easy, the answer rising instantly before his eyes in a vision of a beautiful young face, sweet and open and full of laughter as she had been before the slavers got her.

Marine.

In all he had seen, in all he had endured, no day had been worse than the day she had died, taken irrevocably from him by the evil and cruelty of this life. Or at least, it had seemed irrevocable at the time. No doubt then, when he had been barely a man, more than two decades would have seemed an immeasurable time to live without her, and the age of forty would have seemed incredibly old. But now he was here, the years didn't seem so long, not really. Had he changed so much? Not enough to forget her, that was certain. In his heart he felt young still—why else would his very being reject the idea of death so strongly?

But the dragon had talked of peace with his ancestors. Marine had gone before him, but he hadn't taken so long, really. Surely she would tarry for him this long. Surely she would be waiting.

After all, he could not truly be sorry that she had been spared enduring two more decades of this life. He was strong. The years of struggle, bitter as they had been, had not warped him, had never broken his spirit. But she was not made for this toil and suffering. In the year she had spent in slavery, he had watched, helpless, as she grew weaker. Time and time again he had done all he could to shield her, but still she had weakened, even as he had grown inexplicably stronger. He had seen it in her eyes that day—that she had given up, that she had been unwilling to keep fighting—and it had broken his heart. But perhaps she had been wise after all.

He paused when he finished his labor with the wall, satisfied with his effort. It was strange to think of taking off the talisman. He had not done so since he had fashioned the rock into a necklace, so soon after his mother's death. But he would have no need of it now.

Gone was the frenzied feeling of failure. Somehow peace had stolen in and taken its place. He thought again of Marine as he began to slip the leather thong off his neck. He had no need of any last request. All would be well.

AGAIN JONAN LET GO of the rock, his steps reeling dizzyingly as he tried to process his return to reality. He realized that there were tears in his eyes, and he dashed them away with an arm that shook. The room around him looked strange for its very similarity to the sight Alben had seen as he awaited his execution here.

Much of what he had just witnessed he had already known, at least in summary, but it was somehow vastly different to see it through Alben's eyes. The dream vision with the dragon had been incredible, and was certainly something that no one else could have discovered from Alben in the short time between its occurrence and Alben's death.

Amazingly, the dragon had been familiar not because of Alben's consciousness but because of Jo's own experience. He had no trouble recognizing Qadir from their previous encounter in Kyona's mountains. The mighty beast was difficult to forget for his own sake, but in any event Jo was unlikely to forget the dragon who had shattered his world by revealing that the parents who had raised him were not his blood, and that it was Cal, not Jo, who was descended from Kyona's kings.

At least on that occasion he had been frank. Jonan couldn't help but sympathize with Alben's frustration and confusion. It was so like the dragon-ruler, Jo reflected, to go to such great lengths to communicate with Alben, only to give questions instead of answers. In Jo's limited experience, dragons were almost invariably cryptic.

But at least his guess had been confirmed. Alben's mountain rock did have something to do with the curse. Jo briefly considered whether he should destroy it in the hope that it would end the curse, but he quickly rejected the idea. It would be rash to do anything so irreversible without fully understanding what he was dealing with. Alben had been convinced it wasn't evil, after all.

Jo wasn't ready to delve into any more unsettling visions, so at first he kept his hand off the rock. But looking at it more closely, he realized that a small hole was drilled into it. He knew from his vision into Alben's mind that its original bearer had threaded it onto a leather thong to turn it into a necklace. The leather had obviously not survived the intervening years, but Jo suddenly realized that he didn't need it. He slipped off the chain he had worn around his neck since the night he left his hometown, passing the thin cool metal through the hole in the unnaturally warm rock.

As he placed the chain back around his neck, he felt an empowering sense of rightness. When he had first worn the necklace, with the Kyonan royal signet ring suspended on it, it had felt like the chains of a slave, weighing him down with a burden he didn't want but couldn't fight. But the rock felt comfortable, like it belonged there, like it was supposed to be his. He couldn't help but feel that this was the reason he had kept the silver chain, had worn it empty all this time. He touched the rock briefly. He was determined not to betray Alben's trust in the unknown future finder of the talisman.

Alben had thought that anyone who found the rock in this room would be destined for execution the same as he had been. But Jonan was more determined now than ever to cheat the death the Overseer had planned for him. There was no peaceful acceptance in his heart, no wistful expectation of reunion with departed loved ones. His veins throbbed with life, and his heart and mind were full of a face that was no less precious to him than Marine's had been to Alben, one that hid an incredible strength behind its beauty.

Thoughts of Scarlett cleared the last of the fog from Jonan's mind, and he squared his shoulders. She was not going to die tragically before her time, and neither was he. After all, such an eventuality would frustrate his intention of taking her in his arms and kissing her again, someplace where her blasted father couldn't interrupt them.

But first he had to get out of here. No sooner had he turned his mind to the question than he again heard the sound of approaching footsteps. He hastily replaced the loose piece of wall, thinking that it would be as well not to let anyone know about the hiding place. Then he tucked the chain and its new pendant under his tunic, hiding the mountain rock from sight. He was relieved to find that contact with the skin of his chest didn't set off the startling sequence of memories.

He settled himself against the wall, trying to look nonchalant. But his mind was racing, wondering who could be approaching. It was surely not someone coming to take him for execution. Wasn't there first supposed to be a couple of days of starving him out followed by barbaric attempts to extract information from him via torture? Perhaps Lord Wrendal had decided to move the program forward slightly, or perhaps that bloodthirsty soldier of his was too eager to pay Jo a visit to wait on his master.

But it was neither of those figures that suddenly came into view. And as much as he had improved in his ability to play a part, Jonan couldn't quite hide his surprise at the identity of his visitor.

CHAPTER TWENTY-FIVE

For a moment the two men regarded each other silently. It was Jonan who spoke first.

"Your Highness," he said blankly. "How kind of you to visit me."

"I think we can dispense with the playacting," said Prince Giles dryly. "You must realize I didn't come here to fence with you."

"Must I? Honestly, I don't have any idea what you did come here for," Jo said reasonably.

"I came here," said Prince Giles, his tone crisp, "to better familiarize myself with the man whom my cousin is apparently willing to risk her safety in order to embrace."

Jonan winced at the prince's words. The idea of Scarlett in danger because of him brought back all his distress.

"That wasn't exactly planned by either one of us," he admitted. "I went there to talk to her. But we just sort of...got caught up in the moment."

The prince didn't respond, just looked at Jonan with raised eyebrows. He sustained the expression for so long that Jo began to feel nettled.

"What's it to you, anyway, Your Highness?" he asked tartly. "Don't tell me she was wrong and you were hoping to marry her after all?"

"Of course not," said Prince Giles sharply. "She's a sister to me. And for that very reason, I have a great interest in anyone who aspires to be close to her. Especially anyone who has the capacity to place her in real danger by his very presence in her life."

"So you realize that her father is a danger to her?" asked Jonan quickly. The prince didn't answer straight away, and when he eventually spoke, Jonan had the impression that he was choosing his words with care.

"I didn't say that."

Jonan scowled. "Of course not." He spread his arms wide, still maintaining his seated position against the wall. "Well, you came to have a look—here I am. What do you think? Still mystified by your cousin's 'ill breeding' in allowing such a curiosity to come near her?"

Prince Giles didn't rise to the bait, his expression calm and thoughtful as he looked Jonan over. "I suppose I do have to acknowledge that she allowed it," he said at last, almost to himself.

Jo stiffened as he caught the prince's meaning. "Of course she did! Are you suggesting I accosted her? I'm sure it's a more convenient explanation for your ordered world, but I would never do such a thing!" Jo found himself breathing hard, infuriated at the thought of someone embracing Scarlett against her will. "And just let anyone try," he added fiercely, for good measure.

"It's no good becoming self-righteous," said Prince Giles mildly. "I don't know you, or what kind of man you are. I have no reason to trust your integrity."

"No, I realize you don't know me," shot back Jo, "but if you have as much respect for Scarlett as I thought you did, maybe you should have more faith in her judgment. Ask her—I think you'll find she trusts me."

Prince Giles regarded him for a long moment, his expression unimpressed. "If you are so reasonable, you should be able to consider the matter from the point of view of Scarlett's family."

"If you think I'll see eye to eye with Lord Wrendal on anything," said Jo tightly, "then you couldn't be more right when you say that you don't know what kind of man I am."

The prince sighed, looking suddenly long-suffering. "Do you have any sisters, Jonan?" he asked wearily.

Jo blinked, taken aback by the sudden change of topic. "No," he said blankly.

Prince Giles sighed again. "You are fortunate. They're maddening creatures. You spend your whole childhood wanting to box their ears, then inexplicably spend your whole adulthood wanting to protect them from harm."

Jo coughed, trying to suppress a smile at the prince's harried expression.

"I think I have as strong a protective brotherly instinct as the next man," Prince Giles continued. "I came to Scarlett's house last night, in response to an urgent summons that I won't deny filled me with concern. When I discovered her, despite the hour, being passionately embraced in her rooms by a largely unknown young man, one who has every reason to want to do an injury not just to her father but to our people in general..." He gave Jonan a hard look. "I'll admit to some sympathy with my uncle's desire to run you through."

Jonan felt a slight flush rise up his neck. When the matter was put to him like that... "The whole situation was my fault, not hers," he said quickly. "It wouldn't be the first time my impulsiveness got me into trouble. But I would never mean her any harm." He hesitated. "I suppose you don't trust my word, but it's still true that I did go there to talk to her, and that was the first and only time I'd ever been anywhere near her rooms."

Prince Giles said nothing, his gaze seeming to assess Jonan, and Jo's voice darkened. "I can be reasonable enough to understand your instinct to rip into me. But if you tell me you had any sympathy with Lord Wrendal's instinct to make insulting remarks about Scarlett's virtue, and to strike her across the face, then I have nothing more to say to you."

"No," said the prince quickly, his own voice turning hard. "Of course I didn't. I was as outraged as you were."

Jo remained silent, raising an incredulous eyebrow. Prince Giles could say what he liked, but Jo had been there.

The prince smiled in amusement, as though reading his mind. "You are thinking that if I was really angry at my uncle's behavior, I should have attempted to punish him with violence at the time, as you did. But how successful was that approach, Jonan? I am not one to lose my head, and there are much more effective ways of handling conflict."

Jo raised his eyebrows at the euphemism, and the prince seemed to realize he had chosen his words poorly. With the hint of a grimace, he continued quickly.

"The fact that I do not openly challenge my uncle doesn't mean that I agree with him, or that I trust him. You said before that he is a danger to Scarlett." Prince Giles hesitated. "I can't deny that as her blood father, he has the right to maintain her under the protection of his household. But I have never been comfortable with his decision to so suddenly remove Scarlett from our family. I don't entirely understand his machinations, but I do not think she has ever been happy in his home. And I have been surprised—I may even say dismayed—by the changes I have observed in her since she left us."

Jo stared at the prince, struck by this comment. He had never before contemplated it, but if Scarlett had been the warm and engaging self Jo knew until her father took her away, then her adoptive family would be confused and alarmed by her behavior in playing the part of the haughty Lady Wrendal. He suddenly understood her comment the night before about her aunt and cousins having already lost her. It had never occurred to him before now that her sacrifice had involved more than herself.

"I have on a number of occasions witnessed conduct toward her by her father that has made me uneasy, to say the least," the prince was continuing. His voice turned hard. "But never open violence like last night." He met Jonan's look. "I *was* angry, whatever you might think. I still am. But it doesn't mean I have to behave impulsively. I don't believe I've ever been called reckless."

Jo regarded him in silence for a long moment. "No," he said at last, "I've never heard Scarlett call you reckless. She did say you were stubborn even as a child." He smiled slightly. "I believe her words were 'stubborn as a mule'. And she said you have a will of iron. But she never accused you of being reckless." His tone turned rueful. "She reserved that for me."

The prince stared at him, surprise written clearly on his face. For a moment Jonan wondered if he had gone too far in repeating these personal details about the royal, but Prince Giles didn't look angry.

"She said that to you?" he asked. "She spoke to you so casually about our childhood?" He gave Jonan a long look. "You really have become close, it seems."

Jo reflected that you couldn't get much closer than the way he and Scarlett had been pressed against each other in the embrace in which the prince had discovered them the night before. But he kept his peace, thinking such an observation would be unhelpfully inflammatory.

"I told you, she trusts me," he said instead with a shrug. "Much as you might not want to believe it. Ask her."

Prince Giles frowned, his handsome features creasing, but said nothing.

"Why did you come here, anyway?" asked Jo curiously. "Why did you tell me all this?"

The prince was still frowning. "I suppose I hoped that if I was frank with you, you might return the courtesy."

Jo's expression instantly became guarded, and he could see from the other man's sigh that he hadn't missed it. "Frank about what?" Jo asked cautiously, trying not to betray his hand. "I don't know what Scarlett told you, but—"

"She hasn't told me anything," said the prince heavily. "She hasn't had the chance. If I had realized that it would be my only opportunity to speak with her about the matter, I would not have left her house in such a hurry last night. I had intended to return first thing this morning to talk with her, but it was futile."

"What do you mean?" asked Jo quickly. "Where is she?"

Prince Giles shrugged. "I don't know."

"What?" Jo surged to his feet, approaching the bars with quick strides. "What do you mean, you don't know?"

"Exactly that," said the prince, raising an eyebrow. "Her father has clearly been at great pains to prevent her from discussing last night's events with anyone, especially me. She is not at her home. I have been there repeatedly—I even went to the extent of exploring the building while I knew my uncle to be here at the castle. I'm not sure where he has taken her. He insists that he merely wishes to ensure her safety after her rooms were broken into last night."

The prince's tone was dry. "The explanation seems to satisfy most people, but unlike me they did not have the...benefit of witnessing the precise nature of the 'break in' that happened."

Jo ignored the accusatory note in the prince's voice, starting to pace back and forth in the confined space. "I don't like this," he said uneasily. "What has he done to her? She could be in trouble, and no one knows where she is." He ground his teeth. "She's probably terrified. If he's hurt her—" He shot a look at the prince. "All this time we've been calmly discussing the time of day, and you knew she was missing? Why didn't you open with that?"

The prince sighed. "Because I suspected you would respond this way, and I wanted to make the most of any opportunity for coherent conversation. Besides, she's not exactly missing. I am confident that Lord Wrendal knows where she is."

"Is that supposed to reassure me?" Jo asked with a hollow laugh. "He's the last person I would trust with her."

"He is her father," said Prince Giles, raising his eyebrows.

"He's a cruel and evil monster," spat Jonan, still pacing with restless energy. "You're very resigned about it all—you're either blind or you don't care nearly as much about her as you claim." He clutched at his hair involuntarily. "You don't know how much it's been torturing me to know she's in his power, and now... couldn't you intervene?"

"How do you propose I do that?" asked the prince calmly.

"Can't you talk to the king? Or at least to your father? Surely he would agree that there's something suspicious about him keeping her in seclusion, not even letting her speak with you. Isn't she basically your sister? What justification could Lord Wrendal offer for denying you access to her?"

A look of frustration passed across Prince Giles's face. "I have spoken with my father," he admitted. "If only she *was* my sister by blood, there would be no difficulty. But she's not. My father agrees that it is unusual, but he feels strongly that we have no right to intervene in Lord Wrendal's handling of his own affairs. And I cannot help but see his point."

"They're not his own affairs!" protested Jonan. "They're Scarlett's. She's a person, not a piece of property." The prince said nothing, his expression inscrutable, and Jonan groaned. "But of course you Balenans are used to seeing people as property," he said bitterly. He put his head in his hands, his voice coming out muffled and hollow. "She's no less a slave than any of them," he said. "And he won't hesitate to dispose of her in whatever way he thinks best."

"Really," said Prince Giles, frowning slightly, "I think you exaggerate the situation." Jonan didn't respond, his face still buried in his hands as he struggled not to panic at the thought of Scarlett's unknown circumstances. The elation he had felt at finding Alben's rock was momentarily forgotten as solving the mystery of the curse took second priority to ensuring Scarlett's safety. If only he wasn't locked behind these stupid bars!

"I don't think it's quite as dire as you fear," Prince Giles tried again. "But I will own to some apprehension."

Jonan snorted, out of all patience with the reserved prince and his measured language. Thank goodness he didn't want to marry Scarlett, because she would die of boredom if she was married to such a dull dog. Provided she survived her father long enough. He let out another groan, only half listening to the prince's words.

"I have learned today that Lord Wrendal is leaving the capital for a while. He is probably already gone—he left the castle earlier today with the intention of an immediate departure I believe. I had no idea that he had any plans to make a trip to his estates so soon. I would think he had sent Scarlett on ahead of him there, but from my inquiries that didn't happen."

Prince Giles took a deep breath, obviously not finding it easy to be honest with Jonan. "As he was at great pains to remind me during the unpleasant scene last night, my uncle does have some right to order his own household as he chooses. I can't deny that. But I also can't deny that I don't trust him. He spent the whole morning closeted with the king, and I'm very much afraid that Uncle Siloam has given him some kind of free license to act as he sees fit in relation to the Kyonan crisis. And I can't shake a strange fear that Scarlett is somehow caught up in it all." He gave Jonan a hard look. "She is certainly entangled with Kyonans to some extent in her father's mind now."

Jonan lowered his hands, ignoring the prince's reproach as he frowned over the information. He had been left with a similar impression himself from the Overseer's cryptic taunts. "Do you think the king would have given him authority to declare war on Kyona?" he asked slowly.

"No." Prince Giles's answer was quick and confident. "No, I am sure he would have stopped short of that. I know that Lord Wrendal has been pushing for it, but the king is not quick to take drastic action. He would not embark on war without greater provocation than Kyona has given."

Jonan rolled his eyes at this description of King Siloam. "Not quick to take drastic action" seemed a generous label for the supreme laziness of the man he had glimpsed the night before.

"So Lord Wrendal has left town," he said slowly. "I guess he really meant it when he said he would be too busy to torture me personally." Prince Giles raised his eyebrows but didn't comment on the casual remark. Jo frowned, talking mostly to himself. "Is he intending for me to stay in this cell until he returns? I'll starve before then, but surely he'd prefer to see my head taken off?"

"Actually," said the prince, his tone slightly apologetic. "He has arranged for your execution for the day after tomorrow. I heard him myself. He seemed to think that sufficient time for any...uh...confessions."

Jo snorted again. "Interrogations, you mean," he said grimly. "Well, we'll see. If he thinks I'll break in such a short time, he underestimates me."

"You seem very confident of yourself," said the prince dryly, and Jonan shrugged.

"Well I can't let him have it all his own way. Just because everyone else does."

"Not quite everyone," said the prince lightly.

"What do you mean?" asked Jonan.

"I mean that not everyone is happy to let Lord Wrendal order things as he pleases. Somebody else has plans of their own for you, it seems. Lord Grentan," supplied Prince Giles in answer to Jonan's questioning look. "After the Overseer left, and in the belief that he would not be returning for some time, Lord Grentan took an interest in your affairs."

"How kind of him," said Jonan sarcastically. He narrowed his eyes. "Why is that name familiar?" He mused for a moment, then it hit him. "Oh yes! He's the one who sent his servants to knife me after I left Lord Wrendal's party, when I'd just arrived."

"Is that so?" asked the prince quickly. "I didn't know that. How did you escape?"

"Scarlett was expecting trouble, and she sent her father's soldiers to watch my back," said Jonan absently, realizing only after the fact that he was speaking too freely and that the prince was taking in every word with great interest. "Never mind that," he said quickly. "What did this Lord Grentan say about me today? Don't tell me he's disputing my execution?"

"Hardly. His desire to be rid of you does not seem to have gone away with time," said Prince Giles with irritating calm. "He intends to oversee your execution himself."

"Oh?" asked Jo, not particularly interested. "Why?"

The prince sighed, suddenly looked tired. "I don't know if you're aware, but there has been a great deal of debate in the last couple of days about the best way to respond to the Kyonan king's statement with the trader ship," the prince said. "Everyone understands that King Siloam is not eager to go to war. In light of that position, Lord Wrendal has argued for a diplomatic solution, as he calls it. Lord Grentan, on the other hand, has expressed the view that a show of strength would be more appropriate. Both claim the purpose of preventing war, but anyone who has been paying attention will be aware that both have been eager to see hostilities commence. Lord Wrendal is playing a deep game with his "diplomatic solutions", I am sure. I just don't know what that game might be. Lord Grentan is not so subtle, and his methods are easier to understand."

Jo blinked, trying to keep up with the flow of smooth words. He was hungry, and he was tired, and he was sore. And his anxiety at the mystery of Scarlett's whereabouts made him more than usually impatient with the intricate maneuverings of the power structure.

"It might be easy for you to understand, but I haven't got a clue what you're talking about," he said shortly. "What does all that mean?"

"It means," said the prince, a bite in his voice, "that several very powerful people are very determined to plunge both our countries into war."

"But I thought you said the king was set against it," said Jo. "Surely no one is more powerful than he is?"

A wry look came over Prince Giles's face in spite of his measured tone. "He doesn't want to go to war, it's true. But my uncle the king tends to be very...trusting when it comes to the suggestions of his advisors. He would not look for hidden agendas. When Lord Wrendal tells the king that he will find a diplomatic solution, Uncle Siloam is more than happy to trust the details to him. And when Lord Grentan tells him that we must respond to the statement with the trade ship by sending a strong statement of our own, Uncle Siloam is sure he is right. He is happy to take Lord Grentan's word for it that such a statement will surely deter the young inexperienced Kyonan king from pursuing war. But I suspect that Lord Grentan's intention is rather to provoke war. Which is an outcome that I, for one, do not wish for."

Prince Giles smiled humorlessly. "If the two noblemen worked together, they would be quite a force. However, each believes himself to be too clever to need assistance, and so each charts his own course."

Jo rubbed his head, which ached from the effort of trying to follow the nobles' tortuous schemes. "But what's the strong statement?" he asked. "What does this have to do with me?"

"It has everything to do with you," said the prince curtly. "You are the statement."

"Huh?" asked Jo stupidly. "Me? How so?"

"Well, not all of you," Prince Giles conceded. "Just your head."

"My...head?" repeated Jo, dropping his hand from it as he spoke.

"Yes. Lord Grentan's suggestion is that after your execution, your head should be sent via ship as a clear statement of how Balenol will respond to any further attempt by Kyona to repudiate our...trade arrangement."

"But..." For a moment Jonan was distracted by practicalities in spite of himself. "The voyage takes three weeks. By then..."

"Not at all," said the prince casually. "There are ways to preserve—"

"All right." Jo stopped him with an upraised hand. "I really don't need to know the details." He tried to match the prince's cool tone, but he wasn't quite able to keep his features smooth as he contemplated the nobleman's plans. "And the king thinks that will help *avoid* war?"

Prince Giles lifted a shoulder. "As I said, he is a little too easily convinced. Accounts are that the Kyonan king is very inexperienced, after all. There is some reason to think that he will be easily intimidated."

"Is there?" asked Jo humorously.

He suddenly thought of what Cal's reaction would be upon receiving a communication from Balenol consisting of Jo's severed head. He had a feeling that Cal would have quite a strong reaction, actually, and intimidation would not feature. Even Cal had a temper, despite the fact that he wasn't generally one to lose his head, and—but there was that unfortunate euphemism again. All at once Jo was seized by the comedy of it all, his mind gladly latching onto the morbid humor to avoid contemplating the consequences of the gruesome fate planned for him.

"The king plans to send a disembodied Kyonan head to Kynton?" he said, his voice unsteady.

"Yes," the prince assented.

"And not just any head—my head?"

"That's right."

"He plans to send *my* head to the new king?"

The prince nodded.

"And he thinks that will convince the new king *not* to go to war with Balenol?"

"That's what I said." Prince Giles was starting to sound irritated.

For a moment Jo just stared at him, then he burst into laughter. The prince looked startled, and Jo himself could feel the slightly hysterical nature of his mirth, but he made no attempt to check the outburst. He had never needed a release of tension more.

"Sorry," he gasped. "It's just so...*unlucky*."

"Yes," said Prince Giles, still looking bemused, "I can imagine you would feel that way. Although what there is in that to make you laugh, I can't imagine."

"Not unlucky for me," said Jonan, "for your king." He paused, sobering slightly. "Well, I suppose it is unlucky for me also," he admitted. "But that's not what I was thinking of. How many rebellious Kyonans are floating around Nohl, and I'm the one he picks to make this big statement of his?"

Prince Giles was watching him with narrowed eyes. "Is there a reason that your head in particular would be so inflammatory?" he asked.

"Well, it's such a well-formed one, don't you think?" asked Jonan flippantly, still smiling in an unbalanced way.

The prince looked unimpressed, and Jonan because serious at once. It was a horrible thought, and quite apart from his own feelings on the matter, he wouldn't put Cal through that experience for anything.

"Let's just say that Lord Grentan is right that such an action would provoke war, not prevent it. And I don't want that outcome any more than you do." He shook out his shoulders resolutely. "So I'll just have to not get my head chopped off." He gave Prince Giles a determined look. "Let's talk about more important matters. We need to find Scarlett and make sure she's all right."

"We?" asked the prince, amused.

"Well, you're obviously not going to get it done on your own," said Jo accusingly. "It looks like I need to take a hand."

"And how are you gong to do that?" asked Prince Giles, raising his eyebrows. "Do you have a key to this cell hidden in your pocket?"

"No," admitted Jo, deflating slightly. "I don't suppose you do?"

"As a matter of fact," said Prince Giles calmly. "I do."

Jo just stared at him. The prince met his look steadily, the hint of a smile in his eyes.

"Are you serious?" Jo asked. "You came here to let me out? Again, that seems like something you could have opened with."

"I could have, of course," said the prince, still maddeningly calm. "I must say, you seemed quite convinced of your ability to escape death even without my help."

"I never had any intention of passing beyond the blade," agreed Jonan. "I would have found a way. I always land on my feet."

The prince shook his head slightly, clearly amused. "I almost believe you would have," he said. He cocked an eyebrow humorously. "Would you like me to leave you in there after all so you can prove your resourcefulness?"

Jonan laughed. "No, thanks. I'm not too proud to accept help." He gave the prince a shrewd look. "Are you letting me out because you don't think I should be executed, or for Scarlett's sake? Or simply because you don't want my head to be available as a tool to start a war?"

The prince's face remained smooth, his expression difficult to read. "Does it matter?" he asked.

"Not at all," said Jonan quickly. "I don't care what your reasons are. I'm more than ready to be done with this cell."

"If I let you out," said the prince slowly, "what will you do?"

"Find Scarlett," said Jonan promptly.

"And how will you do that?"

Jo shrugged, his expression veiled. "That's my own concern," he said. "But you can rest assured that I will find her."

The other man regarded him for a long moment, his face giving away nothing of his thoughts. Then, finally, he reached into the folds of his clothes with a fluid motion and produced a key.

Jo's heart pumped with excitement, but he tried to keep his features impassive. Prince Giles clearly didn't fully trust him, and he didn't want to give his would-be rescuer any reason to change his mind.

The click of the key in the lock was the sweetest sound Jo had ever heard, and within moments he was standing next to the prince, shaking out his stiff limbs. The two men regarded each other silently.

"I will distract the guards," said the prince after a moment. "I can get you out into the streets, but the rest is up to you."

Jo nodded. "That's more than enough." He hesitated. "Thank you."

The prince looked steadily back at him. "If you want to thank me, do whatever you can to prevent war between our countries."

"I'm not sure what I can do, but I'll certainly try," responded Jonan.

The prince nodded. "And if you really want my gratitude, ensure no harm comes to my cousin on account of all this."

"That I will most definitely do," said Jonan, his voice fiercely determined. "With my last breath if necessary."

CHAPTER TWENTY-SIX

Although the rain had stopped, it turned out to already be dark in the city above, which suited Jonan's purposes perfectly. He had never moved more swiftly in his passage through Nohl's sleeping streets. Still not entirely sure he could trust the prince, he had circled back several times to ensure he wasn't being followed, but it was still in record time that he found himself knocking on the trapdoor at the base tree.

He had quickly decided that there was no point searching Lord Wrendal's house for news of Scarlett if Prince Giles had already done so without success. He was fairly certain that if anyone knew where Scarlett was, it was Bonnie, and he couldn't imagine her running anywhere else but here in the case of danger.

It was a moment before the door was opened, and for the first time ever he was met with a drawn blade. But when the Kyonan boy saw who it was, he lowered the knife with a cry of delight. Jo hurried down into the hideout, pausing for a moment to take stock of his surroundings. The base was not as full as it had been the night of the slave breakout, but there were still many more people than he was used to seeing in the enclosed space.

His eyes scanned the crowd for a familiar face, but she saw him first, running forward with a shriek.

"Jonan!" She threw herself at him, her relief evident. "How did you get out?"

He gave her a quick squeeze, but let go straight away, in no mood for enthusiasm. "Prince Giles sprung me," he said shortly.

"The prince?" she repeated, astonished. "Why? What did he say?"

"Never mind that," said Jonan. "Where is she, Bonnie?"

The girl's face sobered instantly. "Oh, Jo. You're too late, and no one else could help her. She's already gone."

"What?!" Jo seized Bonnie's shoulders convulsively, his whole body going numb. It wasn't true—it simply couldn't be. "No," he said hoarsely, "I don't believe you. She's not—she can't be—"

"No, no, she's not dead!" said Bonnie hastily, taking pity on his distress. "I didn't mean that. Just that she's literally gone— she's left Nohl. Or at least, she's leaving tonight, but even if she hasn't actually left yet, she's already locked away. But she's still alive. For now at least," she added in a mutter, her face dark.

"What do you mean for now?" asked Jo frantically, letting go of her shoulders.

Bonnie rubbed her face wearily. "Her father," she said. "He's...Jo, I've never seen anything like it. I thought he was angry with her before, but it was nothing to this."

"It's all my fault," said Jo, stricken. He looked at Bonnie beseechingly. "I didn't mean to kiss her, Bonnie. It just happened. And now I've made a mess out of everything."

She started at his words. "Is that what happened?" she demanded, and he nodded. "And her father saw?" He nodded again, and Bonnie's mouth fell open, aghast. "No wonder he was angry. How are you still alive?"

"He didn't intend me to be for much longer," said Jo simply. Shaking her head, Bonnie led him over to the same corner where they had all been in conversation the night of the riot. Stan appeared from somewhere, welcoming Jo with relief. Jo returned her greeting distractedly, frowning at Bonnie.

"Didn't Scarlett tell you what happened?" he asked, confused. "When I saw you at the gate I thought for sure you'd go straight up to her."

"I did," Bonnie assured him. "But she didn't tell me anything I could make sense of. She was…beside herself. I've never seen her in such a state, Jo. It scared me."

Jo's heart seized at her words. He remembered how Scarlett had looked when he had first arrived at her rooms. He had been distressed at the sight, and had wanted nothing more than to lift her burden. How had he managed instead to make it worse?

"She sent me out again straight away," said Bonnie. "She wanted me to find out what was happening to you. I didn't want to leave her on her own, but she didn't exactly ask my opinion." Bonnie shook her head. "I should have stayed. All I could find out was that they'd put you in the execution chamber, and Lord Wrendal had ordered that you weren't to be sent any food or water."

She paused. "By the way, you must be hungry."

"I'm starving," admitted Jonan curtly. "But never mind that. What about Scarlett?" Out of the corner of his eye he saw Stan signal to someone, and a moment later some simple rations were set before him. He devoured them readily, his eyes fixed on Bonnie as she continued.

"By the time I got back, she was gone. Lord Wrendal had bundled her off without delay."

"But where?" asked Jonan desperately.

"To the harbor," said Bonnie. "Onto a ship."

"A ship?" repeated Jo, startled.

Bonnie nodded. "They sail tonight, but he wanted her shut up on the vessel straight away, so she couldn't speak with anyone. And I think so that she wouldn't try to visit you or plead with the royals on your behalf."

"But Prince Giles said that Lord Wrendal was going on a visit to his estates. And he couldn't find any trace of Scarlett."

"I'm not surprised," said Bonnie. "Lord Wrendal was particularly determined that none of her adopted family were to know where she was or what he was planning. He seemed to think they might try to intervene. He didn't want them to find out until after he had left, by which time it would be too late to do anything."

"How do you know so much about what he was thinking?" demanded Jo.

Bonnie gave the ghost of a smile. "I'm good at being neither seen nor heard, remember? I didn't come here straight away when I found her gone. I hung around the house until I heard what I wanted to know. I was eavesdropping when Lord Wrendal gave instructions to that favorite soldier lackey of his. He was supposed to stay behind and deal with you." She gave Jonan a tight look. "I won't trouble you with the details of what he had planned for you, but it wasn't pretty."

"I can imagine," said Jo dryly. "But at least if he was planning to spirit Scarlett away he wasn't actually going to use her to get me to talk, which is what he threatened."

Bonnie shook her head darkly. "He's a monster," she said. "And I wouldn't put it past him, given what he's planning now."

"What is he planning?" asked Jo quickly. "Where is he taking her?"

"To Kyona, of course," she said, as though it was obvious.

"Where else would they be sailing to? Like I said, they leave tonight, if they haven't already."

"Kyona?" Jo repeated, startled. "Why?"

"To secure an alliance," said Bonnie ironically. "A diplomatic solution to the current crisis."

"Why do I find that hard to believe?" said Jo dryly.

"Well that's what Lord Wrendal has been authorized to do by the king," said Bonnie. "But of course he has other plans."

"Why is he taking Scarlett, though?" asked Jonan, for the moment not interested in Lord Wrendal's complicated scheming. "Is it just to keep her from trying to stop me being executed?"

"What? No, of course not. That's just a happy side effect. He needs her for the alliance, obviously."

Jonan frowned. "Why?" He looked up to find both Bonnie and Stan staring at him like he was dense. "What?" he asked. "What kind of alliance are we talking about?"

"A marriage alliance, obviously," said Stan. "What better way for him to exploit Scar's beauty now that she's apparently blown her chances with her cousin?"

"What?" said Jo, aware of his decision to leap to his feet only when he found himself looking down at the two girls. He felt a strange rushing in his ears. "Who is he going to marry her off to?"

"The new king," said Stan, speaking slowly as if to a confused child.

"Oh," said Jo, relaxing instantly and dropping back into his seat. "Well, that's all right then. He won't have any success with that plan."

"You'd better hope you're wrong about that," said Bonnie grimly.

"I'm not," Jo asserted, frowning at her. "Why would you hope I'm wrong? You're the one who told me Scar has no desire to be

Balenol's queen. Why would you think she wants to be Kyona's queen?"

"I'm sure she doesn't," said Bonnie. "But it's better than the alternative." She frowned. "Why are you so sure the king won't want to marry her? She is very beautiful, after all."

"Doesn't matter," said Jo shortly. "He's already betrothed. What alternative?"

"Betrothed isn't married," said Stan skeptically. "And Lord Wrendal is very good at manipulating people from what I hear. Maybe the king will change his mind when he meets Scar."

"He won't," said Jo impatiently. "He's too in love for that."

It was true. Jo had thought it a bit much at the time, to be honest, but now it somehow seemed much less ridiculous.

"What's the alternative, Bonnie?" he pressed.

"Who is he betrothed to?" asked Stan curiously, before Bonnie could respond. "I didn't think kings usually got to marry for love."

Jo took a deep breath, his nerves becoming more and more frayed the longer his question went unanswered. "He's betrothed to your sister," he said curtly. "Now can we stop with all the interruptions and can someone please tell me what the alternative is!"

But it was instantly clear that any such hope was absurdly optimistic after his statement. Both girls were staring at him open-mouthed, bereft of words. He sighed, resigning himself to more delay, and waited.

"Elnora?" asked Stan eventually, dazed. "Elnora is betrothed to the new king? You're making a joke. You must be. I thought you hinted that she was being courted by your best friend, the one you were traveling with when you met her."

"That's right," said Jo patiently. "Cal. Or rather Calinnae. He's the new king."

"Your best friend is the king?" Bonnie asked, her tone unmistakably accusatory.

"Elnora is going to be queen?" said Stan at the same time. "It can't be true."

"It is true, I promise," said Jo earnestly. "I'm sorry I didn't tell you. Honestly, I didn't know how. But it really is the truth." He looked at Bonnie. "You too, Bonnie. I should have told you about Cal earlier. I was going to, the night of the riot, but we got interrupted. That's how I was at Kynton when the false king was overthrown. I was part of the quest to help win back the throne."

"Do you...do you have a way to get a message to him?" asked Bonnie, clearly struggling to process it all. "We could warn him about the true nature of this delegation."

"No," said Jo heavily. "He doesn't even know I'm here. I sort of just...left."

Bonnie rubbed at her temple, her expression perplexed. "Why would you do that?"

"That's not important right now," said Jonan. "Tell me what Lord Wrendal is planning."

Bonnie gave her head a little shake, evidently trying to clear it. "Nothing good," she said slowly. "King Siloam doesn't know this obviously, but if Lord Wrendal can't get control over King Calinnae by maneuvering him into a marriage alliance with milady, he's going to provoke war. That's what he's really wanted all along, but he knows there would have to be serious provocation for King Siloam to take that step." She took a deep breath, and Jo realized that her hands were shaking slightly. "His plan is to have milady killed and make it look like the Kyonans did it. She's basically Balenol's princess. I think he's right that people would be angry enough that King Siloam would have to go to war."

"WHAT?!"

This time Jo was fully aware of leaping to his feet, sending the bowl in front of him flying in the process. His hands balled into fists, opening and closing convulsively. "No," he choked out, his throat constricted by his rage. "That's not happening. I won't let it happen." He was breathing hard, and his gaze was furious as it rested on his companions. "Why aren't you doing anything about it?" he accused. "Why are you just sitting here?"

"You think we don't want to help?" asked Bonnie sharply. "What can we do? She's been under close watch all this time thanks to your little escapade. There's no way we can get her off that ship."

"Then we need to get on the ship," said Jo quickly, but Bonnie was shaking her head.

"We can't, Jo!" she said. "Don't you see? That's why I said none of us could help her. If we stow away on that ship, it'll sink, milady along with it."

Jo paused, realizing the truth of her words. "So she's really all alone," he said quietly. "No one can go with her." He met Bonnie's eyes with determination. "No one except me."

She hesitated. "Yes, it had occurred to me...but what if we're wrong? What if the curse applies to you too?"

"It doesn't," said Jo confidently. "Why would it? I'm not a slave, and neither were my ancestors. I came here by choice, and I'm leaving by choice."

"But it's a big risk to take," said Bonnie nervously. "If the ship goes down in the middle of the ocean, you'll both almost certainly die."

"What other choice is there?" Jo asked. "If I do nothing, her father will murder her for sure, because there's no way Cal will break his betrothal to Elnora and agree to marry Scarlett."

Bonnie chewed her lip anxiously. "I don't know...three weeks is a long time to hide on a ship, and if Lord Wrendal finds you on there..."

"I'm doing this, Bonnie," said Jo firmly. "I don't care in the least about the risk to me. You said it yourself, I'm the only one who has the option, and I'm not leaving Scarlett at his mercy."

Before Bonnie could respond, the trapdoor opened again, and they all turned to see who was entering. Three Kyonans appeared, clearly back from a patrol, Cody among them. When the boy saw Jo, he ran over with a shout.

"You got out!" he cried delightedly. "I knew they'd never get you."

"Hey Cody," said Jo, summoning a smile with difficulty. He was always glad to see the boy, but the revelation about Scarlett's intended murder made it hard to think about anything else.

"We'll be all right now we have you," said Cody confidently.

Jo's heart sank at the trusting expression on Cody's face. "Cody," he said slowly. "I'm sorry, but I can't stay."

Cody's face fell. "You're leaving us?"

"I have to," said Jo pleadingly. "Scar's in trouble, and I'm the only one who can help her."

"Oh," said Cody, his expression becoming heroically determined. "If it's for Scar, then of course..."

Jo took in the boy's dejection, feeling helpless. He looked over at Stan. She still looked dazed, and she hadn't spoken since the conversation had moved away from his revelation about Elnora. But when she felt his gaze on her, she looked up.

"Of course you have to go," she said quietly. "We can't leave Scar to her father. But I won't deny that it's a blow. It's not exactly the ideal time to lose Raldo, Scar, and you."

"I'm hardly as big a loss as Raldo or Scar," Jo protested, but she shook her head.

"Yes, you are. You're the unmarked liberator, remember? You're a symbol if nothing else. Between here and the other bases, we have a lot of new members who don't know the resistance, and don't know us. But they do know about you."

Jo was silent for a moment, considering her words. In his

rush to save Scarlett, he hadn't even thought about the others he would be abandoning. He had taken on a new purpose when he arrived in Nohl, and the way he felt about Scarlett was not reason enough to desert it. He was as determined as ever to break the curse. He just had to make sure Scarlett was safe first. Leaving her to her fate was simply not an option.

The curse. In all that had happened since, he had almost forgotten about his discovery in the execution chamber. But the talisman still sat against his chest, and he was as convinced as ever that its presence brought him one step closer to unraveling the mystery of the curse.

"Cody," he said, turning to the boy. "I do have to go. I'm sorry to leave you all, but Scar will die otherwise, and I can't live with that. Can you understand that?"

Cody nodded, his eyes round and his expression solemn.

"But it doesn't mean I'm giving up on you," Jo continued. "I'm going to break the curse so you can all go home. Once I get Scar away from her father, she and I can figure it out together."

Cody nodded again, but he didn't say anything, and Jo noted that Stan's expression was guarded.

"It's not empty words," he insisted. "I don't have all the answers yet, but I finally have a clue."

"You do?" Bonnie asked skeptically. "Since when?"

"Since today," said Jo. "When I found this, hidden in the wall of the execution chamber, under where Alben carved his name." He drew out the chain from under his clothing as he spoke, until the mountain rock dangled in front of him. The space seemed to still, and more than three pairs of round eyes turned to him.

"Is that—?" Cody whispered, and Jo nodded.

"It's Alben's mountain rock," he confirmed. "And it definitely has magic. When I held it I saw something—Alben's memories. Like I was in his head."

Cody's eyes were wide, his expression awed. "Can I touch it?" he asked.

For a moment Jo hesitated. It wasn't that he didn't trust Cody, but he wondered if letting the boy hold it would violate some dragon code. The only other magical object with which he was familiar was the Esvalere, an ancient and powerful glass sphere that had been gifted by the dragons to the Kyonan kings. Its existence was so secret that by rights Jo shouldn't know anything about it. Jo knew that if he, or anyone but Cal or his heirs, was to look in it, it would unleash disaster on Cal's whole bloodline.

But this rock was different. It must be. It was a rock from the Dragon Realm, certainly, but it wasn't a dragon-made object. And it was no gift from a dragon to him. It didn't belong to him at all—it had belonged to Alben, and Jo had merely found it in the wall. He had no right to deny anyone else the opportunity to wield it.

"Of course you can," he said, slipping it off his neck and holding it out to Cody. The boy took it reverently, squeezing the rock in his fist.

"This was really Alben's?" he asked, and Jo nodded.

"What is it showing you?" he prompted, but Cody just looked confused. "Can you see any memories?" Jo tried again.

Cody shook his head. "No. I don't see anything. Am I supposed to do something?"

Jo frowned, trying to remember when he had held it. "I don't know...I think you sort of ask it a question, in your mind I mean. Like something you want to know about Alben, maybe."

Cody closed his eyes, scrunching up his face in concentration, and everyone waited breathlessly. After a long moment he opened them again.

"Well?" prompted Bonnie, and he shook his head ruefully.

"Nothing."

"Can I take it back for a minute?" Jo asked, frowning, and

Cody handed it over. Jo held it by the chain for a moment, thinking. He tried to focus on Alben, but his thoughts were still full of Scarlett. He didn't think Alben would blame him, somehow. Twenty years after she died, his thoughts had still been full of his Marine, after all. Jo remembered that the boy at the castle records room had told him that Marine didn't come to Balenol at the same time as Alben, but that he had known her before, back in Kyona. Did she come from the mountains too, then?

With the question in his mind, Jo reached out and grasped the rock. He gasped involuntarily as he was instantly transported back into Alben's mind. He felt the grief of homelessness as Alben traveled away from the mountains, with other survivors of the rockslide. Some of them had chosen to go elsewhere in the mountains, but Alben had joined the group heading for the coast, and a new life.

Through Alben's memories, he saw the town of Argath, on the seashore. It was a pleasant enough spot, but Alben had not particularly intended to stay there. Until he saw her, that was. He was only fourteen then, and he hadn't really begun to notice the girls in his hometown yet. But this girl was different. Her face was made for laughter, her expression as open as the sea and her eyes as clear as the sky after a storm. She was kind to him from that first moment, she and her family, when no one else had time for a lonely refugee from the strange mountain folk. He was strong already, and for the few years before the slavers took him, he was able to support himself well enough to meet his physical needs. But it was Marine who gave him something to live for, whose kindness met a different need, one harder to quantify but no less important to survival. The need for friendship, companionship. And—he couldn't help but hope —something more.

Jo let go of the rock, shaking his head to clear it. There was plenty more it could tell him, he was sure, but now wasn't the time to lose himself. He couldn't afford to delay. It was too late for Marine—had been for long generations—but it wasn't too late to save Scarlett.

"What just happened?" asked Bonnie, amazed. "You went all rigid. It looked like you were having some kind of vision or something."

"It was showing me Alben's memories," said Jo, his voice coming out slightly breathless. "Like I said before." He turned to Cody. "You really didn't see anything?"

Cody shook his head, his eyes wider than ever. "It only works for you," he said, awe in his voice. "You were meant to find it. You and no one else."

"What?" said Jo, uncomfortable. "No, that can't be right. That doesn't make sense. Why would it be connected to me?"

"It makes perfect sense," said Cody firmly. "You're the liberator."

Nonplussed, Jo saw heads nodding reverently all around him. A girl he didn't even know stepped forward.

"If anyone can figure out the curse, I believe you can," she said solemnly. "You won't forget us once you're back in Kyona, will you?"

"No," said Jonan, dazed. "I promise you I won't." The girl nodded, satisfied, and stepped back. Jonan took a deep breath, trying to pull himself together. "I definitely won't forget you all," he repeated, looking from face to face. "And if the curse does come from mountain magic, I honestly believe that I'm more likely to figure it out once I'm back in Kyona anyway. I think I know how to look for the answers once I'm there."

"Of course you'll figure it out," said Cody firmly. "We have faith in you."

Looking around him, Jo saw the truth of the statement in the many pairs of eyes trained on him. The now-familiar feeling of discomfort started to tug at him, but he pushed it aside. He was done feeling overwhelmed by the weight of expectation. Instead of shying away from it, it was time to live up to it. He didn't have to be crushed by the weight—he would choose to instead be encouraged by their faith in him, to let it spur him to do all he could for their cause.

"Thank you Cody," he said, standing a little straighter. "I won't let you down." He slipped the rock back around his neck. "But now," he said decisively, "I have to go, without delay. I have to get to Scar before it's too late."

"It might be too late already, Jo," said Bonnie anxiously. "The ship was going to leave sometime tonight. We shouldn't have kept you talking so long."

"It's not too late," said Jo firmly. "I'll get onto that ship if I have to row after it."

"But it'll take you forever to get back under the wall and sneak through the city," Bonnie argued.

Jo shook his head. "I'm not going back under the wall, or sneaking through the city. I'm going straight for the river. It'll take me directly to the port."

"But you can't, Jo!" Bonnie protested. "The gate will be closed now, and swimming under it is a death wish. Especially after all this rain. The river will be swollen."

"And the current faster than ever, which means I'll be at the harbor in no time," said Jo firmly. "Don't worry, Bonnie. I'm a very strong swimmer. I know it's a risk, and I'll be as careful as I can. But it's for Scarlett—it's worth the risk. I just can't afford the time it will take to walk there."

"All right," said Bonnie, still looking anxious but obviously realizing there was nothing to be gained by arguing. "If you make it onto the ship, tell milady we're all safe. You know she'll be worrying. And Jo," she hesitated, "please try not to die."

Jo grinned. "Don't worry," he said. "I excel at not dying."

She rolled her eyes, and Jo became serious, turning to

address Stan as well as Bonnie. "Stan, if I do manage to break the curse, you need to be ready to get everyone out. I know it's not exactly a small task, and I'm hoping that once I'm back with Cal, we'll be in a position to send help, but you should be as prepared as possible. Bonnie, you know the boy Jack, who works for Mundsen?" Bonnie nodded. "He's the one to contact if you want a message to go out to the Kyonans in Nohl. The breadth of his network will amaze you. Tell him you're working with me and he'll help you."

Both girls nodded firmly, and Jo turned to leave. They followed him to the trapdoor, and he looked back down, his eyes resting first on Stan, whose expression was troubled.

"I really am sorry I didn't tell you all about Elnora earlier, Stan," he said softly. "You had a right to know."

"I just hope she really is all right," said Stan quietly. "I'm not sure what to think about it all."

"She's all right," said Jo reassuringly. He saw that Stan wasn't convinced, and he smiled at her. "He's a good man. And she's more important to him than anything. He'll take care of her. And when we break the curse, you'll be able to see that for yourself."

She smiled more genuinely at that, her eyes conveying her gratitude for the encouragement.

"And Bonnie—" said Jo, turning to her.

"Oh enough," she said impatiently. "Go get milady before you miss your window, will you? We'll be fine here. And," she shot him an accusing look, "if you must kiss her again, try to do it when her father isn't around, will you?"

He grinned, his meek tone at odds with the mischievous twinkle in his eyes. "I'll try. See you back in Kyona."

And without another word, he was up the stairs and back into the humid jungle air.

CHAPTER TWENTY-SEVEN

With the rain past and the moon to light his way, Jo reached the river in no time, following the route that he had taken with Scarlett and Bonnie the day they had rescued Stan and the others from the cave in. The current was indeed strong and fast, the river considerably higher in its banks since the twenty four hour long downpour.

But Jonan didn't hesitate, pausing only to seize a large branch before slipping into the water and letting the current pull him to the middle of the river. He used the branch for flotation assistance and didn't try to swim, just letting the flow take hold of him and propel him toward the sleeping city. He watched closely for the approach of the huge suspended gates, knowing that he would have to time his submersion very carefully if he didn't want to be dashed against the wooden surface.

Soon enough he saw the walls rising up before him and he braced himself. He had spoken confidently to Bonnie, but he was perfectly aware that he risked his life by attempting to dive under the wooden gates. Still, he knew no hesitation. To save Scarlett, he would risk his life as many times as it took. As he let go of the branch, beginning to take confident strokes, he felt a sudden and unexpected surge of power from the rock around his neck. It pulsed out and flowed into him, giving extra energy to his efforts and unnatural strength to his arms. It reminded him of the rush of power he had felt when he had been briefly flogged, the one that had made the pain seem temporarily so inconsequential.

He didn't understand what had triggered the rock's magic, but he wasn't about to waste it. Taking a deep breath, he dove as deeply as he could, striking out with the current with every bit of energy he had. He stayed under for longer than he would have imagined he could, the swirling water pulling at him mercilessly, but eventually he had to kick back upward. His head broke the surface, and he took a deep gasp. The river continued to pull him along, but a quick glance back was enough to show that the wall was now behind him. Buildings were racing by on both sides, as the river pulled him toward the sea. Elation filled him. That had been much easier than he had expected.

In much less time than it had taken him to walk from the port that first day, the river carried him through the silent city to his destination. He let the water take him right to the edge of the harbor, his every sense on the alert as he drew close to the ocean. His heart hammered within him as he hoped desperately that he was not too late.

He wasn't disappointed. As soon as he reached the quay, the bustle of departure became evident, around one ship in particular. It was one of the largest vessels in the dockyard, which was not exactly a surprise. Lord Wrendal would surely demand the best for his delegation.

Even with the extra energy from the rock, Jonan's limbs were by now very tired, but he forced himself to push out into the harbor. He swam with careful strokes to the ship, making sure to keep the vessel's bulk in between him and the gangplank, up and down which a number of people were moving in the final preparations for departure.

Scanning the side of the vessel, he saw with a leap of the heart what he was hoping for. There was a round porthole partway up the ship that was open. It was fortunate, he reflected, that he had always been lithe. A broader-shouldered man would not fit through the opening. He swam along the edge of the ship until he found another porthole at water level, this one closed. After peering cautiously inside to ensure he had no audience, he used it to pull himself out of the water. Calling on his climbing skills, he began to scale the side of the ship, first looking quickly into each opening he had to cross, just in case someone might be watching.

He had made it halfway to his destination when he looked in on a scene that almost made him lose his grip and topple back into the water. Holding on with an effort, he stared through the glass at the agonizing sight inside. He had clearly found Scarlett's quarters, a richly furnished state cabin fit for a queen.

But he didn't notice the accommodations. He was too focused on the figure occupying them. Scarlett's slim form was thrown face down across the bed, and even without being able to hear, Jonan could tell that she was sobbing wildly into her out-flung arms. His heart wrenched at her distress, and he raised a hand to knock on the glass, thinking that if she could at least know that he had escaped beheading, it might ease some of her anguish.

But his gaze fell on something else in the room, and he stopped himself just in time. His breath caught in his throat as he took in the soldier sitting in a chair by the door of Scarlett's cabin. The man was watching her with a bored expression. A sense of outrage rose up in Jo at the sight, but his indignation was quickly replaced by a deep uneasiness. He wasn't sure what alarmed him more—the fact that Lord Wrendal had actually stationed a man inside Scarlett's sleeping quarters, or the fact that she was so little in control of herself that the man's presence apparently had no effect on her display of grief.

The soldier turned his head, and Jonan pulled away from the glass quickly, his mind whirring. Clearly Bonnie had not exaggerated when she said Scarlett was being closely watched. He would have to tread with great care. He hated to move away from where Scarlett was, but he couldn't see any benefit to be gained from hovering there. He completed his journey quickly, slipping in through the open porthole into a stateroom that was mercifully unoccupied.

He knew he couldn't stay there—it was too central a part of the ship. He had to wait a fair while before the coast was clear enough to leave the room, but he seized the first opportunity that presented itself, and made his way down deeper into the bowels of the ship. He let himself into a large storeroom right in the ship's hull. There were a few supplies in there, but it didn't seem well stocked enough to suggest it would be regularly trafficked during the journey. Jonan found an old length of sailcloth and settled under it to await the ship's departure.

It was hard to take it all in. A very short time ago, he had been locked in a prison cell, awaiting torture and execution in this harsh foreign land. And now, provided his luck held—and he somehow felt confident it would, despite the odds—he might just be going home.

In spite of everything, he couldn't help the rush of elation that passed through him at the thought.

THREE WEEKS LATER, the rush became a positive flood of excitement as Jonan set foot once again on Kyonan soil. To be fair, he would have been beyond thrilled to be setting foot on any shore, just to get off that blasted boat. But the fact that it was his native land certainly made it all the sweeter. And the knowledge of how incredibly lucky he had been to make it through the voyage undetected lent a certain giddy thrill to his homecoming.

If the journey had seemed long when he had first sailed to Nohl, it had felt interminable on the way back. Jonan had chosen his hiding place well—the storeroom was located right in a back corner and rarely visited. But even so, his position had been precarious at best. It would have been easier to hide in plain sight if he had not been the only Kyonan on board, but of course the Balenans knew better than to take slaves on a voyage to Kyona. Jo had been forced to leave his haven numerous times to supply himself with food and water, and it had taken all his recently acquired skills in stealth, along with a large dose of luck, to avert disaster on these occasions.

He had almost been caught on just the second day at sea, and he had been sobered enough by the near miss to err on the side of caution for the rest of the voyage. It had been foolish, he knew, to venture out of his hiding place after dawn had broken, but he had been unable to stop himself. The cry of distress had penetrated even to his fastness, and he had no difficulty in recognizing the voice as Scarlett's.

He had barely retained the sense to move stealthily as he hastened through the ship, and had he found her in immediate danger, he surely would have given up on avoiding detection and come to her aid. But as furious as he had been at the scene he had overheard from his precarious hiding place in the ship's passage, he had been reasonable enough to realize that no benefit would be gained from attacking Lord Wrendal then and there, afloat on the ocean as they were, in a ship full of his lackeys.

"You will cease this display at once," the nobleman was saying smoothly. "You embarrass me in front of these fine soldiers, and I will not tolerate it. Do you think I told you so that

I could be treated to more of your hysterics? I told you so that we could be done with this topic of conversation once and for all. If you really cared about him, you would be glad that his suffering is over." The Overseer's voice turned nasty. "I am sure he was, by the time my orders were carried out."

Suddenly Jonan had understood. It was dawn on the second day after his escape. According to Prince Giles, this was the time Lord Wrendal had appointed for his execution, and the nobleman had obviously decided to make his daughter aware of the timing. Jonan balled his fists, infuriated by the man's cruelty and wretched over Scarlett's obvious distress.

"How could you?" she had choked out.

"After the insult he had offered to my household, how could I not?" retorted Lord Wrendal. "You are fortunate to be my daughter, so that I do not deal with you in the same manner for your share in the behavior."

"Fortunate to be your daughter?" repeated Scarlett, with a slightly hysterical laugh. Jo didn't need to see her face to read her anguish. "I wish you *had* dealt with me the same way," she said hollowly. "It would be better than this."

"You are being melodramatic," snapped her father. "Honestly Scarlett, when did you become such a fool? I never saw such weakness in you before now. I am even generous—you display an unnatural preference for these Kyonans, and instead of reproaching you, I am going to make you their queen."

"You are not!" came Scarlett's passionate voice. "I will never cooperate with you. I won't marry this king so that you can manipulate his rule."

There was a moment of silence, and Jonan could picture Lord Wrendal attempting to master his anger. "I would advise you to reconsider that position," he said at last, his voice silkier and more dangerous than ever. "You would be wise to pursue this marriage to the best of your ability—one might even say you should pursue it as if your life depended on it."

Lord Wrendal had turned and departed the room without warning, and Jo had only just managed to scramble behind a corner in time to avoid the man walking right into him. As it was, had the nobleman decided to turn left instead of right outside of Scarlett's door, Jonan would certainly have been lost. He had retreated without delay to his hiding place, but had been unable to help pacing restlessly around the storeroom for a space, his blood pounding furiously in his ears, despite the risk that someone might hear the movement. Had he not known there were soldiers in Scarlett's room with her, he would have doubled back once her father was gone, and risked discovery to reassure and comfort her. But she was under watch. She was always under watch. However much he pretended to be in control, Lord Wrendal clearly didn't trust his daughter, and he didn't leave her alone.

It was like that for the rest of the voyage. It was a big ship, and alternating between hiding and sneaking as he was, Jonan was rarely close enough to see or hear Scarlett. On those rare occasions he was always on the lookout for an opportunity to get her alone, but no such opportunity ever arose. She was always accompanied, if not by her father or a soldier, then by a sharp-eyed older woman who seemed to be her chaperone, and whose perpetually unpleasant expression supported Jo's impression that Scarlett found no enjoyment in her company.

And now they were on land, and there had still been no chance to tell Scarlett he was not only alive, but watching her back. After three miserable weeks, they had finally reached the large Kyonan trading town of Alezae. The delegation had disembarked some hours before, and Jo had forced himself to wait until the area was well clear before sneaking from the ship himself.

The daylight was starting to fade by the time he stepped onto the quay, breathing in the Kyonan air deeply and gladly. He supposed it was his imagination that the air tasted better, but despite the hazards and stresses still surrounding him, he couldn't help but rejoice to be back home. Warmth still lingered from the afternoon sun, the last of summer dying away, but there was no moist heaviness in the air. He felt as though an unpleasant weight had lifted from his lungs, and with it went some of the impotent anger and anxiety he had felt whenever he thought about Lord Wrendal and his schemes. This was Jonan's turf now. He had the advantage, and the foreign nobleman would discover it soon enough.

As he crept through Alezae's large dockyard, he couldn't help but remember the only previous time he had been here, when he and Cal had rescued Elnora from a slaver ship, then set the vessel on fire for good measure. It was strange to think that if Elnora had actually been shipped to Balenol, she would likely have been liberated by the resistance without delay, and reunited with her sister. If she had survived long enough, of course, Jonan thought darkly. Elnora was strong, incredibly so, but she had been in a terrible state when the traders got hold of her.

At that time, Jo had thought that if he could stay alive long enough, he would become king in Kynton, and have the power to end the slave trade from there. Never would he have imagined that he would be arriving back in Alezae as a stowaway on a ship from the South Lands. How strange life could be.

Jo was aware that the Balenan delegation was to spend this first night in Alezae, and he had no doubt that they would be settling in the wealthy merchants' sector, far from the filthy dockside district where Elnora had grown up. He was trusting that their presence would be so notable that it would not be difficult to track them once he got close.

He was not disappointed. It was quickly clear that Alezae was buzzing over the distinguished foreign arrival. Reactions were varied—Jo supposed that the last ship that had arrived from Balenol had been the one that was met by a squadron of soldiers and sent back with an uncompromising message.

It was an incredible release to be able to wander freely through the streets, listening in with interest to local gossip, and just generally being inconspicuous without trying. After so long in the minority, it was strange to see Kyonan features everywhere, and to not stand out.

Or at least, not too much. He was a stranger, after all, and he saw a few curious looks cast his way. There was something strange in people's expressions when they looked at him. It took him a while to place what it was, and when he identified it, he was astonished. Respect. It wasn't something he had been accustomed to seeing in people's eyes when they looked at him before he left home.

But he supposed he must look more hardened and imposing than he had before. During the voyage he had drilled himself as much as possible in his large storeroom, and he had maintained the muscled physique that Scarlett had once commented on. No one's eyes flicked unconsciously to his unmarked arm now, but more than once he saw someone's gaze linger on the scar on his cheek from the whip, which he had almost forgotten about. And perhaps he carried himself differently now. He certainly didn't feel like the same restless boy who had boarded a ship out of Kyona a few months ago, bent on aimlessly wandering in search of adventure.

Jo didn't have any coins and so couldn't bespeak accommodation. But he had foraged a dagger in one of his explorations on board the ship, and with his newly gained ability to defend himself, he had no hesitation about spending the night on the street. He didn't know how early the delegation might be leaving in the morning, and he didn't want to miss it, so he took the risk of poking around near the inn where the group was lodging once darkness had fallen.

Any hope he might have had of catching Scarlett unattended was quickly dashed. From what he could gather, she had already retired for the night, her chaperone in close attendance and a soldier stationed outside her door. Jo was hovering outside the inn when he witnessed an arrival, a Kyonan man who asked for Lord Wrendal by name, and was invited to enter a private parlor.

His curiosity piqued, Jonan decided at once that he needed to overhear their conversation. He had not been aware that the Overseer had any contacts here in Kyona. Fortunately, getting close enough to listen in was infinitely easier here in Alezae than it had been on the ship. The inn bustled with servants, all Kyonans of course. Even better, it seemed that a number of additional hands had been called in to cater for the important foreign guests, so that an unfamiliar face would not be likely to stand out.

Jonan put his skills at being inconspicuous into practice, and in no time at all found himself one of a small group of servants carrying food from the kitchen to the parlor where Lord Wrendal was entertaining his guest. Jonan kept his head carefully lowered, a submissive stance that was not out of place among the well-trained servants. He didn't dare to look up at all while in the room, so he didn't see the face of the visitor.

But he took care to be the last servant to withdraw, and he left the door slightly ajar, boldly standing in the corridor right next to it, arms folded behind his back and eyes straight ahead, as if he was standing at attention ready to respond to any instructions from the guests within. A couple of servants gave him curious looks as they bustled past, but no one challenged him. He restrained a smile. It was almost too easy.

"Thank you for coming promptly," Lord Wrendal was saying smoothly.

"Certainly, My Lord," responded an unfamiliar voice, the accent clearly Kyonan. "Your message was a surprise but, if I may say so, a welcome one. I received your original contact, the one brought by the traders' ship. I am pleased that Mundsen recommended me to you, and I am more than willing to work with you for our mutual benefit. I dispatched a reply with the same ship, despite its, uh...unfortunate failure to acquire its usual cargo. But given how quickly you have arrived, I would have thought there would not have been time for my message to reach you before you left on your voyage."

"It did reach me," said Lord Wrendal. "Only a couple of days before I departed Nohl. My departure was sudden, certain circumstances having arisen that required me to act without delay. One of those circumstances, I need hardly add, was the state in which the trader vessel returned to us."

"Yes, I can imagine King Calinnae's little message caused something of a stir in Balenol," said the unknown man, his sneering tone turning Cal's title into an insult. "Rest assured that there are still many of us in Kyona who do not wish to so hastily end the...understanding that has flourished between our countries in recent decades."

"I am glad to hear it," said Lord Wrendal, his voice grim. "I was disappointed to find no information in your reply about this young envoy who came to us in Nohl."

"Yes, the boy you inquired about," repeated the Kyonan. "I am sorry to say I know nothing of him. My sources at the castle assure me that the new king has not sent anyone to Balenol since his takeover. It is puzzling. What has happened to him?"

"He was arrested and executed," said Lord Wrendal dismissively. "I did not stay to oversee the event myself. I had my reasons for not wishing to delay. I left my best man in charge of extracting from the boy anything he might know. But it hardly seemed necessary to await his information when I was coming here myself. My man can be trusted. He will send me anything he thinks I should be aware of."

"Of course, My Lord."

"What of the state of things at Kynton? I have sent a messenger on ahead to the castle with King Siloam's message. Will the king receive our delegation formally?" asked Lord Wrendal.

"Yes, My Lord, I am confident he will," said the visitor quickly. "The royal brat is certainly determined to end the trade —the little display with the trader ship was all his own idea I understand. But my sources at the castle assure me that he does not wish for open war if he can avoid it. He will receive you with at least the appearance of diplomacy."

"Good," said Lord Wrendal. "Then the rest will take care of itself, one way or the other. What of my proposed alliance? I was disappointed to read in your earlier message that the king is already betrothed. I trust that his marriage has not yet taken place since the time you wrote to me?"

"Certainly not," said the stranger, his tone derisive. "That marriage will never take place. There are too many powerful players set against it. She is some simple common girl, who the royal brat brought with him when he stormed Kynton."

The man hesitated, and Jo frowned to himself outside the door. So they'd been giving Elnora a hard time, had they? Cal wouldn't like that.

"I must confess," the man was continuing, "that despite considerable efforts, those against the union have not yet succeeded in separating her from the king's side, or in deterring him from his intended course. But the process has been begun at least. And if your daughter is as beautiful as you claim, and as well-connected with the Balenan royals, I have high hopes that she will change his mind. He is very young after all, and young men are always susceptible to beauty. And if he wants to avoid war as much as he claims, how can he justify rejecting the proposed alliance?"

"Excellent," said Lord Wrendal, his voice smug.

Jonan's hand itched to strike the older man, to wipe from his face the smirk that would certainly be spread across it. He wasn't sure what made him angrier—Lord Wrendal's arrogance in trading off Scarlett's beauty as though it was a possession of his, or his insulting assumption that Cal would be so easily manipulated.

"And should things take a less desirable turn," Lord Wrendal went on, "what assistance can you offer me?"

"I will follow you to Kynton," promised the conspirator. "I have a contingent of men still loyal to me. I need to take care in showing my face—the brat has reason to recognize it, and he has no love for me. But we will stick close. You and I can talk further as we progress. And in the meantime, I will make contact with those among the court who will be sympathetic to your cause."

"Excellent," said Lord Wrendal again. "I see Mundsen showed unusual intelligence in giving your name to me."

The other man laughed unpleasantly. "Aye, he's a coward if ever I met one. But he knows how much the royal brat has robbed me of, and he's not wrong that I have enough reason of my own to do him harm."

"I see we are in agreement." Lord Wrendal's voice was silky, and Jo knew him well enough to guess that he had every intention of using the unknown Kyonan for his purposes, then turning on him as soon as it was convenient. "One other thing," the Balenan nobleman continued. "I did not understand what you meant by the cryptic comment in your communication."

"Cryptic comment, My Lord?" the Kyonan repeated in confusion.

"The reference to dragons," clarified Lord Wrendal. There was a moment of silence, and Jonan could almost feel the Kyonan man's discomfort.

"I did not intend to be cryptic, My Lord," he said at last. "I spoke quite literally. The claimant was assisted by a dragon in his coup."

The silence that followed this pronouncement was even longer than the previous one. Jonan wished he could see both their faces.

"Well," said Lord Wrendal finally, and it was clear from his tone that he placed no credibility on the other man's words. "We can discuss the matter more in future, I daresay."

"If you wish it, My Lord," said his companion, his stiff tone suggesting that he could read the nobleman's disbelief as easily as Jo could.

The men began to take their leave of each other, and Jonan moved away from the door, deep in thought. Once he would have been enraged by what he had overheard, but he had enough sense now to realize that the conversation was actually a windfall, not an insult. Much better to be aware of what was being plotted against Cal. He wished he could discover the identity of the Kyonan traitor, but no name had been used, and while Cal would apparently recognize the man's face, it seemed unlikely that Jo would.

Nevertheless, he loitered near the door of the inn, hoping for another glimpse of the visitor as he left. He got his wish. Night had truly fallen by now, but the doorstep of the inn was well-lit by the lamplight that pooled out of the open door. The man glanced casually around him as he stepped through the portal, and Jonan got a good look at his countenance.

For a moment he frowned, sure that he did recognize the

Kyonan after all, but unable to place him. But his interest in the man's face was fleeting, his eye drawn instead to something just below it. Something wholly unexpected, and yet all too familiar.

Because there against the man's chest, suspended on a short leather strap, dangled an unremarkable gray rock.

CHAPTER TWENTY-EIGHT

Jonan's consternation over the sight stayed with him throughout the entire trip to Kynton, although he didn't again glimpse the man. The initial shock that had kept him frozen in place for minutes after the traitor had disappeared had worn off, but he still could hardly believe what he had seen.

He rejected out of hand the idea that the other rock was no more than some unrelated keepsake. It was too absurd a coincidence, and in any case, he could have sworn he had felt some kind of throb from the rock against his own chest, a sudden angry warmth. He couldn't fully explain it, but he was sure his rock had recognized the other as kin.

While on the ship there had been plenty of opportunity to wield the stone, and on a number of occasions he had viewed Alben's memories. But nothing he had seen had led him to imagine that there was a second rock. He didn't dare to explore it during the night he spent on the streets of Alezae—he needed his wits about him and couldn't afford to get lost in visions. But he found a quiet moment the next day to seek an answer.

As soon as he grasped the rock in his hand, his curiosity

aflame about the origin of the second rock, he witnessed again the moment when Alben had followed his fanciful impulse to keep some of the rock that had crushed his mother. But hard on that memory followed another one, of Alben turning the rock into a keepsake. Jonan peered inside Alben's mind as the young boy acted on a sentimental urge and made a second necklace. When he left the ruined town with the group of refugees headed for the coast, he approached Liam, the boy who had been inadvertently saved by Alben's mother's final act.

Alben had felt slightly guilty when saying goodbye to the other boy, not wanting to admit how pleased he had been to discover that Liam was not coming to the coast. He had instead opted to join those of the townsfolk who intended to seek a new home elsewhere in the mountains, in one of the many towns further south. Alben had never gotten on well with the other boy, and the sight of him brought back his grief over the loss of his mother. He could only be glad that they were parting ways, most likely forever. He suspected that Liam would not leave the mountains. Like many of the mountain folk, his love of their alpine home was strong to the point of pride, leading him to look down on those who lived on the plains.

Alben had no sympathy with such an attitude. But he felt—perhaps because of his sentimental nature—that he and Liam were somehow tied together by the price that had been paid for their survival. When they said goodbye, he gave Liam the other rock, expressing the hope that he would keep it in memory of their home, and of Alben's mother's sacrifice. Liam had not shown any marked enthusiasm, but he had accepted the token readily enough.

That much Jonan had found out with ease. But when he tried to ascertain how the rock had passed from Liam, Alben's contemporary who had lived generations ago, to the unnamed stranger whom he had seen wearing it, he saw nothing. It was as though his rock didn't have the answer.

This experience supported the conclusion Jonan had reached based on his previous explorations. For the rock to show him something of Alben's story, he had to have some idea of what he was looking for. It was as if the talisman only responded to what it was asked.

And as curious as he was about this unexpected discovery, he didn't want to spend hours sitting around attempting to extract information from a rock. He wanted his senses to be on the alert for what was happening in the real world around him.

At first Jonan had worried that he would fall behind the Balenan travelers in their hired carriages. But the journey from Alezae to Kynton took almost a week, and felt ponderously slow even to Jonan, following on foot, and scrounging food as best he could. Lord Wrendal moved at a pace he presumably considered dignified. Jonan was quickly out of patience with the pompous Overseer, because the impractically slow pace made it difficult to blend in as an unrelated traveler for more than the first day. After that he had to be more creative in finding ways to maintain enough distance to avoid being recognized but still stick close enough not to lose the delegation.

He had been confident that once they were no longer confined to the ship, he would be able to get Scarlett on her own and reveal his identity to her. But maddeningly, this had not proved to be the case. He saw her from a distance, many times, but she was always closely guarded. More than once he thought he could have caught her eye if she would just look up, but she seemed to take no interest in her surroundings. Her eyes were almost invariably cast downward, her posture docile and her general demeanor unresponsive.

It was a pity, Jo thought, because the landscape through which they passed was beautiful, at least to his eyes. The very familiarity of the scenes lifted his spirits, and he wished he could have shared it with her. It was strange to see her in his own environment—she was even dressed in the attire favored by Kyonan women now. It was nothing at all like her jungle home, and he wondered whether she liked what she saw, or whether the air felt too dry, and the open fields too empty.

But of course he couldn't ask her. He watched her from afar, anxious to ensure that she was all right, but it brought him no reassurance to look at her. It wasn't that she was visibly unhappy. Since that distressing morning in her cabin, there had been no more outbursts or storms of tears that Jo could see. Scarlett seemed to have regained control of herself in the wake of what she believed to be Jonan's fate. She moved and spoke with both the coldness of Lady Wrendal and the poise of the rebel leader Scar.

Jo thought that Lord Wrendal seemed to have relaxed around her also, as if the return of his daughter's former manner reassured him of her renewed compliance. But Jo could only suppose that Scarlett was back to playing a deeper game of her own, one that would not be served by allowing her father to see her emotion. And in actual fact, he didn't think she had returned to her former manner exactly. She was unexpressive, sure, but it went beyond that. There was a deadness in her eyes that was new. It filled Jonan with acute distress every time he saw it.

Despite his concern for Scarlett, Jo enjoyed the journey north toward Kynton much more than he had enjoyed the voyage across the sea. Being able to move freely was a relief, and Kyona had never been more appealing. Perhaps it was just the result of his precarious position in unfamiliar Balenol followed by his confinement aboard the ship, but it seemed to him that the country through which he now traveled was noticeably more pleasant than the Kyona he had left.

Was it the influence of the new, legitimate king that made

faces everywhere seem lighter, and the very air seem cleaner? He remembered being struck by the climate of fear last time he had traveled through his homeland, but he formed no such impression now.

Certainly recent events had made an impact. They passed through several towns, and Jonan had the opportunity to wander through various markets. He didn't know whether to be disapproving or amused at the regular appearance of products that had certainly not been on offer in any Kyonan market three months ago. Powdered dragon teeth to make the hair grow thickly, blades that had been sealed by dragon fire and would therefore remain sharp indefinitely, dragon talons that, if worn on the person, would ward off danger.

One woman, trying to convince Jonan to pay an exorbitant price for a jar of dragon scales that would apparently guarantee him long life, swore that she had clandestinely removed the scales from a dragon herself while traveling through the Kyonan mountains. As Jonan was not only one of just three humans to enter the Dragon Realm in centuries, but had also grown up in a coastal fishing village, he had good reason to recognize the scales of both dragons and codfish. But he held his peace. Remembering Lord Wrendal's patent disbelief at his unknown conspirator's mention of dragons, Jonan wondered what the nobleman made of this evidence of widespread acceptance of their existence.

When they finally arrived at the capital, Jonan slipped ahead, wanting to reach the castle before the Balenans. He was glad he had done so, because as Lord Wrendal's group drew close, a squadron of Kyonan soldiers rode out to meet them, escorting them the rest of the way in a tight formation. Jonan, on the other hand, was free to make his way through the city without drawing attention to himself.

He hadn't spent much time in Kynton before leaving the

country, but it wasn't difficult to find the castle. Unlike last time, when he had entered the city from the forest to its east, the delegation used the large southern entrance. Jonan passed through the enormous wooden gates without attracting any notice, but a swift glance upward showed that archers were positioned along the wall above, their faces expressionless and their eyes fixed on the approaching Balenans. Jo smiled grimly. He was glad to see that Cal wasn't underestimating the supposedly diplomatic envoy.

The main thoroughfare ran from the gate right through the heart of the city, curving eastward toward the castle. Jonan had fully intended to gain entrance to this structure ahead of the group so that he could find Cal, but this proved not to be as simple as he had expected. He reached the castle without difficulty, but he couldn't just walk inside. Whether the Kyonan castle was always more closely guarded than the Balenan one, or whether it was a result of the approaching delegation, he didn't know. But either way, the imposing intricately carved doorway at the top of a broad flight of steps was flanked by guards, and they flatly refused him entry.

He was still arguing with them, attempting to convince them that the king would be glad to speak with him, when the Balenan group approached. The guards instantly lost interest in him, turning their attention to the foreigners, their faces tight. Jo cursed softly and fell back, not wanting to run the risk of being recognized by Lord Wrendal before he had found the chance to speak with Cal.

He took no interest in the formal exchange occurring between one of the foreign officials and the head guard at the castle's entrance. Instead, he joined the crowd of interested locals who had gathered behind the Balenans, waiting for his opportunity. From behind, he saw Scarlett look up briefly at the castle, and wondered what she thought of it. He remembered how dour he had found the Balenan castle upon first sight. But Scarlett had grown up there—perhaps she had a fondness for it. He had never asked her. Still, he thought that Cal's was much nicer. It looked just as strong, but much more beautifully designed. And there were no permanent structures of punishment or execution positioned directly outside it.

The guards were apparently satisfied with whatever discussions occurred, because after a moment they stepped aside, and the big doors opened. For all the apparently tightened security, it was not difficult for Jonan to slip inside at the back of the group. Once inside, he detached himself from the others as speedily as possible, instead trying to blend in with the many servants who scurried across the space, obviously expecting the foreign group.

Jo may not have explored the city much, but he had done a fair bit of wandering about the castle when he had stayed here last, and he knew his way around a little. He was just wondering how likely he would be to succeed in finding Cal if he just went poking around, when the question became irrelevant. A stillness fell over the scene in the entranceway, and looking up, Jo could instantly see why.

A broad stone staircase rose up from the area where Jo stood, leading to a wide landing, where it split into two staircases to right and left, reaching the level above. Word of the arrival had obviously spread, and their host had arrived, entourage in tow, to greet them.

Cal! Jo only just managed to clamp his mouth shut on the cry of greeting that rose to his lips. It felt like an eternity since he had seen his friend, and his heart leaped at the sight of him. But at the same time...he couldn't help but stare in amazement at the serious young ruler before him, resplendent in a formal outfit in the traditional Kyonan blue and gold.

With his innate sense of how best to play to the setting, Cal had paused dramatically on the landing, looking calmly down upon his visitors. He made an impressive picture, his advisors arrayed behind him, and even Jo felt a bit overawed by the presence of the young king. Cal approached with confidence in his every movement, his silent regard somehow communicating more strongly than words that he was in command of the situation.

"King Calinnae, we are honored," Lord Wrendal opened, and Jo wondered if Cal could hear the oily falseness of the man's voice as clearly as he could. Rolling his eyes, he tuned the Balenan out. He had no interest in listening to the official greetings, tedious as they were sure to be.

Instead he looked around for Elnora, surprised that she was not standing at Cal's side. He spotted her after a moment, ranged on one of the staircases behind Cal. She stood next to a tall man whom Jo recognized as Leander, one of Cal's distant kin who had been instrumental in reclaiming the throne. Jo felt a warmth spread through him at sight of Elnora, too. It hadn't felt like he was really back home until he had laid eyes on his friends.

Leander was looking at the Balenans as a whole with hard, suspicious eyes, but Elnora's gaze was fixed unblinkingly on one person in particular, her eyes widening slightly in an otherwise expressionless face. Jo followed the trajectory to see Scarlett, her face upturned to take in Cal's approach. Neither Cal nor Elnora had noticed Jo. And why would they? They were fully focused on the Balenan delegation, and had no reason to look closely at the Kyonan servants ringing the room.

After an exchange of civilities, throughout which Cal continued to conduct himself with an icy politeness that told Jo, at least, that he had no trust for the visitors whatsoever, the group progressed up the staircase and down a wide passage. Jo followed at a discreet distance. Truth be told, he was not conspicuous, as a number of servants were doing the same, their official roles clearly a flimsy front for avid curiosity. He glanced involuntarily into the throne room as they passed it. Last time he had been in there he had been taking part in an armed conflict, fighting desperately for his life against the former king's guards.

But it wasn't their destination today. They continued past it to a smaller, but still imposing, receiving room. The whole group entered, with the exception of Jonan and the nosy servants of course, but only briefly. The castle steward seemed to be awaiting them inside, and while Lord Wrendal and Scarlett stayed in the room, the rest of the Balenan delegation emerged straight away and were led off to their accommodations. A short time later, most of the Kyonans exited the room also, presumably returning to their previous activities. Peering quickly in through the open doorway, Jo was surprised to see that only Leander and his twin Laramie were left with Cal, although guards were stationed right outside the door.

He looked around, and caught sight of Elnora moving off with the rest of the Kyonans. He had somehow missed her when she came through the door. He hesitated, tempted to run after her, but decided against it. He felt uneasy for both Cal and Scarlett, being shut up in close proximity with Lord Wrendal. He could vaguely hear the nobleman continuing to make pompous speeches. It was tempting to burst in and claim Cal's attention right now, just to see the look on Lord Wrendal's face. But he knew that the impression Cal made at this moment was important, and he held himself in check.

He was astonished, however, only a few minutes later, to see Lord Wrendal emerge as well. He was flanked by both Laramie and Leander, who were watching the Balenan nobleman with expressions that told Jo that they had no trouble identifying who they needed to keep a close eye on. Lord Wrendal didn't look discomfited by their scrutiny. On the contrary, he looked well pleased with himself.

Jo, who had retreated some distance down the corridor in an attempt to hide his observation, looked between the three figures who were now moving away from him and the open door. Were Cal and Scarlett alone, then? He blinked. Lord Wrendal certainly didn't waste any time.

He moved eagerly back toward the room then paused, taking in the guards still standing to attention at the door. Looking around, Jo saw a servant going past with a platter of food.

"I'll take that," he said quickly, whisking it out of the boy's hands, deaf to his protests. Jo walked quickly up to the door and nodded at the guards. "Refreshments for His Majesty's guest," he said confidently, and passed through. The room was empty, but he could hear Cal's voice coming through a doorway into an adjoining room.

"Your father seemed very certain of your interest in our records room, but I daresay he was mistaken."

Jo, pausing just next to the open doorway, suppressed a smile at his friend's frigid tone. Cal's words might be diplomatic, but he clearly had no difficulty seeing through whatever maneuvers Lord Wrendal had employed to leave the two young people alone.

"Not at all, Your Majesty. It is a well-appointed room," said Scarlett, her tone equally colorless. She sounded very much like her Lady Wrendal persona.

"I shall be sure to ask our records keeper to give you a thorough tour, then," Cal replied, his voice short. "There can be little to interest you in my instruction, as I am not well versed in these records. I can assure you I have no intention of monopolizing your attention while you are with us."

Jo grinned. The subtext was clear. Cal seemed to have grown skillful at diplomatic speech. Jo supposed he could hardly say outright, *I have no intention of marrying you, and you can tell your father to forget it.*

"I would not wish you to be put to the trouble," said Scarlett, but Jo had heard enough of this terse politeness. Abandoning the platter on a nearby table, he slipped through into the small records room occupied by Cal and Scarlett, closing the door softly behind him.

"Will the two of you stop trying to out-freeze each other?" he said cheerfully. "You both sound ridiculous."

CHAPTER TWENTY-NINE

"Jo!" cried Cal and Scarlett simultaneously, and he grinned, not sure whose shock he enjoyed more.

Scarlett seemed to be frozen, but Cal strode across the room with quick strides, and Jo grasped his offered arm firmly.

"What are you doing here?" Cal demanded.

"Saving the day, of course," said Jo, still grinning. His gaze traveled past Cal to Scarlett, but she was still immobilized, her hand gripping the back of a chair and her expression blank as she met his eyes almost unseeingly.

Cal, however, raised his eyebrows in an endearingly familiar expression, the perfect mix of reproach and amusement. "Is that so? What makes you think I need saving, you impudent fiend? Don't you know I'm the king now?"

"Not you, idiot," said Jonan cheerfully. "I've come to rescue Scarlett from being forced into a political marriage with the dullest king alive." He turned to her, eager to coax her out of her shocked silence. "Trust me Scar," he said, his expression pious, "that young face hides the most boring old man's personality."

Scarlett met his eyes, her expression stricken, but Jo was

momentarily distracted by the choking sound that greeted his words. He turned away to locate the source, emerging from behind a tapestry.

"Elnora!" he cried gladly. Apparently Scarlett was capable of even more astonishment, because in his peripheral vision he saw her start in surprise.

"You're a sight for sore eyes," Jo said to Elnora. "It's a relief that you haven't jumped ship on Cal yet, because I don't think he can pull off this royal racket by himself."

Elnora laughed, coming forward to embrace him eagerly. "Jo, you're as outrageous as ever. And I'm glad to see you in one piece."

"You're calling me outrageous?" he protested. "When I just caught you hiding behind a tapestry, eavesdropping on a royal conversation?"

He had expected her to match his banter, but her face fell slightly. "Yes," she said, her attempt at lightheartedness suddenly less convincing. "I'm not quite proper enough to pass as royal, am I?"

Jo couldn't help but notice the distress on Cal's face as he frowned at Elnora, and the fact that she wouldn't meet Cal's eyes. He saw her gaze lingering instead on Scarlett's perfectly shaped, immaculately dressed form, and hastily changed the subject.

"Lord Wrendal's a nightmare, isn't he?"

"You're not kidding," said Cal with feeling, then seemed to suddenly remember Scarlett's presence. "Apologies," he said, his voice once again formal as he inclined his head in her direction. "I forgot myself. I meant no offense to you."

"None taken," said Scarlett, her voice faint. She was still grasping the chair back, and she hadn't quite regained her usual poise, her face pale and her eyes wide.

"Of course she's not offended," said Jo, smiling at Scarlett, whose eyes were still fixed on him. He reminded himself that while being in Cal and Elnora's presence made him more comfortable than he had been in months, they were perfect strangers to Scarlett. And hard as he had found their separation, it had been much worse for her, believing him to be dead. Knowing her as he did, it was clear to him that her battle to conceal her reaction to his reappearance was making her feel more vulnerable than ever. So he tried to keep his tone light to mask his own rush of emotions at their reunion.

"No," she said dryly, taking a deep breath as she clearly tried to master herself. "I don't think anyone could dislike my father more than I do. But never mind that. Can someone please explain to me what in the kingdom is going on?"

"I have a feeling that only Jo can do that," said Elnora, a laugh in her voice.

"Yes," said Cal, turning back to Jo. "You have some explaining to do! What have you been doing with yourself, and how do you know—wait a minute." Cal's expression grew horrified. "You haven't been in Balenol, have you?"

"That's right," said Jo cheerfully. "Just sailed back a week ago, on Scar's ship actually. Stowed away."

"Jo!" Cal exclaimed in horror, over the top of Scarlett's astonished protest. "Don't tell me you were caught by the traders!"

"Of course not," said Jo scornfully. "You know me, I always land on my feet."

"Then how..." Cal's look went from confusion to rebuke as understanding dawned. "Jo, tell me you didn't. You went there by choice?"

"Why are you acting so surprised?" demanded Jo. "I told you myself I wanted to go find my own adventure. Where did you think I was going, back home to Nerita?"

Cal groaned. "Of course not, but I assumed you'd go over the mountains to Valoria or something, not straight onto a ship bound for the country that has been enslaving our people for centuries!" He paused for a moment. "No offense," he said again, as an aside to Scarlett.

"No, I agree," she said promptly, her voice stronger. Jo was heartened to see that her color was starting to return as she looked him over. "It was a bit stupid, Jo."

He spluttered a protest, his expression hurt. "Even you're turning on me now, Scar?"

"Well, they're not wrong, are they?" she said reasonably.

"I don't know what you mean," he said, his voice stubborn.

"Really?" Cal's tone showed that he wasn't convinced for a moment. "Tell me Jo, how long did it take you after arriving in Balenol to fall afoul of whatever authorities are in charge there?"

Jo considered the question, unable to hold back his grin. "Three hours, give or take," he said cheerfully, and Cal groaned.

"It's not all bad," Jonan assured him, pointing to his cheek. "I got a scar out of it, to impress the ladies."

"Not to mention a sound beating," added Scarlett dryly. "And more than one knifing."

"Oh Jo!" said Elnora, sounding distressed. He waved her concern aside.

"It's nothing, I'm fine! What a lot of fuss you all make." He turned to Scarlett accusingly, hoping she could see the warmth in his eyes behind the banter. "You're pretty high and mighty considering I seem to recall one of those knife wounds being inflicted by you."

She flushed as Cal and Elnora turned astonished eyes on her, and Jo tried not to be distracted by the way the warm color brought out the soft beauty of her face. She had looked pale and drawn for too long.

"I—I mean—I didn't," she stammered, but Jo came to her rescue with a grin.

"It's all right, I was only teasing," he assured everyone. He smiled at Scarlett. "To use your own words, it didn't do me any harm to be reminded that I'm not invincible."

Scarlett still looked embarrassed, but Cal's eyes had taken on a gleam of appreciation. "You and I might get on much better than I had anticipated," he said humorously, addressing himself to Scarlett. He turned back to Jo.

"Although going to Balenol for a sightseeing tour was the action of the reckless fool you've always been, I can't deny that I'd be enormously pleased to have any information you can give me on what's happening there."

Jo nodded quickly. "Of course," he said. "I'll tell you everything I've learned, and there's a lot to tell." His eyes flicked over to Scarlett. "But first I need a minute alone with Scarlett. I need you to cover for me with her father—the man sticks to her like bog stench. The only reason he's not in here right now is because he thinks you're alone with Scarlett, succumbing more hopelessly to her charms by the second, I imagine. And he'll definitely try to kill me on sight if he gets wind of me being here. Fact of the matter is, he thinks I'm dead already. Thinks I had my head chopped off back in Nohl."

Elnora just blinked at this rapid flow of information, but Cal groaned. "Why am I not surprised?" he asked grimly.

"Jo," Scarlett protested faintly. "Surely King Calinnae has the right to your information without delay. You can't ask your king to 'cover for you'."

"Sure I can," said Jo promptly. "I've been trying to catch you alone for almost four weeks, without success. Helping me out is the least Cal can do. After all, I cleared out and gave him privacy enough times when he was trying to win Elnora over while the three of us were traveling together."

"I don't remember you showing any such consideration," muttered Cal, while Scarlett blushed rosily at Jonan's implication. But Elnora was grinning.

"Of course we can cover for you," she said quickly. She pointed across the room. "There's a withdrawing room through there. We can make sure no one interrupts you."

Jo didn't hesitate, merely sending her a grateful grin as he grabbed Scarlett's hand and pulled her toward the door indicated. He heard Elnora speaking to Cal behind him, her tone placating.

"Don't begrudge him the time, Cal, there'll be opportunity enough for you two to catch up and for him to tell you everything that's happened."

"Do you hear me complaining?" returned Cal's familiar voice. "You may not have realized, but it hasn't escaped my notice that if they get a minute alone to uh...talk, so do we. I'm sure I've been trying to achieve that for more than four weeks."

Jo grinned more broadly as he pulled the door closed behind him. He didn't think his friends would be trying to cut short his interview with Scarlett in a hurry. But the expression fell away as he turned and took in Scarlett's ashen countenance. She had moved halfway into the small room before turning, and her eyes were stuck to him as if he was an apparition.

He took a step toward her, but the look on her face made him pause. He had intended to take her immediately in his arms, but he could see at a glance that she was in no mood for such a greeting.

"Scarlett," he said uncertainly, taking another tentative step forward.

"I thought you were dead, Jo," she whispered. "I thought they executed you because of me, and it almost killed me too." She drew a shaky breath. "I've been...in anguish, picturing you being beaten for information first, with me far away and unable to do anything. It was...more than I could bear."

"I know," he said quickly, stepping forward and taking her hands. "I know, and I'm so sorry Scarlett. It was all my stupid fault. I really did stow away on your ship, and I could see how distressed you were. It was almost more than I could bear, too. I tried so many times to get you alone, but it was too risky."

"You were deterred by the risk?" she asked with a hint of dryness. "Is this just another dream, after all? Because surely you wouldn't say that in real life."

He squeezed her hands involuntarily, his heart full at the idea that she dreamed about him. "I know I'm reckless and pigheaded," he said. "I don't deny it. But that doesn't mean I'm incapable of learning from my mistakes. I probably would have taken the risk on my own account, but it would have put you in danger too, and that I wasn't willing to do. Not again. I deserved to have my head removed for endangering you so stupidly back in Nohl."

"Don't say that!" she said with a shudder. She raised her eyes curiously to his. "How did you get out? I thought they took you to the execution chamber."

"They did," he assured her. "But your cousin broke me out."

"Giles?" she asked in surprise, and he nodded. "So did you tell him everything, then?" she asked, looking slightly hesitant.

"No," said Jo quickly. "I told him basically nothing. I wasn't sure if you would want me to."

"And he still helped you?" she asked, her eyes glowing. "I knew I couldn't be mistaken to trust him. I was sure you two would like each other if you were given the chance."

"I don't know if I'd go so far as to say he likes me," said Jo ruefully. "He saved me from having my head cut off, sure, but I think that was more to do with not wanting Lord Grentan to provoke war by sending my head to Kynton in a bottle."

"What?" Scarlett gasped, but Jo waved the topic aside.

"Never mind that. I don't care what his reasons were, I'm still grateful for his help. I just don't think he exactly approves of my interest in you. He had some words to say about, well, this kind of thing." Jo gestured to their situation, alone in the small room.

Scarlett smiled. "Yes, Giles is very serious. I could tell we had offended his sense of propriety that night, when he discovered us..." she hesitated, her color rising.

"Kissing," supplied Jo helpfully. "We were kissing. Had you forgotten? Did you need me to jog your memory?"

"Hardly," she said, laughing a little even while her cheeks still flamed red. She looked up at him shyly. "How could I forget?"

His breath caught at the look in her eyes, and his words tumbled over each other. "Scarlett, I know my timing was..."

"Unwise?" she suggested, and he laughed unsteadily.

"I was going to say idiotic," he said. "But it was real. I mean, I meant everything." He hesitated, and his next words came out in a whisper. "I was so afraid for you, Scarlett. I was determined to protect you, and instead I..." He swallowed. "I know you were worried about me, but I couldn't bring myself to care in the least about what became of me. I was just terrified about what might happen to you because of me. Being parted from you was worse than any beating would have been."

"I understand," she said simply. "I felt the same way."

He reached for her then, attempting to pull her into his arms. But she stepped back, her eyes darting nervously to the door.

"What are you doing?" she demanded. "My father—"

"Is not going to burst in this time, as you know perfectly well," said Jo patiently.

"Well, I know, but we have to be serious, Jo. There might be a lot of people depending on us. If we can't prevent war—"

"No one is depending on us in this moment," said Jo, his voice soft as he took one of her hands in his. She didn't meet his eyes, but his gaze roamed over her face perceptively. "Surely we're past playing a part, Scarlett," he said gently. "Don't hide behind Lady Wrendal, and don't hide behind Scar." He put a hand under her chin, gently tilting her head up until she finally looked him in the eye. "If you don't want me to kiss you again, say so, as yourself, and I won't."

His face was slightly stern as he glared down at her, but the look in her exquisitely shaped eyes made the expression slide away. They both stilled, and Jo lost his train of thought briefly. But as the moment stretched out, he suddenly remembered his own words, and he realized with a thrill what Scarlett was communicating by her silence.

He reached out a hand, more tentatively this time, and stroked her cheek with his thumb. Her skin was incredibly soft against his fingers, calloused as they had become. She reached out with unsteady hands to clutch the front of his shirt, and the way she was looking at him made his heart thump erratically.

She was almost too beautiful to be real. It seemed excessive for someone so stunning to also be brave and selfless and intelligent and kind. And entirely implausible for her to even consider him. But Jonan wasn't about to argue.

He leaned down, touching his lips to hers in a gentle movement, trying to contain his eagerness and take his cue from her. He hoped that she would respond enthusiastically, as she had last time. For a moment she was frozen, her hands still curled up in his tunic, then she let out a soft groan at the kiss, and her whole body relaxed against him. He gathered her instantly into his arms, exulting in the way her soft form seemed to fit so perfectly there. She reached up to wind her arms around his neck, and he deepened the kiss. His every nerve tingled at the fervor with which she returned the embrace, her lips moving eagerly against his.

There was no interruption this time, but the moment still felt all too short. Jo couldn't help but let out a protest when Scarlett eventually pulled away. He tried to pull her back in, but she stopped him with a shaky laugh, placing her hand flat against his chest.

"I need a minute to take it all in," she told him breathlessly. "It's all right for you—you've been following the delegation all the way here from Nohl. But I thought you were dead all this time. I never thought I'd get to see you again, let alone...you know..." she gestured toward him with her free hand, and he caught it, pressing his lips to it impulsively. She smiled, her expression uncharacteristically shy. "I feel like I'm in a dream."

"Well I'm in no hurry to wake up," he said hopefully, but she shook her head, a smile on her lips.

"I have way too many questions," she said. "My father forced me onto that ship in such a rush, I have no idea how much of a mess I left behind me." She looked up at Jonan, her face suddenly apprehensive. "Do you know if Bonnie made it out safely?"

He squeezed her hand, his own demeanor instantly becoming serious. "Yes, she did," he assured her. "Last I saw her she was safely at the base tree, with Stan and the others." He gave a sudden jerk, remembering a crucial omission. "Stan! I have to tell Elnora!"

"So it really is her?" Scarlett asked in amazement. "That really is Stan's sister?"

Jo nodded.

"And she's going to marry the new king?"

"Well, unless you cut her out," said Jo humorously, but she just glared at him.

"The new king, who is clearly a close personal friend of yours," she went on, her tone accusing. "I think you have a lot to explain, Jonan."

"I suppose I do," he said sheepishly. "It's a long story, and I'd like to tell it to you sometime, but for now I'll just say that Cal and I grew up together, like brothers. A bit like you and your cousins, really. Except that we're not blood relations. And we come from a small fishing village, like I told you, and neither one of us had the smallest inkling of Cal's royal ancestry until very recently."

Scarlett was silent for a moment, and there was something in her expression that Jo didn't like.

"What is it?" he asked anxiously.

"It's just..." She hesitated. "For a long time my life has been a deadly patchwork of secrets and deceptions and playing the part. I hardly knew myself anymore. But so quickly, almost as soon as I met you, I let you into all of it, perhaps more than anyone. And I started to feel like you really knew me." She looked him in the eye. "I came to trust you."

He squeezed her hand again, gratified but confused. "You can trust me, Scarlett," he said. "You know you can."

"But you don't trust me," she said, an ache in her voice. "You didn't tell me the truth, and I'm trying to understand why."

"Oh Scarlett," he said, gathering her against him. She leaned her head on his chest wearily, and the confiding gesture only increased the remorse he felt at the hurt he had seen in her eyes. "I should have told you everything. I'm sorry. It wasn't because I didn't trust you. Or at least, not after the first couple of days, once I found out about your identity. I hardly know why I kept it to myself. Partly I was afraid of raising expectations. Cal really didn't send me—you heard him yourself, he had no idea where I even was. I thought if people knew about our friendship, they would think I had some kind of power or authority to act on the crown's behalf, and that surely wouldn't end well. And I really was going to tell you at the base tree that night, all of you. But then we got word of the revolt in the logging camp, and there was no time for anything else."

He paused. "But there was more to it than that." He sighed,

the sudden insight into himself pricking his consciousness uncomfortably. "It was pride, I suppose. You see, there was a mistake. I thought—Cal and I both thought—that I was the one who was supposed to be king. We were already most of the way to Kynton before we found out the truth. Our parents switched us at birth."

Scarlett pulled back to stare up at him in astonishment, and he shook his head with a rueful smile. "Part of that long story I'll tell you sometime. Don't get me wrong, I don't want to be king. I never did. I hated the very thought of it. But it was still something of a shock to go from thinking I was the long-lost heir of a noble royal bloodline to finding out I really was just Jonan, an unremarkable kid from a fishing village."

Scarlett leaned up to give him a quick kiss on the cheek, planting it right on his scar. "You are anything but unremarkable," she said softly.

He smiled gratefully at her, smoothing a strand of her hair behind her ear before continuing. "I had always wanted to set off on an adventure, even before all of it. But after Cal came into his own...there was really no question for me. I don't begrudge him the role, and I want to see him succeed more than anything, but I didn't want to stick around to fade into the background while he did. And," he said, giving her an ironic look, "I had no interest in getting caught up in court intrigue or mingling with nobles."

She laughed suddenly, appreciating as he had known she would the twist of fate that had landed him in the midst of the Balenan court.

"I left without clear intentions, but when I got to Balenol, I was determined to help the slaves," Jo went on. "I didn't plan to make a stir like I did—it just happened. But it was a bit hard to stomach the fact that I was suddenly in a position of privilege— precarious as it was—and it was nothing to do with me, and everything to do with Cal's ascension to the throne. I hadn't fully realized it until now, but I guess I wanted to succeed on my own. I didn't want to throw his name around and get results just because of my connection to him."

He shook his head. "As I say it, I'm disgusted with myself. The stakes were so high for so many people. I was utterly foolish not to use every resource at my disposal. But I didn't even realize I was doing it." He pulled Scarlett against him again suddenly, placing his head on top of hers to hide his face. It wasn't easy, even with her, to admit to such weakness. "Pride and arrogance," he said bitterly.

"No," she said softly. "A very natural desire for independence from someone who was never born to follow." She gave him a quick squeeze. "Don't be so hard on yourself. Few of us are as self-aware as we should be."

"You're too good to me," said Jonan warmly, and she laughed again.

"Having someone miraculously restored to you from the dead will do that," she said. Her face sobered slightly. "I just wish you were out of danger now. But you were right that my father will do his utmost to kill you if he finds out you're here."

"Forget about me," said Jonan, his arms tightening protectively around her as he suddenly remembered what had sent him racing after her in desperate haste. "There's a lot I need to tell you. You're in more danger than you realize."

"What do you mean?" she asked, frowning up at him.

"Cal and Elnora should hear this too," he said. "We need to figure out what we're going to do."

With his usual impulsiveness, he seized her hand and headed for the door without another word.

CHAPTER THIRTY

He didn't particularly intend to be stealthy, but moving without being detected had become habitual to him, and he entered the records room so quietly that neither of its occupants heard his entrance. He hovered in the doorway, seeing clearly that he was interrupting.

Cal held Elnora in his arms, quite as tightly as Jo had just been holding Scarlett, and his voice sounded a little breathless as he spoke to her.

"That's what I think of that comment," he said, as Elnora raised adoring eyes to his. "And if I hear one more word out of you about suitability and alliances, I'll—"

"You'll what, Your Majesty?" Elnora teased, her voice cheeky. "Lock me in the dungeons?"

"I wouldn't recommend it," Jo cut in cheerfully. "I have some experience now, and they're mighty uncomfortable."

The couple jumped at his voice, Elnora springing away from Cal, her expression guilty. Cal maintained one arm around her waist, scowling at his friend.

"You're a nuisance, Jo," he said. "Can't you learn to knock?"

But Jo just grinned at his friends' discomfiture. He knew

exactly how they felt, although at least he wasn't about to pull out a sword on them. "Well how was I to know that you wouldn't want to be interrupted? I thought you would simply be having a civilized conversation."

"Which is exactly what you were doing, I'm sure," muttered Cal belligerently, and Jonan grinned more broadly.

"Of course."

Elnora gave Cal's arm an admonitory whack, addressing herself to Jonan. "Don't listen to him, Jo. He's missed you terribly."

Cal's face softened as he pulled Elnora against his side. "She's right," he admitted, looking at Jo warmly. "I've missed you every day."

Jo returned the smile, encompassing Elnora with his glance. "I've missed you too. Both of you." He grimaced. "Not that I could ever get away from you exactly. The good people of Nohl won't shut up about the mysterious new Kyonan king."

"Really?" asked Elnora, throwing a glowing look up at Cal. "I'm glad." Her gaze hardened. "I hope they're afraid." She suddenly seemed to remember Scarlett, standing a step behind Jo, and looked at her hesitantly. "I mean...maybe that seems rude, but—"

Jo sighed, tugging gently on Scarlett's hand to pull her up to stand next to him. "I think we should explain some basics so everyone can stop walking on eggshells. Scarlett is on our side. She's the absolute best of Balenol." Scarlett started to protest, but he cut her off. "You are, Scar, don't argue with me. Her father, on the other hand, is the worst of them. He's the Overseer of Slaves and he's cruel for fun. Unknown to him, Scarlett started a secret resistance, and for the last few years has been living a double life with the aim of undermining the slave trade and freeing as many as they can."

Cal and Elnora both turned their gazes on Scarlett, their

expressions astonished and impressed. She seemed uncomfortable with their admiration, but the sight made Jo's heart glow.

"The result, of course," he said grimly, "is that she's in constant danger of discovery. And with the father she has, it's no exaggeration to say that puts her life at risk." He turned serious eyes on Scarlett. "And that's never been more true than now. Lord Wrendal came here with the stated intention of securing an alliance through a marriage between Cal and Scarlett—trusting in her charms to win you over, Cal—which he believes would allow him to control you as a puppet ruler. And if it looked like that would work, I think he would be willing enough to follow through with it."

"And if it doesn't look like it will work?" Cal prompted, and Jo looked over at him. He could see Elnora glowering next to him, and he could tell that one part of Lord Wrendal's plan in particular had annoyed her more than the rest.

"If it doesn't look like it will work, he'll be able to turn to his backup plan, which is what he would have done in the first place if King Siloam wasn't so difficult to rouse to action."

"What's the backup plan?" Cal asked.

"War," said Jonan simply, and both Cal and Elnora drew in sharp breaths, throwing each other a glance.

"But, Jo..." said Scarlett, a frown on her face. "King Siloam doesn't want war. My father has a lot of influence, but he can't declare war unless he has the king's authorization. And the king won't give it without serious provocation."

"Which is why your father has every intention of making sure there is that provocation," said Jo grimly.

"What do you mean?" asked Scarlett uneasily, but Cal seemed reassured by Jo's words.

"I'm not so easy to manipulate," he said. "I'll take great care not to do anything to provoke war. As angry as I am about the slave trade, I don't exactly want to lead the country into an armed conflict only months after ascending to the throne."

"You won't have to actually do anything," said Jo, his arm going protectively around Scarlett's shoulders in an involuntary movement. "Nothing except reject a marriage alliance. But when that rejection is followed by Lord Wrendal's daughter being murdered in cold blood within your castle, it won't be difficult to persuade everyone that you have offered Balenol an insult that can't be tolerated. You should know that Scarlett is a cousin to the royal family through her mother's side. She was raised by them, and people see her basically as a princess. Killing her would be seen as an act of aggression against their crown. I think it would be enough to start a war."

Cal and Elnora were both staring at Jo in undisguised horror, but Scarlett nodded slowly, even while she pressed closer to Jonan's side, apparently unconsciously.

"It makes sense," she said softly. "Now I understand some of his veiled comments. And I didn't think he was trying quite hard enough to force me into this marriage." She shuddered. "I'm sure he would prefer his backup plan."

"But..." Elnora's voice was horrified. "You're his daughter. Surely he doesn't want you to die. Surely he won't really kill you himself?"

Scarlett gave a hollow laugh. "No, I suspect he'll have someone else do his dirty work," she said. "But he wouldn't exactly shed tears over my death. As far as he's concerned, I live to serve his purposes. And if I can help him start his war by dying, he won't hesitate. He's been angry enough to want me dead since he found out about me and Jo. And that's without even knowing I was involved in the resistance! If he knew that, he probably would want to do it himself."

"That's awful," said Elnora softly. "I'm so sorry." She stepped forward, placing a reassuring hand on Scarlett's shoulder. "We won't let it happen, don't worry. You're a guest in our castle now, and we'll protect you. Won't we, Cal?" She turned to him, and he stepped forward quickly, nodding.

"Of course we will!" He smiled at Elnora. Jo hadn't missed the way his face had lit up as Elnora talked about "our castle". "If you're a friend of Jo's, you can count on our support."

Jo gave him a look at the word "friend", which Cal returned blandly. Elnora looked between them, amused, and the sight of her suddenly jogged Jo's memory again.

"Scar has another claim on your friendship beside me!" he said suddenly, addressing himself to Elnora. "She's close with Stan. Constance, I mean. Your sister."

Elnora jerked convulsively, her eyes flying between Jo and Scarlett as the color drained from her face. Cal's mouth fell open.

"Are you serious?" he asked, locking eyes on Scarlett. "You know Elnora's sister? She's alive?"

"Yes," said Scarlett quickly. "She's not just alive, she's one of the leaders of the resistance. One of the very best of us."

"I can't believe she's alive," whispered Elnora. "I didn't dare to hope..." Tears started to fill her eyes, and Cal drew her close. She turned her face up to his. "We have to bring her home, Cal!" she said. "We have to save her. Even though she can surely never forgive me for not doing anything to stop her being taken, I still have to see her."

"Forgive you?" repeated Scarlett, startled. "She doesn't blame you! You're all she cares about! Ever since I've known her, she's been determined to get back here to make sure you're all right. Every new intake, she would insist on scouting the camp herself, to make sure you hadn't been captured."

Elnora's tears welled over at that, and heedless of the audience, she turned her head and buried her face in Cal's chest. He held her tightly, talking soothingly.

"We'll bring her home, Elnora, I swear. We'll bring all of them home, whatever it takes."

"It's going to take more than you think," said Jo grimly. "The resistance has freed a lot of slaves, and there's a reason none of them have ever come back to Kyona."

"What do you mean?" asked Cal, but before Jo could answer, the four of them all turned at a noise coming from the receiving room.

"It's probably my father!" Scarlett whispered, her color draining away again as she looked at Jo. "You need to hide."

Jo frowned, grasping her hand more tightly. "No, thanks. I've had my fill of hiding. This is my home ground now."

"Of course you don't need to hide," said Cal sharply. "This is my castle, and you're under my protection now. Anyone who suggests that you shouldn't be here will have me to deal with."

"I applaud the sentiment," said Scarlett quickly, "but if you're going to reveal everything to my father, you'd better be ready to fight it out right now. Once he sees Jo, I'm not sure what he's going to do."

"And where does that leave Scarlett?" Elnora asked, raising her head from Cal's chest and running a shaky hand across her eyes. "He'll expect her to go with him, and unless you want to give exactly the provocation he's trying to create, how can you refuse?"

"She's right," said Scarlett. "We have to play along for now."

Jo growled in frustration, tightening his hold on her hand even more. "I'm sick of playing a part," he said. He captured her gaze, lowering his voice. "I don't want to let you go again. I don't like leaving you in his power."

She touched his cheek gently. "It will be all right," she said, her own voice soft. "Now I know you're alive, and nearby, I'm not even afraid of whatever he's planning." She dropped her hand. "Now get out of here," she said more firmly.

He hesitated for one more moment, soaking in the sight of her. "Not for much longer," he promised her. "Soon I'm going to get you away from him, whatever it takes, and then we stick together." She met his look, her eyes glowing, and he leaned in abruptly, heedless of Cal and Elnora, to place a quick kiss on her lips.

Suddenly they heard Lord Wrendal's voice in the receiving room, deceptively cheerful. "Still in the records room, are they? My, my."

"Quick!" hissed Scarlett, and Jo let go of her, grabbing Elnora's hand and racing into the withdrawing room that he and Scarlett had recently vacated. He shut the door behind him and turned to find Elnora beaming at him. He grinned back easily, giving her a quick hug. It was so good to be among friends again.

"Tut tut," she teased in a whisper as he let go. "Your Scarlett will think you're very fickle, closeting yourself in here with her one minute and with me the next."

He chuckled. "Forget Scarlett, what will Cal say? Now he's got the might of the crown behind him, I'd better watch my step. He must be feeling insecure now that he's no longer the best looking guy in the castle."

Elnora rolled her eyes at him, and they both fell silent for a moment, straining to hear what was happening on the other side of the door. From what Jo could make out, Lord Wrendal had joined the two in the records room and was making veiled comments about how long they had been in solitary conversation, clearly well pleased with the success of his maneuvering. Jo scowled.

"They do make a very good looking couple, don't they?" said Elnora softly, responding to Jonan's joke. "She's magnificent, Jo, I could hardly believe my eyes when she walked in. She looks like a queen."

Jo opened his mouth to agree in glowing terms, but something in Elnora's demeanor checked him. She was clearly troubled, but surely she couldn't doubt Cal's constancy.

"Yes," he said lightly. "What a shame you and I didn't suit. We could have freed them both up to make an alliance and make everyone happy."

"Yes," she said, sounding miserable. "It is a shame."

"Elnora!" Jo protested, only just remembering to whisper as he gave her a little shake. "I was joking. What's going on with you? Surely you're not having second thoughts about Cal!"

"Of course not!" she said. "As if I ever could."

He frowned at her. "Well don't try to tell me he's having doubts about you, because I wouldn't believe it. Why were you hiding in there, anyway? I was surprised you weren't right there with him when you all came to receive the Balenans, and surprised that you left with the others after everyone came into the receiving room. Aren't you two formally betrothed? Shouldn't you be up front and visible with Cal?"

She sighed. "Betrothed isn't married," she said. "Some of the advisors didn't want to offend the foreign delegation by seeming to reject the marriage alliance without even hearing them out." Her voice darkened. "What they mean of course, is that they hope our marriage will never happen."

"And you're telling me Cal let them wheedle him into excluding you?" asked Jo, incensed.

She laughed grimly. "Of course not. He wanted me beside him, but I didn't want to cause more trouble than I already have, and he couldn't force me to agree. I wouldn't have been there at all if he hadn't absolutely insisted. I could see he wanted me to stay when everyone else was leaving, but I thought it would be best not to push it."

"How considerate of you," said Jo ironically. "And, being so compliant and eager to please these advisors, you snuck back around and hid behind a tapestry to eavesdrop. Wouldn't it have been easier to just stay in the room?"

Elnora grinned in spite of herself. "Well, I didn't plan to eavesdrop," she whispered reasonably. "But I didn't expect that foreign lord to leave, or the twins to follow him. When I realized Cal and the foreign princess were on their own, can you blame me for feeling an...overwhelming curiosity to know what they were talking about?"

He grinned back. "No, I guess I can't. And she's not actually a princess, you know."

Elnora shrugged. "Whatever." Her smile was gone, and she had wound one arm around her slim form defensively.

"At least Cal didn't seem put out to find you listening in," offered Jonan, trying to be encouraging.

She sighed. "No, he wasn't in the least annoyed with me, even though it's exactly the kind of behavior that makes them all think I'm not fit to be queen. He should have told me off really, but all he could do was say he was glad to know I was close by after all."

"Well I'm glad he's not letting them turn him into an insufferable prig!" said Jo, with feeling.

Elnora shushed him, even as she smiled half-heartedly. "No, he's too stubborn for that." She dropped her voice even lower. "And I love him for that stubbornness. But—oh Jo!" she said, turning a suddenly distraught face to him. "I want him to succeed, and—"

She began to pace restlessly. "How naive we all were, thinking we could stroll in and take on these exalted roles without the least bit of preparation. You had it right all along—I should have taken off before the waters could get muddied. But I couldn't have brought myself to do it. I wanted to be near him too much, and that's what he wants too. But you don't know how complicated all this court maneuvering is. I'm a millstone around his neck, Jo!"

She was wringing her hands as she spoke, and Jo stepped forward and took them in a reassuring clasp. "You're not," he said firmly. "You make each other stronger, you always have. And I do have some idea of how tortuous court intrigues can be. Scarlett is a master at navigating it all, but it makes me want to escape through the nearest exit."

Elnora smiled unconvincingly. "Yes, I'm sure she is," she said. "She was raised to it, I suppose."

Any further conversation was cut off as the door was opened at that moment without ceremony. The two of them blinked up at Cal, standing in the doorway regarding them with a long-suffering look. Elnora turned slightly pink, pulling her hands out of Jonan's, but Jo just met Cal's look humorously, a twinkle in his eyes.

"Curse you, Jo," said Cal without heat. "I leave the room for five minutes—can't you refrain from holding Elnora's hands?"

Jo laughed, not bothering to respond. He was perfectly aware that Cal knew he was no threat. "Is Scarlett gone, then?" he asked, and Cal nodded.

"She left with her father. I think they're settling in somewhere."

Jo sobered at once. "I don't like letting her out of my sight," he admitted. "Not when her father is involved."

"Would he really have her killed, Jo?" Elnora asked, her eyes wide.

He nodded grimly. "I really think he would, if it would benefit him."

"I don't think you need to be worried for the moment, Jo," said Cal reassuringly. "You can bet that I've got people watching every member of that delegation very closely. We're not exactly trusting when it comes to the South Lands."

Jo nodded, his expression serious. "Things are bad over there, Cal," he said. "Worse than I had imagined. I have a lot to tell you."

"And I'm eager to hear it," said Cal. "But not right now. I've already stretched my absence to breaking point. Believe it or not, I can't really get away with disappearing for hours at a time these days." He sighed. "To tell you the truth, the timing of this delegation is not ideal. We have enough going on already, between stupid court dramas, and the defection of some of the guards."

"Some of the guards defected?" asked Jonan sharply, and Cal nodded.

"The ones still loyal to Yaeger. Some of Yaeger's men stayed, of course, to infiltrate my own guard. But the bulk of the traitors left, which is probably for the best, really. Fortunately we were able to replace them quickly with foresters who came with Laramie and Leander."

Jo raised his eyebrows. "You seem pretty calm about it, given you know you've got traitors hiding among your people."

Cal shrugged. "I never thought it would be smooth," he said. "The thing that really troubles me is that we still don't know where Yaeger is."

Jo frowned. "Remind me *who* Yaeger is?"

"He was Chief of Filip's Royal Guard," said Cal. "He was at the battle, but he got away."

Cal's expression was dark, his eyes flicking to Elnora, and suddenly Jo remembered with blazing clarity the man who had targeted Elnora during the battle in an attempt to fatally distract Cal from his own duel. His mouth fell open.

"Yaeger!" he cried. "That's who it was!"

"What?" Cal and Elnora were both staring at him.

"I've seen him!" said Jo eagerly. "In Alezae, when we landed! I knew I recognized him, but I couldn't remember where I'd seen him before. He was the one with the second rock."

"Second rock?" repeated Elnora blankly, but Cal wasn't to be distracted.

"He's in Alezae?" he said, his voice fierce. "I'll send a squadron at once." He paused. "Maybe I should go myself, actually."

Jo shook his head. "No, don't do that. He's not there anymore. He was in league with Lord Wrendal. He was going to follow us here at a distance, with his men. He might already be in Kynton."

"What?" thundered Cal, putting out a protective arm and pulling Elnora close. "He's here?" His eyes grew hard. "And this Lord Wrendal is working with him? I'll have his blood for that."

"Get in line," said Jo dryly. He paused. "For Lord Wrendal, I mean. Yaeger I couldn't care less about."

Cal didn't answer, his stormy gaze lingering on Elnora. Jo was still enraged every time he thought about Lord Wrendal striking Scarlett, and he couldn't exactly be surprised that Cal wasn't in a hurry to forgive Yaeger for attempting to run his sword through Elnora's heart.

"How do you know he's in league with Lord Wrendal?" asked Elnora calmly, the only one who seemed not to have become distracted from the main point.

"I was eavesdropping," said Jo, and briefly told them everything he had overheard at the inn in Alezae.

Cal seemed to have a hold on himself again, his expression becoming thoughtful, but Elnora's reaction was wholly unexpected. A smile had begun to grow on her face as Jo spoke, and in the momentary silence that followed his words she let out a quickly stifled laugh.

"What?" asked Jo, surprised. Even Cal was staring at Elnora in confusion.

"Sorry," she chuckled. "It's just...Cal's been worried about Yaeger's whereabouts for three months, and has tried without much success to discover the extent of what he's planning." She grinned. "It's just so like you, Jo, to disappear without a hint of where you're going and what you're up to, to be gone for months without sending any word to let us know you're alive, and then to turn up completely out of the blue, at a crucial moment, not only in one piece, but having conveniently picked up all the answers along the way."

Jo couldn't help but grin himself. "When you put it like that," he said. "I am rather remarkable, aren't I?"

"Don't let it go to your head." Elnora's tone was severe, but she was still chuckling. Cal, on the other hand, had given only a perfunctory smile at her mirth, clearly still deep in thought about the problem at hand.

"She's right, this information is invaluable. I don't exactly like the idea of Yaeger nearby, but this could be our opportunity to stop him once and for all. Maybe it's a good thing."

"I'm just sorry I didn't find out more," said Jo. "They didn't use any names, and I don't know who in your court is working against you, for example."

"Don't worry about that," said Cal absently. "I have a pretty good idea who they are."

"You do?" asked Jo, surprised. "How?"

Cal gave him a meaningful look. "I may be inexperienced, but I have some tools at my disposal that my doubters are not aware of. I have my own way of finding out who can be trusted."

Jo sucked in a breath as he realized Cal's meaning. He glanced around quickly, making sure they were really alone before lowering his voice. "The Esvalere?"

Cal nodded. "It's been absolutely crucial. I don't think I would have made it this far without it. I know a lot of things no one suspects I know. But there are limits." He looked frustrated.

"I'm still learning to use it, and believe me, I don't know everything."

Jo nodded, easily able to understand Cal's frustration. He had come up against similar limitations with his own talisman, after all.

Cal seemed to come out of his thoughts with a sigh. "I have to go," he said. "I'm supposed to be meeting with some key members of the court right now, to discuss the Balenan arrival." He offered Jo his arm, and Jo grasped it in the traditional Kyonan greeting. "It's good to have you home, Jo," he said. "And there's a lot to talk about. I'll have you put up in a suite in the royal wing. We can talk tonight, after the welcome banquet." He cocked his head questioningly. "How do you want to play it with Lord Wrendal? Do you want to stay unseen for a while longer, or come out into the open?"

Jo sighed. "As much as I hate to say it, I think I'd better not show myself just yet. Not until we have a plan. Lord Wrendal is going to lose it when he finds out I'm alive, and here, and it might put Scarlett in danger."

"Good," said Cal, seeming surprised by Jo's caution but clearly in agreement. "I'll have food sent to your room, then, so you can avoid the banquet hall. And I'll keep your arrival to myself for now, except for Laramie and Leander. They should know. We can talk tonight, in my private receiving room, where we can be sure no one will overhear. I'll send a servant to show you the way once I'm free."

"You'll send one of your servants, will you, Your Majesty?" said Jonan with a grin. "How you've risen in the world."

"Oh shut up," said Cal amicably, slipping from the room.

CHAPTER THIRTY-ONE

The rest of the day passed quickly for Jonan. Despite his decision not to reveal himself, he felt incredibly free as he wandered around the castle. Unlike on the boat, he didn't have to hide from everyone, just the visiting delegation. There was no one else who would recognize him, with the exception of the forester twins, and Cal had informed them of Jo's presence. They each took the time to greet him, but separately, and Jo was glad to discover that at least one of them was keeping Lord Wrendal under discreet observation at all times. The thought made him chuckle, remembering how Lord Wrendal had ordered that Jo be watched almost from the moment of his arrival in Nohl. It was satisfying to see the tables turn.

He knew he would be wisest to stay away entirely from the area where the Balenans were being accommodated. But he couldn't quite stop himself from making a quick trip to identify the area. He wanted to know where Scarlett was. He didn't see her—she was of course caught up in official undertakings. He fantasized about the idea of sneaking her out of the castle in the middle of the night and running away, someplace far from her father and royal expectations.

But it was just an idle thought. Scarlett deserved something better than spending the rest of her life on the run, and Jo found that he didn't want that for himself either. He was glad he had left Kyona—even if his lack of purpose in doing so had been a bit childish—but he was even more glad to be home. In his absence, he had discovered a love for his native land that had surprised him by its strength, and he found that he wanted to make his home in Kyona after all. But not in the royal court. That thought still made him shudder.

It was just that attitude that made Jonan only too glad to have gotten out of the welcome banquet, which was certain to be an unbearably stuffy affair. Still, in spite of his stated intention of being cautious, he couldn't quite resist loitering on the landing near the banquet hall, buried in a mass of curious servants, to witness Scarlett's arrival at the welcome feast.

He was not disappointed. She was nothing short of glorious, once again arrayed in a glowing crimson to match her name, as she had been the night of the party at her father's house. He had thought her shallow and despicable then, her beauty only skin deep. When he looked at her now, it was hard to believe he had ever thought her anything short of perfection. Surely she had never seemed haughty—surely her goodness and selflessness and incredibly kind heart had always glowed out of her as they did now. Her dress did not leave her shoulders and arms bare, as her Balenan ones had done, but the Kyonan fashion sat equally well on her, making her look regal as well as exotic.

The sight of her took his breath away, and he couldn't help but stare at her. Fortunately this didn't make him conspicuous, as most of the servants were also staring at her. Her eyes skimmed over the throng of people and picked him out with a tiny start. Her face crinkled slightly in sudden alarm, but he just winked at her, and her features once again returned to their impassive mask, although he could have sworn her eyes twinkled.

He met her gaze with unabashed admiration, a small smile curving his lips, and had the satisfaction of seeing her blush ever so slightly as she cast her eyes down, trying to hide a smile of her own. For the first time his resolve to stay out of sight wavered as he thought what it would be like to go in to dinner with her, to sit next to her through the meal, maybe even to dance with her if such an entertainment was planned. But his eyes slid quickly across to her father beside her, and he remembered why he had to be cautious for a little while longer.

Cal was nowhere to be seen—presumably he was already within the banquet hall, ready to receive his guests. Glancing around at the other important people arriving for the meal, Jo saw Elnora not far behind the Balenans. She was looking at him reproachfully, but he thought he saw a twinkle of amusement in her eyes. Her glance flicked from him to Scarlett's back as Scarlett passed into the hall, and she shook her head slightly, a smile on her lips. She had clearly witnessed the whole silent exchange. Jo grinned unashamedly at her, passing his eyes up and down her trim person and giving her a curt nod of her own. She was wearing a dress of the deep blue that was a traditional color for Kyonan royals. He had no trouble in recognizing it as a small act of defiance, of which he heartily approved.

Once the hubbub had died down, he slipped away, shaking his head to himself. They were all of them playing a deep game that made his head hurt. He was only too glad to get out of this round, and enjoy a solitary meal in the peace and quiet of his room.

After surviving on stolen scraps for weeks, and choking down the unfamiliar Balenan food for weeks before that, the hearty Kyonan fare was the sweetest thing Jo had ever tasted. He had expected a simple spread, but Cal arranged for someone to send up a dizzying array of dishes, each more delicious than the last. It seemed like Jo had been sent a small portion of every type of food being served at the banquet currently underway. Mentally promising himself that he would thank Cal profusely when he saw him, he fell on the food with enthusiasm and made a very solid meal.

He hadn't intended to fall asleep before speaking with Cal, but with his stomach more full than it had been in months, he found that he was incredibly weary, and the next thing he knew he was being woken by a persistent knocking on the door of his elegant suite.

Still half asleep, he looked involuntarily at the window, half expecting the sound to be coming from there. But of course Cody was far away, safe at the base tree, he could only hope. He shook his head to clear it, pulling open the door with a yawn. The waiting servant conducted him to the king's private receiving room without delay, betraying his curiosity only by the regretful way in which he bowed himself out once his task was complete.

"There you are, Jo," said Cal, sounding as weary as Jo felt. He cast a knowing look over Jo's foggy expression. "Fell asleep, did you?" he asked with a grin. "Lucky you. I just got back."

"How late is it?" Jo asked, settling himself into a chair. Cal was far too comfortably attired to still be in his formal dinner outfit. Jo could only be glad—it was strange enough seeing his friend in the richly embroidered clothes that passed as his casual wear. He couldn't imagine trying to chat normally with Cal if he had been in full court dress.

"It's almost midnight," said Cal.

"How was the banquet?"

"Ugh." Cal made a face. "Tedious. At least once Elnora and I are married we'll be able to sit together at these types of things. That would make it much more bearable."

Jo raised his eyebrows. "Couldn't you sit together now, since you're betrothed?"

"Of course we could," Cal growled. "Good luck convincing her of that." He sighed. "But never mind that. Tell me what you've been doing, Jo. What's happening in Balenol?"

So Jo told him, as concisely as he could manage, all that had happened to him since he had left Kyona. He intended to be brief, knowing how tired Cal was, but additional details kept popping into his mind, too entertaining or moving or enlightening not to be shared. It had been so long since he and Cal had properly talked like this. Not just since he'd been away, since before they'd left Nerita. Cal listened attentively, laughing in the right places, poking fun at Jo with his uncomfortable ability to read any omissions Jo might make in an attempt to save face, and asking such searching questions about the Balenan authorities that Jo could see at once that he wasn't the only one who had been receiving a sudden education in court politics.

Cal was amazed by the magical visions Jo had seen both before and after finding Alben's rock, but he accepted the truth of Jo's story without question. He asked to hold the rock, and Jo complied. He told him what he had learned about needing to direct the rock's revelations, but remembering how it had showed nothing to Cody, he didn't expect that Cal would actually see anything. He was astonished, therefore, when Cal's whole body stiffened, his face tightened in concentration for a long moment before he suddenly relaxed, shaking his head in amazement as he handed it back to Jonan.

"Remarkable," he said calmly. "Definitely dragon magic."

Jo stared at him in astonishment. "Did you see something?" he asked, and Cal looked faintly surprised.

"Sure," he said. "I asked about the origin of the rock, and I

saw the rockslide at Alben's home town, just like you described."
He raised his eyebrows at Jo's expression. "What?"

"It's just, I didn't actually think it would work for you." Jo
described Cody's attempt, and Cal frowned, perplexed.

"That's odd. I wonder why it didn't work for him. It certainly
worked for me."

Jo just grunted. He didn't want to admit it, but he felt a bit
nettled. Cal carried it lightly, but he was a very powerful man
now, not just because of his crown. The burden of the Esvalere,
and even the ownership of his magic sword, which Jo had
noticed Cal always kept with him, gave him an unusual authority. Jo had kind of liked the idea that the mountain rock might be
his own, admittedly much less potent, magical talisman. But he
shook the thought off, recognizing it as childish.

His description of the curse had the effect of sobering Cal
considerably, and he didn't seem to have any difficulty believing
that it was somehow connected to the rock. Or perhaps rocks.
The discovery that Yaeger possessed another mountain rock
brought the first real flicker of alarm to Cal's face that Jo had
seen throughout the whole conversation. He showed an inclina-
tion to get caught up in discussions about what the former Chief
Guard might be planning, but to Jo's mind there was a more
pressing matter.

"What are we going to do about Scarlett, Cal?" he asked seriously. "I won't be able to relax until she's out from under her
father's thumb. I'm worried that at any moment he might lose
patience with the whole alliance sham and decide he prefers his
backup plan."

"Yes," said Cal, frowning. "We need to get her safely away
from him before we do...whatever it is we're going to do. He acts
very smooth, but I can tell he's constantly watching me. I get the
sense that he's not too pleased to find me so strong-willed."

"That's just it," said Jo, standing up and starting to pace. "The whole marriage alliance only serves him if he can control you like a puppet once you're his son-in-law. If he realizes that's never going to happen, what's to prevent him moving straight on to provoking war?" He stopped, looking down at Cal. His friend was watching him with a frown, and he knew that Cal could read his distress on his face.

"I can't imagine you love the idea, and to be honest neither do I, but could you maybe pretend to go along with him for now? Could you make it seem like you're considering marrying Scarlett?"

Cal was shaking his head before Jo finished speaking. "I can't do that Jo," he said, his voice apologetic but firm. "Please don't ask it of me. We *will* protect Scarlett, but we have to find another way to do it. You don't understand how much opposition Elnora and I have been facing. I thought we'd be married by now, but it's proving much more complex than I expected. If I gave the impression, however temporarily, that I was going to marry this Balenan Lady Wrendal, it would undermine Elnora and my betrothal so much that I'm not sure she would ever recover her position. I'm sorry Jo—you just don't realize how complicated these things are."

Jo sat down again with a sigh. "I understand. And you're wrong—I do realize that these things are complicated, and that you can't afford to put a foot wrong."

"You do?" Cal was clearly surprised, and a little amused, at Jo's readiness to consider the political ramifications.

"Of course I do," said Jo. He didn't add that he was not altogether sorry on his own account that Cal had rejected his suggestion. "I gathered things were not going quite as smoothly as hoped."

Cal grunted at the understatement. "It's not that everyone is against me marrying Elnora. Far from it. The common people absolutely love her." He smiled crookedly. "I understand that people find the whole idea very romantic—an everyday girl, orphaned and growing up in the slums of Alezae, meeting the king by chance, capturing his heart and becoming royal. Well it's no surprise they're taken with the story."

He paused. "The members of the court are not quite so easily enchanted. Don't get me wrong—even if they're not enthusiastic, most of them are at least willing to accept her. But the few who aren't are very vocal and very influential." He shot Jonan a look. "You won't be surprised to learn that they're mainly the same ones whose loyalty I have reason to doubt. They don't insult her outright, of course, but it would almost be better if they did. It's all I can do to stop myself from milling them down when they make their snide little comments, or look at her in that way that makes her—"

He cut himself off, making a frustrated noise in his throat. "Elnora's the strongest person I know, and I'm confident there's nothing we can't face when we stand together. But the worst of it is that she lets them get into her head, and then I'm wasting half my energy trying to persuade her of what she already knows perfectly well, instead of working on the stupid nobles."

He scowled. "We should have eloped when we were still in the forest, and I could have ascended to the throne already married. I thought arriving betrothed would be enough, but these oily courtiers see our betrothal as a starting point from which to negotiate." He gave a hollow laugh. "You can bet if I'd been betrothed to one of their daughters they would see it as binding enough."

Jo had listened patiently to this embittered tirade. He could sympathize with Cal's frustration—he didn't envy the idea of lots of powerful and opinionated people trying to have a say in his love life.

"And I suppose the arrival of this delegation, with an offer of a marriage alliance with Balenol, didn't exactly help your cause."

"Not exactly," agreed Cal dryly. "Some of my advisors were horrified by my little stunt with the slave ship. They didn't approve of such a blatantly aggressive response. Well, you already know that Filip was explicitly approving the trade by agreement with the Balenan royals, which I now suspect means with Lord Wrendal. From what you say he would have had no difficulty getting King Siloam's approval. Of course none of the nobles own up to being part of that. They all pretend to be shocked and horrified that Filip was selling Kyonans. But some of them were surely in on the racket, and the idea of an alliance with Balenol, especially with a party as sympathetic to their interests as Lord Wrendal, is undoubtedly very appealing to them."

Cal scowled. "Never mind that the proposed alliance would involve marrying me off like some eligible maiden, or that it would leave Elnora out in the cold." He looked at Jonan seriously. "She might not seem it here in the castle, right on the edge of becoming queen, but she's actually very vulnerable. If they were to succeed in pushing me into marrying someone else, do you realize that she would have nowhere to go? No family, no home, nowhere safe. I can't imagine she'd be eager to stay here to watch someone else take her place."

His expression hardened. "That's not why I'm standing my ground, of course. It wouldn't matter if she had the best home and the most powerful family in the country, I would still be just as determined to marry her, because I love her and I want her by my side. It's just that there are those who would be only too glad to cut her adrift and remove her from the equation to ensure she didn't ever exercise her undesirable influence over me. Especially if they think that she's all that's standing in the way of an advantageous marriage alliance."

Jo nodded slowly. "Don't worry, Cal. We won't let them have their way. But I can see that you have your hands full, and that

Scarlett's arrival hasn't helped any." He clapped his hand on his friend's shoulder sympathetically. "I'm sure it doesn't help that she's so unbelievably beautiful, either."

"I don't know what you mean," said Cal loftily. "I don't think she's all that pretty. I don't mean any offense to your Scarlett, of course, but Elnora is much more beautiful." He took in Jo's expression of outraged disbelief, and gave him a look. "And don't try to tell me that she's not *your* Scarlett, because I have eyes in my head, Jo, and—"

"I wasn't going to say anything of the kind," cut in Jo, incensed. "Of course she's my Scarlett, and I'll thank you to keep your distance, king or not."

But Cal just grinned, refraining from pointing out that he had just been ranting at length about how little interest he had in Scarlett, or in fact anyone but Elnora.

"Well, well, well," he said instead. "Someone's changed his tune, I see."

"What do you mean?" asked Jo, grumpy, and Cal's grin broadened.

"I believe your words were, 'all girls are as inconvenient as the plague'," he said.

Jo snorted. "Well, I'm not eleven any more, am I?"

The grin slid slowly from Cal's face, and he sighed, suddenly becoming serious again. "Sometimes I feel like I'm no more than eleven," he admitted, running a hand through his hair. "That's certainly how half the court sees me—an incompetent child. And honestly, as much as I hate to admit it, I am out of my depth far too often."

"You're not," said Jo suddenly. "You must feel like you're drowning, surrounded by snobbish nobles who've been playing politics all their lives. But you can't see yourself from the outside. I've been away for months, and coming back I can see how much you've grown. You were born to this role, Cal, and you're carrying yourself like a king. The statement with the slave ship was brilliant, and believe me, it had the desired effect in Nohl. Your determination to marry Elnora in spite of opposition does you credit, but so does your sensitivity in trying to win everyone over before actually taking the step. You're going to be the greatest king Kyona has seen since King Cael, and I mean that."

Cal was silent for a moment, looking surprised but gratified at this praise. "Thanks, Jo," he said at last. "It's certainly nice to have a real friend nearby again. And you've grown too. I can hardly recognize you under all that wisdom and caution." Jo grinned, and Cal returned the look easily. "You're a good man, Jo," he said. "And you wear responsibility surprisingly well. I wish I *had* sent you as an official envoy to Nohl, to chip away at the slave trade from that end."

Jo laughed. "We both know I would have refused to go if I was sent with any official purpose." He grinned. "The perversity of youth, right?"

Cal laughed too. "Well, I'm glad you did go. And I'm even more glad you're back."

"Me too," said Jo.

"That still leaves us with the question of what now, of course," said Cal wearily. "How are we going to thwart Lord Wrendal's plans and catch Yaeger?"

"With a good night's sleep behind us, that's how," said Jonan firmly. "I don't even want to know what the time is now, and you're dead on your feet. Everything else can wait until tomorrow."

Cal groaned. "Except that tomorrow I have to sit in a room with that pompous prig of a Balenan lord and listen to him drone about treaties and trade agreements with a straight face, as if I didn't know he was the kind of filthy scum who would have his own daughter killed to fill his pocket, not to mention conspiring against me with the man I've sworn to kill."

"Sure," said Jo lightly, "but are you busy before then? Maybe we could plan our sweeping counterstrike over breakfast?"

Cal's laugh died in his throat at the unexpected sound of someone banging urgently on the door. They exchanged uneasy looks, neither needing to speak the cause of their alarm. Any message carried to the king with urgency at this time of night could not be a good one.

Jo surreptitiously placed his hand on his weapon as Cal crossed the room with quick strides and pulled open the door. A grim-faced man stood there, something indefinable about his demeanor convincing Jo that he was a former forester.

"What is it, Louis?" asked Cal quickly.

"She's gone, Your Majesty," the man said. "I came straight away."

Cal's whole body stiffened. "Who?" he asked in unison with Jo, who had leaped to his feet. The man looked at him in surprise, obviously not having noticed his presence until that moment.

"Who's gone, Louis?" Cal prompted impatiently, and the man's eyes returned to his king, his face grimmer than ever.

"The Lady Elnora."

CHAPTER THIRTY-TWO

For the space of one agonized heartbeat, Cal stood frozen, his horror evident in every line of his frame. Then he took off sprinting without a backward glance, Jo hard on his heels and Louis following close behind.

Jo didn't know his way around the castle like Cal did, but as he followed Cal through the dark corridors, he could only assume that they were headed for Elnora's suite. It was evidently not located in the royal wing like Jo's temporary lodgings were, but it was still only a short space of time before Cal skidded to a stop outside a door that had been left slightly ajar.

Cal pushed his way into the room without hesitation. Jo, barreling in after him, almost ran into his friend's back. It was immediately obvious why Cal had stopped short. Jo's eyes widened as they passed over the scene. They had entered a richly furnished receiving room, and any hope that this was all a mistake evaporated at the obvious evidence of a struggle. Chairs had been knocked over, ornaments lay smashed in pieces, and an elegant tea tray had been upended all over the lush rug that was spread across the stone floor.

Cal strode wordlessly to a nearby door and pushed it open to reveal a large bedchamber. One glance was enough to confirm that the bed had not been slept in. Jo's gaze returned to the mess in front of him, his eyes catching on one particular detail.

"Cal," he said, not quite managing to keep his voice steady.

His friend was at his side in a moment, but Jo couldn't bring himself to articulate it. Instead he pointed silently at the smeared puddle of liquid that spread across the edge of the rug and onto the stone. It was unmistakably blood.

Chancing a look at Cal's face, Jo felt his own fear spike as he saw the last bit of color drain from his friend's face.

"How did this happen?" Cal demanded, his voice curt. For a moment Jo was at a loss for how to respond to the accusatory question, but then Louis stepped forward and Jo realized that Cal hadn't been speaking to him.

"I don't know about how, Your Majesty," Louis said quickly, "but I have a fair idea of when. It can't have been more than an hour ago. That's when the shift changed. I wasn't on myself tonight, but Armistad was. He finished his shift an hour ago, and came to the guardroom, to take a meal before retiring. He's been there ever since, gossiping about these Balenans with the rest of them, but he only mentioned in passing a few minutes ago that it had been Sean who had relieved him."

"Sean?" repeated Cal sharply. "I didn't think he was on the list approved for this duty."

"He wasn't," said Louis grimly. "And I knew it. As soon as Armistad mentioned that it was Sean who took over watching Her Ladyship, I felt uneasy, and I thought I'd better come along to check all was well." He gestured at the room. "When I found no one at the door, I took the liberty of checking inside, and this is what I found. I came to Your Majesty's rooms immediately."

"But how did he gain access?" Cal insisted, his face still deathly pale. "He should never have been put on duty! There is a very limited list of guards with authority for this role."

"I don't know," said Louis carefully. "But I know that the order was given recently to increase the watch on Lady Elnora."

Cal cursed quietly, running a hand up his face and through his hair. "This is my fault," he said, his voice hollow.

"Don't be ridiculous, Cal," said Jo sharply. "You can't blame yourself for this."

But Cal just shook his head. "I knew that we were stretched to our limit with the visiting delegation, but I still insisted that the guard on Elnora be increased. When I heard that Yaeger was probably already in Kynton, I didn't want to take any chances. But that's exactly what I did! There's a very short list of guards I trust to watch her—only those I'm absolutely confident are loyal —and how I thought they could stretch themselves so thin without calling in others..."

He trailed off, his hand still clutching at his already disordered hair as he attempted to master himself. His glance fell again on the blood on the floor, and without warning he seized a china ornament from the mantel and hurled it across the room. The resulting smash seemed to loosen his tongue.

"We have to find her, immediately," he said. "If it's been no more than an hour, they won't be out of reach. Louis," he barked, turning to the guard. "Wake the chief, and have him round up our cohort. I want the city searched immediately, and messengers sent to every gate. Find out when Sean was last seen, and who he's known to associate with. And send Laramie or Leander to me, whichever is available. I want a full report on the delegation's activities this afternoon."

The guard was gone on the last word, and Jo and Cal were left alone, Cal beginning to pace restlessly.

"Do you really think this Sean would have betrayed you?" Jo asked tensely.

"It's possible." Cal's voice was terse, the tension rolling off him in waves. "I told you that I'm sure some of Yaeger's men are still among the guards. But no one who's even slightly under suspicion should have ever been given responsibility for Elnora's security."

"Does Elnora know she's under such close watch?" Jo asked shrewdly, his eyes on his friend, who was still pacing.

"No," said Cal, a slightly guilty look crossing his face. "She would almost certainly have protested, but like I said earlier, until we're actually married, her position here is incredibly vulnerable." He stopped pacing, turning to Jo with a pleading look. "I know it seems bad to have her under guard without telling her, but I couldn't risk losing her, Jo. She's too precious to me."

"I understand," Jo said quickly. And he did understand, perfectly. How many times had he been tormented by the thought of Scarlett's danger, hidden in plain sight in her father's household? He recognized the barely contained panic lurking behind Cal's eyes, and his heart went out to his friend.

He remembered all too clearly how he had wished momentarily for the power of a crown so that he would have the ability to protect those he cared about. And now Cal was in the position of knowing, not only that his crown hadn't kept Elnora safe, but that she would likely never have been in danger if he hadn't worn it.

"We'll find her, Cal," said Jo, trying not to show how desperately he hoped he was right.

"Yes," Cal agreed, his voice tight. "And when we do, whoever did this is going to wish they were never born."

For a moment Jo didn't answer, absorbing the uncompromising look on his friend's face.

"What?" Cal snapped, noticing Jo's scrutiny.

"Nothing," said Jo quickly. "It's just...I know you're angry, but—"

"If you of all people are going to tell me to exercise restraint

—!" Cal began furiously. "Angry! You'd better believe I'm angry. I'm angry enough to kill the man who did this with my bare hands! I'm angry enough to—"

"Angry enough to go to war?" Jo said quickly, and Cal paused, his eyes leaping to Jonan's.

"You think Lord Wrendal is behind this?" he asked sharply.

Jo shrugged. "The timing is astonishingly coincidental if he isn't. The thought hadn't occurred to you?"

"Of course it had!" said Cal, still angry. "But I thought he might have wanted to remove Elnora from the picture to try to improve his chances of a marriage alliance. You're saying you think he's moved beyond that plan? You think he's found a way to provoke war without having to sacrifice his daughter?"

"I don't know," said Jo grimly. "But I hope it wasn't him. Because..." He hesitated, but he couldn't see anything to be gained by being less than candid. "Because if it was Lord Wrendal, I can't think of any benefit to him from keeping her alive."

The words were followed by a pause, during which Cal met Jo's eyes unblinkingly. The expression Jo saw belonged not to the easygoing country boy Jo had grown up with, but to a powerful and dangerous king, enraged beyond the limit of reason. Somehow Jo knew a moment before Cal moved that his friend was not going to wait passively an instant longer. Jo could only imagine that the guards Cal had summoned would arrive any minute, but he made no attempt to talk Cal into staying put and waiting for backup. He certainly wouldn't have done so in Cal's situation.

Instead he followed as his friend took off through the corridors, once again running, this time in the direction of the wing occupied by the visiting delegation. All thought of remaining hidden from the Balenans was gone. Jo wasn't even sure himself whether he was following Cal in order to keep him from doing anything he would regret, or to help him punish Lord Wrendal should he prove to be behind the abduction. He just knew that he needed to stick close to his friend.

With this thought in mind, he was hard on Cal's heels when they rounded a corner, still some distance from the relevant wing. The halls had so far been empty, the castle still asleep, so it came as a great surprise when they turned the bend only to run straight into someone, moving stealthily through the corridor.

Cal literally did run into the person, and both he and the other man stumbled involuntarily back. Jonan pulled up short as well, his breath caught on a gasp. Cal's shout of outrage told Jo that he was not the only one to have suddenly recognized the intruder as Yaeger. In the same moment, Jo grasped that Yaeger had also needed only an instant to recognize the identity of the man confronting him. There was no time for conscious thought as Jonan saw Yaeger's hand flick out, something flashing along with it in the moonlight that filtered in through a nearby window.

With a wordless shout, Jo threw himself in front of Cal, his duty to protect his king and his desire to shield his best friend jumbled together into a single surge of potent determination.

It was all so quick Jo barely understood what was happening. One moment Yaeger's dagger, aimed at Cal, was headed instead straight for Jo's heart, Jo bracing himself uselessly against the thrust. Then the blade hit rock instead of flesh, almost as though Jo's mountain rock talisman had swung of its own accord to meet the attack. The force of Yaeger's momentum should still have had its effect, but Jo felt barely a thing. At the moment he had thrown himself between the blade and Cal, his senses had been overwhelmed by a rush of power, much stronger than the one he had felt at the whipping post, or in the river the night he escaped Nohl.

He may have felt no pain from Yaeger's dagger, but there was no escaping the impact of what followed. The last thing he saw was Yaeger's own rock swinging out on its leather thong, but there was no time to get a good look. As Jonan's rock absorbed the brunt of Yaeger's attack, there was a loud explosion.

Jonan felt his rock burn blazing hot against his chest as all three men were thrown backward with enough force to lift them off their feet. Jo felt his head slam against a stone wall, before he slid down to the floor in a heap. His senses swam alarmingly as he struggled in vain to retain consciousness. The last thing he was aware of before he blacked out was a terrifying uncertainty. Was Cal all right?

WAS THE BOY ALL RIGHT? Alben squinted uncertainly in the direction from which he had heard the cry. He had just seen a boy walk around that corner, and he had seemed fine when he disappeared.

Alben followed quickly, taking the precaution of peering around the corner before committing himself. What he saw sent a dual wave of anger and horror crashing over him.

Traders. There could be no doubt. He had heard rumors of their presence, of course. The raids had increased in frequency in recent months, even here in Argath. That's why soldiers had been posted in all the seaside towns. But this was the first time he had seen them with his own eyes.

The poor boy looked terrified. Alben had seen him before. He was one of Argath's street kids—there weren't many, but they were around. He was young, probably three or four years younger than Alben. Certainly no older than fourteen. Alben hesitated, his first instinct to run immediately to the boy's rescue. But a moment's reflection made him think better of it. There were half a dozen of them, and only one of him. It was for this purpose that soldiers had been billeted in the town, and his best course would be to make them aware of the traders' activity. The South Landers were not setting sail this instant —there was still plenty of time to intervene in the boy's fate.

Alben took off running in the opposite direction, his lungs protesting as he pushed himself to his limit. He reached the makeshift guardhouse in minutes, pushing his way without invitation into the building commandeered by the soldiers for the purpose.

"Traders!" he panted. "Near the quay! I just saw them grab a boy."

"Slow down, kid," said one of the soldiers, his voice maddeningly unconcerned as he looked up from his game of dice with another soldier. "What's your hurry?"

"I tell you, I saw them just minutes ago!" Alben shouted, frustrated. "If you go now, you can catch them before they move on!"

"Could we?" asked the second soldier, amused. "How fortunate for us." He rolled the dice, giving a small shout of triumph at the way the numbers fell.

For a moment Alben just stared, nonplussed, his chest still heaving from his sprint through town.

"Well?" he demanded at last. "Aren't you going to go after them? I'm telling you, they just grabbed a boy off the street!"

"Tut tut," said the first soldier lazily. "Quite unacceptable. We'll have to check it out." But neither of them made any move to get up, instead continuing calmly with their game.

"What are you waiting for?" Alben cried. "Isn't this the only reason you're here?"

"Relax, kid," said the second soldier, his eyes still on the dice. "We'll round them up in good time. Don't worry about it."

"But—" Alben's outraged protest was cut short as a door into a further room opened and another figure strolled out. Alben froze in shock when he saw the newcomer, the young man's face easily recognizable despite the three years that had passed since he had last seen it.

"Liam?" he faltered, momentarily distracted from his purpose. "What are you doing here?" His eyes were drawn irresistibly to the

mountain rock hanging from around Liam's neck, so similar to the talisman he still wore.

"Alben?" said Liam, his cool voice holding a hint of mockery. "Well, well, well. I didn't know you'd ended up here. You been here since you left the mountains?"

Alben nodded slowly, his unease growing as he got the sense that he was missing something crucial. "What about you?" he asked carefully. "I thought you didn't want to leave the mountains. I thought you were going to settle in one of the towns further south."

Liam's face twisted into a sneer that was clearly intended to be derisive, but that didn't quite conceal his anger. "Oh, apparently the southern mountain folk didn't want to taint their precious towns with our presence, since the mountains had seen fit to expel us. They seemed to think we should take the message and leave the mountains altogether." He ground his teeth, seeming to speak to himself for a moment. "As if they had the right to cast us out—as if it was nothing for us to lower ourselves to settle on the plains."

"Oh," said Alben lamely, unsure what to say. "I'm...I'm sorry." He glanced between Liam and the soldiers, who were still focused on their game and seemed to have paid little attention to the conversation between the former neighbors. "So are you working for the soldiers now?"

"That's right," said Liam silkily, smoothing his features into a smile that was still not quite pleasant. "What about you? What brings you here?"

"He says he saw some traders snatch a boy not far from here," piped up one of the soldiers, for some reason sounding amused. "Seems to think we should round them up."

"Well, shouldn't you?" demanded Alben, his irritation resurfacing.

"Sure, kid, of course," said the other soldier absently. "All in good time."

"Actually, boss," said Liam, his sneer once again pronounced, "no

need to act the part for this one. I think he'd be quite a nice addition himself."

"Oh?" said the soldier, looking up and showing real interest for the first time. "Would he now? You know something of him, then? On his own, is he?"

"Oh yes, completely on his own," said Liam comfortably. "He comes from the same town as I do, and his parents were killed in the rockslide. He's got no one."

"What do you—" started Alben, confused but starting to get angry, but the soldier cut him off.

"Excellent. He looks strong. Our associates will be pleased." He gave a shrill whistle, and a number of other soldiers appeared from the room where Liam had been concealed. Before Alben fully understood their intent, they had him surrounded. He struggled, but he was outnumbered, and his shock made his efforts ineffectual.

"What are you doing?" he cried, finally grasping the magnitude of their treachery. "You're the king's soldiers! You're supposed to be here to stop the traders! Not round up victims for them!"

One of his captors gave a nasty laugh. "If the king wants loyal soldiers, he should pay us more."

They began to drag him out of the building, but Alben made a final effort, lunging back toward his former contemporary.

"Liam, how can you be part of this?" he shouted, enraged. "How can you betray your own people like this?"

"My own people?" repeated Liam, striding forward with a very ugly look on his face. "Plain-dwellers? Coast-dwellers? These aren't my people! The mountains are my country—what do I care for Kyona? I owe no loyalty to anyone here!"

"No loyalty!" shouted Alben. "How can you say that? Didn't we grow up together? Weren't we raised on the same street?" Liam just shrugged, his expression unconcerned, and Alben's voice rose in volume. "You snake! My mother saved your life that day, and she died doing it! You wear her rock around your neck even now!"

"My *rock!*" Liam shouted, his young face twisted so that he looked almost mad. "Your mother has nothing to do with it. We both know she didn't do what she did for my sake. The rocks of the mountains are my birthright. You think I wear this for her, or for you?" He was breathing hard as his eyes fell on Alben's own rock, dangling on its leather thong. "You are the one who has no loyalty," he spat. "You chose to leave the mountains. You don't deserve to wear that."

He strode forward the last few steps. Alben, his arms still held by soldiers, gave a furious cry as Liam reached out to rip the rock from around the captive's neck. But he was not destined to lose his talisman. The moment Liam's hand touched it, Alben felt the rock burn hot. Both boys were thrust backward as an invisible shock wave seemed to boom out from the point of contact, and Alben could feel rather than see the ripple as it ricocheted away from him, toward the ocean, a few blocks away.

Alben's own exclamation of shock and pain was drowned out by Liam's agonized cry. Alben could see that Liam's shirt, like his, was singed under where his rock sat, but the other boy seemed hardly to notice it, instead cradling the hand that had grabbed at Alben's rock. Alben felt a surge of savage satisfaction at the sight of the mangled flesh on Liam's palm, the skin burned and disfigured.

"What in the kingdom..." started one soldier, his voice uneasy as he glanced between the two boys. But the first soldier, who seemed to be in charge, was not so easily daunted.

"Get him out of here," he barked. "Mountain tricks don't impress me. He'll sail tonight, along with the rest, and none of his mountain superstitions will save him."

Alben could barely comprehend his change in fortunes as the soldiers dragged him outside. Were Kyonan soldiers really conspiring with the South Land traders? Had he really just been betrayed by Liam of all people? And what had just happened with his rock? He didn't understand the nature of the explosion that had burst out from *it, but there was no question that it had been powerful and destructive, beyond his own situation.*

He thought suddenly of Marine, and he barely kept a cry of despair from bursting out. What would she think when he didn't show up to walk with her as usual? Would she ever know what had happened to him? She would guess, perhaps, when whispers spread that a number of young people had gone missing today. Would he ever see her again?

Yes, he promised himself with grim determination. He might have allowed himself to be subdued far too easily today, but they would find that his spirit was not so easily broken. He was no quickly intimidated fourteen year old. They would regret taking him—they would regret taking any Kyonans, these barbaric South Landers. He would make sure of it—whatever it cost him.

"J‌onan. Jonan! Wake up! Are you all right?"

Jonan returned to wakefulness with a gasp, sitting bolt upright. He instantly regretted the swift movement, groaning as he put his hand to his aching head, remembering suddenly the way he had slammed into the wall.

He blinked rapidly, his vision coming into focus in the dark corridor as he took in Laramie's face, concern etched on his features.

"Cal!" he said quickly. "Where is he? Is he all right?"

"His Majesty is fine," said Laramie, a hint of reproach in his voice, and Jo barely refrained from rolling his eyes. Trust the reserved former forester to take issue with Jo's failure to use Cal's title at a moment like this. Leaning sideways to peer around Laramie, Jo saw with relief that Cal was indeed conscious, propped against the opposite wall. Even as Jo watched, Cal pushed himself to his feet, ignoring the protests of Leander, who was bent over him in obvious concern.

"Where is he?" Cal demanded furiously.

"Jonan?" asked Leander uncertainly, glancing toward Laramie and Jo. "He's fine, he's just over there."

"No, Yaeger!" said Cal, his tone impatient.

"Yaeger?" repeated Laramie, on his feet in a moment. "He was here, in the castle?"

Cal nodded, his eyes sweeping the corridor frantically, as if Yaeger might still be hiding behind a suit of armor. "We happened upon him, and he attacked us."

"What?!" Leander was beside his twin in a moment, the two of them drawing their swords in a simultaneous movement.

"Search the immediate area," Laramie barked, and only then did Jo realize that he had brought a small squadron of guards with him.

"He can't have gone far," said Jo quickly. "Unless...how long were we out? Were you knocked unconscious too, Cal?"

Cal nodded, his expression grim.

"You can't have been out for long," said Laramie. I heard the explosion, and came straight away."

"As did I," said Leander. "What's going on, Your Majesty?" he added anxiously. "Why were you running through the castle alone, at this hour of the night?"

"I wasn't alone," said Cal curtly, clearly impatient with his kinsman's disapproval. "Jo was with me."

"I hardly think that—" Leander began dryly, but Cal cut him off.

"He saved my life, for your information." Cal's tone softened for a moment as he turned to Jo. "Thank you, by the way." He grimaced. "Since you somehow didn't die, I won't reproach you for throwing yourself into danger on account of my reckless-ness." He paused. "Not until this is all over anyway."

Jo smiled weakly. "You would have done the same, so don't get high and mighty with me."

"But where were you going?" persisted Leander.

"To confront Lord Wrendal," said Cal grimly. "Elnora's gone, Leander. She was taken out of her suite—there was clearly a struggle."

"What?" Leander looked at his twin, his shock evident on his face. But Laramie showed no sign of surprise.

"Yes, Louis told me as much," he said. "I pulled together a squadron and we were on our way to Lady Elnora's suite when I heard the explosion and redirected here. What caused it, Your Majesty?"

Cal hesitated, looking at Jo. "I don't know exactly," he said. "It wasn't entirely natural, that much is certain. But that's not important right now. Leander," he turned to the man, "were you with Laramie and his squad?"

Leander shook his head. "No, I was stationed near Lord Wrendal's suite. I've been keeping watch. I heard the explosion also, and came immediately. You said you were going to confront Lord Wrendal? You think he's behind Lady Elnora's disappearance?"

"You tell me," said Cal quickly. "If you've been guarding him. Could he have done it?"

"Not directly," said Leander. "He returned to his rooms immediately after the banquet, and he hasn't left since then. But that doesn't mean he isn't behind it of course. It just means he wasn't working alone."

"Given Yaeger's presence in the castle, that much we could have worked out, I think," said Jo grimly. "We're not far from where the Balenans are staying. Could Yaeger have been on his way to consult Lord Wrendal, do you think?"

"Very likely," said Cal curtly. "But he will have abandoned the attempt now. I can only imagine he got himself out of the castle as fast as possible." He clenched a fist, suddenly letting out a curse. "We almost had him, Jo! If only we hadn't both been knocked out!"

"I know," said Jo, "but there's no use dwelling on it now. At least we know who we're looking for. There can be no doubt he was involved, now we've found him prowling around an hour after Elnora went missing."

"Yes," said Cal, his voice hard. "But he was obviously not working alone." He turned to one of Laramie's guards who had stayed behind in case of further instructions. "Wake everyone up," he said curtly. "Start with the master of protocol, and get him to help you make sure you don't miss anyone. I want everyone assembled in the throne room in fifteen minutes."

"And...who do you want assembled, Your Majesty?" asked the man faintly, and Jo could see he didn't relish the job of rousing important people from their beds.

"Everyone," said Cal impatiently. "The whole court, the visiting delegation, all of them."

"But—it's still two hours until dawn, Your Majesty," protested the soldier.

"Do you think I care about that?" Cal said furiously. "If Lady Elnora wasn't too important to be disturbed from her rest, the rest of them certainly aren't!"

"Stop gawking and do as your king has instructed," said Laramie sharply, and the man hastened to comply, mumbling apologetically.

The four of them who remained began walking briskly toward the throne room, Cal in the lead, his strides strong and purposeful. Jo struggled to keep his mind on the crisis at hand, his thoughts circling in spite of himself around the strange incident with the rock, and the most recent vision into Alben's past.

He was certain that the memory of Alben's capture by the traders held crucial revelations, if he could only marshal his thoughts enough to figure them out. He felt like he should tell Cal what he had seen, but one glance at his friend's face was enough to convince him that this was not the moment. He put a hand surreptitiously to his chest, where the burned skin still stung. A hole had been singed straight through his shirt.

"What are you going to do, Cal?" he asked as he followed in the young king's wake.

"I'm going to end this," Cal said, his voice grim.

CHAPTER THIRTY-THREE

I t was rather more than fifteen minutes later that Cal raised a hand for silence, bringing to an end the angry mumbling of his offended court. They were clearly unimpressed about being hauled from their beds, and the stony silence Cal had maintained until this moment had done nothing to mollify them. Nevertheless, even Jo could sense the icy authority emanating from Cal's person, and he was not surprised when the young king's imperious gesture brought instant stillness to the room. The Balenans had still not arrived, but Cal was evidently done waiting.

"You are all wondering why I have called you from your rest, so I will get to the point without delay," he said curtly. "The crown has been the subject of an attack tonight. Lady Elnora has been abducted from her rooms, and there can be no doubt that those responsible were assisted by someone within the castle."

While Cal spoke, Jo scanned the faces before him carefully, aware that Laramie and Leander were doing the same as they stood beside him. Many wore expressions of blank amazement, and a few exclaimed in shock or horror, but one nobleman looked unsurprised. Jo made a mental note of the man's face, but it was unnecessary, as whoever it was showed no reluctance in making his response visible.

"If Your Majesty permits," the man said, clearing his throat and stepping forward. "A most unfortunate incident, but...are we certain that the lady's disappearance is...suspicious? It strikes me that it is possible that Your Majesty has roused us all from our sleep on the basis of a misapprehension."

Cal turned cold eyes upon the nobleman, for a moment saying nothing. Jonan could see that his friend resented giving the speaker the satisfaction of asking him to explain his comment.

"Meaning?" Cal said eventually, his anger barely contained.

The man cleared his throat again, glancing appealingly at those around him. Everyone was watching him with great interest. "A most delicate matter, Your Majesty," he said, his apologetic tone at odds with the malicious glint in his eyes. "But I cannot help but wonder if she perhaps left...of her own volition. She has not seemed entirely comfortable in the court since her arrival some months ago. And, if you will permit, I imagine we all noticed how struck she was by the young Balenan noblewoman who is, we must acknowledge, uncommonly beautiful—"

"No, I will most certainly *not* permit your insolence," Cal cut in furiously. "How dare you suggest that she ran away? From the start, you have—"

Cal broke off in response to the silent pressure of Leander's hand on his arm. For a moment he struggled to master himself, breathing hard. Jo admired his restraint, but envied him his restricted position less than ever. In his place, Jonan would have wanted nothing more than to wipe the nobleman's smarmy smirk off his face with his fist. The way Cal's hands were clenched at his sides suggested the same thought had occurred to him.

"There can be no question," Cal continued through gritted teeth, "that Lady Elnora was removed from the castle forcibly. Her suite shows obvious signs of a struggle, and a former guard, known to be a traitor, was seen nearby."

Jo noted with interest that the nobleman looked genuinely surprised at this information. But perhaps he was simply a good actor. Any response the man might have made, however, was prevented by a new voice, its angry tones carrying over the assembled crowd. Apparently the Balenans had arrived, Lord Wrendal at their head.

"What is the meaning of this, Your Majesty?" he demanded. "This is an outrage! Little did I think when my king sent me here that we would be treated in such a manner!"

Cal turned toward the new arrivals, his voice level but his eyes hard. "I regret the necessity of disturbing your rest, My Lord," he began, "but a situation has arisen that—"

"Forget my rest!" Lord Wrendal interrupted, righteous anger in every line of his frame as he strode through the assembled courtiers, who parted to let him through. "Where is—" He broke off suddenly as his eyes fell on Jonan, standing just behind Cal on the raised dais at the end of the room. "You!" he bellowed, his eyes popping.

Cal looked quickly between Lord Wrendal and Jo, obviously having forgotten that the Balenan was not yet aware of Jonan's presence. Truth be told, Jo had forgotten himself.

"Me, My Lord? Do I know you?" he asked outrageously, taking a vindictive satisfaction from the nobleman's fury. "You don't look familiar."

"Why you little—" Lord Wrendal took a step forward, but pulled up short as Cal shifted slightly to the side, interposing himself between Jo and the Balenan.

"Is there a problem, Lord Wrendal?" the young king asked coldly.

Lord Wrendal's eyes flicked between the two of them, clearly unsure of his next step. Jo knew him well enough to recognize that he did not take kindly to being placed on uncertain ground. For a moment Jonan wondered if Lord Wrendal would just let his presence slide, but he was not surprised that the nobleman's diplomatic front could not be stretched quite that far.

"Yes, there is a problem, Your Majesty," he said, his chest heaving. "You have been imposed upon. This whelp is a criminal, sentenced to be executed in my country."

"Indeed?" asked Cal blandly. "And for what crime, may I ask?"

Again Lord Wrendal hesitated, his expression murderous as it rested on Jonan. Jonan smiled unpleasantly back at him, fully aware of his dilemma. Given that he was ostensibly trying to push Cal into a marriage alliance with Scarlett, he could hardly declare that Jonan had been sentenced to be executed because he had been caught kissing her in her rooms. His usual all-encompassing accusation of insubordination would also not serve him in this situation. He would hardly want to remind the Kyonan king of the enslaved position of his countrymen in Balenol.

"He...he broke into my home," said Lord Wrendal stiffly. He was clearly aware that the delayed answer sounded lame and unconvincing.

Cal raised his eyebrows. "You seem to impose heavy penalties in your country, Lord Wrendal," he said. "Execution for a housebreaker."

"We take thievery seriously, Your Majesty," snapped Lord Wrendal.

"So I should hope," said Cal dismissively. "But I am certain there is a mistake in the present instance. I can vouch for this man personally, and I assure you he is no thief."

For a moment Lord Wrendal's jaw worked as he looked

between the king and Jonan. Jo knew the situation was still unstable, but he made no attempt to hide his satisfaction at this reversal of positions. Still, he didn't take the nobleman's poorly concealed fury lightly. The need to remove Scarlett from his vicinity was fast becoming urgent. Jo looked away from Lord Wrendal, scanning the arriving Balenans for her familiar figure. She didn't seem to be there yet.

"I will not argue with Your Majesty on a matter of such little importance," Lord Wrendal was saying, pulling himself together with an effort. "Not when I have a much more pressing grievance. Your Majesty will answer for—"

"I was attempting to answer your question when you became distracted," Cal pointed out crisply. "The reason you were woken at this hour—"

"I tell you I don't care about being woken!" interrupted Lord Wrendal. "I care about the safety of those under my care. We are your guests here, and you will answer for it if harm has befallen her. Now, where is my daughter?"

"Where—what?" asked Cal blankly, thrown off course. "What do you mean?"

"What I mean, Sire," raged Lord Wrendal, "is that my daughter is not in her room. In fact, she is unaccounted for."

"What?!" Jo shouted, taking a step forward. There was a sudden ringing in his ears that made it hard to think straight.

Lord Wrendal's eyes flicked to him, venom in his expression. "I might have known as soon as I saw you," he said, his voice quieter and more savage than before. "I suppose I can thank you for this insult. I don't know by what means you have—"

"Liar!" Jo shouted over the top of him. He could feel Cal's hand on his arm, but his panic was fast overwhelming his restraint. "What have you done to her?!"

"How dare you make accusations against me?" gasped Lord Wrendal. His tone was the perfect blend of outrage and astonishment, but Jo could see the gleam of malicious satisfaction lurking underneath. He felt the last of his control evaporate, and he lunged forward, his voice rising furiously, hardly able to see for the rage and terror that blinded him.

"*Murderer!* You killed her, like you said you would! You killed her to start your war! You'll pay for this with your life! I'll kill you myself!"

He had broken free of Cal's restraining hand with ease, and he was only prevented from carrying out his threat then and there by Laramie and Leander, who seized him from either side and bodily held him back. He struggled blindly against them, his whole focus on Lord Wrendal, oblivious alike to Cal's sharp command to stop and to the shocked faces of his audience. His mind was consumed with the horrifying thought of Scarlett finally falling victim to her father's violence, and the poorly concealed glee on Lord Wrendal's face only fueled the fire of his rage.

"So you vouch for this man, do you, Your Majesty?" said Lord Wrendal smoothly. "You countenance such threats against your guests? He speaks of murder and war—I little knew what a barbaric land I was coming to when I set sail from my home. But I can tell you this—if my daughter *has* been murdered, I will certainly take it as an act of war and so, I can assure you, will my king!"

"Enough!" said Cal, his voice icy and furious. "You dare to threaten me with war, as though it is your country and not mine that has been wronged? You said your concern is for those under your care, and your daughter must certainly be one of those people. If she is missing it is you who must answer for it. I do not know where your daughter is, and anyone with the least sense can clearly see that this man doesn't either." He gestured to Jonan, still struggling against the hold on his arms.

"Easy now," muttered Leander in Jonan's ear. "Don't play into his hands." Jo looked around at him furiously, but his eyes slid past Leander's to lock on Cal's face. He stilled at the look of blazing reproach Cal was directing toward him, and realized suddenly that he was only making matters worse. He deflated, and he suddenly needed Laramie and Leander's grip to hold up his sagging form as the rage that was fast seeping from him was replaced with cold horror.

"A search will be made for Lady Wrendal if you wish it," Cal was continuing, "but do not think it will deter me from my purpose in calling you all here. Lady Elnora's forcible abduction from this castle is an outrage that will not be tolerated, and I will not hesitate to deal swiftly and decisively with anyone involved."

Jo tuned out the rest of Cal's speech, his eyes still focused on Lord Wrendal. It was hard to be certain—the man was so experienced in playing a deep game—but Jo thought that his start of surprise at the mention of Elnora's disappearance seemed genuine. He was so absorbed in his contemplation of the despised Overseer that he didn't even realize Cal had finished addressing the assembled group until his friend directed a curt command toward him.

"Jo. A word." Laramie and Leander had relinquished their hold on Jonan. Leander stepped forward now to take control of the situation while Laramie followed Cal and Jo into a small antechamber opening out behind the raised dais. As soon as they were inside with the door closed behind them, Cal rounded on Jo.

"What were you thinking, Jo, threatening him to his face in front of all those people? Are *you* trying to start a war now?"

"You heard him, Cal!" returned Jo furiously. "We know he planned to kill her if the marriage alliance wasn't successful, and now she's conveniently missing?"

"It doesn't help anything for you to lose your head!" Cal shot back.

"Because you were so calm when you found out someone had taken Elnora!" Jo accused. For a moment he stared furiously back at his friend, but the very familiarity of the face before him reminded him that Cal was the last person he should be directing his rage toward. All of a sudden his anger left him, and he felt his shoulders slump in defeat. Cal regarded him in silence for a long moment before he was apparently satisfied that Jo wasn't going to do anything irrevocable. Cal turned to Laramie.

"Find the guard who went to rouse the Balenans," he said curtly, and Laramie disappeared instantly back into the throne room. Cal turned back to his friend, his expression becoming softer. "We'll get to the bottom of this, Jo," he said.

"I don't know where she is, Cal," Jo said, his voice barely more than a whisper. "I don't know if she's all right, or if she's even alive."

"I don't know either," said Cal gently. "But I know the feeling." He gave Jo a long look, his expression rueful. "And I know that we both need to pull ourselves together, or we're not going to be any use to either one of them."

Jo acknowledged this, running his hands over his face wearily. "Do you think it's part of the same attack?" he asked. "Did the same person target them both?"

"It seems too big a coincidence if it's not," said Cal, "but it doesn't make any sense."

Jo was prevented from responding by the reappearance of Laramie, a guard in tow.

"You went to Lady Wrendal's room?" Cal asked the man quickly, and the guard nodded. "Are you confident she isn't there?"

The man nodded again. "Yes, Sire."

"Was there any sign of a struggle?" Jo asked quickly.

"No," the guard said confidently. "The bed was untouched. It didn't look like anyone had been there at all."

Cal and Jo exchanged frowns, trying to make sense of it all. "Thank you," said Cal to the guard. "You can go." He looked over at Laramie. "You too, Laramie. Leander may need your assistance out there."

Laramie hesitated, clearly reluctant to leave, but Cal's expression was unyielding, and he had no choice but to comply. As soon as they were alone, Cal turned back to Jo.

"You know Lord Wrendal much better than I do," he said with a frown. "Is it like him to act so rashly? He's been here less than a day. Surely it's too soon for him to decide to give up on the alliance and move to his backup plan."

Jo thought for a moment, realizing the sense in Cal's words. "It is rash, isn't it?" he said slowly. "And he's certainly not that. No, it isn't like him to be so hasty."

"That's what I thought," Cal mused. "I don't think he's killed Scarlett, Jo. It doesn't add up. If he wanted to make it look like she was murdered by one of our people, surely he'd need more time to set it up. And surely he'd be parading her body before us, not declaring her missing."

Jo said nothing. His legs felt strangely weak as he contemplated the image of Scarlett's lifeless body. He sank into a nearby chair. Cal's explanation made sense, but he felt no less alarmed by the mystery of Scarlett's whereabouts. It was easy for Cal to be reassured by these logical arguments—Scarlett's well-being wasn't a matter of quite such vital importance for him. But Cal's next words reminded Jo that his friend had as much to lose as he did.

"In which case I hope they are together," Cal said, his voice breaking slightly. "Because then if Scarlett is alive, surely Elnora is too." He met Jo's eye. "We need answers, Jo. Answers neither one of us has."

Jo frowned at him for a second, not immediately taking his meaning. Then suddenly the realization hit. "The Esvalere!" he said. "That's why you sent Laramie away."

Cal nodded absently. "I need to go, to see what I can find out."

"Of course!" Jo's voice was eager. "It can show you where they both are."

"I hope so," said Cal uncertainly. "It's not that simple, though. And it's a risk. Every minute might be crucial. I can't afford to disappear for hours."

"Hours?" asked Jo, startled. "Surely you don't need that long."

Cal shrugged. "It's hard to keep any sense of time when I'm using it. The real world just kind of...fades away. I was accidentally gone for an entire day once. Elnora had to cover for me, and even so I almost created a security crisis."

Jo nodded slowly. He had found the same thing, to a lesser extent, when he had been lost in Alben's visions. He suddenly remembered that he hadn't told Cal about the latest one of these, after Yaeger had attacked.

"Cal," he said quickly. "There's something else you don't know." As concisely as possible, he recounted what he had seen after he had been knocked unconscious in the corridor. Cal's frown grew as the story unfolded.

"I don't like this," he said when Jo had finished. "There's too much that we don't understand. And the last thing we need is for Yaeger to have some kind of magic power at his disposal." He frowned silently for a moment. "Although, it would explain why he was so hard to overcome in the battle...he seemed to be able to withstand even my sword in a way no one else could." He glanced down at Jo's own rock, his eyebrows rising at the sight of the blackened hole in the fabric underneath it. "It would be great if you could figure out how to call up that surge of power at will, Jo."

"I know it would," said Jo, nettled. "But how am I supposed to do that? It's not exactly a magic sword that I can slice through the air to call down dragon power."

Cal gave a humorless laugh. "I had no more idea how to use the sword than you know how to use your rock," he said. "I had to figure out the hard way in the middle of a deadly battle. I'm just saying it would be great if you didn't have to do the same."

"I agree," said Jonan dryly. "But I don't have the answers."

Cal sighed. "It seems no one does."

"Not no one," contradicted Jo. "This is mountain magic, remember? I'm pretty sure the dragons could unravel it all if they wanted to." He scowled. "Although they'd probably just say it's not their problem."

"It doesn't matter what they'd say," said Cal. "We can't exactly afford the time it would take for a trip to the mountains and back."

Jonan was silent for a moment, thinking. "Maybe we don't have to," he said at last. He looked up at Cal. "Didn't Elddreki say you would be able to use the Esvalere to communicate with him?"

Cal nodded slowly.

"Would he come, do you think?" Jo asked eagerly. "If you asked him to?"

"Honestly? I have no idea," Cal said. "I know he's not quite as aloof as Qadir, but I don't think he would see Elnora's disappearance as the crisis it is to us. He'd probably say we should just give it time, or something maddening like that."

Jo shook his head quickly. "It's not just about that. I know it's hard to think about anything else while she's unaccounted for. Believe me, I know! But there's a bigger picture here. If my rock has something to do with the curse, Yaeger's rock must, too. It's not just about finding Elnora and Scarlett, or even stopping a war. Surely the dragons want to see the curse broken. They were happy enough when you broke the curse on your family last time."

"Happy might be a stretch," said Cal dryly, and Jo acknowledged his point with a grimace. It was true that the dragons did not seem to be given to displays of emotion. Cal thought over Jo's words for a moment longer before giving a decisive nod. "I'll try," he said. "It won't do any harm to try."

"Good," said Jo, leaping purposefully to his feet.

Cal looked at him, hesitating. "I'm sorry, Jo," he said tentatively, "but I can't take you with me."

"Of course you can't," said Jo briskly. "The last thing we need is the dragonwrath unleashed on the lot of us."

"So where are you going all of a sudden?" Cal's voice was suspicious.

"I'm going after Lord Wrendal," said Jo with determination.

"No you're not," said Cal grimly. "I know you're mad, Jo, but you need to leave it alone until we have all the information."

"I'm not going to attack him," protested Jo. "I'm just going to follow him, see if I can find out what he knows."

Cal raised his eyebrows incredulously, and Jo scowled.

"Curse you Cal, have a little faith in me! I can show restraint."

"Restraint? You?" said Cal waspishly. "Forgive me for being skeptical, but ten minutes ago you announced in front of my entire court that you were going to kill Lord Wrendal yourself."

Jo grimaced. "I'll admit, I lost my cool for a moment there. But you can trust me to do this. I want information as much as you do, and since I don't have a magic all-knowing royal sphere that I can take my questions to, I have to find other means."

Cal ignored the flippant remark, clearly still unconvinced. "If he catches you snooping around him, Jo—"

"He won't," said Jonan confidently. "I'm good at being inconspicuous."

"Since when?" asked Cal incredulously.

"Since I joined Scar's spy network," said Jo simply. "Now stop wasting time. Do you know what room Lord Wrendal has been put in?"

Cal nodded, his expression suspicious.

"Does it have a window to outside?"

"Of course it does, but it's not on the ground floor."

"Doesn't matter," dismissed Jo. "You know I've always been good at climbing. Describe to me where it is."

Cal still looked skeptical, but he complied. Jo listened attentively, giving a satisfied nod when Cal finished. Cal eyed him dubiously.

"I'm relying on you to show restraint, Jo," he said, his voice serious. "Don't let me down."

"I won't," Jonan assured him. "Now go do your part."

"Yes, Your Majesty," muttered Cal, and Jo allowed himself the briefest of grins. He had stayed away too long—it wouldn't do for Cal to get too used to giving all the orders.

But the smile was gone in an instant. There would be time enough to share a joke with his friend once Scarlett and Elnora were safe. Despite his earlier outburst, he was not going to contemplate the possibility that it was already too late for that.

Jo exited the antechamber by a route that would not take him back through the throne room. He wasn't sure how many of the courtiers and foreigners might still be assembled there. He hoped Lord Wrendal would leave soon, if he hadn't already. There was no hope of overhearing anything useful as long as the nobleman remained in the midst of a crowd.

It wasn't far from the throne room to the broad staircase that led up from the castle's wide entryway. Jo was down the steps in no time, but he didn't make for the firmly fastened front entrance, which would take him out to the street. Instead, he headed for a smaller side door that he knew would open up outside the building but still within the castle grounds.

It was still an hour before dawn, but the castle's various servants were already stirring, and although the guard at the door gave him a sharp glance, he didn't prevent Jonan from leaving. It was dark outside, the slightest hint of gray in the black the only indication that dawn was gradually approaching. Jo moved stealthily around the edge of the castle, hoping that Cal's description had been accurate as he came to a halt in front of the appropriate stretch of wall.

The visiting delegation had been given rooms that looked out on a pleasant garden, although the scene was currently shrouded in darkness. Creepers made their way up the walls sporadically, but even without them, the rough stonework afforded holds enough for a skillful climber. Jo scaled it up to the second floor without difficulty, counting windows as he went. He couldn't see into the room past the heavy brocade curtains that hung over the window, but at least that meant he wouldn't be in danger of being seen from inside.

He balanced precariously on the ledge jutting out from the window, attempting to ease the window open. At first it held fast, and he pulled harder and harder in his attempt to raise the glass. When it finally came unstuck, it shot upward with unnecessary force, almost causing him to fall backward and making him wince at the loud screeching scrape that accompanied the movement.

For a moment he hovered anxiously, wondering if he should cut his losses and climb back down to safety before the occupant of the room came to find the source of the noise. But as the silence stretched out, he realized that he had gotten lucky. Apparently no one was inside yet. He contemplated slipping into the room to search it, but it seemed unlikely he would find anything of interest. Instead he curled himself uncomfortably into the window frame and settled down to wait.

Almost ten minutes had passed, and his limbs were becoming painfully cramped, when he finally heard the door to the room open. He tried to breathe silently, holding his whole body stiff and still. He could have crowed with delight when he heard Lord Wrendal's quiet voice and realized that the nobleman had not entered the room alone. Clearly he was accompanied by one of his lackeys.

"This is unacceptable," the nobleman was saying crisply. "Where is she? This could ruin everything."

"We will find her, My Lord." Beyond the Balenan accent, there was no clue as to the identity of the second man, but Jonan could only assume he was one of the soldiers who had accompanied Lord Wrendal from Nohl.

"You had better," the nobleman snapped. "And how is that insolent pup here? I left him in the execution chamber. His head should have been taken from his shoulders weeks ago. How did he not only escape, but beat us to Kynton?"

The other man remained silent. The question was clearly rhetorical.

"And he seems to have the ear of that young fool of a king," Lord Wrendal continued, and Jo couldn't help but smirk at the anger in the Balenan's voice. "That complicates things considerably. Who knows what he's said to him?" There was a moment of silence, then Jonan heard Lord Wrendal drumming his fingers restlessly on a wooden surface. "When I saw him there, I thought for certain he must be behind Scarlett's disappearance, but his childish display of emotion makes me think he really doesn't know where she is."

Jo pricked up his ears. So Lord Wrendal hadn't been feigning ignorance as to Scarlett's whereabouts. He didn't know whether to be relieved or more concerned than ever.

"Yes, my Lord," agreed the soldier blandly. "He certainly seemed convinced that you were responsible for her...absence."

"Curse you, how should I be responsible?" snapped Lord Wrendal, and Jo noted with interest that this man was obviously not as deep in his master's confidence as the head lackey back in Nohl had been. He wondered if anyone on the delegation knew of Lord Wrendal's despicable backup plan to sacrifice Scarlett for his purposes. "The boy's accusation was the outburst of a lovesick fool with more passion than sense," Lord Wrendal added, but his haughty tone was undermined by his subsequent muttering. "Although if my ungrateful brat of a daughter has run away in defiance of me and ruined any more of my plans, I might just *have* to kill her myself like the stupid boy suggested."

Jo curled his hands into fists, his anger toward this terrible man returning. For a moment his thoughts strayed to the dagger concealed at his side. Lord Wrendal had only one man with him, and maybe if Jo took him by surprise...but no. He shook his head to clear it. He had assured Cal he could rely on Jo's restraint, and to kill Lord Wrendal in cold blood because his words made Jo angry wouldn't exactly be keeping that promise.

"Do you have any idea where Her Ladyship might have gone, My Lord?" asked the soldier delicately. "I will have my men begin a search, but I cannot deny that we are disadvantaged, since we don't know our way around the castle or the city."

"No idea whatsoever," said Lord Wrendal shortly. He paused. "Unless...I wonder if that former guard could be behind it? But surely he wouldn't dare..."

Jo leaned involuntarily forward to hear better as Lord Wrendal's voice dropped musingly. He was talking about Yaeger—he must be.

"I can only assume that he's the one behind the kidnapping of the king's peasant girl," Lord Wrendal was continuing. The nobleman's tone turned dark. "I wonder how he dared do even that. The fool is no doubt trying to force my hand. Making the girl disappear was only one of a number of strategies we discussed. He should not have acted without my direction, and it seems he bungled the whole affair. It was supposed to appear that she had run away, and instead his men leave obvious signs of an abduction." He broke off, and a sharp slap sounded, as though he had slammed his palm down on a desk. "I should have known better than to entrust any part of my plans to a Kyonan. They're halfwits, every last one of them. The idiot told me to my face he believes in *dragons*."

Jo rolled his eyes at the soldier's derisive snort. If this whole saga could only end with Lord Wrendal being eaten by a dragon, he would consider all his restraint in not killing the man himself well worth the effort.

Lord Wrendal was once again drumming his fingers. "Have the men search for Scarlett," he said decisively. "And make as much fuss as possible in the process. For all the king's smooth words, if harm has befallen her, I will make sure he bears the consequences for it. I will make contact with this Yaeger, and find out what the dolt has done."

"Yes, My Lord," responded the soldier quickly, and Jonan immediately heard the door open and close. He strained his ears, wondering if he was likely to hear anything else of interest. But Lord Wrendal didn't seem the type to talk aloud to himself, and Jonan wasn't exactly surprised when the minutes stretched out in silence. Jonan wished he knew how the nobleman intended to make contact with Yaeger, but he didn't dare to look past the curtains to see what Lord Wrendal might be up to.

Just as he was thinking of easing back down the exterior wall, he heard the door once again open and close. He hovered for a long moment, trying to decide whether to take the risk. But he was fairly certain that the room was now empty. On impulse, he decided to be bold. If Lord Wrendal had gone to contact

Yaeger, it would be too late to follow him by the time Jo crept down the wall, back into the castle and up through the corridors to this wing.

He peered around the curtain, noting with relief that the room was indeed unoccupied. He slipped silently through the window and padded across the floor, pausing with his ear against the door into the corridor. Hearing nothing, he eased the door open and slid out. He could just see Lord Wrendal disappearing around a corner up ahead, and he hurried along as stealthily as he could in the same direction.

Apparently he was not stealthy enough, however, because he was just about to round the corner himself when he felt an iron grip on his arm. With difficulty he repressed a cry of surprise, putting all his energy instead into wrestling against the hold.

"Be still!" hissed a vaguely familiar voice, and realizing who had grabbed him, Jonan stopped fighting at once.

"What are you doing?" he whispered furiously. Even as he said it, though, he remembered that one of the twins was supposed to be watching the Balenan nobleman at all times.

"What are *you* doing?" Laramie returned, his own voice icy. "Did you just come out of Lord Wrendal's rooms?"

"I was eavesdropping," Jonan hissed shortly. "Now let me go, before we lose him!"

"Does King Calinnae know what you're doing?" Laramie asked grimly.

"As a matter of fact, he does!" Jo whispered, and although Laramie's disapproving expression didn't disappear, he did loosen his grip on Jo's arm.

"Did you overhear anything useful?"

Jo nodded impatiently, rattling off the essentials in a tight voice. "He genuinely doesn't know where his daughter is. He had a plan with Yaeger to make Elnora disappear and make it look like she ran away. But it was only one of many ideas, and if it was Yaeger, he acted without Lord Wrendal's approval."

Laramie looked impressed in spite of himself.

"Now let me go!" Jonan whispered. "We've probably lost him already, and he was on his way to contact Yaeger right now!"

"I will follow him," whispered Laramie firmly. "You should make your report to the king."

Jo shook his head frantically. "Lord Wrendal doesn't know where either of them are. If he leads me to Yaeger, I can follow him instead. Yaeger won't recognize me, but he *will* recognize you." Laramie hesitated for a moment, and Jo pressed his advantage. "We don't have time to argue about it!"

Laramie let him go with a soft curse, clearly not happy but unable to deny the need for haste. Jo didn't wait for further discussion, sprinting off in the direction Lord Wrendal had gone. There was no sign of the nobleman, and he could have screamed in frustration. They had probably just thrown away their best hope of finding Yaeger, and with him Elnora, if not Scarlett as well. He barreled along the corridor, reaching the end of the passageway in moments, with no idea which way Lord Wrendal had gone. Making a split second decision, he turned left, racing down the new corridor as quickly as stealth would allow.

There was no sign to suggest that he had chosen the right direction. So he was taken completely by surprise when a figure emerged suddenly from a side passage as he passed. Jonan barely took in the flicker of movement before he felt the hilt of Lord Wrendal's sword connect with his chin and was sent sprawling, his senses swimming.

He struggled to rise, but Lord Wrendal's foot was on his chest in an instant, the point of the nobleman's sword against Jo's throat. Cursing his own carelessness, Jo glared up into his enemy's eyes.

"I knew I was being followed," the Balenan said softly, his silky voice at its most dangerous, "but I never imagined that even the boy king would be fool enough to give the task to you." Jonan said nothing, his mind racing as he tried to think of a way out of this mess. He felt the rock cold against his chest and willed it, desperately, to send that surge of power through him. But it rested unresponsive against his burned skin. It may as well be an ordinary piece of stone for all the good it did him.

"How much I would like to kill you where you lie," Lord Wrendal said, his voice hardly more than a whisper. "But it seems you may be more use to me alive, at least for now." He sighed. "A pity."

And with that deadly speed that never failed to take Jo by surprise, Lord Wrendal's arm shot out, twisting his sword around to bring the hilt smashing down on the top of Jonan's head. For the second time in as many hours, Jo's vision went black as he crashed inevitably into unconsciousness.

CHAPTER THIRTY-FOUR

The first thing Jonan was conscious of was an almost unbearable throbbing in his head. The second was the dappled light dancing against his closed eyelids.

That didn't seem right. Wasn't it still nighttime?

His eyes shot open, and he groaned involuntarily at the way even the dim light stung them.

"How kind of you to join us," said a smooth voice, and suddenly memory came crashing back. Jonan whipped his head around, wincing at the increased throbbing.

Lord Wrendal stood nearby, his expression infuriatingly smug. Jo ignored him, looking around instead in an effort to identify his surroundings. He didn't think he could have been out for too long. Dawn had certainly broken, but the scene was still colored with the gray of early morning. He was no longer in Kynton—he was surrounded by trees. He frowned. They must be in the Forest of Rune, which ran almost to the eastern wall of the city.

He shifted uncomfortably on the forest floor. The undergrowth was not dense, so he could only assume they had not traveled far into the forest. For a moment he wondered how

Lord Wrendal had gotten him there, but a quick glance around showed that the nobleman had quite a number of his Balenan soldiers with him. They must have carried—and if Jo's aching body was any indication, dragged—him from the castle. His hands were bound tightly behind his back, and his mouth was gagged.

He once again berated himself for being so foolish. He remembered his overconfidence in assuring Cal that he wouldn't be caught and groaned internally. It had all happened so quickly that he hadn't even put up a fight.

"How much further?" he heard Lord Wrendal ask impatiently. "I thought you said Yaeger wasn't far into the forest."

"Not far now, My Lord," answered an unfamiliar voice. Looking over at the man, Jo realized with surprise that one of the soldiers was actually Kyonan. At least, he carried himself like a soldier, but he didn't wear a uniform. Presumably one of Yaeger's defectors. The man seemed to feel Jo's gaze, and he glanced uncertainly down at the captive. "I'm not sure what he'll think about you bringing the boy," he said to Lord Wrendal.

"Do you think I care what he thinks?" snapped the nobleman. "He's lucky I don't abandon our agreement altogether after he made such a mess of things."

The Kyonan man looked resentful but was evidently unwilling to openly challenge the Balenan lord.

"Besides," continued Lord Wrendal with a malicious glance at Jonan, "this boy is a friend of the king's, I gather. He will be useful if your master holds to his plan for an ambush."

Ambush? Jo's breathing quickened in alarm. Were they trying to draw Cal into a trap? It would probably work, too, he thought bitterly, if they had both Elnora and Jonan as bargaining chips. He growled internally. How many times had he wished he could communicate with his friend about Lord Wrendal's schemes? But this time was so much worse than all the rest—maddening to be so close to Cal, but just as incapable of warning him.

He closed his eyes, trying with all his might to call up the latent power contained in the mountain rock that still hung around his neck. He thought about Alben, bringing to mind every detail he had learned about the deceased rebel. But there was no answering flicker from the talisman. He thought about when it had responded to him previously. When Yaeger attacked him in the castle only a matter of hours ago, when he was in the river just outside Nohl, when he had been flogged in the square.

But no—he hadn't even heard of the rock then, let alone had it on his person. For a moment he forgot his surroundings as he frowned over the anomaly. That had been the day of his arrival in Balenol, and although he had seen Alben's mark on the ship the day before, there had been no thought of mountain magic in his mind. He hadn't claimed the talisman yet—how could its power have coursed into his chest?

Lord Wrendal's group remained halted, the nobleman talking with the Kyonan traitor. Jo had tuned them out in his attempt to figure out the mystery of the rock. One of the Balenan soldiers wandered past and, evidently feeling that Jonan was in his way, kicked the captive's foot to one side with unnecessary force. Jonan scowled at the man for the briefest of moments before freezing where he lay. Because the contact with his foot had sparked the memory of the flogging incident. It hadn't been through his chest that he had felt the rush of power. It had come from his feet, spreading up through his body. From his feet—or could it be from under his feet? He remembered the words of the stranger in the square the day Raldo had been executed. The execution chamber was located right underneath the square.

Could that have been the first time Jonan had felt the rock's power, after all? Had it somehow rushed up through the flag-stones, from the talisman's hiding place in the wall of the cell?

Jonan felt a rush of excitement at the revelation, but he quickly deflated at the realization of how little good the information was to him in his current situation. If the rock had responded to him that day, why had it done so? And why couldn't he feel its power now, while he wore it against his skin?

"It's quite convenient that you were able to join us, as it turns out." The hated voice of Lord Wrendal broke into Jonan's musings, as he approached Jonan lying on the ground.

"I don't know how you have gained friendship with the king —probably another relic of his peasant past, I imagine." The nobleman shuddered. "Such an ill-bred pup to sit on the throne...I suppose it's what I should expect from a kingdom of slaves. He probably thinks his crown will let him get away with his impudence. But he will soon learn his mistake. Whether or not the halfwit guard's coup is successful, you can rest assured the trade will continue. I would ship your precious King Calinnae himself across the water just to prove the point if you hadn't demonstrated to me the danger of giving the slaves a rallying point." He regarded Jonan in silence for a moment, his expression thoughtful.

"But unlike you, I do not fail to learn from my mistakes," he continued, dismissing whatever thought had been occupying his mind with a flick of his head. "In any event, it's gratifying to know that your connection with him might be of use to me. I must confess that I am impressed you managed to escape the execution I ordered. But your use of your undeserved freedom only confirms your stupidity. I can only imagine that you raced after us to Kynton in the hope of being reunited with my daughter." The nobleman's eyes grew hard. "I told you once before that you would never set eyes on her again, and you will find I am as good as my word."

Remembering his recent kiss with Scarlett in the withdrawing room, Jonan wanted to roll his eyes. Lord Wrendal's posturing came a little late. He would like to know, since the nobleman apparently had no idea where his daughter was, how he was going to keep his word.

But the gag in Jonan's mouth most unfortunately prevented him from open defiance, and he had to be content with directing a murderous glare toward his tormentor. At least Scarlett wasn't currently at the man's mercy. In spite of all the other ways in which the situation had spiraled out of control, that was one source of comfort.

Lord Wrendal didn't seem at all deterred by Jonan's inability to respond. On the contrary, he seemed to be enjoying his opportunity to insult his enemy uninterrupted.

"You may count yourself lucky to be alive, of course," he continued. "I daresay you thought I would kill you when you so conveniently put yourself at my disposal in the castle. I have no doubt you would have killed me if our positions were reversed. But I am not so shortsighted." He rested his hand comfortably on the hilt of the sword he wore at his side. "As much as I would enjoy running my blade through your heart, I didn't get to where I am by being unable to sacrifice my inclinations for the sake of my greater interests."

Jonan frowned back at the nobleman, forgetting to be mutinous as his mind was arrested by a sudden impression. The mention of sacrifice sparked a nebulous thought. It tugged at the edge of his mind, but he couldn't quite pin it down.

"I think, My Lord," broke in the Kyonan man, "that I'd still better get the boss's orders before bringing him into camp." The man gestured at Jonan. "He never said nothing about another hostage."

Jonan's heart leaped at the word "another". Hopefully they meant Elnora—hostage was much better than dead.

Lord Wrendal made an irritated noise in his throat, whether because of the interruption to his gloating monologue, or because of the Kyonan man's refusal to recognize his authority, Jonan wasn't sure. Either way, the nobleman evidently didn't think it was worth arguing the point, because he ordered three of his men to stay and guard the captive while the rest went ahead with their Kyonan guide. Apparently sick of the delay, Lord Wrendal headed up the departing group, pausing only to promise Jonan a painful end to the morning's adventures, one way or the other.

Jonan received the threat without concern, his spirits lifting slightly at the reduction in the number of enemies in his immediate vicinity. He couldn't immediately see how he could turn it to his advantage, bound, gagged and unarmed as he was, but it was still nice to have better odds. His legs weren't bound, but he quickly dismissed the idea of trying to run away. They would be sure to catch him immediately, and in addition to looking foolish, he would probably find himself trussed up and dragged the rest of the way.

He was deeply engrossed in his attempt to think of an escape plan, so it took a few minutes for his mind to register that something was off. He stilled, trying to identify whether it had been sight, sound or smell that had triggered the indefinable sense of something abnormal.

There it was again! Sound, then. The bird call repeated, its soft but clear note cutting through the forest's early morning calm. Jonan peered through the trees in the direction of the sound, but he couldn't see anything. He glanced at his minders, none of whom seemed to have noticed anything amiss. Surreptitiously, he shifted his weight, trying to get in position to struggle quickly to his feet should the need arise.

The bird call came again, and he frowned. Why did it seem so out of place? With the appearance of the sun, a number of birds had woken up and begun to make themselves heard. In his short time since regaining consciousness, Jonan had heard more than one of them singing in the trees.

Once more the melodious whistle came, and with a sudden rush he identified the sound. No wonder it hadn't seemed to fit. It was a bird call he had heard in the jungle during his time in Balenol, but not one he had heard in Kyona before. He remembered Stan making just such a sound as a signal, and it had been totally unfamiliar to him at the time. Whatever bird she had been mimicking, it wasn't one that could be found in his homeland.

His heart leaped. He knew Stan couldn't be here—she was far away, wrestling with the impossible task of keeping a staggering number of escaped slaves alive and hidden until the curse could be broken. Jonan wasn't sure exactly what the call meant. But he felt at this point like he didn't have much to lose, and he knew no hesitation as he decided to follow his instincts.

Using his bound hands to assist, he rolled from his back to his side, pushing himself to his feet as rapidly as possible. One of the guards gave an inarticulate shout at the sudden movement, but Jo ignored him, taking off without pause and running as quickly as his awkward posture would allow in the direction of the bird call.

The cries of the guards behind him sounded more annoyed than alarmed, and Jonan could imagine that they thought, as he had a moment before, that they would have no difficulty in catching him. He could hear one close on his heels, but the other two seemed to be following more slowly.

He had no idea how far away the source of the call might be, so he was still running blindly at full speed when he passed a particularly large tree. As he went past it, he caught a flash of movement and spun violently around mid-stride, almost overbalancing. He turned in time to see a crimson-clad figure step out from behind the tree and take the first guard, only a few steps behind Jonan, completely by surprise. Before the man could so much as shout, Jonan's rescuer had plunged a blade straight into his heart. The man dropped like a stone.

Without hesitation, the newcomer retrieved the knife, straightening again in the same fluid motion. After the briefest of pauses to line it up, the figure threw the knife with unexpected skill, catching the second guard in the chest, and cutting off his cry of astonishment. Another moment was all it took for Jo's rescuer to draw the sword of the first fallen guard, lying at their feet, and step forward to meet the third and final opponent. The man hesitated, clearly unsure what to do as he took in the identity of his challenger, and the delay cost him. In a move reminiscent of Lord Wrendal's recent attack on Jonan, the hilt of the stolen sword flashed upward, hitting the man's chin so hard that his head snapped back and he dropped, unconscious, to the forest floor.

Throughout this entire astonishing performance, Jonan had stood uselessly, frozen in shock. In the sudden stillness, he turned his startled eyes on Scarlett, who had discarded the sword and was losing no time in retrieving and cleaning her own, smaller blade. She stepped up to him without a word, spinning him around with a firm grip and slicing quickly through the bindings on his hands. As soon as they were free, Jo used them to rip the gag from his face, turning back around to face his rescuer.

"Scarlett!" he cried, his relief and astonishment mingling together into a confused jumble. He hardly knew how to articulate his reaction to what he had just witnessed. He remembered that Scarlett had scoffed at the idea that she would have been able to operate as a rebel leader without learning to fight, but other than his own unintentional knife fight with her, he had never seen her put that particular skill set to use before.

"Are you all right?" she asked, meeting his eyes with an anxious expression.

"Yes," he said, a shaky laugh escaping. "Thanks to you! Did you really just incapacitate three grown men single-handed?"

"I'm just glad you recognized the call," said Scarlett, her voice tight. "I didn't know how long we had, and I didn't want to waste the opportunity while there were only three of them."

"Yes," said Jo, still dazed. "*Only* three." He took in her tense form. "Never mind me," he said quickly. "Are *you* all right? I've been so worried! When you went missing—oh Scar, I thought your father had killed you like he threatened!"

She shook her head, for a moment unable to speak. Disregarding the grisly scene around them, Jo reached toward her, placing a hand softly on her cheek.

At his touch, her fierce demeanor seemed to crumble, and she threw herself suddenly into his arms, which he closed firmly around her.

"Oh Jo!" she said, her voice catching. "When I saw them dragging you through the forest, and realized my father had gotten his hands on you...I thought we were going to be safe now. I thought we were past all of that."

"I know," he said soothingly. "I know. I've been beside myself since I found out you were missing. I keep saying I'm going to protect you, and then I keep failing dismally."

She shook her head again, before pressing her face against his chest. He continued to hold her tightly, his whole body trembling with relief at the feel of her, whole and unharmed and leaning against him for support.

It wasn't that he was glad of her distress. But truth be told, as grateful as he was for her intervention, he had been unnerved by what he had just seen her do. There were so many sides to this incredible girl, and it was somehow reassuring to be reminded that the soft heart he had come to love was as real a part of her as the lethal skill that commanded his admiration.

He had almost forgotten their danger in the bliss of their reunion, but as usual Scarlett was more level-headed. After a long moment she pulled back from him, her tone once again businesslike.

"We need to get out of here before the others come back for you." She looked at him appraisingly. "I assume you're not armed?" He shook his head, and she stepped forward, away from him, to pick up the sword of the first guard, which she had dropped.

It was as she was bent double that Jonan's eyes slid past her, and he realized with a thrill of horror that the third man had regained consciousness while Jo and Scarlett had been embracing. Taking in his two dead comrades, the man's eyes moved to Scarlett, his expression changing from astonishment to fury as he clutched the sword that had fallen at his side.

Starting forward, Jo gave a wordless cry of alarm. Scarlett's gaze jumped to him, startled, but he didn't look at her, instead leaping past her to put himself between her and the guard just as the man raised his arm.

Jo was still unarmed, but as he jumped in front of Scarlett, the rock around his neck finally granted him the sought-after rush of power, and he felt his every muscle tense with an unnatural strength. His hand shot out and seized the guard's wrist, forcing his arm upward so that the sword pointed uselessly into the air.

For a long moment they struggled, but not for an instant did Jo doubt the outcome. The guard was much bigger and burlier, but the magic of the rock seemed to course through his veins, and he forced the man's arm inexorably up, twisting it around until the guard dropped the sword with a cry of pain.

Jonan's fist shot out, catching the man full in the face, and the guard dropped to the ground, once again knocked senseless. Jonan hesitated for a moment. He knew the man had recognized Scarlett, and he wasn't sure what the outcome of his report to Lord Wrendal would be, but still Jo couldn't quite bring himself to run a sword through an unconscious man.

Scarlett made no comment on his forbearance, but it seemed she shared his view, because she also made no move to permanently silence the downed guard. She did, however, have something to say on Jonan's previous action.

"Jo, what were you thinking?" she accused, her face unusually pale. "You were unarmed, and he had a sword. You know I can defend myself. I don't know how you overpowered him like that, but I wish you would stop trying to be heroic. How many times do I have to tell you that I don't want you to put yourself in danger for my sake?"

But Jo just scoffed dismissively. "I'm not being heroic, Scar!" His face softened as he looked at her, still reveling in the discovery that she was safe after all. "You're right that I got lucky with overpowering him—I haven't even told you about Alben's rock, and I'm as surprised as you are that it came to my rescue. But even if it hadn't, how could I have stood by while he attacked you? You're so important to me that putting myself in danger for your sake isn't even going against my own interests. It doesn't count as a sacrifice."

Even as the word came out of his mouth, the realization hit, and he felt his eyes grow wide. Scarlett opened her mouth to argue, but fell silent, her expression uncertain as she took in Jonan's suddenly rigid posture.

"That's it!" he cried. "That's the key. Sacrifice. I knew there was some connection I was missing!"

"What are you talking about?" she asked uneasily. "What sacrifice? And did you say Alben's rock saved you?"

He nodded. "There's a lot I need to tell you." He glanced

around at their immediate surroundings. "But not here. You're right that they'll be back any minute." He frowned at the trees around them. "I suppose the best thing to do is to go back to the castle and warn Cal. But it's a shame that I didn't see exactly where they're keeping Elnora."

"I did," said Scarlett quickly, and Jo looked at her in surprise.

"You did? How? And now that I think about it, what are you doing here? Where have you been, and why did you leave without saying anything to anyone?" He took a good look at her for the first time, and realized that she was still in the crimson gown she had worn to the banquet the night before, although it was hardly recognizable for its disheveled state. The flowing skirt was so reduced that he suspected she had torn it herself in order to increase her own mobility. "I think you have quite a bit to tell me as well," he said dryly.

"Yes," she agreed. "But you first. I'll show you where they are, while you tell me about the rock."

Jo nodded his agreement. Pausing only to each retrieve a sword from their fallen opponents, the two of them set off through the trees, moving stealthily. It was so similar to their excursions through the jungle outside Nohl, and yet so wildly different. Jo wondered if Scarlett was also thinking of those occasions.

At first they traveled in silence, putting some distance between themselves and the scene of the recent fight. Scarlett wasn't going in the same direction as Lord Wrendal and the others had gone, and Jonan assumed she was taking a round-about route to avoid the risk of running into them. When they had been moving for several minutes, Scarlett nodded at Jo, apparently feeling that it was safe to speak.

Keeping his voice low, he told her about finding the moun-tain rock in the execution chamber, and about the vision he had seen when he grasped it. She listened in amazement, and he couldn't quite decipher the look on her face when he finished his tale.

"What is it?" he asked quietly, and she shook her head in wonder.

"It's just...I don't know. It's so strange. When my father hauled you off to the execution chamber, it was the worst moment of my life. I couldn't imagine a worse outcome. But if you'd never been put in there, you wouldn't have found the rock. And if it really is the key to breaking the curse...it's just odd to think that being put in the execution chamber might actually be the best thing that happened to you in Nohl."

"Not the very best thing," Jonan contradicted. "The thing that came just before it was still better."

Scarlett blushed rosily. "I'm being serious," she reproached him. But Jonan could see that she was pleased, and he grinned, unrepentant. "What did you mean before?" Scarlett pressed. "About sacrifice being the key?"

"The rock," said Jonan, becoming enthusiastic as he remembered his revelation. "It has some kind of power in it, and it's like I can draw on the power every now and then. It seemed random, but I think I've finally figured it out! It's a rock from the Dragon Realm, with some kind of mountain magic involved, I already knew that much. But it's not just any random rock—it's part of the rock that crushed Alben's mother."

"And she sacrificed her own life to save his," said Scarlett quietly, catching on.

"Exactly!" said Jonan, his voice eager.

"So you have to sacrifice your life, or attempt to, in order to draw on its power?" asked Scarlett, alarmed. She shot the talisman a look that suggested she was contemplating snatching it away from him before he could throw himself in front of any more blades, and he couldn't help but smile.

"I don't think so," he reassured her. "It wasn't my life on the line—or at least not directly—when I intervened in that boy being whipped."

Scarlett pondered this. "But you were willing to sacrifice your well-being for someone else's," she said at last. "And the same with the attack just now."

"And Yaeger's attack against Cal in the castle," said Jonan, mostly to himself. He frowned. "I'm not sure about in the river, though. Maybe if I could remember exactly what was happening when the rock responded…" He thought for a moment, then realized the answer. "I know! I was getting ready to dive under the gate. I knew it was risky, but I had just been thinking that it was worth risking my life a hundred times over if it meant I could save you from your father." He beamed at her, pleased with his powers of deduction. "It still fits!"

"Oh Jo," said Scarlett, her beautiful eyes showing distress. "That river is dangerous at the best of times, let alone after a downpour—you could so easily have been killed!"

"Not me," said Jo cheerfully. "I always—"

"Always land on your feet, yes, yes, I know," said Scarlett testily, and Jo grinned.

"Well, don't I?" he asked, raising a cheeky eyebrow, but she shushed him with a gesture.

"We're getting close," she said, her voice low. "We shouldn't talk any more."

"Hang on!" hissed Jo, pulling her to a stop. "Don't think you're getting out of telling me what happened to you last night! Why did you leave? And why didn't you tell me?"

"I didn't *leave*," protested Scarlett indignantly. "I was abducted, the same as Elnora."

"But why?" Jonan insisted. "What's Yaeger's interest in kidnapping you when he's supposed to be helping your father marry you off to Cal?"

"Well for one thing," said Scarlett dryly, "I think he has no more intention now of doing that than my father does. From what I can gather, this Yaeger wants King Calinnae's blood at any cost, and I seriously doubt he was ever planning to cooperate with my father. He was probably always just intending to use him for his own ends."

"Making them the perfect pair," said Jonan ironically.

"Exactly," Scarlett agreed. "But in answer to your question, Yaeger had no interest in kidnapping me. I wasn't the target—Elnora was. They didn't expect me to be there."

Jo frowned. "To be where? How did you get caught up in it?"

"I was with her, in her suite," said Scarlett, surprised. "Hadn't you figured that out? We had been talking after the banquet, and she invited me back to continue our conversation. Time ran away with us. I'm pretty sure the men Yaeger sent expected her to be asleep and vulnerable. I'm very sure they didn't expect there to be two of us. But having entered the room by way of the window, armed to the teeth, they couldn't exactly back out. I guess they had no choice but to grab us both."

Jo blinked, feeling incredibly stupid. It was such a simple explanation of why both girls were missing, but it hadn't even occurred to him. It should have, he supposed, since he and Cal had been doing the exact same thing at the time of the incident. His first reaction was alarm at the thought that Scarlett had been forcibly abducted after all. But as he pictured the scene, he couldn't help a slow smile spreading across his face.

"So they thought they were grabbing a sleeping girl from her bed, and instead they found the two of you, awake and together? They must have gotten quite a surprise."

Scarlett smiled grimly. "You could say that. I must say, Elnora is tougher than she looks. She told me about her history—you wouldn't guess it to look at her. But I guess I should know better than anyone that someone's appearance can be misleading. Still, I think it's a mistake that she doesn't take the precaution of being always armed. Well, she didn't—I'm guessing she will from now on."

Jonan regarded his lady with increasing respect. "Whereas you do take that precaution?"

"Of course." She flashed him a grin. "I got one of them a pretty decent gash, too. But there were just too many of them."

Jo shook his head, still smiling faintly. "So that's whose blood it was. We assumed it must be Elnora's. You should have seen poor Cal's face."

"He must be so worried," she said, her own face creasing. "And I wish I could say he has no reason to be, but Elnora is still in danger."

"How did you get away?" Jo asked, and she shrugged.

"While they were dragging us through the forest, we figured out pretty quickly that if we put our heads together, we could get one of us free." She gave a quick smile. "It didn't hurt that they hadn't located my second dagger. By then it was clear that they weren't planning to kill Elnora immediately, and she insisted I go." Scarlett sighed. "I didn't want to leave her behind, but she's just as stubborn as Stan is. And I knew I could do it. They chased me, of course, but it didn't take them very long to give up."

She smiled grimly. "No one expected the young Balenan noblewoman to be experienced in the forest. But honestly, compared to our jungle, this place is a breeze. I gave it some time, tracked them to where they're camped, and got out of there." She suddenly looked a bit guilty. "I was supposed to go straight back to the castle to raise the alarm, but when I came upon you, looking like a corpse and being dragged through the forest by my father, I got a little bit sidetracked."

"Well, I can't deny I'm glad you did," Jonan admitted, giving her hand a quick squeeze. "But let's not waste any more time. Show me this camp."

Scarlett nodded, and the two of them started moving again, falling silent. After a few more minutes, Scarlett motioned upward with her head, and Jo followed her lead in scaling a nearby tree. He had to admire her dexterity as she passed from one treetop to the next—it was all he could do to keep up, and he was sure even that would have been beyond him if he hadn't had so much recent experience with rooftops. In a short space of time, they started to hear noises through the trees, and not long after that he caught a glimpse of activity below them, not far ahead.

He crawled carefully along a sturdy branch, trying to see past the greenery without exposing himself to view. What he saw caused him to draw in a sharp breath. The renegades had camped in a large clearing. He could see Lord Wrendal speaking with Yaeger at the center of the space, neither man looking particularly impressed with the other. Even from a distance, Jo thought he could make out the rock around Yaeger's neck, the extent and nature of its power still uncertain.

A quick scan of the area also showed Elnora, bound against a large tree on the edge of the clearing. She looked disheveled but perfectly conscious and aware, glaring daggers at everyone passing by. It wasn't the unknown magic at Yaeger's disposal, or Elnora's precarious position, that filled Jo with alarm—it was the scene that surrounded them. He glanced at Scarlett, further back in the tree, and she returned the look grimly.

Jo had known that Yaeger had a band of defectors with him, and had accepted that a fight was brewing. But his impression was that Cal was expecting maybe two dozen men to be traveling with Yaeger, and he could only assume that if Cal came, he would come prepared to meet such a force. The problem was, the group gathered in the clearing below him was no motley band of two dozen. It was closer to two hundred. Armed, organized, and unscrupulous, as evidenced by the callous disinterest with which they passed by the place where Elnora was bound.

Jo inched back along the branch toward Scarlett. "So many of them," he breathed. "This is much worse than I realized. Cal's not going to be ready for this—he really would be walking into an ambush. We need to get back to the castle and warn him."

But even as the words left his lips, a shout went up in the camp below. For a moment Jo thought they had been detected in their hiding place, but then his ears picked up the sound that had obviously sparked the alarm. Thundering hoof beats, coming from the direction of Kynton.

They had left their warning too late.

CHAPTER THIRTY-FIVE

Jo cursed softly, hovering for a moment on the branch, unsure of what to do. Even as he hesitated, he caught a glimpse of movement almost immediately below them. The Balenan soldier whom they had twice knocked unconscious had made his way back to the camp, and was running without delay toward the two men in the middle of the clearing.

Yaeger ignored him, already issuing orders to his men, who sprang into action at the sound of the distant hoof beats. But Lord Wrendal listened closely to what the man was saying, his growing rage evident even from a distance. Jonan couldn't resist a small smirk as he contemplated how furious the nobleman would be that his quarry had once again slipped out of his reach. But when Lord Wrendal's expression changed suddenly from anger to astonishment, Jonan sobered again.

He glanced at Scarlett, and saw that she also was watching her father, her expression hard to read. What exactly Lord Wrendal would make of the information that his missing daughter had not only reappeared unexpectedly for the purpose of rescuing Jonan, but that she had skillfully and unhesitatingly killed two soldiers in the process, Jonan wasn't sure. It was more imperative than ever that she didn't come within her father's power again, but even in the midst of his concern, Jonan felt a small measure of relief that her charade was finally over, and this time irrevocably.

But there was no time to dwell on it now. Jo's first instinct was to try to intercept Cal, to stop him before he reached the ambush set up for him. It looked to him like the men Yaeger was sending out of the clearing were intending to form a wide pincer and surround the group approaching from the city. But it took only a moment for Jonan to realize that it was too late for him to warn Cal. As he ran his eyes over the scene below, trying to identify the most strategic assistance he could give to his friend's cause, his gaze settled on Elnora. As long as she was in danger, Cal was doubly vulnerable.

"We need to get Elnora free," he whispered to Scarlett, not taking his eyes from the clearing. She followed his gaze and nodded at once, not needing him to explain.

Even as he spoke, he saw Yaeger stride over to Elnora. Jonan tensed as the man pulled out his sword, but Yaeger just sliced through the rope binding Elnora to the tree. He pulled her roughly to her feet, her hands still bound in front of her. Keeping his sword at her throat, he dragged her by the arm until they were in the middle of the clearing, facing toward the city. Jo felt a rush of pride at the steadiness with which his friend held herself. Elnora looked mutinous, but not in the least afraid.

Jonan was surprised, glancing around the clearing again, to see it almost empty. Yaeger's men had moved with impressive speed, and it seemed that whatever plan the former Chief Guard had in mind required him and his captive to be standing alone in the middle of the clearing. It was certainly a dramatic picture. Jo couldn't help but think that Yaeger was right that arriving to such a scene would set Cal at a huge disadvantage. Especially as he could have no idea just how many men were lurking nearby, ready to attack.

The stone felt heavy around Jo's neck as he thought about how to change the balance of the situation. Now that he understood the nature of the power the talisman held, he thought he would have a much better chance of drawing on it at need. Even now, as he thought about throwing himself into the fray in Elnora's defense, he could feel a potent flicker against his burned skin. Strong as Yaeger looked, Jonan thought he could take him on if he could get the man one on one. It seemed hard to believe that Yaeger could be gaining much power from his rock if to do so required him to sacrifice his own interests.

The trouble was that Yaeger wasn't alone in the clearing. Lord Wrendal was still there, and he seemed to now be accompanied by most of the soldiers he had brought with him on the delegation. They stood some distance behind Yaeger and his captive.

"If we could distract them somehow," Jo muttered to Scarlett, gesturing toward the Balenans, "I could take Yaeger, I think."

"Jo," she said warningly, her face creasing in her anxiety.

"I know, Scarlett," he said quietly. "I really do, but there isn't time to argue about it." He held her gaze for a moment, and saw that she knew he was right. "Can you think of a way to distract them?" he asked.

"Yes," she said concisely. "Quite easily."

And before he could ask her to elaborate, she swung herself down from the branch, reaching the ground in seconds.

"Scarlett!" Jo hissed in alarm, but if she heard, she ignored him. She strode purposefully forward, only a few quick strides needed to place her in the clearing.

Jonan stifled an oath with difficulty, knowing there was no benefit to be gained from giving away his position. If he had guessed what Scarlett meant to do, he would have done all he could to prevent it. But as one of the Balenans gave a shout at her appearance, Jo realized that to waste the advantage she was giving him by trying fruitlessly to pull her back was the worst thing he could do. Already he could hear shouts and the clash of metal from the force approaching from Kynton, and he knew there wasn't a moment to lose.

He dropped to the ground himself and sprinted around the edge of the clearing, trusting in Scarlett's diversion to prevent anyone from noticing the movement behind the tree line. He passed around behind the Balenans, sprinting at Yaeger and Elnora from behind. Yaeger didn't notice him, his attention divided between the still unseen approaching group, and the unexpected reappearance of his disheveled former prisoner.

Although his eyes were on Yaeger, Jo was keenly aware that the Balenans had converged on Scarlett. From the resultant shouts, it sounded like she was giving a good account of herself. Probably the man she had previously knocked unconscious was not the only one to make the mistake of hesitating when he saw who she was. As much as he liked Elnora, and didn't want to see harm come to her, Jo's own priority was inevitably Scarlett. Every nerve in his body was screaming at him to run to her aid, but he knew that there were bigger issues at stake than his own emotions, and he resolutely forced the impulse down, continuing on his course.

Even as he steeled himself, he felt a surge of strength from the rock pour into his chest and throughout his aching limbs. He felt suddenly full of energy, the magic itself mingling with his sudden elation at having figured out how to access the talisman's power. He hadn't yet even drawn the sword he had slung across his back, and he didn't do so as he ran. Instead he pulled up as he reached the still unaware Yaeger, gathering his newfound energy into a powerful kick that landed squarely in the middle of the former guard's back and sent him flying forward onto his face with unnatural force.

Elnora hadn't seen Jo either, her wide eyes watching Scarlett's fight with alarm. But she didn't waste the unexpected opportunity. She dove away from Yaeger as soon as his sword, falling to the ground at his side, was no longer at her throat.

"Jo!" she cried in amazement.

Already Yaeger was struggling up, and Jo didn't take his eyes from him as he sawed quickly through the bindings around Elnora's hands.

"Run!" he shouted as soon as the severed rope fell away. He didn't look to see if she had obeyed, just moving to put himself between her and Yaeger, who was back on his feet. Jo's movement had been unconscious, but he felt another wave of power surge through him, and he gripped his sword confidently, feeling stronger and more energized than he had in his life.

Yaeger had retrieved his sword, which had fallen right next to him, and he drew it up in front of him as he rose. His expression changed rapidly from anger to surprise to derision as he took in the slim young challenger who was staring him down with such grim determination.

"Don't think you'll so easily take my prize from me, boy," he said, his tone almost indulgent. "That was a clever trick, but you won't catch me unawares again."

A shout from the group of Balenans distracted Jonan for a moment. He started to look around, his fear for Scarlett rising back to the forefront suddenly, but a flicker of movement from Yaeger drew his attention back to his own fight. He raised his sword instinctively, blocking the older man's attack. Yaeger tried again, and again Jonan parried, the swords locking dangerously. He was taken by surprise by the force of Yaeger's attack, and he knew that without the unnatural strength given to him by the mountain rock, he would never have been able to hold it off. But his arms held steady, his muscles straining. Yaeger pushed harder, his eyes narrowing in confusion, but Jonan mustered his strength for a counter push, and threw the other man's sword off with a shout.

Yaeger retreated a step, his eyes still narrowed shrewdly as he assessed his opponent. The two began to circle, and Jonan turned his head quickly, trying frantically to locate Elnora, and make sure the change in position wasn't bringing her within Yaeger's reach. He caught sight of her, running across the clearing, and for a moment he hoped that she was headed for safety. But as she stooped down a second later, he realized that she wasn't planning to run and hide. The ongoing struggle of the Balenan group had moved them several feet, leaving exposed the inert form of a soldier whom Scarlett had clearly brought down. Elnora had seized the opportunity to arm herself, and when she straightened again, she clutched the man's sword.

Glancing past her, Jo's eyes locked on Scarlett, finally subdued by the soldiers she had so boldly attacked. Two of the men held her arms firmly, pulling her before her father, who had a look on his face that made Jonan's blood run cold.

All this Jonan took in in a moment before his attention was dragged back to his opponent as Yaeger rushed at him. His nerves humming with frantic energy, Jonan raced forward to meet him, the blades once again ringing together as Jonan parried Yaeger's thrust and brought his own sword back in an attempted riposte. Yaeger was a much more experienced swordsman, however, and although he staggered under the strength of Jonan's attack, he had no difficulty deflecting it.

He was clearly surprised at Jonan's continued success in withstanding his assault, and his eyes roamed over the young man's person, as if looking for a weakness. Jonan saw them settle on the rock on its chain around his neck, and didn't miss

Yaeger's dramatic start of astonishment. The man's eyes flew to Jonan's, their expression calculating.

"I don't know where you got your hands on that, boy," he said softly, "but something tells me you don't have the stomach to make use of it."

It was Jonan's turn to frown in confusion, but before he could respond, a shout drew his attention back toward the Balenans. It took a moment for him to make sense of the flurry of movement, but he quickly realized that Elnora had made good use of her stolen weapon, taking one of the soldiers who held Scarlett by surprise. Whether it would be enough to enable Scarlett to fight her way free again rather than ending in both Elnora and Scarlett being taken captive by Lord Wrendal, Jonan didn't have time to observe.

The sounds of fighting he had heard earlier had been growing louder, and at that moment a group of mounted Kyonans burst into the clearing, Cal at their head. Leander, riding beside Cal, gave a shout of triumph as they emerged, and Jo realized that they had just pushed their way through a thin line of defense. Jo's heart sank at the number of guards Cal had with him—he judged it to be no more than three dozen.

Cal, his face grim, took in the scene at a glance. He gave a curt command, the exact content of which Jo couldn't catch, although he could guess the gist from the way Cal's eyes were locked on Elnora's slim form as she struggled against a large Balenan man. A number of Cal's guards surged forward, but Jo felt his heart drop into his stomach when the movement was met by an answering shout from the trees.

Yaeger's hidden forces raced in from both sides in an attempt to close the challengers in. Cal's guards were forced to turn their attention outward, abandoning the attempt to join the fight going on in the middle of the clearing. Jo could see the dismay on their faces as they realized that they were surrounded and outnumbered. He supposed that they had been fooled into thinking the small group of renegades they had overcome in order to enter the clearing had been the sum of Yaeger's force. That part of the former guard's plan had worked.

But Jo couldn't afford to wait for the outcome. Yaeger seemed to take the king's appearance as a good opportunity to deal with the pesky interruption once and for all and free his attention for his more important quarry. He raised his sword high, attempting to bring it down on Jo's head with furious speed. But Jo raised his own blade in time to hold off the attack, letting out a roar as he put all his strength into his attempt to repel the older man's sword. The force with which Yaeger pressed his weapon down felt irresistible, but somehow Jonan resisted it.

"So you *have* figured out how to use the rock's power," panted Yaeger, still pushing untiringly. "I congratulate you. You don't have the look of someone who's capable of killing."

Jo was confused by the other man's words, but he wasn't about to let himself be distracted. Remembering his knife fight with Scarlett all those weeks ago, he kicked out suddenly, his foot connecting with Yaeger's shin with such unnatural force that he almost expected it to shatter the bone. But Yaeger just stumbled back a step, his growl more of anger than pain.

"No matter," the traitor spat. "You cannot have called on its power as much as I have. And when I kill the royal brat's peasant girl before his eyes, it will make me more than strong enough to finish him off this time." His eyes flicked over to where Elnora was still fighting, and following his gaze, Jonan saw her and Scarlett back to back, struggling against Lord Wrendal's soldiers. Most of Cal's guards had been unable to reach them, locked in their deadly struggle with the defectors who surrounded them, but a few had raced forward to engage the Balenans, their focus on Elnora and their expressions determined. It was clear to Jo that Cal had ordered his men to defend Elnora at whatever cost.

Jonan's eyes flicked quickly back to his adversary. The two of them began to circle each other, and Jonan was able to take in the scene more clearly. Yaeger's men now had Cal's small force mostly surrounded in a wide horseshoe shape, their lines several men deep as they pushed the defenders further into the center of the clearing. The result was that Jonan's fight with Yaeger was being pushed closer and closer to the group of struggling Balenans.

Cal was clearly trying to fight his way to Elnora, but he was being constantly beset by Yaeger's men, who threw themselves at him with unwavering focus, despite the way Cal's supernaturally powerful sword cut their fellows down before him. For a moment Jonan was unable to locate Lord Wrendal, but he realized with a flash of scorn that the nobleman had drawn back out of harm's way and stood at the open end of the horseshoe, surrounded by half a dozen soldiers. His attention was divided between the renewed attempt to subdue his daughter, and the struggle between Jonan and Yaeger. His expression was still furious, but Jo could also detect a characteristic gleam of shrewd calculation.

Yaeger saw Jonan's eyes on the Balenans and glanced over at them himself. "I might take out the Balenan girl personally as well," he mused. "She seems important, and much more capable than she looks—perhaps her power will be stronger than I had at first supposed."

Jonan gave a cry of rage, throwing himself at the former guard with renewed energy. Yaeger parried his thrust easily, and for a moment their blades rang together in a swift exchange of attacks, each quickly disengaged. Yaeger fought with a deadly strength to match Jo's own unnatural power. But Jo's whole being was aflame with his determination to die before he allowed his opponent to touch any one of the three targets he had named, and when their blades once again locked together, he leaned into the struggle, willing his sword to push past Yaeger's.

The rock around his neck swung forward, clinking against metal, although whether Jo's blade or Yaeger's he couldn't tell. There was a small explosion, less potent than the one in the castle, but enough to throw both combatants backward off their feet, their swords spinning out of their hands. Yaeger's sword had fallen close to him, but Jo's was well out of reach, so he rushed unarmed at his opponent, trying to reach him before he could retrieve his blade.

Yaeger was forced to abandon his scramble for his sword to meet Jo's onslaught, and the two of them collided with enough force to send anyone else back to the ground. But neither man even stumbled, instead grappling with grim determination. Yaeger rained down blow after blow on his smaller, younger opponent, but Jo barely felt them. His energy was unabated, but so was Yaeger's, and although Jonan landed several blows of his own, it wasn't enough to end the fight. The surrounding ring of beleaguered Kyonans continued to close in on them, and as he struggled Jo was aware of how many of his countrymen were falling, only increasing the advantage of Yaeger's men, with their superior numbers. Through the melee, he heard a shout that he was sure came from Cal, and all at once he knew he had to act quickly if they were to avoid annihilation.

He was starting to feel the pain of the repeated blows of Yaeger's enormous fists, but he felt as strong as ever, and he was inclined to think that he could overpower the other man eventually. But it wouldn't happen quickly, and there wasn't time. Changing tactic, he lunged forward suddenly, closing his hand on the rock around Yaeger's neck before his opponent realized his intention. With a mighty tug, Jonan ripped the rock from its leather thong. He had wondered if it would burn his hand like

Alben's rock had done to Liam in Jo's most recent vision, but instead it felt painfully cold, as though he was gripping ice.

He had only a moment to register this, however, as the moment the rock was ripped away from Yaeger, an invisible force rebounded out from the point of contact, throwing Jonan flying. He landed on his back, feet away from his adversary, and despite his best efforts, he was unable to hold onto his prize. As his hand hit the ground, his fist was thrown open and the rock burst out, tumbling and cartwheeling over itself until it came to rest on the grass of the clearing.

CHAPTER THIRTY-SIX

Jonan scrambled up, throwing himself after the rock, aware from his peripheral vision that Yaeger was doing the same. But before either one could take more than a few steps, their view of the talisman was obstructed by a moving mass of bodies. The ring was closing ever tighter, and their own struggle had finally merged with that of the Balenans. Jonan drew up short, his eyes searching the grass frantically, looking for the rock beneath the trample of many feet.

But even as he searched, he was jostled from the side by a thickset Balenan. Turning, he prepared to defend himself, before remembering that he was unarmed. The man wasn't looking at him, locked in a struggle with one of Cal's guards who had rushed to Elnora's aid. Jonan took advantage of his distraction to knock him senseless with a single, powerful blow to the head. The man's Kyonan opponent didn't pause to thank Jo, who was bending down quickly to relieve the unconscious man of his sword, instead pushing forward to take on another Balenan. Following the man's trajectory, Jonan saw that Elnora had been seized not by a Balenan but by a Kyonan—clearly one of

Yaeger's men who had broken through the inner ring of Cal's fighters.

The man was making no attempt to kill Elnora, but he had her in an iron grip as he dragged her away from the fight. Jo could only suppose that Yaeger had ordered his men to keep her alive, in light of his expressed intention to kill her by his own hand once Cal had arrived.

Jo heard a shout and recognized Cal's voice. The young king had evidently seen Elnora's predicament, and was attempting to reach her through the mass of people separating them. But he had only taken a step in her direction when he was mobbed, half a dozen of Yaeger's men throwing themselves on him in their attempt to keep him from moving across the clearing. Jo's head was whipping back and forth, unsure who more desperately needed his assistance, when another familiar voice cut across the chaos.

"Elnora!"

He turned frantically at the sound of Scarlett's call. She was not far from Elnora, and she seemed to have reclaimed her dagger. He saw her toss it with unerring aim, and Elnora caught it, unable to restrain a wince as the blade sliced into her hand. But it didn't slow her down—twisting her hand around, she plunged the dagger into the leg of the man holding her. Jonan, acutely aware that Scarlett was now unarmed, didn't stay to watch any longer. Instead he sprinted to Scarlett's side, arriving in time to dispatch a Balenan who was attempting to capitalize on her sudden vulnerability.

"Jo!" she cried, turning to him breathlessly. "What happened? I saw you fighting Yaeger."

"He's still here somewhere," said Jo bitterly, bending down to take the sword from the man he had just taken out. "I couldn't bring him down. But I did get that rock off him."

"Where is it?" she asked frantically, taking the sword Jo was offering her without even looking at it. "Do you have it?"

He shook his head. "I lost it. It's somewhere on the ground."

She looked wildly around, as if she might spot it between the crush of people.

"I don't think he'll be able to access its power now, at least," Jonan said, but Scarlett didn't answer straight away, her expression growing grim as she looked past him.

"I don't think that's going to be enough," she said.

Jo followed her gaze, and his heart sank as he saw the truth of her words. Yaeger's men were closing in rapidly, the small ring of defenders wavering under the superior numbers. The horseshoe had become a full circle, and only Lord Wrendal and his companions were now outside it. All around Cal's guards fought fiercely, acquitting themselves well against their adversaries, even though it was clear they couldn't hold out much longer. Still, something didn't add up. Yaeger's men certainly had the advantage of numbers, but there didn't seem to be enough of them, not compared to the scene Jonan had first witnessed in the clearing.

Even as Jonan tried to figure out what to make of it, a cry caught his ears. Looking across the increasingly small battleground, he saw that Elnora was once again in trouble. He started forward, but before he could do anything useful, a figure charged past him, falling on her attacker with such ferocity that it was over in a moment. Cal had finally broken free from Yaeger's men. In spite of the battle raging around them, he allowed himself the briefest moment to pull Elnora close, although Jo couldn't hear what he was saying. The next second he had spun around again, placing her behind him as he scanned their immediate vicinity for further threats.

"Cal!" Jo cried, and the king's eyes snapped to him. There wasn't much space between them anymore, and Jonan reached his friends in moments, Scarlett in his wake. "I'm sorry Cal," Jo said as soon as he was close enough to be heard. "I wish I could've warned you that there were so many."

"I knew," said Cal grimly, and Jonan's eyes flew to his, surprised.

"You did? How?"

Cal just looked at him meaningfully, and suddenly Jo realized. The Esvalere. "Why didn't you bring more men?" Jo asked, his tone a little exasperated.

"This was as many as I could spare, at least at such short notice," said Cal curtly. "I left Laramie in charge to muster the rest and defend the castle."

"Defend the—" Jo started, but Cal cut him off.

"This is only half of Yaeger's men. There were two parts to his plan."

Of course. That's where the rest of them were. He should have known Yaeger wouldn't have made his move against Calinnae without a well laid strategy.

"So what do we do now?" Jo asked, looking around again. Now that Cal and Elnora were in one place, Cal's guards were no longer divided in their focus, and the four friends found themselves temporarily out of the battle, surrounded by a protective ring. But the fight raged on, and the outlook was grim.

"Stop!"

Yaeger's clear commanding voice carried over the tumult, and his men instantly drew back, giving the king's beleaguered force a moment of respite. Leander appeared out of the throng and struggled his way to Cal's side, his eyes on the former guard. Jo also glared at Yaeger, noting with a tiny spurt of relief that he didn't seem to have found the rock. But he knew Yaeger was still dangerous—and his fury at the loss of his treasure would make him more so.

"I thought I'd give you the chance to surrender, *Your Majesty*," said Yaeger viciously, striding toward Cal.

"Not likely," spat Cal.

"Not even to save your little peasant friends?" taunted Yaeger, gesturing at Elnora, whom Cal still shielded with his body, and Jo, who was glaring murderously back at Yaeger, Scarlett at his side.

But Cal just snorted. "As though I didn't know you would kill us all anyway if I gave you the chance."

Yaeger grinned unpleasantly. "You're smarter than you look," he sneered. "It's a shame—I would have liked to see you beg before I kill you. But don't worry, you have a little longer. I'll make sure you're last."

Yaeger's eyes lingered meaningfully on Elnora as he spoke, but Jo could see that Cal was well in command of himself and was not going to be goaded into doing anything reckless.

"This is between us, Yaeger," said the young king calmly. "Why don't we dispense with the dramatics and settle this man to man?"

Yaeger's eyes lit up, and for a moment Jo was sure he would agree. But then the guard's hand leaped halfway to his chest before he could stop himself, and Jo could tell that he had remembered the loss of the rock. Yaeger's eyes fell on him, and Jo couldn't help a little smirk. Yaeger's gaze hardened furiously as he turned back to Cal.

"How can I settle anything man to man with a foolish boy?" he said. "Besides, you'll have to trust my age and experience that it's much better to be thorough. By now I imagine the rest of my force has taken your poorly defended castle, and there will be time enough to enjoy killing you once I've wiped out those of your forester allies who you brought with you."

Yaeger raised his hand, ready to order his men forward again, and Jo braced himself. He glanced sideways at Cal, and was surprised to see that although his friend had raised his sword, he had closed his eyes and had a small smile on his face.

Even as he noted the strange reaction, Jonan felt a powerful tingling where the stone sat against his chest, and heard a distant rushing noise.

"You may find that not all of my allies are so easy to overcome," said Cal conversationally.

The words had barely left his mouth when a mighty wind swept through the clearing, forcing everyone present to throw their arms up over their faces. For a moment the growing morning light was overtaken by a monstrous shadow as everyone looked involuntarily up at the darkened sky.

The impressive reptilian form of Elddreki hovered for a moment in the open space above the clearing, every eye fixed on him as shocked cries rang out from both sides. Then he came to rest on top of an enormous tree, his mighty talons wrapped around a branch as the sunlight glinted off the purple, green and blue of his armored scales.

A hushed silence fell over the clearing as all activity stopped. Jonan could feel his rock pulsing frantically at the proximity of such a raw source of dragon magic. He supposed that in a similar way Cal's sword had given him warning of Elddreki's approach.

Most of the challengers were clearly terrified, but Yaeger looked more angry than afraid. The Balenans seemed completely immobilized by their shock, and even Scarlett clutched convulsively at Jonan's arm. He squeezed her hand reassuringly, perfectly understanding her awe. He had believed in dragons before he first saw one, but no amount of description could prepare you for the reality of seeing one in the flesh.

Jonan couldn't help glancing over at Lord Wrendal, and was satisfied to see the nobleman frozen, rigid with astonishment and fear. It seemed that for once he would have to acknowledge that he was not the most powerful presence in the situation.

For a moment the scene remained still, Elddreki regarding

the humans below him with an expression of bright interest, so unlike the disconnected demeanor of the dragon-ruler Qadir in Alben's vision. His eyes found Cal, and he gave a stately nod of recognition. His gaze took in Elnora and Jo as well before traveling over the rest of the assembled combatants. He looked faintly surprised at the unmoving posture of the fighters, all of whom were staring up at him with open mouths.

Without any change in expression, he opened his own mighty mouth wide, displaying an alarmingly large row of viciously sharp teeth, and let out a ferocious roar. Cal's fighters drew closer together in their circle around their king, their expressions nervous, but Yaeger's men turned tail and fled into the trees, many of them throwing down their weapons in their haste. Yaeger shouted his rage at them, and a few of the hardier ones hesitated.

Seeing this, Elddreki opened his mouth again experimentally, letting out a tiny spurt of fire, for good measure. The last holdouts abandoned their master, following their fellows into the forest. At a nod from Cal, his remaining guards gave chase, shouting battle cries as they ran. Ally or not, Jo had the impression that Cal's forces were only too glad to remove themselves from Elddreki's vicinity as well.

Cal strode forward until he was right in front of Elddreki, who looked down at him serenely.

"Thank you, my friend," he said earnestly.

"You are welcome, young king," said Elddreki pleasantly. "I didn't do a great deal."

Cal looked around the mostly deserted clearing. "It was enough." He returned his gaze to the dragon, adding with a touch of humor, "I didn't actually know that dragons roared."

"Well, they didn't quite seem to have gotten the message," explained Elddreki conversationally. "I thought they needed a little prompt." He glanced at Jonan, his catlike eyes resting on the rock around Jo's neck. "But there was another reason you called me. One I would like to know more of."

"Yes," said Cal quickly. "But if it isn't asking too much, there's something else I could use your help with." Elddreki looked at him inquiringly, and Cal hurried on. "The castle is under attack as we speak. I think the forces I left to defend it will be enough, but I can't be sure. And I would avoid unnecessary bloodshed if I could."

"I am willing to assist you," said Elddreki. "But are you sure you wish me to leave? I think your task here is not finished." His gaze lingered on Yaeger, who had joined the Balenans in the absence of his own men. The whole group was hanging back just behind the tree line, Yaeger presumably because he was not ready to relinquish his attempt to kill Cal, and the Balenans because they had nowhere else to go. Or so Jo assumed.

"I'm sure," said Cal, in answer to Elddreki's question. "We can handle them."

The dragon gave him a long look before he responded. "Yes," he said at last. "Perhaps this is your fight." His eyes slid across to include Jonan. "But be careful," he warned. "I sense a dark power here. I need time to fully understand it, but it is strong."

"I understand," said Cal quickly.

Jo, still clutching Scarlett's hand, was watching Lord Wrendal, and he felt vaguely uneasy at the realization that the nobleman was following the conversation closely. He seemed to have recovered from his stupefaction much more quickly than his men.

Jonan didn't realize that Elddreki had finished speaking with Cal until he felt the rush of wind that heralded the dragon's departure.

"Yaeger," Cal called once the clearing was still again. "You deserve to be killed as a criminal, but I am still willing to offer you a fight, man to man."

"Cal," said Elnora warningly. She put a restraining hand on his arm, but he removed it gently.

"You heard Elddreki, Elnora," he said. "This is my fight, and I intend to finish this." He raised his voice again. "What do you say?"

Jonan's attention was still on Lord Wrendal, who had been watching Scarlett with narrowed eyes, so he didn't immediately see why Yaeger hadn't answered the challenge. The first he knew of what was happening was when Scarlett pulled her grip suddenly from his, darting forward.

He gave an involuntary cry of alarm as he saw that Yaeger was also scrambling forward, racing Scarlett for her target. Even as he started after her, Jo saw it, too. Lying on the grass, looking deceptively innocuous. Yaeger's rock, once again revealed by the exodus of fleeing fighters.

Scarlett reached it first, her fist closing over it moments before Yaeger caught up to her. His hand, robbed of the prize for which it had been reaching, grabbed at her throat instead. For a moment they grappled on the forest floor, Jonan leaping forward with a furious shout to rush to Scarlett's aid. But someone beat him to it. He skidded to a halt at the flash of a blade, for a moment unable to make sense of the sight of Lord Wrendal's sword held to Yaeger's throat.

Scarlett leaned back, panting, the rock still clutched in one hand. Her eyes were fixed on her father, her expression showing shock, and something else harder to read, at the sight of him coming to her rescue.

But the nobleman wasn't looking at his daughter, and his words weren't addressed to her.

"What is it?" he demanded. "What power does it have?" For a moment Yaeger was silent, his expression resentful, held in his ignominious position on the ground by the sword still to his throat. "Well?" Lord Wrendal demanded, pressing his blade down more firmly, causing a trickle of blood to run down Yaeger's neck. "What is it?"

"I don't know what it is," spat Yaeger. "But it has magic."

"What kind of magic?" asked the Balenan smoothly. Gone was the derision with which he had greeted Yaeger's previous mention of anything magical. Jonan could only suppose that the appearance of a living, breathing dragon had changed his perspective.

"It makes its bearer powerful, unnaturally strong," said Yaeger, his voice sullen. "But only for a cost. It requires sacrifice."

"Sacrifice?" Lord Wrendal asked, his voice tinged with an eagerness that made Jonan uneasy.

"You pay for your strength with someone else's life," said Yaeger. "The more you take, the stronger you become."

Jonan had been listening, spellbound, to this warped version of his own discovery about Alben's rock. So he was a moment late in recognizing the speculative gleam in Lord Wrendal's eyes as he turned to his daughter, still frozen in place on the ground.

"Give it to me, Scarlett," he said, his voice quiet.

She shook her head, beginning to scramble backward away from him. But he was quicker, his sword flashing from Yaeger's throat to hers in a heartbeat.

"Give it to me," he repeated calmly.

"I won't." Her face was pale, but her voice was resolute, even as her father pressed the blade down harder.

Jonan started forward with a furious growl, but he stopped short as the nobleman reached out, pulling Scarlett to her feet in a fluid motion, his blade never leaving her throat.

"Stay where you are," said Lord Wrendal, his voice at its silkiest. "Do you think I won't kill her? Do you care to bet on it?"

Jonan hesitated, terror and rage chasing each other around his head. He had no doubt that this monster was capable of killing his own daughter for the power the rock promised him.

Out of the corner of his eye he saw Yaeger, freed from Lord Wrendal's sword, pulling out his own blade, his eyes also on Scarlett.

Before Jo's panic could rise further, however, a flash of movement to his side solidified into Cal, running forward to engage Yaeger at last. The guard was forced to relinquish pursuit of the rock for the moment, turning with a growl to meet the young king. Jo was vaguely aware of the clash of their swords, but he had no attention to spare for his friend's fight, his whole focus locked on Scarlett's perilous predicament.

"Do you really want to die for this, Scarlett?" Lord Wrendal was saying. "What would be the point? If I kill you, I'll take it just the same. Or do you hope to claim it for yourself? Yesterday I would have said it was no use to you, as you surely wouldn't have what it takes to make use of it. But now I'm not so sure. I had a very surprising report about you today. It seems you have been hiding some things from me."

Scarlett didn't answer. Her face was still pale, and Jonan saw a tremor pass through her. He was shaking himself, furious at his own impotence. A shout from where Cal was still fighting Yaeger tugged at his attention, but he kept his eyes on the Balenan pair, terrified that any second Lord Wrendal might decide to be done with it all.

"Where did you learn to fight, Scarlett?" Lord Wrendal said, his voice so soft Jo could barely hear him. Scarlett swallowed hard, and the blade was so firm against her throat that the motion caused it to prick the skin. Jo clenched his hand on the hilt of his sword as he saw a trickle of red make its way down her neck.

"I would almost be proud of you," that hated voice continued, "if I didn't so strongly suspect that the application of your skills has been as offensive as the direction of your affections." The nobleman's gaze flicked momentarily to Jonan, his sneer becoming more pronounced. "Tell me you haven't been helping these animals, Scarlett," he said, his words all the more terrifying for the icy calm of his voice. "Tell me you haven't been part of that cursed resistance."

"Part of it?" choked Scarlett. "I started it!" Jo could feel her relief as her facade, straining under the weight of years, finally cracked. But the relief was edged with desperation, and it filled him with fear.

"Scarlett!" he cried, his voice charged with warning, even though he knew the damage was already done.

She ignored him, her eyes bright and her voice breathless as she tumbled on. "I've been the greatest enemy of your trade for years. You've always thought I was foolish and useless, but it's you who has been played for a fool."

Jonan took an involuntary step forward, unable to bear the tension of inactivity. But Lord Wrendal twisted Scarlett's arm cruelly behind her back, and her little cry of pain drew Jo up short, as the nobleman had clearly known it would.

"You will die for your defiance," Lord Wrendal said to his daughter, his voice still quiet, but for once not quite steady in its suppressed rage. "And when I return to Nohl, I will crush your pathetic resistance."

Jo's gaze was riveted on the sword against Scarlett's throat, and he saw the infinitesimal tightening of Lord Wrendal's hand on the hilt. All at once it was terrifyingly clear that the nobleman truly was going to kill his daughter. Jo threw himself forward with a shout.

His intervention bought Scarlett a few seconds more, as Lord Wrendal paused, drawing his blade back the tiniest amount as he gave a curt nod. Several of the Balenan soldiers, whom Jonan had almost forgotten about, raced forward to restrain him. One of them wrested the sword from his grip, throwing it aside.

He struggled against them, his thoughts swirling in panic as

Lord Wrendal's blade moved lazily from Scarlett's throat to just above her heart. The nobleman's eyes traveled to Jonan's face, his expression malicious. Jonan understood perfectly. The strike might be moments away, but as always Lord Wrendal was not acting in the heat of passion. He could afford the extra seconds to make sure Jonan was watching.

Still wrestling against the soldiers, Jo swept his horrified gaze down Scarlett's person, and his heart leaped. Scarlett was armed after all. Her once-magnificent dress was so torn that he could see the flash of her dagger, where she had sheathed it in its hiding place on her leg.

For the briefest of moments he thought everything would be fine. He knew she was capable of disabling the man next to her, and he wondered if she had been drawing the confrontation out for some purpose he couldn't discern. But as his eyes passed to her face and their gazes locked, his brief optimism was violently shattered by the fear he saw there. It was the same uncharacteristic panic he had first seen the night of the riot in the slave camp—the fear that only her father could bring out. He realized all at once, with absolute certainty, that as deadly as Scarlett could be, she was incapable of raising her blade against the man who now held her in his power.

And if he killed her, he would get the rock, which would apparently give him power from sacrificing other people's lives. His willingness to kill his own daughter to get it showed that Lord Wrendal was the last person who should ever be allowed to get hold of it. Jo could easily imagine the Overseer slaughtering every Kyonan in Nohl in his quest for the unnatural power. Elddreki had been right when he called it a dark power, dark and strong.

All of this passed through Jo's head in seconds, the thoughts following one another in successive blasts. His eyes were still locked with Scarlett's, and Lord Wrendal's arm was still tensed, ready to strike.

Casting around for help, he saw Cal still dueling Yaeger, the former guard a much more experienced swordsman, even without the unnatural strength of the rock. Elnora's focus was wholly centered on Cal's battle.

So he was alone. But not alone. Strong though the dark power might be, it wasn't going to claim Scarlett's life. Because the power coursing into Jonan from the rock hanging around his neck was at least as strong. The talisman had become a familiar presence, linking him to Alben, whom he had long felt to be a friend rather than a stranger from the past.

Lord Wrendal had been watching Jonan's panicked resistance with amusement, but Jo tuned him out. He stopped struggling, closing his eyes for the briefest of moments, visualizing himself drawing strength from the rock, calling on the powerful imprint left by Alben's mother, by Alben, even by Jonan himself. Those others had been willing to die for the people they loved, and without a shadow of hesitation Jonan was ready to do no less for Scarlett.

The rush of power came easily this time, its secret unlocked at last. With an involuntary roar, he thrust his arms outward, throwing off the several Balenan soldiers who had been holding him with such force that they flew through the air, limbs flailing. Jo didn't pause to look at them, seizing his sword from the ground and rushing on Lord Wrendal with grim ferocity. He had the briefest moment to register the shock in the Overseer's eyes before his own blade made contact. Lord Wrendal's sword, yanked around by its owner in an attempted defense, sliced shallowly along Scarlett's chest. But it was too late to intercept Jonan's sword, which passed unchecked straight into his adversary's heart.

CHAPTER THIRTY-SEVEN

Jo didn't even stay to watch his enemy's body hit the ground. He threw his sword aside, reaching steadying hands toward Scarlett's swaying form.

"Are you all right?" he asked frantically, assessing her wound with anxious eyes. The fabric was ripped jaggedly, the red of Scarlett's blood lost in the crimson of her gown, but the gash didn't look deep.

She didn't answer immediately. She seemed unable to tear her eyes away from the sight of her father's body, sprawled unceremoniously on the ground.

"Scarlett?" Jo asked in concern, and she pulled her gaze up to him with an effort.

"I'm fine," she gasped, feeling at the cut on her chest with a wince.

Jo felt like he should say more, but he wasn't sure where to start, and his attention was pulled away by the continued clash of metal that accompanied Cal and Yaeger's fight. He had almost forgotten that his friend was still in danger.

But he could see that, skilled as he was, Yaeger was no match for the young king who was wielding the sword that had lain for centuries in the heart of the Dragon Realm, imbibing its magic. The older man was holding out with an effort, but it was clearly almost over. It didn't hurt that Cal had obviously been training in swordplay over the months of Jo's absence.

A mere minute after Jo turned his attention to the pair, he saw Yaeger waver, and all at once he knew the fight was done. Cal didn't waste the opening. With a final, powerful lunge he drove his point home. Yaeger dropped as heavily—and as irrevocably—as Lord Wrendal had done minutes before, and the clearing was suddenly still.

Turning away from his adversary, Cal met Jo's eyes. His gaze passed to Lord Wrendal's prostrate form, and he gave a small nod, acknowledging the end of the crisis. The Balenan soldiers from whom Jo had broken free were beginning to stir, but even as Jo wondered what to do with them, he heard Leander's voice and turned to see him emerging from the trees. A number of other members of Cal's guard followed, a couple of prisoners dragged between them.

"Your Majesty! Where is the dragon?" Leander's eyes passed over the slain bodies of Yaeger and Lord Wrendal in alarm. Jo was sure that if he had known Cal was going to send Elddreki away, Leander would never have left his king's side.

"I asked him to assist at the castle," said Cal. He gestured around the clearing. "As you see, our challengers have been dealt with." His gaze lingered on the Balenan soldiers, and his tone became ironic. "Although some of our foreign guests are still with us."

Leander instantly took charge of the situation. At a few curt orders, his men surrounded the Balenans and began to bind their hands. Cal turned away with evident relief and was instantly joined by Elnora. She clutched his arm for a moment, before her hand fluttered to his chest, then his face, then back to his arm, as if trying to reassure herself that he really was alive.

Although his eyes were on his friends, Jo sensed Scarlett's presence as she approached behind him, coming to stand at his side. He took her hand, and they made their way over to the others.

Cal and Jo clasped arms in the familiar greeting, the gesture firm with wordless relief, but none of the four of them asked if the others were all right. The question seemed superfluous.

"What happened to Yaeger's—" started Cal, but he cut himself off as his eyes found the answer to his question. Scarlett still clutched the second mountain rock in her hand.

"We need to get back to the castle," said Cal instead, his voice grim, and Jo nodded. Hopefully his friend still had a throne to return to. Jo wondered uneasily how many of Yaeger's traitors had still been hidden in the guard, in addition to those he had sent to Kynton from the forest.

Leaving Leander to follow with the prisoners, the four of them left the clearing without further delay. For quite a while they wended their way through the trees in silence, but when Elnora engaged Scarlett in conversation, Jo took the opportunity to step forward and address Cal.

"Do you think Laramie will have held them off until Elddreki got there?"

"I hope so," said Cal. "They were relying on some pretty substantial inside help, and if Laramie followed my orders quickly enough, he should have disabled most of the conspirators." He grimaced. "The difficult part was issuing those orders without revealing the source of my information."

"So you saw his plan?" Jo asked quickly. He glanced back at the girls and saw that they were several steps behind, engrossed in their own quiet conversation. "In the Esvalere?"

Cal had followed the direction of his gaze, and for a moment he didn't answer, his eyes lingering on Elnora. Given his own recent experiences, Jo had no difficulty interpreting the myriad of emotions in the glance. But since he intended not to let Scarlett out of his sight for the next decade or so, and he couldn't talk about the Esvalere in front of her, he didn't want to waste the opportunity to get answers.

"Cal?"

"What?" Cal asked, starting slightly. "Sorry. Yes, I saw his plan. I also saw that Elnora was alive, and where she was." He frowned. "I tried to find out about Scarlett, too, but I couldn't see her." He gave Jo an apologetic look. "It's not the first time I've found that it responds to what's closest to my heart, and I guess I couldn't fool it into thinking that Scarlett's whereabouts were quite as critically important to me as Elnora's. But I'm glad she's all right." He smiled wearily. "And apparently I care about your fate a sufficient amount, because my train of inquiry was interrupted by the image of you being bound and dragged out of Kynton. I decided it was time to stop digging for answers and start moving." He gave Jo a long-suffering look. "So much for not getting caught."

Jo grimaced, but didn't respond.

"I reached out to Elddreki before I finished with the Esvalere, but there wasn't time to see if he received it, and I wasn't sure whether he'd come. When I reemerged, Laramie told me what you had reported to him. It simplified things once I knew Lord Wrendal was headed for Yaeger and we didn't need to mount a separate search." Cal rubbed a hand across his eyes as he walked, and Jo remembered that his friend had not slept at all the night before. "At least neither of them can do any more damage now."

"Yes," Jo agreed, but his eyes strayed involuntarily back to Scarlett. He wished it was so simple, but he knew the damage her father had done in her life would not be so quickly forgotten. His heart ached at the memory of the look in her eyes—shock and hope and a hundred other inexpressible emotions—when Lord Wrendal had seemed to rescue her from Yaeger.

They had just left the trees, and were making their way across the short stretch of grassland between the forest and the city, when a whooshing sound made them all look up. Elddreki's arrival was not accompanied by the gale force wind that usually announced that a dragon was approaching at the impossible lightning speed of their kind, so Jo assumed he had only come a short distance to meet them.

The dragon came to land on the grass in front of the group, his eyes on Cal.

"Greetings, King Calinnae," he said placidly.

"Greetings," Cal responded quickly. "Have you come from the castle?"

Elddreki inclined his head. "I have. Your forces were in some difficulty, but a very little persuasion was required to convince the attackers to abandon their attempt."

Jo snorted. He could imagine the nature of that "persuasion".

"But what is this?" Elddreki continued, his eyes on Scarlett. "I thought you had overcome your foes."

"We have," said Jo with a scowl, stepping defensively in front of Scarlett. "She's with us."

"The power I'm speaking of comes not from her but from the item she carries," said Elddreki with his usual calm.

"Oh," said Jo lamely. He had momentarily forgotten about the mountain rock.

"It is a most interesting signature," mused the dragon. His gaze transferred to Jonan. "Both of them."

"They come from the mountains," said Jo quickly. "I think—I think from the Dragon Realm."

Elddreki inclined his head again. "That is right," he said. "I never saw them myself, but I remember talk of the group of mountain folk who built their ill-advised town on the edge of our realm. I remember too that when they left, some kind of powerful magic went with them."

"It was these rocks, I suppose," said Jonan. "Someone called Alben took them with him. They were part of the rock-slide that crushed his mother, and their power seems to be linked with her sacrifice. With sacrifice in general, from what I can tell." He touched the rock at his chest. "This one gives power when you sacrifice your own interests for the sake of others. That one," he pointed to the rock in Scarlett's hand, "apparently gives power when you sacrifice someone else's life."

"Indeed?" To Jonan's surprise—and annoyance—Elddreki looked faintly amused. "What a crude summary. I wonder how much basis it has in truth?"

Aggrieved, Jo opened his mouth to argue, but Cal caught his eye and shook his head, frowning slightly. Jo subsided, still scowling.

"May I?" asked Elddreki, bending his neck so that his head snaked down toward Jo. His tone was polite, but it was somehow not a request. After a moment of hesitation, Jo slipped the chain off his neck and held it out, the rock dangling freely from it. There was a moment's expectant silence before Scarlett realized that the dragon was now looking at her, obviously waiting for a response.

Her color rose rapidly as, mumbling incoherently, she hastened to hold out the rock in her hand. It looked dull and unremarkable as it sat just next to where Jo's rock was still swinging. Jo had expected Elddreki to take the rocks, but instead he brought his head very close to them, closing his eyes and breathing in deeply, as though he could inhale their essence.

The scene was silent for a couple of long minutes as Elddreki maintained his position. Jo could see Scarlett's hand tremble slightly under that enormous reptilian head. At last the dragon opened his eyes, exhaling mightily as he pulled his head back to its usual height.

"Most interesting," he said thoughtfully. "Sacrifice is indeed central to the enchantment."

"That's what I said," muttered Jo, but no one paid him any heed.

"The latent magic in the Dragon Realm is powerful," said Elddreki to the group at large. "Certainly these rocks should not have been removed from their place of origin. But the consequences were particularly potent in this instance, because of the magic that was activated by the sacrificial act of this Alben's mother."

"But Alben's rock doesn't seem to be evil," said Jonan. "Why were the consequences so bad?"

Elddreki looked at him in surprise. "Neither rock is evil," he said. "At least, not in itself. But it is true that the magic in the rock Alben gave to Liam has become warped beyond reclaim."

"So why does it give power to the wearer if they kill someone?" Jo asked, and the dragon wrinkled his snout.

"What an interpretation. But I suppose I can see how it came to be understood that way. Its power is not attached to death, but to sacrifice, the same as its partner. When the rocks came together again, only for the bearer of one to betray the bearer of the other for his own gain, it splintered them apart, changing the nature of the rock this fair maiden now holds."

Scarlett blinked at the description of herself as a fair maiden, but Jo wasn't about to be sidetracked now he was finally getting to the bottom of the rocks.

"I suppose sacrificing someone else's interests for your own is the opposite of what Alben's mother did."

"Precisely," agreed Elddreki. "And since that time, the magic of the rock is in part released every time its bearer does the same. Killing another person is not a necessary part of the process, but it is certainly a potent example of the kind of action that would draw on the darkness inside this talisman." He looked again at Jo's rock. "That one, as you have surmised, works in the opposite way. You might say that a barrier was created between them at the moment of betrayal. One of the bearers turned on his own, and I suppose you could say it activated a curse, fueled by the magic in the rocks."

Scarlett had started at the word "curse", and her voice was eager as she addressed the dragon, her awe seeming to be momentarily forgotten. "Could that have created a larger barrier? Did the curse extend beyond the two people involved?"

"Of course," said Elddreki simply. "As I said, the consequences were particularly potent. Liam's action was only one instance of a plague that was already defiling the land. The involvement of Kyonans in selling their countrymen was already dark enough—the addition of a twisted magic was disastrous. A division was created between Kyona's people, those in exile, and those who betrayed them. It is a gulf that cannot be crossed."

"And since then no Kyonan sold into slavery, or their descendants—has ever been able to cross back over the sea to come home," finished Jonan. Elddreki nodded, apparently pleased to have made his point so clear.

"So if we destroy the rock, will it break the curse?" Scarlett asked, her voice more eager than ever. Elddreki looked at her curiously.

"Is that what you want, young Balenan?" he asked.

"Of course!" said Scarlett. "More than anything."

"Well, I think you should try it, and find out," said Elddreki, unruffled.

Scarlett turned to Jo, holding the rock toward him with a shaking hand. "You should do it, Jo."

He took it without a word, his hands tingling unpleasantly at the reunion of the two halves of this puzzle. How did one destroy a powerful magic rock? His eyes traveled around the group, coming to rest on the weapon at the king's side.

"Cal," he said quietly. "Can I borrow your sword for a minute?"

Cal handed it over silently, his whole body stiff with the tension that held them all in thrall. Jo put the two rocks down on the grass and gripped the sword with both hands. He could feel its magic now, his exposure to the rocks having awoken an extra sense that he had not previously been able to exercise. The power of the sword had a different substance, but he could recognize a kinship between it and his rock, reflective of their shared source.

He raised the sword above his head, pausing for a moment to think of Cody and Bonnie and Stan, and all the others still waiting and hoping for their freedom, and of Raldo, who had sacrificed his life to give it to them. Then he brought the sword down in an unerring arc, bracing himself instinctively as the tip of the blade made contact with Yaeger's rock.

The instinct wasn't wrong. Illogically, the sword shattered the rock into dust, and the shock wave that burst outward was a hundred times more intense than the one set off by Yaeger's blade in the castle. Jonan was thrown from his feet, dimly aware that the invisible boom wasn't bursting in all directions, but was undeniably traveling south, toward the distant coast.

Jo's vision spun for a moment, but when the world righted itself, he saw that Cal, Elnora, and Scarlett were all on the ground as well. Elddreki, of course, remained calmly in precisely the position he had been in before.

"That seemed to work," he said mildly. "Interesting."

Jo couldn't help but laugh as he struggled to his feet, the others following suit. He went to return Cal's sword, but hesitated, looking toward Elddreki.

"Should I destroy the other rock, too?" he asked, a bit regretfully. "Or return it to the Dragon Realm?"

"I don't think so," said Elddreki cheerfully. "On its own, it won't do any harm. Its magic hasn't been twisted. And besides," he gave Jo an appraising look, "its signature has wrapped around you quite intimately." He gave a decisive nod. "I think you can keep it, young man."

That was good enough for Jonan. Giving Cal back his sword, he scooped the rock back up from the ground and passed the chain around his neck once again. It felt complete somehow, being reunited with it.

"I don't understand how I was able to feel its magic," he said. "Even before I had it. Even before I knew about it. In fact," he frowned, "I felt the magic, or some hint of it, on the ship, before I was even in the same country as the rock. When I touched Alben's carving."

Elddreki nodded serenely, as if the explanation was obvious. "Clearly a powerful magic lingered around Alben due to his possession of this item. Some trace of it remained in his carving. When you touched it, you were able to sense it. I imagine that heightened awareness contributed to the way the magic of the rock responded to you when you sacrificed your own safety for another while standing directly above its resting place."

"But *how* could I sense it?" asked Jonan, still confused. "Would anyone have?"

"Of course not," said Elddreki patiently. "Ask your Balenan friend if she felt anything when she held the other rock."

Jo turned to Scarlett inquiringly, and she shook her head, looking perplexed.

"It can't be because I'm Kyonan, though," said Jo slowly. "Because Cody couldn't feel it."

Elddreki made the strange, slightly alarming noise that Jo had previously discovered to be dragon laughter. "Being Kyonan doesn't give you the ability to sense dragon magic, young man. Dragons do not favor one kingdom over the others. But you in particular had good reason to recognize dragon magic. Perhaps you do not realize the significance of the quest during which you met me. It has been generation upon generation since any human entered the Dragon Realm. Until you three," his gaze swept over Cal and Elnora as well as Jo, "were brought there a few short months ago."

"That's why Cal could use the rock as well," Jonan said, suddenly understanding. He shook his head. "It's almost unbelievable, the chance that took me to Nohl on that ship, and brought all those factors together to reach this outcome."

"Chance?" repeated Elddreki in faint surprise. "I don't think so. These things are mysterious, certainly, and difficult to predict, even for the wisest. But there is not much chance in magic. Chance is merely the name humans give to any purpose that they cannot understand."

Jo pondered this for a moment, but could think of no reply. It didn't matter—his thoughts quickly turned in a more important direction. "So the curse really is broken?" he asked, the excitement of the victory starting to set in. "The Kyonans in Balenol can really come home?"

Elddreki smiled. "It seems you did what you set out to do, young man." His gaze rested again on the talisman around Jo's neck. "I think you can be trusted with the care of that object. But don't use it lightly."

"To tell you the truth," said Jonan, a touch of humor in his voice, "I'm hoping I won't be called on too regularly to sacrifice my life for others."

Elddreki smiled even as he shook his head. "As I told you before, life and death is not the key. Sacrificing your own interests for those of others is much more commonly a matter of mundane, everyday decisions."

Jonan couldn't help but smile as he looked over at Scarlett. A future of having the opportunity to make sacrifices for her in the everyday matters sounded pretty good, all things considered.

"I think I will return to the mountains now," Elddreki said, looking around at them all. "I hope we will meet again, but then, your lifespans are so short...I can't be at all certain that we will."

For a moment, the four humans just blinked, unsure how to respond to this depressing observation. Cal was the first to pull himself together.

"Thank you," he said earnestly. "I'm more grateful than I can say. That's twice you've saved both me and my kingdom. I know it's unlikely that you need my help, but if there's ever any assistance I can offer you, I would consider it an honor."

"Would you?" asked Elddreki with interest. "As a matter of fact, there is one matter in which you might be able to assist me."

"Name it," said Cal readily, despite his obvious surprise.

"Oh no," said Elddreki airily, "I think you'll have your hands full here for a while. You may come and find me once things settle down. Perhaps in twenty of your years."

"Twenty years?" repeated Cal, startled. "I hope it doesn't take that long to get things in order!"

"Well, unlike you humans, I'm not in a hurry," said Elddreki reasonably.

"It's not that I'm in a hurry," laughed Cal. "And I'm ready to do whatever I can. I'm just worried that I might be past the age of adventuring in twenty years."

Elddreki just smiled. "Humans always take things so literally," he said indulgently. "You are not the final keeper of our friendship, Calinnae. If you consider yourself too old, send your son." He looked at Elnora, who was suddenly blushing furiously, and amended, "or your daughter." Cal didn't seem to know how to respond to this, but Elddreki apparently didn't mind. "Until then," he said, smiling in amusement. Then, with a mighty whoosh, he shot into the air and out of sight with such impossible speed that Scarlett gave an involuntary gasp.

Jo couldn't help grinning at her. "So that's a dragon," he said. "And believe it or not, that one is smaller, more approachable, and less cryptic than most of them."

She was spared the necessity of replying by the appearance of Leander, leading his remaining men and their various prisoners out of the forest. Jo had the impression that they'd been nearby for a while, waiting for the dragon to disappear before emerging. Jo couldn't blame them. He wasn't afraid of Elddreki, but even he could feel the release of tension at the dragon's departure. It was finally over.

It was clear as soon as they entered the city that news of dramatic events had spread. But as Elddreki had indicated, they found the castle doors still manned by Cal's own guards. A crowd was beginning to gather behind them, and they passed through into the castle without delay, weary but triumphant.

The wide entrance hall was packed with shocked courtiers and curious servants, and as they entered Jonan's attention was caught by an exaggerated noise of disgust. Locating the source, he recognized the man as the nobleman who had suggested that Elnora had merely run away. The man's eyes were fixed on Elnora now, as she limped along at Cal's side, her dress torn and bloodied, and a sword still held loosely in her hand.

"And *this* is to be our queen?" he muttered audibly.

Cal took a furious step forward, a very ugly look in his eyes, but was pulled up short by the sound of Elnora's voice, razor-sharp in its icy politeness.

"Certainly I am going to be your queen, My Lord," she said. "I don't pretend to be as knowledgeable in royal protocols as you are, but even I know that's how a betrothal to the king usually works."

The nobleman looked taken aback, but quickly recovered himself. "Bold words, Maid Elnora, but—"

"I beg your pardon, sir," interrupted Elnora, her tone frigid, "but the correct title with which to address me is My Lady."

"Indeed?" sneered the man. "I was not aware that you could claim any noble lineage—"

"On the contrary, My Lord," cut in Elnora coldly, "you are perfectly well aware that my betrothal to King Calinnae confers on me the status of a lady." She looked around at the packed space, in which every eye was now turned to her. "But you're right. I imagine everyone in this room knows as well as you do that I was raised on the streets of Alezae. And," she fixed her accuser with an eagle eye, "we can all be extremely glad that I was."

"And why would you imagine that?" The man's expression was sour.

"Because," said Elnora calmly, "had I been raised in a noble household, I would most likely not be able to defend myself. Meaning I would almost certainly have been killed today by attackers consisting of the king's enemies from both Kyona and Balenol, with the likely result that our country would have been plunged into war." Her eyes narrowed to slits as she continued to stare down the nobleman. "An outcome that I am certain no loyal Kyonan could wish for."

There was a long moment of silence as the man glared back at her. Then, just as the tension seemed stretched to breaking point, the nobleman lowered his eyes, affording Elnora a small half-bow.

"No indeed, My Lady," he muttered resentfully. "Certainly none of us wish for war."

In the stunned silence that followed this dramatic encounter, Jonan, watching on in astonishment, heard Cal's voice next to him. His friend sounded dazed.

"Is the master of protocol here somewhere?"

"Yes, Your Majesty, I am here!" A man bustled up.

"What's the shortest possible time in which you can plan a royal wedding?" Cal demanded.

"Uh…" The man blinked, surprised. "Well, Your Majesty, I suppose, considering the necessary—"

"No, don't answer that," Cal cut him off, his eyes still fixed on Elnora in awe. "Take whatever period you were going to say, halve it, and make it happen."

"But, Your Majesty—!"

Cal ignored the man's sputtered protests, striding forward to join Elnora, his eyes glowing with admiration. She turned to him, a smile on her face.

"That," she said brightly, "was *extremely* satisfying."

Cal laughed delightedly, taking her hands in his. "You took the words out of my mouth, *My Lady*."

Elnora grinned, her gaze passing over Jonan and Scarlett, both of whom smiled warmly back at her. "Not even lunchtime," she said cheerfully, "and today's already the best day I've had in ages."

"What?" Cal protested. "You may have, but I haven't forgotten that you were abducted and almost killed this morning!"

"Of course I haven't forgotten," she said. "But I'm glad it happened."

"How can you be—?" Cal started to demand, but she cut him off.

"I've spent the last three months feeling incapable and insufficient," she said softly. "When I was dropped suddenly into the world of the court, I felt completely useless—a burden for you to carry, with no skills to offer." Cal frowned, but she ignored the expression, continuing on.

"People like him," she indicated the offended nobleman,

who was glowering at them from across the room, "were at great pains to remind me of everything I didn't know, and all the training I didn't have. But when Yaeger's men charged into my suite expecting an easy victim, and grabbed Scarlett and me, they underestimated us both. I didn't spend years in Bryant's gang for nothing. I just needed a little push to be reminded that there are a great deal of things I do know, and lots of skills I can offer once I'm queen."

"A little push?" repeated Cal faintly, and Jo could see him tighten his hold convulsively on Elnora's hands.

She just flashed him a grin. "If I could learn to pick a lock at age eleven, and scale a three story building without making a sound, surely I can pick up all this court stuff with a little bit of application."

"Of course you can," said Cal, his whole face alight with his love and admiration. "I think that little showdown demonstrated that you're already well on the way." He put a hand gently on her cheek. Jo felt like he could read Cal's mind, sure that his friend wanted desperately to take Elnora in his arms and kiss her then and there, but was restrained by the interested crowd. Even so, the look passing between them was so intimate that Jo coughed, looking away to share an amused look with Scarlett.

The sound seemed to draw Elnora's attention to them, and she smiled warmly at Scarlett. "I have you to thank for helping me figure out how stupid I was being, by the way."

"Me?" asked Scarlett, startled. "I don't think I did anything useful!"

"No, nothing much. Just little things, like taking out about half of Yaeger's men, rescuing Jo, and coming back for me when Yaeger had a sword to my throat," said Elnora dryly, and Jo squeezed Scarlett's hand. "But that's not what I meant," Elnora continued. "I was struck by what you told me, back at my suite, about your parents. How your mother was a wonderful person and a much better wife than your father deserved, but how he thought she had nothing to contribute because of her common birth. Well, when I saw what he tried to do back there, and realized what kind of person that attitude had turned him into...I realized that was the last type of thinking I should give any weight to."

"I'm glad," said Scarlett, but Jo thought her smile seemed strained, and as soon as Elnora's attention was back on Cal he addressed Scarlett quietly.

"What is it, Scarlett? Is it your injury?" He looked anxiously at the gash on her chest. It wasn't bleeding anymore, but it was still alarming to see the blood staining her clothes. "We need to get you looked at."

She sighed, looking down at their joined hands. "No, it's not that. It's...I just wish I'd been as successful in facing down my demons," she said. "After everything, I still couldn't stand up to my father."

"What are you talking about?" Jo demanded. "Of course you stood up to him! He had a sword to your throat, and you still refused to give him the rock."

"Yes, but I wasn't brave like you were. Nothing had changed —I was still afraid of him. Years as a supposedly fearless rebel leader, and I've always been afraid of him. He had a hold on me that no one else did."

"He was your father, Scarlett," said Jonan gently. "Of course he had a hold on you. And how can you possibly say you weren't brave? Being brave doesn't mean you can't be afraid. I don't think you can even really be considered brave if you're not scared. I mean it," he insisted as she made a disbelieving noise. "The fact that you stood up to him *even though* you were afraid is what makes you brave. Plus, you're wrong if you think I wasn't scared," he added, smoothing her hair behind her ear. "I was terrified when I saw him with a blade to your throat."

She looked up at him, her expression still sad. "I was certain he was going to kill me," she said. "But I didn't fight him. I had no trouble fighting back against any of the others, but with him, I still froze up."

"You don't have to be invulnerable, Scarlett," said Jonan gently. "No one can be. We all have weaknesses. The last thing I want is for you to be some kind of indestructible unreachable rock. You have a softness about you, a gentleness that I loved from the start. Don't let it make you doubt your unbelievable strength. The two things are not enemies."

She said nothing, but the look on her upturned face spoke volumes, her eyes shining with the joy of being known so deeply.

"And if you're berating yourself for not taking him down," said Jonan, his voice still soft, "then stop. I would never wish it on you to carry the burden of killing your own father."

"I didn't wish it on you, either," she whispered.

Jonan shook his head. "It's not the same. I'll admit that there have been times these last few months when I've been so angry with him that I wanted to kill him in cold blood, and that would have been a mistake. But what happened today—that won't keep me up at night. Not when the alternative was letting him kill you."

He captured her gaze and held it, glorying in the sight of her, whole and mostly unharmed and breathtakingly beautiful. "That I couldn't live with, because it would mean living without you, and I'm not brave enough to do that." He let go of one of her hands to lay his palm against her cheek, his fingers tangling in her hair. "I love you, Scarlett," he said, his voice clear. "I love every part of you."

Her eyes seemed to glisten as she met his look, her own voice coming out soft but strong. "I loved you as soon as you stepped in front of that whip, Jonan, and I'll love you as long as I live."

Jo beamed back at her. He took just one moment to delight in the fact that he wasn't king and Scarlett wasn't going to be queen, and he didn't have to care one jot for the opinion of all the interested onlookers. Then he forgot all about them as he pulled Scarlett close and kissed her, with all the passion of their first stolen embrace, and all the confidence of knowing that there was no longer anything to part them. Either now or in a future that seemed full of the promise of a different kind of adventure.

EPILOGUE

Jonan stood on the quay, watching eagerly as the ship was docked. He could see the other vessels in the armada approaching Alezae's harbor. Scarlett's grip on his hand was painfully tight, but he just smiled down at her barely contained excitement. It was hard to tell who was more impatient out of her and Elnora, who stood nearby with Cal. Cal was more restrained, clearly torn between entering into Elnora's nervous excitement, and presenting the calm and authoritative face of a king receiving a large group of his subjects, freed from a long and undeserved exile.

It was hard to believe this day had finally come. There had been times in the weeks that had passed since the curse was broken when Jonan had wondered if it would ever happen. The surviving soldiers and other representatives of the Balenan delegation had been sent back to Nohl without delay, but the time required for them to carry their message to Balenol's king, and for the first of the Kyonans to sail across the sea, still felt interminable.

At first Cal had been concerned that Lord Wrendal's death might spark war in just the way the nobleman had planned for

Scarlett's death to do. But Scarlett seemed to think it was very unlikely. Her father's plan had relied on his own role in exercising his considerable influence over King Siloam to act against Scarlett's supposed killers, playing the part of a bereaved father. Plus, the Balenan soldiers had seen Elddreki in the forest, and the rest of the delegation had seen him when he descended on Kynton.

From all accounts the image of the dragon perched upon the turret of the castle's highest tower, spewing flames from his ferocious mouth, would be hard to forget. The Balenans had clearly formed the impression that the young Kyonan king could call dragons to his aid at will. When the delegation, significantly reduced in both number and spirits, set sail for Balenol Jo was confident that its members would report to their king that to resist the demands of King Calinnae would be to court disaster.

Still, more than once since then, Jo had been gripped by the fear that King Siloam would be convinced by someone like Lord Grentan that he should refuse to release the captives after all. Scarlett, sending a long and persuasive letter to Prince Giles along with the ship, had told Jonan that he could count on her cousin's influence. She had placed her faith in Prince Giles's readiness to do what was right, now that it could at least be argued to align with the interests of the kingdom. And it seemed she had been right.

"You must be eager to be reunited with your friends," said Leander, coming up alongside Scarlett now. "To be honest, I was surprised you didn't want to return with the delegation yourself, to oversee the process."

"I thought about it," said Scarlett. "But I didn't think it was safe for Jo to return to Nohl, not until things settle down, and he wouldn't hear of me going without him." She looked over at Jonan, her cheeks flushing delightfully. "He seemed to think it was wiser to wait until we're married before I return there."

Jo smiled at her, returning the pressure of her hand. That day couldn't come fast enough as far as he was concerned. He turned to Leander with a dry grin. "What she means," he said, "is that her family on her mother's side would try to talk her out of throwing herself away on me, and her family on her father's side would try to forcibly restrain her from returning to me."

Scarlett laughed reluctantly. "Yes, he's right," she admitted. "Besides, I wasn't in any hurry to leave. I like it here. The air is so clear. I don't know if it was because I was always playing a part, but so much of the time I used to feel like I was suffocating. Here I can really breathe." Jo let go of her hand to slide an arm around her waist and give her a quick squeeze. She leaned her head against his shoulder fleetingly, the confiding gesture characteristic of her.

"I'll need to return to Balenol sometime of course," Scarlett continued. "Just for a visit, and to tie up loose ends. And I would like to see my aunt and my cousins now that I don't have to hide anything from them. But if Jo and I go together, already married, it will make things much simpler."

"You are, in fact, learning from someone else's experience," said Leander with the hint of a smile, his gaze resting on the young king and his future queen standing nearby.

Jo flashed him a grin and didn't try to deny it. He felt a bit sorry for Cal that his wedding still hadn't happened, but it seemed that such a royal celebration took an unbelievable amount of planning. Cal had been ready to defy convention and insist on a hasty ceremony, but once Elnora had confessed that with the curse broken she would like to wait so that her sister could be present, Cal had swallowed his impatience.

And it seemed that everyone's patience was about to be rewarded. The ship's gangplank was lowered at last, and crew members began to bustle about as they prepared to disembark. Jonan ignored them, his eyes straining for any familiar figure. A moment later he saw a small form throw itself eagerly down the walkway, and he exchanged a brief grin with Scarlett. It was no surprise that Cody would be first to put himself forward. They started toward him, and his eyes, roaming the area excitedly, latched onto them.

"Scar! Jo!" he cried, launching himself at them. "You did it! You broke the curse! I knew you would—I told them all, they'll do it, don't worry. This is the liberator we're talking about! And Scar is—well, it's Scar! And when you broke the curse, everyone saw I was right. We could tell—they felt it right throughout the city, and even in the jungle! It was like a tidal wave, but without the water. Everyone was knocked flat!"

"Slow down, Cody," said a long-suffering voice. "Give them a minute to breathe."

"Bonnie!" Scarlett cried, embracing her friend eagerly. "You made it!"

"Yes, milady, we made it," said Bonnie with a grin. "And thank goodness the voyage is over." She sent a fond but exasperated glance in Cody's direction. "I thought this one was stir crazy at the base tree, but being stuck on a ship with him for three weeks was even worse."

"Oh stuff," said Cody scornfully. "Being at sea was great fun!"

"Maybe for you," said Bonnie darkly. She turned to Scarlett again. "But are you really all right, milady? Your father didn't carry out any of his awful schemes?"

"I'm really all right," said Scarlett warmly. "And you don't need to call me milady anymore, Bonnie. There's no audience to perform for now."

"Audience or not, you're still Lady Wrendal," said Bonnie stubbornly.

"Not for much longer," Scarlett smiled, once again blushing adorably as she glanced up at Jo.

"So that's how it is, is it?" asked Bonnie, raising an eyebrow at

Jo, even as she grinned. "You'd better look after her, or you'll have the whole resistance after you."

Jo grinned back. "That's my plan," he assured her.

"Yes, yes, never mind that," said Cody impatiently, not interested in discussion of Jo and Scarlett's betrothal. "Did you really run the Overseer through the heart, Jo?"

Jo hesitated, glancing down at Scarlett, but she didn't seem upset. She just smiled faintly at the young rebel's bloodthirsty enthusiasm.

"Yes, I did," acknowledged Jo. He drew his brows together a bit as Cody crowed in delight. "But not because I didn't like him, Cody. He was about to kill Scar, and I did it to stop him."

Bonnie turned distressed eyes on Scarlett, but Cody ignored the qualification. "And was there really a dragon there? An actual dragon?"

Scarlett laughed. "Yes, there really was."

"Did you see it, Scar?" asked Cody eagerly.

She nodded, her smile indulgent. "I didn't just see him, Cody, I even got to talk with him."

"Wow," breathed Cody, his eyes round and his tone a bit wistful. Apparently being sold into slavery as a child, then escaping, joining a dangerous resistance, and living a guerrilla lifestyle full of daring feats and espionage wasn't enough adventure to satisfy Cody. Not when there were dragons on offer.

"I can hardly believe we're in Kyona," said Bonnie, looking around. "It's even more beautiful than I remembered."

"It is beautiful, isn't it?" said Scarlett softly. "I just wish Raldo could have been here for this moment. He never even got to see Kyona."

Jo squeezed her hand as they all fell silent for a moment, remembering the bravery of their friend. He looked around at the disembarking Kyonans, frowning as he took in who was missing.

"Where's Stan?" he asked. "Don't tell me she wasn't on this ship. Elnora would be so disappointed."

"She's here," said Bonnie. "Just nervous. Probably hiding at the back."

"Stan, nervous?" asked Jo, raising his eyebrows. "That's hard to picture."

Even as he said it, he caught sight of Stan. As Bonnie had predicted, she was lurking at the back of the group, looking anxious. A sudden cry told Jo that Elnora had also seen her sister. Letting go of Cal's hand, she threw herself forward. At sight of this undignified approach, Stan's eyes lit up and she hurried forward too. The sisters embraced, laughing and crying at the same time, their words tumbling over each other. Cal had been speaking quietly with the ship's captain, but he hurried forward eagerly to be introduced. Jo thought that Stan looked wary, but not for nothing had Cal been working hard to develop his natural aptitude for diplomacy. Jo couldn't hear their conversation, but even from a distance he could see that Cal's open manner and kind words soon put Stan at ease.

In fact, from what Jo could observe, the arriving Kyonans all seemed to be quite taken with their handsome young king. Observing his friend critically, Jo saw with approval that Cal carried himself with confidence and grace, the calm sense and good humor that had characterized him when they were growing up somehow not lost under the dignity and authority conferred on him by kingship.

Jo was getting plenty of attention himself, lots of the new arrivals eager to swarm their beloved Scar and the liberator, and to thank them personally for breaking the curse. Jo saw Cal watching with some amusement as Jo was mobbed by a group of awestruck girls who had not until now met the liberator in the flesh. Jo grimaced slightly back at his friend, and Cal turned away with a grin.

"Did you see Giles before you left?" Scarlett was asking Bonnie. "I assume he got my letter?"

Bonnie nodded. "He got it. The royals were pretty upset that you weren't with the delegation when it returned, but the prince calmed them all down a bit after he read your letter."

Scarlett sighed. "I don't envy them the task ahead." Seeing Bonnie's look, she hurried to add, "Don't get me wrong, I'm glad King Siloam is releasing all the slaves. But they're going to leave behind an incredible mess to clean up, and somehow I don't think King Siloam will do much to bring things into order. My uncle, and probably my cousin too, will have all the work without the benefit of the actual crown."

"I'm sure you're right," said Bonnie, although she didn't look too troubled by the plight of the Balenans. She looked across at Cal, her expression shrewd. "It strikes me that there's a pretty overwhelming job to do at this end, too. There are a lot of us coming, you know, and the reentry won't be easy. It's been generations for some. Is the new king really up to the challenge, do you think?"

"Oh yes," said Scarlett confidently. "He's more capable than you think."

"Good," said Bonnie with a smile. "Because I for one am glad to be home."

"Me too," said Jonan emphatically.

Scarlett smiled, her voice soft and her heart in her eyes as she looked up at him. "Me too."

WITH THE LONG-AWAITED arrival of the first ship behind them, the castle threw itself into preparations for the royal wedding with a fervor Jo found alarming. Scarlett was to be one of Elnora's attendants, and Cal had even guilted Jo into agreeing to stand up beside him for the ceremony. Cal said it was the least Jo could do given that he intended to once again desert Cal and leave Kynton.

But Jo knew Cal was just using dirty tactics to get him to agree about the wedding. They had discussed plans for the future at length, and Cal was fully supportive of Jonan's intended course. He had looked a bit sad, and Jo knew that Cal would miss Jo as much as he would miss his friend, but Cal had to acknowledge that Jo wouldn't thrive in the court. Scarlett had the capacity to do so, of course, but she had assured Jo earnestly that she wanted nothing more than to be free of that lifestyle.

But at least they wouldn't be far away. The problem of how to reintegrate the large number of returning Kyonans naturally occupied a great deal of conversation between the two couples. It had been Jonan who had the idea of establishing a community in the Forest of Rune for those who were interested. He thought that the forest setting might be more familiar for those who had spent years, or even their whole lives, living in the jungle. And the close proximity to Kynton would help to ensure that they didn't isolate themselves so much that they failed to integrate.

Cal was quite taken with the idea. It solved another problem he was facing, which was that some of the foresters who had helped him take the throne—Laramie and Leander's people— had not settled well in the city. They missed their forest lifestyle, and they would have the skills to help the new arrivals to settle into that environment. It helped that there was already quite a lot of infrastructure left by the first forest community.

The idea had taken, and a very little conversation was needed for Jonan and Scarlett to confirm that they were in perfect agreement about being part of the group. Jo had spurned the offer of a title, but Cal had brought him around to the idea of an official role. The new settlement, which at Scarlett's suggestion was to be called Raldon, would need leaders, and Jonan and Scarlett were an obvious choice.

It was the veiled relief in Scarlett's eyes that fully reconciled Jo to the idea. She was born to lead, and she had the respect of many of the arrivals already. By contrast, if they were to stay in Kynton, as the only Balenan she would probably always feel like an outsider, constantly having to work to prove her loyalty and earn her position. It was exactly the type of maneuvering she had been caught in back in Nohl. Jo had seen how it had worn away at her, and it was precisely what he most wished her to be free from.

Nevertheless, neither the fact that they were all well satisfied with the plan, nor the fact that Jo and Scarlett would be only a few hours' ride from Kynton, prevented Cal from using their imminent departure to bully Jo into being part of the wedding.

But Jo fully intended to get his revenge. Cal bore up under all the fuss pretty well, but Jo caught the harassed look in his friend's eye when no one was looking, and he knew that Cal was accepting it all with good grace mainly for Elnora's sake. The bride-to-be, although at times overwhelmed by some of the formalities, was clearly much more inclined to enjoy the magnificence of it all than her prospective groom. Cal grumbled to Jo that he hardly got to see Elnora, given she was so caught up in preparations, but Jo didn't take the complaint too seriously. He could see Cal's happiness every time Elnora went past, laughing and excited and accompanied by Stan. The joy of having her sister with her during her wedding was something that Elnora had never expected to have, and Cal's satisfaction at her delight was obvious. Stan, who was once again going by the name Constance, had decided to stay in Kynton rather than move to the forest. Scarlett would miss her, but they were all glad to know she would have her long-missed sister at her side.

Any time Jo ribbed Cal on the unbelievable fuss of it all, Cal told him with vindictive delight that he would get his own back soon enough. Neither Jo nor his bride might be royal, but they were notable figures—Scarlett was even a member of a foreign nobility—and Cal promised a bit maliciously to make sure their wedding was an event of kingdom-wide interest.

Jonan just grinned, determined to have the last laugh. His pious expression when he fetched Cal for a final fitting the day before the royal event was to take place should have put the young king on his guard. But Cal clearly had no thought of treachery in mind as he followed with a groan, grumbling about the ineptitude of any seamstress who would not have the groom's outfit completed before the eve of the wedding.

His first clue that something was amiss was when Jo led him between open double doors into one of the castle's beautiful gardens.

"Wait, where are we going?" asked Cal, confused. "Why are we outside?"

"The bride thought this garden would be a beautiful place for a wedding," said Jo innocently.

"What are you talking about?" said Cal, staring at him. "She never mentioned it to me. Elnora knows as well as I do that we have to get married in the throne room. Some kind of royal tradition, apparently."

"I wasn't talking about Elnora," said Jonan, unable to hold back a grin.

Cal frowned in confusion, looking around the garden. His eyes fell on the figure of Scarlett, dressed in a simple but beautiful white gown. She was standing beside a fountain and accompanied by Elnora, Bonnie and Constance, all of whom were dressed more elaborately than a garden stroll justified. Cal's gaze passed last to the master of ceremonies, hovering nearby, and Jo saw the moment that understanding hit.

"You little rat!" Cal cried, turning wrathfully to his friend. "You're stealing a march on me?"

"Is that any way to speak to your best friend on his wedding day?" asked Jonan in mock offense.

"This is a dirty trick, Jo," said Cal bitterly. "Here I've been waiting all these endless months, and putting up with an unbearable fuss and carry on, and you sneak in at the eleventh hour, and—"

"I know, I know," said Jo placatingly. "But can you honestly tell me you wouldn't do the same if you had the option?"

Cal regarded him belligerently for a moment longer. But then he looked over at the girls, his eyes locking on Elnora who was looking gorgeous in a pale pink gown and was laughing back at him with a rueful twinkle in her eyes, and he grinned reluctantly.

"I suppose I would," he admitted.

"Then just look at it as a practice run for tomorrow, and stop arguing with me," said Jo, his severe tone at odds with the roguish look in his eyes.

It was a simple ceremony, sincere and to the point. Jo couldn't remember ever thinking about his wedding when he was growing up, but he was sure that if he had, this intimate and unpretentious gathering would be exactly what he would have wanted. His best friend was beside him, his future was an unwritten and unfettered adventure, and his bride...well, his bride was perfection personified as far as he was concerned. Brave and kind, sweet and intelligent, incredibly strong but wonderfully soft and gentle.

And beautiful. So inexpressibly beautiful that it was almost painful to look at her. The simplicity of her gown only accentuated her breathtaking beauty—she needed no embellishment. The autumn had so far been mild, and she had chosen a gown that was a tasteful blend of the styles of their two kingdoms. The fabric was that of Kyona, but the sleeves were no more than short caps, offset from her shoulders, so that her neck and arms were bare but for the lacy divider. The rich caramel of her skin seemed to glow in the afternoon sun, and the sight made Jonan's heart race unevenly.

Her expressive eyes overflowed with emotion as she repeated her vows softly, and Jonan could hardly believe he would really get to call her his. When the master of ceremonies finally stopped talking, and invited an impatient groom to kiss his bride, Jonan drew Scarlett against him eagerly. She laughed at his enthusiasm, but he held her so close that he could feel her heart beating as quickly as his as he gazed down into her eyes. Then he leaned down to close the gap and pressed his lips against hers with a heart more full than it had ever been. And as she returned his kiss with a passion that sent a tingle all the way down to his toes, he exulted in the knowledge that he finally had the right to make good on his determination never to be parted from her again.

Of course, he had to tolerate being a very small distance apart the next day, as he and his bride stood on either side of the raised dais at the end of the impressive throne room. But, he reflected, it was at least a good position from which to admire her, stunningly attired in a gown befitting an attendant of the soon-to-be queen. He looked at her so often that she shot him a look of reproach, but he wasn't fooled. The smile in his new wife's eyes was just for him.

And it was worth it to be there for Cal. He wouldn't have missed the joy on his best friend's face for anything. The look in Cal's eyes as Elnora walked down the aisle toward him suggested that the moment was worth every minute of the frustratingly long wait for this day to come. Cal looked every inch the king, young, strong, and handsome in the blue and gold of Kyona's royal house. With amusement, Jo saw more than one sentimental damsel in the audience, wiping their eyes at the romance of the occasion. He was sure Cal hadn't noticed them—his friend's eyes never left his bride for a moment.

And Jo didn't blame him. Although in general he only had eyes for Scarlett, even Jo could see that Elnora was looking absolutely glorious. Her elaborate white gown was fit for a queen, with a richly embroidered train that trailed gracefully behind her as she walked. Her golden hair was piled elegantly on top of her head, jewels glistening from a delicate tiara. It was thoroughly unlike Scarlett's simple outfit from the day before, but somehow Elnora wasn't lost under it all. She moved with a stately confidence, her eyes fixed unwaveringly on her groom and her love and happiness radiating from every part of her.

The ceremony was full of formality and speeches, but the look that passed between the couple as they said their vows was as raw and real as in the private garden wedding the day before.

Jo's eyes slid past the king and his queen to lock on Scarlett, and she smiled back at him, her eyes full of the promise of the future. Alben's rock sat warm against his chest, but it was eclipsed by the fullness of the heart beating just underneath it. There were plenty of challenges ahead, but each of them had found their place, and Jonan didn't doubt their ability to overcome any challenge together. It was hard to imagine how life could get any better than this.

NOTE FROM THE AUTHOR

Thank you for reading *Captives of the Curse*. I hope you enjoyed reading it as much as I enjoyed writing it! I would be so grateful if you would consider leaving a review on Amazon—it would really make a difference!

If you want to find out what happens next for Jonan and Scarlett, check out *Captive's Return: A Novella*, the third installment of the Kyona Chronicles, where more adventure, fantasy, mystery, and romance await.

Join up to my mailing list at deborahgracewhite.com to be kept up to date on new releases, specials, and giveaways, such as bonus chapters. You will also receive *Dragon's Sight*, an 8,000 word prequel to the series, told from Elddreki's perspective.

Again, thanks for entering the world of the Kyona Chronicles! I hope to see you back again.

ACKNOWLEDGMENTS

When I first began to imagine the world of Kyona, back in high school, I never really thought it would become an actual novel one day, let alone a whole series. When picturing the first book, I always loved the idea of an open end for Jonan, with adventures of his own in his future.

But after *Heir of the Curse* was written, Jonan's story demanded to be told. I wanted to travel with him to lands beyond the sea, and see what he would discover there. So I did.

I would never have been able to go on that adventure with Jonan without the support of my incredible husband Ray, who has encouraged and enabled me to keep writing. He is my alpha reader, and the first to hear the books as they come. He, and our two gorgeous pint-sized children, have been so gracious in tolerating me spending hours and hours writing long before we ever got to the point of actual publication.

I also owe a huge thank you to my beta readers: Mum, Dad, Andrew, Adrian, Tamara, Jana, Ali, David, and Cherilyn. Your feedback has been both encouraging and challenging, and has helped make this book much better.

And again, a double thank you to Mum for your line editing,

and to Dad for your developmental and copy editing. A further thanks to Dad and to Mel for all your help with publication and release.

Karri, thank you again for creating such a fantastic and professional cover. And Rebecca, the map is even better now we can zoom out to include the whole thing.

To you, the reader, thank you for giving me the privilege of being an author.

And most importantly, to God, the source of creativity, the ultimate dreamer of big dreams. Thank you for putting the love of words in me, and giving me the chance to explore it.

ABOUT THE AUTHOR

I've been a reader since I can remember, growing up on a wide range of books, from classic literature to light-hearted romps. The love of reading has traveled with me unchanged across multiple continents, and carried me from my own childhood all the way to having children of my own.

But if reading is like looking through a window into a magical and beautiful world, beginning to write my own stories was like discovering that I could open that window and climb right out into fantasyland.

I cannot believe how privileged I am to actually be living that childhood dream and publishing my own novels. I do so from my hometown of Adelaide, Australia, where I live with my husband and our two, soon to be three, little munchkins.

I've never outgrown my love of young adult stories, and my first series, The Kyona Chronicles, is a young adult fantasy series of four novels and two novellas.

Feel free to email me at deborah@deborahgracewhite.com and introduce yourself! Or subscribe to my mailing list at deborahgracewhite.com for free giveaways, sales, and updates.